USA TODAY bestsellin[g] books and writing eve[...] tions, she finally sold her first manuscript. she has written fifty-plus books and novellas. Janice lives in Tennessee with her husband, Charles. They love hiking, traveling and family time.

You can connect with Janice at
www.janicemaynard.com
www.Twitter.com/janicemaynard
www.Facebook.com/ janicemaynardreaderpage
and www.Instagram.com/ janicemaynard.

Sheri WhiteFeather is an award-winning, bestselling author. She lives in Southern California and enjoys shopping in vintage stores and visiting art galleries and museums. She is known for incorporating Native American elements into her books and has two grown children who are tribally enrolled members of the Muscogee Creek Nation.

Visit her website at www.sheriwhitefeather.com.

911200003887185

Discover more at millsandboon.co.uk

BLAME IT
ON CHRISTMAS

JANICE MAYNARD

NASHVILLE
REBEL

SHERI WhiteFeather

MIX
Paper from
responsible sources

FSC
FSC C007454

This book is produced from independently certified FSC™
paper to ensure responsible forest management.

For more information visit: www.harpercollins.co.uk/green

Printed and bound in Spain
by CPI Books

MILLS & BOON

First Published in Great Britain 2018
by Mills & Boon, an imprint of HarperCollinsPublishers,
1 London Bridge Street, London, SE1 9GF

Blame It On Christmas © 2018 Janice Maynard
Nashville Rebel © 2018 Sheree Henry-Whitefeather

ISBN: 978-0-263-93631-5

BLAME IT ON CHRISTMAS

JANICE MAYNARD

This book is for every guy or girl who has
found the courage to ask someone out
and then been shot down. It hurts.
But true love finds a way. ☺

One

"The answer is no!"

Mazie Tarleton ended the call, wishing she had a good old-fashioned receiver she could slam down on a cradle. Cutting off a phone conversation with the tap of a red button wasn't nearly as satisfying.

Behind her, Gina—her best friend and coworker—ate the last bite of her cinnamon crunch bagel and wiped cream cheese from her fingers. "Who's got you all riled up?"

The two women were in Mazie's office, a cramped space behind the elegant showroom that drew tourists and locals to All That Glitters, Mazie's upscale jewelry store in Charleston's historic business district.

Mazie dropped into a chair and scowled. "It's J.B.'s real estate agent again. He's making her badger me."

"You mean J.B. who wants to offer you a ridiculous amount of money for this building that's falling down around our ears?"

"Whose side are you on anyway?" Mazie and Gina had met as freshmen at Savannah's College of Art and Design. Gina was aware of Mazie's long-standing feud with Charleston's highly eligible and incredibly sexy billionaire businessman.

Gina flicked a crumb from her cashmere-covered bosom. "We have dry rot in the attic. A heating system that dates back to the Civil War. And do I need to mention that our hurricane policy rates are set to triple when the renewal is due? I know you Tarleton people are richer than God, but that doesn't mean we should thumb our noses at a great offer."

"If it were anybody but J.B.," Mazie muttered, feeling the noose of inevitability tighten around her neck.

J.B. Jackson Beauregard Vaughan. The man she loved to hate. J.B. Vaughan had been on her personal hit list since she was sixteen years old. She loathed him. And she wanted to hurt him as much as he had hurt her.

"What did he ever do to you?" Gina asked. Her perplexed frown was understandable. J.B. Vaughan was the prototype for tall, dark and handsome. Cocky grin. Brilliant blue eyes. Strong features. And shoulders that were about a million miles wide.

"It's complicated," Mazie muttered, feeling her face heat. Even now, the memories were humiliating.

Mazie couldn't remember a time when J.B. hadn't been part of her life. Way back when, she had even loved him. As an almost-brother. But when her hormones started raging and she began seeing J.B. in a whole new light, a spring formal at her all-girls prep school had presented itself as the perfect opportunity to do some very grown-up experimentation.

Not sex. Oh, no. Not that. She was aware, even then, that J.B. was the kind of guy who *knew things*, and she wasn't ready to go down that road.

She called him on a Wednesday afternoon in April. With her nerves humming and her stomach flopping, she blurted out her invitation.

J.B. had been oddly noncommittal. And then, barely four hours later, he had showed up on her doorstep.

Her father had been locked in his study with a nightcap. Both Jonathan and Hartley, her brothers, had been out on the town doing something or other.

Mazie had answered the front door.

Because she felt weird about inviting J.B. inside—though he'd been there a hundred times before—she stepped out onto the wide veranda and smiled at him tentatively.

"Hey, J.B.," she said. "I didn't expect to see you today."

He leaned against a post, his posture the epitome of cool, high school masculinity. In a few weeks he would be eighteen. A legal adult. Her heart beat faster.

"I wanted to talk to you face-to-face," he said. "It was nice of you to ask me to the dance."

"Nice?"

It seemed an odd choice of words, especially coming from J.B.

He nodded. "I'm flattered."

Her stomach curled defensively. "You didn't actually give me an answer on the phone," she said. Suddenly, her hands were ice, and she was shaking all over.

J.B. shifted from one foot to the other. "You're a cute girl, Mazie. I'm glad you're my friend."

He really didn't have to say anything else. She was smart and perceptive and able to read between the lines. But she'd be damned if she'd let him off so easily. "What are you trying to say, J.B.?"

Now a dark scowl erased some of his cocky charm, but none of his brooding sexuality. "Damn it, Mazie. I can't go to that dance with you. You shouldn't have asked me. You're little more than a baby."

Her heart shriveled. "I'm not a child," she said quietly. "I'm only a year younger than you are."

"Almost two."

The real surprise was that he had kept track. Because of the way their birthdays fell on the calendar, he was right. She took three steps toward him. Inside, she was falling apart. But she wouldn't let him see what he was doing to her self-esteem. "Don't make excuses, J.B. If you won't go out with me, please have the guts to say so."

He cursed vehemently. With both hands, he scraped his slightly-too-long blue-black hair from his face. "You're like a sister to me," he said.

The words were muttered, barely audible. In fact, he spoke them in the direction of the floor. A less-convincing lie would have been hard to find. Why was he throwing up walls between them?

Mazie was breathing so rapidly she was in danger of hyperventilating. Clearly she had misread the situation. J.B. hadn't come here tonight because he was fond of her, or because he wanted to see her.

He was standing on her front porch because he was too much of a Southern gentleman to say no to her over the phone.

A nicer person might have made the situation easier for him. Mazie was tired of being nice. She slipped her arms around his waist and rested her cheek on his broad chest. He was wearing a navy T-shirt and faded jeans with old leather deck shoes. Decades ago, he would have been a classic James Dean. Bad boy. Rule breaker.

When she touched him, his entire body went rigid. Nothing moved. Except one thing. One startling and rather large thing.

Jackson Beauregard Vaughan was aroused. Since Mazie had plastered herself against his front, it was rather impossible for him to hide. She found his mouth with hers and threw every ounce of her undiluted teenage passion into an eager, desperate kiss.

J.B. tasted wonderful, exactly like he did in her dreams, only better.

For a moment, she thought she had won.

His arms tightened around her. His mouth crushed hers. His tongue thrust between her lips and stroked the inside of her mouth. Her legs lost feeling. She clung to his shoulders. "J.B.," she whispered. "Oh, J.B."

Her words shocked him out of whatever spell he'd been under. He jerked away so hard and so fast, she stumbled.

J.B. never even held out a hand to keep her from falling.

He stared at her, his features shadowed in the unflattering yellowish glare of the porch light. The sun had gone down, and the dark night was alive with the smells and sounds of spring.

Very deliberately, he wiped a hand across his mouth. "Like I said, Mazie. You're a kid. Which means you need to stick to the kiddie pool."

His harsh words, particularly coming on the heels of that kiss, confused her. "Why are you being so mean?" she whispered.

She saw the muscles in his throat work.

"Why are you being so naive and clueless?"

Hot tears sprang to her eyes. She wouldn't let them fall. "I think we're done here. Do me a favor, J.B. If you ever find yourself in the midst of an apocalypse—zombie or otherwise—and if you and I are the only two humans left on the planet, go screw yourself."

"Mazie…hello… Mazie."

Gina's voice shocked Mazie back to the present. "Sorry," she said. "I was thinking about something."

"About J.B., right? You were ready to tell me why you loathe the man after all these years, and why you won't sell this property to him, even though he's offered you three times what it's worth."

Mazie swallowed, shaking off the past. "He broke my heart when we were teenagers, and he was kind of a jerk about it, so yeah… I don't want to hand him everything he wants."

"You're being illogical."

"Maybe so."

"Forget the money. Hasn't he also offered you two other

properties that are prime locations for our shop? And he's willing to do a trade, easy peasy? What are you waiting for, Mazie?"

"I want him to squirm."

J.B. had bought up every single square foot of property in a two-block strip near the Battery. He planned a massive renovation, working, of course, within the parameters of historic Charleston's preservation guidelines. The street-level storefronts would be glitzy retail space, charming and Southern and unique. Upstairs, J.B.'s vision included luxurious condos and apartments, some with views of the picturesque harbor and Fort Sumter in the distance.

The only thing standing in J.B.'s way was Mazie. And Mazie's property. And the fact that he didn't own it.

Gina waved a hand in front of Mazie's face. "Stop spacing out. I understand wanting to torment your teenage nemesis, but are you seriously going to stonewall the man just to make a point?"

Mazie ground her teeth until her head ached. "I don't know if I'm willing to sell to him. I need time to think about it."

"What if the agent doesn't call you back?"

"She will. J.B. never gives up. It's one of his best qualities and one of his most annoying."

"I hope you're right."

J.B. slid into the dark booth and lifted a hand to summon a server. He'd worn a sport coat and a tie for an earlier meeting. Now, he loosened his collar and dispensed with the neckwear.

Jonathan Tarleton was already sitting in the opposite corner nursing a sparkling water with lime. J.B. lifted an eyebrow in concern. "You look like hell. What's wrong?"

His friend grimaced. "It's these bloody headaches."

"You need to see a doctor."

"I have."

"Then you need to see a better one."

"Can we please stop talking about my health? I'm thirty, not eighty."

"Fine." J.B. wanted to pursue the issue, but Jonathan was clearly not interested. J.B. sat back with a sigh, nursing his beer. "Your sister is driving me crazy. Will you talk to her?" He couldn't admit the real reason he needed help. He and Mazie were oil and water. She hated him, and J.B. had tried for years to tell himself he didn't care.

The truth was far murkier.

"Mazie is stubborn," Jonathan said.

"It's a Tarleton trait, isn't it?"

"You're one to talk."

"I've literally put my entire project on hold, because she's jerking me around."

Jonathan tried unsuccessfully to hide a smile. "My sister is not fond of you, J.B."

"Yeah, tell me something I don't know. Mazie refuses to talk about selling. What am I supposed to do?"

"Sweeten the pot?"

"With what? She doesn't want my money."

"I don't know. I've always wondered what you did to piss her off. Why is my little sister the only woman in Charleston who's immune to the famous J.B. Vaughan charm?"

J.B. ground his jaw. "Who knows?" he lied. "I don't have time to play games, though. I need to break ground by the middle of January to stay on schedule."

"She likes pralines."

Jonathan drawled the three words with a straight face, but J.B. knew when he was being taunted. "You're suggesting I buy her candy?"

"Candy...flowers... I don't know. My sibling is a complicated woman. Smart as hell with a wicked sense of humor, but she has a dark side, too. She'll make you work for this, J.B. You might as well be prepared to crawl."

J.B. took a swig of his drink and tried not to think about Mazie at all. Everything about her flipped his switches. But he couldn't go there. Ever.

He choked and set down his glass until he could catch his breath.

Hell's bells.

The Tarleton progeny were beautiful people, all of them. Though J.B. barely remembered Jonathan's poor mother, what he recalled was a stunning, gorgeous woman with a perpetually sad air about her.

Jonathan and Hartley had inherited their mother's olive complexion, dark brown eyes and chestnut hair. Mazie had the Tarleton coloring, too, but her skin was fairer, and her eyes were more gold than brown. Amber, actually.

Though her brother kept his hair cut short to tame its tendency to curl, Mazie wore hers shoulder length. In the heat and humidity of summer, she kept it up in a ponytail. But during winter, she left it down. He hadn't seen her in several months. Sometimes J.B. dropped by the Tarletons' home on Thanksgiving weekend, but this year, he'd been tied up with other commitments.

Now it was December.

"I'll take the candy under advisement," he said.

Jonathan grimaced. "I'll see what I can do," he conceded. "But don't count on any help from me. Sometimes if I make a suggestion, she does the exact opposite. It's been that way since we were kids."

"Because she was always trying to keep up with you and Hartley, and you both treated her like a baby."

"I suppose we could have been nicer to her. It wasn't easy growing up in our house, especially once Mom was gone. Poor Mazie didn't have any female role models at all."

J.B. hesitated. "You know I would never do anything to hurt her business."

"Of course I know that. Don't be an ass. Your wanting to buy her property makes perfect sense. I can't help it if she's being deliberately obstructive. God knows why."

J.B. knew why. Or at least he had a fairly good idea. One kiss had haunted him for years, no matter how hard he tried not to remember.

"I'll keep trying. Let me know if anything works on your end."

"I'll give it my best shot. But don't hold your breath."

Two

Mazie loved Charleston during the holidays. The gracious old city was at her best in December. The sun was shining, the humidity occasionally dipped below 60 percent, and fragrant greenery adorned every balustrade and balcony in town. Tiny white lights. Red velvet bows. Even the horse-drawn carriages sported red-and-green-plaid finery.

She'd be the first to admit that summer in South Carolina could be daunting. During July and August, tourists had been known to duck into her shop for no other reason than to escape the sweltering heat.

She couldn't blame them. Besides, it was the perfect opportunity to chat people up and perhaps sell them a gold charm bracelet. Or if they were on a tight budget, one of Gina's silver bangles set with semiprecious stones.

Summer was definitely high season. Summer brought an influx of cash. The foot traffic in All That Glitters was steady from Memorial Day until at least mid-October. After that it began to dwindle.

Even so, Mazie loved the holiday season best of all.

It was funny, really. Her own experience growing up had certainly never been a storybook affair. No kids in matching pajamas sipping cocoa while mom and dad read to them in front of the fire. Despite the Tarleton money, which provided a physically secure environment, her parents were difficult people.

But she didn't care. From Thanksgiving weekend until New Year's Day, she basked in the season of goodwill.

Unfortunately, J.B.'s sins were too heinous to include him on Santa's good list. Mazie still wanted to find a way to make him suffer without putting her own business in danger.

When the real estate agent called the following day with another offer from J.B., Mazie didn't say no.

Not immediately.

Instead, she listened to the Realtor's impassioned pitch. When the woman paused to catch her breath, Mazie responded in a well-modulated, exceptionally pleasant tone of voice. "Please," she said politely, "tell Mr. Vaughan that if he is hell-bent on buying my property, perhaps he should come here and talk it over with me in person. Those are my terms."

Then once again, she hung up the phone.

This time, Gina was polishing an enormous silver coffee service they kept in the front window.

She hopped down from the stepladder and capped the jar of cleaner. "Well," she said. "You didn't hang up on her. I suppose that's progress."

Mazie frowned at a smudge on one of the large glass cases. "I thought I was nauseatingly nice."

"Most people think being nice is a good thing."

"True. But not always. We'll see what happens now. If J.B. wants this place, he's going to have to show his face."

Gina blanched and made a chopping motion with her hand.

Mazie frowned. "What's wrong with you?"

The other woman was so white her freckles stood out in relief. And her eyes bugged out of her head. She made a garbled noise.

When Gina continued her impersonation of a block of

salt, Mazie turned around to see what was prompting her friend's odd behavior.

A gaggle of middle-aged women had entered the shop together. The tiny bell over the door tinkled, signaling their presence.

While Mazie and Gina were deep in conversation, J.B. Vaughan had slipped in amid the crowd of shoppers, topping the women by a good six inches.

"I think she's surprised to see *me*," he said. His smile was crooked, his gaze wary. "Hello, Mazie. It's been a while."

His voice rolled over her like warm honey. Why did he have to sound so damn sexy?

The man looked like a dream. He was wearing expensive jeans and a pair of even more expensive Italian leather dress shoes. His broad shoulders were showcased in an unstructured, raw linen sport coat that hung open over a pristine white T-shirt. The shirt was just tight enough to draw attention to his rock-hard abdomen.

Oh, lordy. She had demanded he come in person, but she hadn't realized what she was asking for.

She swallowed her shock and her confusion. "Hello, J.B." A quick glance at her watch told her there was no way he could have gotten there so quickly. Unless he had *already* decided to challenge her refusal to sell face-to-face. "Have you talked to your real estate agent this morning?"

J.B. frowned. "No. I just came from the gym. Is there a problem?"

Mazie swallowed. "No. No problem."

At that precise moment, J.B.'s phone rang.

Mazie would have bet a million dollars she knew who was on the other end of the line. Because she saw his expression change. A huge grin flashed across his face. The Realtor had just passed along Mazie's message.

Damn the man. *She* had wanted to call the shots...to *make* him come plead his case in person.

Instead, he had cut the ground from beneath her feet. J.B. had walked into her shop because it was *his* idea, not because he was toeing some imaginary line or meeting a challenge she had thrown down.

Her temper sparked and simmered. "What do you want, J.B.? I'm busy."

He lifted an eyebrow. "Cleaning a glass counter? Isn't that above your pay grade, Ms. Tarleton?"

"It's my shop. Everything that happens here is *my* business."

Gina squeezed past Mazie. "Excuse me," Gina muttered. "I need to check on our customers."

Mazie should have introduced her redheaded friend to J.B. The two of them might have met at some point in the past, though it was unlikely. But Gina seemed bent on escaping the emotionally charged confrontation.

J.B. held out a red cellophane bag. "These are for you, Mazie. I remember Jonathan saying how much you liked them."

She stared at the familiar logo. Then she frowned, sensing a trap. "You brought me pralines?"

"Yes, ma'am." His arm was still extended, gift in hand.

It might as well have been a snake. "You realize the shop is half a block from here. I can buy my own pralines, J.B."

His smile slipped. The blue irises went from calm to stormy. "A thank you might be nice. You weren't spanked enough as a kid, were you? Spoiled only daughter..."

She caught her breath. The barb hit without warning. "You know that's not true."

Contrition skittered across his face, followed by regret. "Ah, damn, Mazie. I'm sorry. You always bring out the worst in me." He grimaced and pressed the heel of his hand to his forehead. "The candy was a peace offering. Nothing sinister, I swear."

She grabbed the bag of pralines and set it on the counter behind her. She and J.B. were standing at the far back of the store in front of a case of men's signet rings. Hopefully, all of the current customers were shopping for themselves.

"Thank you for the candy." She straightened her shoulders. "Is that all?"

J.B. stared at her, incredulous. "Of course that's not all. Do you really think I wander around Charleston dropping off candy to random women?"

Mazie lifted one shoulder. "Who knows what you do?"

Watching J.B. rein in his temper was actually kind of fun. It helped restore her equilibrium. She *enjoyed* getting the upper hand.

After a few tense moments of silence, he sighed. "I'd like to show you one of my properties over on Queen Street. You could double your square footage immediately, and the storage areas are clean and dry. Plus, there's a generously sized apartment upstairs if you ever decide to move out of Casa Tarleton."

The prospect of having her own apartment was tempting, but she and Jonathan hadn't been able to leave their father on his own. Stupid, really. He'd been a less-than-present parent, both emotionally and otherwise. Still, they felt responsible for him.

Over J.B.'s shoulder, Gina telegraphed her concern like a flamingo playing charades.

Mazie decided to play J.B.'s game. At least for a little while. What she really wanted was to make him think she was seriously considering his offer. And then shut him down. "Okay," she said. "I suppose it couldn't hurt to take a look."

J.B.'s reaction to her quiet statement was equal parts pole-axed and suspicious. "When?"

"Now is good."

"What about the shop?"

"They don't need me." It was true. Mazie was the owner and CEO. In addition to Gina, there were two full-time employees and three part-time ones, as well.

J.B. nodded brusquely. "Then let's get out of here. I'm parked in a loading zone."

"You go ahead. Text me the address. I'll be there in fifteen minutes. All I need to do is grab a coat and get my purse."

He frowned. "I can wait."

"I'd rather have my own car, J.B."

His eyes narrowed. He folded his arms across his chest. "Why?"

"Because I do, that's why. Are you afraid I won't come? I said I would, and I will. Don't make a big deal out of this."

He ground his jaw. She could almost see the hot angry words trembling on his lips. But he said nothing.

"What?" she whispered, still very much aware that they had an audience.

J.B. shook his head, his expression bleak. "Nothing, Mazie. Nothing at all." He reached in a pocket and extracted his cell phone, tapping out a text impatiently. "I sent you the address. I'll see you shortly."

J.B. should have been elated.

The first hurdle was behind him. He had finally convinced Mazie Tarleton to look at another location for her jewelry business. That was *huge*. And it was certainly more than his real estate agent had been able to accomplish in the last twelve weeks. Even so, his skin felt itchy. Being around Mazie was like juggling a grenade. Not only was she an unknown quantity, he was in danger of being sabotaged by his own uneasy attraction.

He was determined to keep his distance.

Nothing with Mazie was ever easy, so he paced the sidewalk in front of the empty property on Queen Street, praying she would show up, but fearing she wouldn't.

When her cherry-red Mazda Miata turned the corner at the end of the street and headed in his direction, he felt a giant boulder roll from his shoulders. Thank the Lord. He was pretty sure Mazie wouldn't have come today unless she was ready to take him up on his offer.

She parallel parked with impressive ease and climbed out, locking her snazzy vehicle with one click of her key fob. He saw her, more often than not, in casual clothes. But today, Mazie was wearing a black pencil skirt with an ivory silk blouse that made her look every inch the wealthy heiress she was.

Her legs were long, maybe her best feature. She walked with confidence. In deference to the breezy afternoon, she wore a thigh-length black trench coat. To J.B. she seemed like a woman who could conquer the world.

As he watched, she tucked her car keys into her coat pocket and joined him. Shielding her eyes with one hand, she stared upward. He followed suit. Far above them, etched in sandstone, were the numerals 1-8-2-2, the year this building had been erected.

He answered her unspoken question. "The most recent tenant was an insurance firm. The building has been sitting empty for three months. If you think it will serve your purposes, I'll bring in an industrial cleaning crew, and we can get you moved with little to no interruption of your daily business."

"I'd like to see inside."

"Of course."

He'd made sure there was nothing to throw up any red flags. No musty odors. No peeling paint. In truth, the building was a gem. He might have kept it for himself if he hadn't so badly needed a carrot to entice Mazie.

For years he had tried to make up for his youthful mistakes. Becoming a respected member of the Charleston business community was important to him. The fact that he had to deal with Mazie and a very inconvenient attraction that wouldn't die was a complication he didn't need. He'd learned the hard way that sexual attraction could blind a man to the truth.

"Look at the tin ceiling," he said. "This place used to be a bank. We're standing where the customers would have come to speak to tellers."

Mazie put her hands on her hips. Slowly she turned around, taking in every angle, occasionally pausing to use her smartphone to snap a picture. "It's lovely," she said.

The comment was grudging. He knew that much. But at least she was honest.

"Thanks. I was lucky to get it. Had to scare off a guy who wanted to use it for an indoor miniature golf range."

"Surely you're joking."

"Not really. I'd like to think he'd never have been able to get the permits, but who knows?"

"You mentioned storage?"

"Ah, yes. There's a finished basement below us, small but nice. And more of the same above. The best part for you, though? There's a safe. We'll have to bring in an expert to get it working again. But you should be able to secure your high ticket items overnight, and thus eliminate any concerns about theft when you're not open."

When he showed her the ten-foot-square safe— stepping aside for her to enter—she lifted an eyebrow. "Kind of overkill, don't you think? My jewelry is small. I don't need nearly this much room."

He followed her in. "Not the way you do it now. But you've been removing every item and putting it all back each morning. If you use the shelves in this safe, you can carry entire trays in here at night and save yourself a ton of hassle."

Mazie pursed her lips. "True."

Her lips were red today, cherry red. It was impossible not to think about those lips wrapped around his—

"Tell me, J.B.," she said, interrupting his heated train of thought. "Is a bank safe this old really secure?"

He swallowed against a dry throat. "Well, it hasn't been used in some time but..."

Mazie pushed on the door. "It's crazy heavy. I suppose it would make a good hurricane shelter, too."

The door was weighted more efficiently than it seemed. Before J.B. could intervene, it slipped out of her grasp and slammed shut with a loud *thunk*.

The sudden pitch-black dark was disorienting.

Mazie's voice was small. "Oops. Guess I should have asked if you have the keys."

"Doesn't matter," he said. "They told me this thing isn't operational." He stepped forward cautiously. "Stand back. I'll grab the handle." That part was easy. Unfortunately, when he threw all his weight into it, nothing moved. "Damn."

He heard a rustle as Mazie shifted closer. "Isn't there a light?"

"Yeah." Reaching blindly, he slid his hand along the wall until he found the switch. The fluorescent bulb flickered, but came on.

Mazie stared at him, eyes huge. "I am *so* sorry. I didn't mean to close it."

"I know you didn't." His heart raced. Aside from the uncomfortable situation, he didn't want to get too close to Mazie. The two of them. In the dark. Very bad idea. "Don't worry," he said. "We'll be fine." He tried the handle a second time. Nothing budged. He pulled out his phone. "I'll call somebody."

He stared at the ominous words on the screen.

No service.

Of course there was no service. The vault was constructed of steel-reinforced concrete, designed to keep out intruders. And the building itself was of an era when walls were built several feet thick. The nearby coffee shop he frequented had terrible cell service because it also was housed in a historic structure.

"So you really *don't* have keys?" Mazie gnawed her lower lip, her arms wrapped around her waist.

"I have keys to the building. Not the safe."

"Someone will notice we're missing," she said. "Gina, anyway. She and I text twenty times a day. What about you? Did you tell anyone you were coming here?"

"I called your brother."

Mazie frowned. "Jonathan? Why?"

J.B. grimaced. "Because he knew I was having a hard time convincing you to sell. I told him you had agreed to at least consider this Queen Street property as an alternative."

"I see." She stared at him. "How often do you and my brother talk about me?"

"Almost never. Why would we?"

Mazie shrugged. "Maybe Jonathan will want to know whether or not you convinced me."

"If he calls, it will just go to voice mail. He'll assume I'm busy and leave a message."

"Well, that sucks." She exhaled sharply and kicked the wall. "You realize that if we die here, I'm going to haunt you for eternity."

"How can you haunt me if I'm dead, too?" He swiped a hand across his forehead, feeling the cold sweat. Her nonsense was a welcome distraction. He would focus on the woman in touching distance.

"Please don't ruin my fantasy," she said. "It's all I've got at the moment." She wrinkled her nose. "We don't even have a chair."

J.B. felt the walls move inward. He dragged in a lungful of air, but it was strangely devoid of oxygen. "Fine," he stuttered. "Feel free to haunt me."

Three

For the first time, Mazie noticed that J.B. seemed decidedly tense.

"Are you okay?" she asked, moving closer and putting a hand on his forehead.

She almost expected to find him burning up with fever, but he was cool as the proverbial cucumber. To her alarm, he didn't move away from her touch or offer even a token protest, and he didn't make some smart-ass remark.

"I'm fine," he said.

"You're definitely not fine."

She got in front of him and put both hands on his face. "Tell me what's wrong. You're scaring me."

His entire body was rigid.

He swallowed, the muscles in his throat rippling visibly. "I'm a tad claustrophobic. I might need you to hold me."

Fat chance. Her heart stumbled at his teasing. And then she remembered. When J.B. was eight years old, he'd been playing in a junkyard with some friends and had accidentally gotten closed up in an old refrigerator during a game of hide-and-seek. He had nearly died.

The incident traumatized him, understandably so. His parents had hired a therapist who came weekly to their house for over a year, but some deep wounds were hard to shake.

She stroked his hair, telling herself she was being kind and not reveling in the chance to touch him. "We're going to be okay. And I'm here, J.B. Take off your jacket. Let's sit down."

At first she wasn't sure he even processed what she was saying. But after a moment, he nodded, removed his sport coat, and slid down the wall until he sat on his butt with his legs outstretched. He sighed deeply. "I'm not going to flake out on you," he muttered.

"I never thought you would." She joined him, but it was far less graceful. Her skirt was unforgiving. She shimmied it up her thighs and managed to sit down without exposing too much.

For an eternity, it seemed, they said nothing. J.B.'s hands rested on his thighs, fists clenched. He was breathing too fast.

Mazie was no shrink. But even she knew he needed to get his mind on something else besides their predicament. "How are your parents?" she asked.

J.B. snorted and shot her a sideways glance. "Really, Mazie? I'm having an embarrassingly public meltdown, and that's the best you can do?"

"You're not having a meltdown," she said. "You're fine."

Maybe if she said it convincingly enough, he would believe her. They were sitting shoulder-to-shoulder, hip-to-hip with less than twelve inches separating them. It was the closest she had been to J.B. in forever. Close enough for her to catch an intoxicating whiff of his aftershave mixed with the entirely ordinary and yet exhilarating man smell of him.

He was big and strong and darkly masculine. Her stomach quivered. *This* was exactly why she normally kept her distance.

J.B. was dangerous.

When she glanced toward the ceiling, she saw tiny air vents up above. They were in no danger of suffocating. Even so, J.B.'s response was understandable. Her skin crawled, too, at the thought of being stuck here for hours.

J.B. was expending every ounce of concentration on not surrendering to the phobia. So any chitchat or small talk would have to be initiated by *her*. The trouble was, she knew J.B. too well, and not well enough.

Charleston wasn't that big a place. Anytime there was a charity gala or a gallery showing or a theater opening, Charleston's elite gathered. Over the years, Mazie had seen J.B. in formal wear on dozens of occasions, usually with a gorgeous woman on his arm. Not ever the same woman, but still…

Because he and Jonathan were best buds, she had also seen J.B. half-naked on the deck of a sailboat and at the basketball court and by the beach. If she really applied herself to the task, she could probably come up with a million and one times she had been in the same vicinity as J.B. and yet never exchanged two words with him.

That was her choice. And probably his. He had been inexplicably cruel to her at a vulnerable point in her life, and she had hated him ever since.

Now here they were. Stuck. Indefinitely.

The tile floor underneath her butt was cold and hard. She drew her knees up to her chest and circled them with her arms. J.B. was right beside her. It wasn't like he was going to look up her skirt.

She sighed. "You doin' okay, stud?" His shallow breathing was audible.

"Peachy."

The growled word, laden with surly testosterone, made her grin. "Why have you never married again?"

The words flew from her lips like starlings disturbed by a chimney sweep. They swirled outward and upward and hung in the air. *Oh, crap.*

Her muscles were paralyzed. Out of the corner of her eye she saw J.B.'s head come up. He went perfectly still. Not looking at her. Gazing straight ahead. The seconds ticked by. A minute passed. Maybe two.

"My parents are well," he said.

It took half a second for the subtext to process, and then she burst into laughter. "Very funny. Message received. The oh-so-mysterious J.B. Vaughan doesn't talk about his private life."

"Maybe I don't have a private life," he said. "Maybe I'm a workaholic who spends every waking hour trying to coax beautiful jewelry merchants into selling their property to me."

With one carefully placed adjective, the dynamic in the room changed. J.B. added flirtation to the mix. Did he do it on purpose? Or was he so accustomed to schmoozing women that the word *beautiful* slipped out?

She pretended not to hear. "If you're a workaholic at this age, you'll be dead before you're fifty. Why do you work so hard, J.B.? Didn't you ever want to stop and smell the roses?"

"I tried it once. Roses have thorns." He sucked in a breath of air. "Are you going to give me your property or not?"

"Did you lock me in here on purpose to make me say yes?"

"God, no. Even I'm not that desperate. Try *your* phone," he said. "You use a different carrier. Maybe it makes a difference."

She glanced at her cell. "Nope. Nada."

J.B. groaned. "How long have we been in here?"

Mazie peered at her watch. "Twenty-two minutes."

"Maybe your watch stopped."

She reached out and squeezed his hand. "Think about something else. Do you have all your Christmas shopping done? What do your sisters want?" J.B.'s two siblings were both younger and female. That's probably why he spent so much time hanging around the Tarleton house when he was growing up.

"They're great," he said. "Do we have to do this?"

"You're the one who didn't want to talk about anything serious."

"Are those my only two choices?"

She hesitated half a beat. "We *could* talk about why you were such an ass to me when we were teenagers."

J.B. cursed beneath his breath and leaped to his feet. "Maybe we shouldn't talk at all."

For the next five minutes, he paced the small space like a tiger in a cage. Mazie stayed where she was. His body language shouted louder than words that he was unraveling.

At last, he paused in front of the impregnable door and slammed it with his fist. He bowed his head, his shoulders taut.

"I can't breathe," he whispered.

The agony in those three words twisted her heart. J.B. was a proud, arrogant man. Having her witness his weakness would make his frustration and anger and helplessness worse.

Without overthinking it, she scooted to her feet and went to him. "Listen to me." Fluorescent lighting was the most unflattering lighting in the world. It made both of them look like hell. His skin was sallow, cheekbones sharply etched. She took his face in her hands again. "Look at me. I want you to kiss me, J.B. Like you mean it. If you can't breathe, I might as well join you. Do it, big guy. Make me breathless. I dare you."

He was shaking, fine tremors that racked his body. But gradually, her words penetrated. "You want me to kiss you?"

"I do," she said. "More than anything." She touched her lips. "Right here. I haven't been kissed in ages. Show me how J.B. Vaughan woos a woman."

He blinked and frowned, as if sensing danger. "You're not serious."

She went up on her tiptoes and brushed her mouth over his. "Oh, yes I am. I'm so damn serious it ought to be against the law." She slid her fingers into his silky hair, cupping his skull, massaging his neck. "Kiss me, J.B."

If this worked, she was going to write a book about curing claustrophobia.

His hands landed on her shoulders, but she wasn't entirely sure he knew what he was doing. There was still a glassy-eyed element to his gaze.

"Mazie?" The way he said her name made the hair on her nape stand up. She knew exactly the moment his arousal broke through the grip of the visceral fear.

This time, the shudder that racked him was entirely hedonistic.

She didn't have to ask again for a kiss.

J.B. took control as if he had been kissing her always. His mouth settled over hers with a drugging sensuality that took the starch out of her knees and left her panting and helpless in his embrace.

Her arms linked around his neck. "This is nice."

"Screw nice…"

His rough laugh curled her toes. No wonder she had kept her distance all these years. At some level she had always known this could happen. She wanted to kick off her shoes and drag him to the floor, but everything was dusty and cold and hard. Not a soft surface in sight.

Once upon a time she had fantasized often about kissing J.B. Vaughan. The reality far outstripped her imaginings.

He was confident and coaxing and sexy and sweet, and she wanted to give him everything he asked for without words.

Thank God there wasn't a bed in sight. Otherwise, she might have done something really stupid.

His tongue stroked hers lazily. "I know what you're doing, and I don't even care. I should have kissed you years ago."

"You did," she reminded him.

"That didn't count. We were kids."

"Felt pretty grown-up to me." In fact, the adult J.B. was reacting much as the teenage J.B. had. His erection pressed against her belly, making her feel hot and dizzy and very confused.

This wasn't real. All she was doing was taking his mind off their incarceration.

He tugged her shirt loose and slid his hand up her back, unfastening her bra with one practiced flick of his fingers. Stroking her spine, he destroyed her bit by bit. "I always knew it would be like this," he groaned.

"Like what?" The two words were a whisper, barely audible over the loud pounding of her heart.

"Wild. Spectacular. Incredibly good." He put just enough space between them to let him cup her breasts in his hands. "Ah, Mazie."

His hands were warm. When he thumbed her nipples, the rough caress sent fire streaking throughout her body.

"Wait," she said. "My turn." She tugged at his soft shirt and sighed when she uncovered his muscled rib cage and taut abdomen. He was smooth and hard and had just enough silky hair to be interesting. She stopped short of his belt buckle.

J.B. nibbled the side of her neck. "Have you ever had sex standing up?"

"Um, no." Her brain was screaming at her to slow things down, but other parts of her body were having so much fun that sensible Mazie didn't stand a chance. "Have you?"

"No. I think it's one of those movie things that might not be so great in real life." He paused, his chest heaving. "But I'm willing to give it a try."

This was insane. They had gone from Mazie trying to distract J.B. from his claustrophobia to jumping each other's bones at warp speed. Though she knew it was suicidal, she couldn't seem to stop herself.

"Kiss me again," she begged. Anything to keep his mind off doing something they both would surely regret.

He granted her wish and then some. First it was her breasts. He bent and tasted each one with murmurs of approval that did great things for her self-esteem. Then he moved up to her neck and her earlobes, and finally, her lips.

Oh, wow, the man knew how to kiss. She didn't even care how many women he had practiced on. The result was mesmerizing.

There were really only so many ways a man and a woman could put their lips together. Yet somehow, J.B. managed to make each ragged breath and groaning caress new and desperate.

He tasted her, and shuddered when she slipped her tongue between his lips and returned the favor. Need—hot and heavy—poured through her limbs and pulsed in her sex. It had been an eternity since she had experienced this level of arousal. Suddenly, she knew she would die if she couldn't have him right here, right now.

Trembling and weak, she clung to his broad shoulders. "I'm not on the Pill," she said. "I don't have any protection."

He bit her bottom lip, tugging it, turning her legs to spaghetti.

"Condom," he moaned. "Wallet."

"Yes." One part of her stood as an onlooker, marveling at her reckless behavior.

Really, Mazie? J.B. Vaughan? After he shot you down all those years ago and ignored you ever since?

Do you really want to do this?

She did. She really did. Maybe she always had.

J.B. removed her top and bra and draped them carefully over the door handle of the safe. Then he turned and stared at her.

She crossed her arms over her chest, unable to pretend sophistication. There had been two men in her life. Not a big number.

He ran his hand from her bare shoulder down her arm, manacling her wrist and reeling her in. "You're exquisite, Mazie."

The recollection of a teenage J.B. had always messed with her head. The popular boy with the raw sexuality and the wicked grin had rejected her and made her feel less than feminine, less than desirable.

It was difficult to reconcile that memory with the present.

"I'm glad you think so."

His slight frown told her he recognized her equivocation. He kissed her temple.

"I love your hair." He ran his hands through it. "It bounces with life and passion. Like you, Mazie."

The sudden segue from frantic hunger to tenderness unsettled her. It was one thing to get caught up in the moment. She didn't trust J.B.'s quiet gentleness. A man could use sex to get what he wanted. Maybe in the midst of their madness, J.B. had recognized her vulnerability where he was concerned. Maybe he hoped to use it to his advantage.

"Kiss me again," she begged. Boldly, she cupped the length of his sex through his pants. He was hard and ready, so ready that the evidence made her want to swoon like some fainthearted Victorian maiden.

Mazie had been abstinent by choice for the past two years. No man had tempted her, not even a little. Now here was J.B. All wrong for her in every way. But at the moment, oh so right.

When she touched him intimately, he shuddered. This

time, she knew the tremors that racked his big frame had nothing to do with a fear of enclosed spaces. J.B. wanted her. Badly. The realization was exhilarating.

They were still mostly clothed, though her bare breasts nestled delightfully against his warm, hard chest. It should have felt weird and odd to be standing here like this. Instead, it was the most wonderfully terrifying thing in the world. In his embrace, she felt torn in a dozen dizzying directions.

She hated this man. Didn't she? Or was this a delightful dream?

The illusion was worth any price. She had waited a decade and more for J.B. to admit that he wanted her. Surely the fates would grant her one outrageous walk on the wild side.

She could call it off. The end would be ugly and awkward and far more scarring than what had happened when she was sixteen. But J.B. would never force himself on a woman, even if Mazie had been the one to initiate the encounter.

"I want you, darlin' Mazie." When he whispered her name and touched her thigh beneath her skirt, she knew the moment was at hand.

It was no contest. "I want you, too, J.B."

What happened next was sheer madness. He scooped her up and backed her against the wall. Her hands tangled in his hair. They were both panting as if they had run a marathon.

He cupped her bottom, grinding his lower half against hers until she wanted to scream with frustration.

He slid his hands beneath her skirt and found bare skin. "Put your legs around my waist."

"The condom," she said. "Don't forget the condom."

"In a minute." He kissed her wildly, his teeth bruising her lips. She pulled his hair, fighting to get closer. Her bikini panties were damp. Her entire body wept with the need to have him inside her.

She crossed her ankles behind his back, ripping at his shirt. "Take this off," she pleaded.

He managed it without breaking the kiss. Now she could run her hands over acres of warm male skin. His body was toned and tanned and sleekly muscled. For a man who supposedly spent a lot of time with spreadsheets and architectural plans, he had the build of an athlete.

"Hang on tight," he demanded. With a muffled groan, he ripped her underpants and held the scraps aloft. "Mission accomplished."

"Those were new," she protested.

J.B.'s grin was feral. "I'll buy you more."

Now he could go where no man had gone in a very long time. He caressed her intimately, inserting one finger…feeling the embarrassingly welcome state of her sex.

"Oh, wow…" She dropped her head to his shoulder and closed her eyes.

J.B. chuckled. "If you like that, I've got lots more."

Without warning, a thunderous pounding on the huge door reverberated in the enclosed space. A muffled shout sounded. "Anybody in there?"

"Holy damn. Lord have mercy."

J.B.'s incredulous response would have been hysterically funny if Mazie hadn't been poised on the brink of a really spectacular orgasm. She groaned and buried her face in his neck.

The voice came again. "Stand back. I'm going to open the door."

"Oh, my God." She jerked out of J.B.'s arms and grabbed for her bra and shirt.

J.B. stared at her, his gaze hot enough to melt all of her inhibitions. "Saved by the bell…"

She should be glad—right? Glad that she hadn't done something stupid and self-destructive?

What was he thinking? His expression was grim.

Her heart sank, incredulous at the way she had let herself fall into old patterns. Suddenly, the situation seemed a thousand times worse.

Four

J.B. cursed beneath his breath, stunned at his run of bad luck. Then again, maybe he should admit the truth. No matter his physical frustration, he had escaped certain catastrophe. He'd spent years avoiding Mazie Tarleton, and yet he'd come perilously close to doing the very thing he knew he couldn't do.

His beautiful enemy was barely decent when a loud scraping ensued, and the heavy door began to swing inward. At the last second, J.B. shoved her torn underwear into his pocket and slipped his shirt on again.

The lights from outside the vault were so bright they both blinked. Their rescuer crossed his arms over his chest. Jonathan Tarleton. Mazie's brother. With a smug smile on his face. "Well, look at you two."

J.B. took a step forward, shielding Mazie in case she had anything else she needed to tuck away. "What are you doing here?"

Jonathan moved back, allowing them to exit. "I though maybe I could convince Mazie to give you a fair hearing. When I arrived, I saw both of your cars, but neither of you. So I put my CSI skills to work and found footprints leading to the vault. Fortunately for you, this hardwood floor is dusty as hell."

For J.B., the rush of cool air was blissful. He inhaled deeply, feeling the last tentacles of his brief ordeal slip away.

Truth be told, Mazie had rescued him quite effectively.

Her methods were almost beguiling enough to make him drag her back into the vault and shut the door again.

Almost, but not quite.

"Thanks for rescuing us," he said. "If you hadn't come by, we might have spent an uncomfortable few hours locked up in there."

"The mechanism was jammed on the outside. I had to hit it with my shoe to knock it loose."

Mazie hadn't said a word up until now, though she had hugged her brother briefly. She edged toward the front of the building. "It was my fault. I didn't mean to close the door." She grimaced. "Not to be rude, but I'm in dire need of the ladies' room. I'll see you later, Jonathan." She gave J.B. an oddly guarded look for someone who had only recently been wrapped around him like a feather boa. "Thanks for the tour."

And then she was gone.

He stared out the window, wondering if the sick feeling in the pit of his stomach was sexual disappointment or something far more alarming.

Had he actually *connected* with his prickly nemesis? Surely not. He couldn't. He wouldn't. The only reason he was spending time with her at all was to seal a deal. He dared not let himself get sidetracked by an almost irresistible attraction.

That kind of thing made a man stupid. He should know.

Jonathan cuffed his shoulder. "Well," he said. "Did you convince her? What did she say?"

J.B. ran his hands through his hair. "She didn't say anything. We'd barely started looking the place over when we got stuck. I have no idea if she liked it or not."

"Of course she liked it," Jonathan said. "Mazie is a sucker for historic buildings. This one has tons of original features, but unlike the dump she's in now, your building is rock-solid."

"Yeah." J.B. nodded absently, reliving every incredible moment of his incarceration. Now that it was over, the whole thing seemed like a dream. Did Mazie Tarleton really let him touch her and nearly make love to her?

"Hey, J.B." Jonathan eyed him strangely.

"What?"

"You have lipstick on your chin."

J.B. froze inwardly. This was a minefield. Mazie wasn't a child anymore, but Jonathan was very protective. That was part of the reason J.B. had kept a healthy distance from her over the years. "Do I?" he said.

Jonathan's expression segued into a frown. "What the hell went on in that vault?"

"None of your damn business. Your sister is an adult. Besides, nothing happened. I got claustrophobic, and Mazie tried to distract me with a little kiss."

"Claustrophobic?" Jonathan's distrust vanished. "Oh, man, J.B., I'm sorry. You must have freaked. That was nice of her, especially considering she doesn't like you all that much."

She seemed to like me just fine a few minutes ago when she had her tongue down my throat.

J.B. swallowed the sarcastic words and managed a noncommittal nod. "Not my finest hour. It's humiliating as hell to have something that happened almost twenty-five years ago still yank my chain. For a minute in there, I thought I was going to lose it."

"You should be glad it was Mazie with you and not someone else. At least she won't ever tease you about it. That girl has a tender heart."

"She's a lot like Hartley in that way. The two of them were always bringing home strays. Have you heard from him at all? I still can't believe he simply vanished."

"No. But it's only a matter of time. Hartley was born and bred here. The Lowcountry is in his blood."

"You don't sound happy about that."

"He abandoned the family business…left me to deal with Dad. I don't have a lot of sympathy for my brother right now."

"He's your twin. Twins are close."

"We were at one time. Not anymore."

"You say that, Jonathan, but I know you. And I know Hartley. The two of you were practically inseparable when we were growing up. You can't pretend that tie isn't there. It always will be."

"Not if I don't want it…not if I don't want *him*."

J.B. let the subject drop, but only because he saw beneath Jonathan's angry response to the deep hurt that still festered.

He rotated his shoulders and took one last look around the room. "I think this will work for Mazie. I didn't get a firm *yes* from her, but I'll follow up."

"And I'll continue to put in a good word for you."

They exited the building. J.B. locked up. "You on for basketball next weekend?"

"Yeah. Seven o'clock?"

J.B. nodded. "I'll see you then."

When Jonathan climbed in his car and drove away, J.B. should have followed suit, but he felt oddly out of sorts. Perhaps because he wanted to get this project settled. He needed Mazie's property.

Who was he kidding? Every bit of his current angst was because of a frustrating, completely off-limits woman who had bedeviled him for years. He wanted her. End of story.

He took out his phone and pulled up her contact info. A short text in this situation would be perfectly acceptable.

Hope you liked the property. Let me know what you think.

But he couldn't do it. Mazie had muddied the waters. Or

maybe they both had. He was accustomed to closing deals. In business. For pleasure. Never both at the same time.

This was exactly why he was screwed. He had resisted temptation all this time, and then in one short afternoon he'd undone all his good intentions.

Thinking about Mazie was a mistake. Half an hour ago, he had been primed to make love to her. His body had been denied satisfaction, and now he was itchy, restless.

One thing he knew for sure.

Kissing Mazie Tarleton was an experience he planned to repeat. Some way. Somehow. Maybe *she* didn't know it, but J.B.'s intentions were crystal clear.

Now that he had touched her, tasted her, there was no going back…

Mazie wanted to go straight home and take a long cold shower, but it was too early in the day to be done with work, and besides, Gina was expecting her to return.

There was no choice but to brazen it out.

Which was not easy when a girl was commando under her skirt.

Fortunately, the shop was swamped with customers. Mazie barely did more than wave at Gina and say hello to her other employees before she was pulled into the fray. Thank goodness for tour ships that dispatched groups of passengers ashore, eager to tick off items on their Christmas lists.

At last, the furor subsided. Mazie sent two of her employees on lunch break. She glanced at her watch. It was almost one.

Mazie had advertised heavily during the last year in several of the cruise lines' brochures. Her print ads were paying off, despite the digital age. Today, she'd had several customers come in clutching their maps of the historic district. All That Glitters was clearly marked, along with the small rectangle showcasing a beautiful necklace and the store's phone number with other contact info.

She glanced in one of the larger cases. "We're going to need more sweetgrass basket charms in gold."

Gina nodded. "Yep. One lady bought six of them for her granddaughters. I'll call Eve this afternoon and place an order."

They were eating pizza standing up, a common occurrence. Gina swallowed a bite and grinned. "Don't keep me in suspense. How did it go with Mr. Gorgeous? Did you like the building?"

"Honestly, I did. The place J.B. wants us to have was originally a nineteenth-century bank. He was showing me the vault when we had a little accident and got locked inside."

Gina's eyes rounded. "You got locked in a bank vault with J.B. Vaughan? God, that's so romantic."

"Um, no. Not romantic at all." You couldn't call what happened with J.B. romance. Sexual frenzy, maybe.

"So it was too scary to be romantic?"

The other woman's crestfallen expression might have been funny if Mazie hadn't been walking on eggshells. She wasn't going to betray J.B.'s secret weakness. Instead, she skirted the truth. "Not so much scary as tense. We were awfully glad to get out of there when Jonathan showed up."

"So are you going to take it? The building, I mean? Will it work for our purposes?"

"It's perfect. Doesn't mean I'm ready to give J.B. what he wants. Surely there's another way."

"Has anyone ever told you that you're contrary?"

"You," Mazie said, finishing her meal. "Every other day." She wiped her hands on a napkin. "My...*conversation* with J.B. got derailed when my brother showed up. I'm sure I'll hear from him soon. J.B., that is."

"And what will you say when he asks you again?"

Mazie flashed to a mental image of the real estate developer's chest. His tousled hair. His eyes, heavy-lidded with desire. Her throat tightened. Her thighs pressed together. "I don't really know."

Unfortunately, the afternoon crowd picked up, and Mazie never found a moment to scoot home and restock her wardrobe. By the time the shop closed at five, she was more than ready to call it quits.

The Tarleton family had lived for decades on the tip of a small barrier island just north of the city. They owned fifteen acres, more than enough to create a compound that included the main house and several smaller buildings scattered around.

An imposing, gated iron fence protected the enclave on land. Water access was impossible due to a high brick wall Mazie's grandfather had erected at the top of the sand. The beach itself was public property, but he had made sure no one could wander onto Tarleton property, either out of curiosity or with dangerous motives. Hurricanes and erosion made the wall outrageously expensive to maintain, but the current Tarleton patriarch was by nature paranoid and suspicious, so security was a constant concern.

At times, Mazie felt unbearably strangled by her familial obligations. Perhaps that was why being around J.B. felt both dangerous and exhilarating all at the same instant.

She punched her security code into the keypad and waited for the heavy gate to slide open. She and Jonathan both wanted to move out, but they were trapped by the weight of love and responsibility for their father. She suspected her brother kept an apartment in the city so he could have a private life, but she didn't pry. Someday she might find a place of her own, as well.

She had let the long-ago debacle with J.B. cast too long

a shadow over her romantic life. Heartbreak had made her overly cautious.

It was time to find some closure with J.B., one way or another. Time to move on.

The house where she had grown up was a colossal structure of sandstone and timber, on stilts, of course. Supposedly, it had been built to withstand a Category Four hurricane. Though the family home had suffered damage over the years, the original structure was still mostly intact.

An imposing front staircase swept upward to double mahogany doors inlaid with stained glass. The images of starfish and dolphins and sea turtles had fascinated her as a child. When she grew tall enough, she liked to stand on the porch and trace them with her fingertips.

The sea creatures were free in a way that Mazie couldn't imagine. All her life she had been hemmed in by her mother's illness and later, her father's paranoia. Jonathan and Hartley—when they had been in a mood to tolerate her—had been her companions, her best friends.

And J.B., too.

The Vaughan family was one of only a handful in Charleston as wealthy as the Tarletons, so Gerald Tarleton had condoned, even promoted his children's friendship with J.B. But Mazie was younger, and Hartley was a loner, so it was always Jonathan and J.B. who were the closest.

Mazie had adored J.B. as a child, then had a crush on him as a teenager, and finally, hated him for years. No matter how she examined her past, it was impossible to excise J.B. from the memories.

Mazie found her father in the large family room with the double plate-glass windows. The ocean was benign today, shimmering shades of blue and turquoise stretching all the way to the horizon.

"Hi, Daddy." She kissed the top of his curly, white-haired head. Her father was reading the *Wall Street Jour-*

nal, or pretending to. More often than not, she discovered him napping. Gerald Tarleton had been an imposing figure at one time. Tall and barrel-chested, he could bluster and intimidate with the best of them.

As he aged, he had lost much of his fire.

He reached up and patted her hand. "There you are, pumpkin. Will you tell cook I want dinner at six thirty instead of seven?"

"Of course. Did you have a good day?"

"Stupid doctor says I can't smoke cigars anymore. Where's the fun in that?"

The family physician made twice yearly visits to the Tarleton compound. Mazie wasn't sorry to have missed this one. "He's trying to keep you alive."

"Or take away my reasons for living," he groused comically.

Her father had married later in life, a man in his midforties taking a much younger bride. The story wasn't so unusual. But in Gerald's case, it had ended tragically. His bride and her parents had hidden from him the extent of her mental struggles, leaving Gerald to eventually raise his young family on his own.

Mazie and her brothers had each paid an invisible price that followed them into adulthood.

She ignored his mood. "I'll speak to cook, and then I'm going to change clothes. I'll be back down in half an hour or so."

"And Jonathan?"

"He's home tonight, I think."

After a quick word with the woman who ran the kitchen like a drill sergeant, but with sublime culinary skills, Mazie ran upstairs and at last made it to the privacy of her bedroom. She stripped off her clothes, trying not to think about J.B.'s hands on her body.

His touch had opened her eyes to several disturbing

truths, not the least of which was that she had carried a tendresse for him, an affection, that had never been stamped out.

She had spent a semester in France her senior year, only a few months after he had rejected her. The entire time she was abroad, she had imagined herself wandering the streets of Paris with J.B.

What a foolish, schoolgirl dream.

Yet now, when she stared in the mirror and saw her naked body, it was impossible to separate her former daydreams from the inescapable reality. She had allowed J.B. Vaughan to caress her breasts, to touch her intimately.

Had Jonathan not intruded to *rescue* them, would she have regrets?

Confusion curled her stomach. She wasn't the kind of person who jumped into bed with a man. Especially not J.B.

Something had happened in the vault.

Yet however she replayed the sequence of events, J.B. didn't come out the villain. *Mazie* had been the one to accidentally close the door and lock them in. *Mazie* had been the one to kiss J.B. *Mazie* had been the one who decided that a nod to her past infatuation would serve to distract J.B. from his claustrophobia.

Was it any wonder he had taken her invitation and run with it?

She stayed in the shower a long time, scrubbing and scrubbing again, trying to erase every vestige of his touch from her skin. She still wanted to hate him. He was still off-limits. And damn it, she *still* wanted to see him squirm.

Today had weakened her position in their face-off.

J.B. was a highly sexual man. When a woman gave him every indication she *wanted* sex, it was no wonder he had obliged.

Mazie had to live with the knowledge that she had done something extremely foolhardy. Self-destructive even.

Circumstances had saved her from the ultimate humiliation.

She didn't have to face J.B. as an ex-lover. Thank God for that.

But the unseen damage was worse, perhaps.

Now she knew what it felt like to be in his arms, to hear him whisper her name in a ragged groan that sent shivers of raw pleasure down her spine. Tonight when she climbed into bed, she would remember his hands on her breasts, her bare body, her sex.

How could she think about anything else?

Five

Even now, her hands trembled as she dried herself with a huge fluffy towel that smelled of sunshine and ocean breezes. The housekeeper liked pinning the laundry on an old-fashioned clothesline when weather permitted.

Mazie put on soft, faded jeans and a periwinkle cashmere sweater with a scoop neck. A short strand of pearls that had been her mother's dressed up the outfit enough to meet her father's old-school dinner requirements.

Sooner or later, J.B. would call about the property swap. She would have to speak to him as if nothing out of the ordinary had happened. And she would have to give him an answer.

His offer was generous. There was no denying the truth.

But she didn't want to give him what he wanted.

Though it was childish and petty on her part, something inside her wanted to hurt him as much as he had hurt her. For J.B., that meant she needed to hurt his business. She was certain he didn't have a heart or real emotions. All he cared about was stacking up more money and more accolades for his financial acumen.

If he really cared about *her*, he'd had plenty of years to make up for the past. But he hadn't.

At last, she could delay no longer. The sun had set in a blaze of glory, and darkness had fallen over the island. She heard a car in the driveway and recognized her brother's voice as it floated up from the foyer.

This mess with J.B. would have to wait.

She had time. Time to come up with a plan. When she saw him again, she wanted to be in control.

Passionless.

Absolutely calm.

There was a very good chance he had used their interlude in the vault to sway her to his side. Though he had not instigated the encounter, he was intuitive and fiercely intelligent. If he had sensed her weakness where he was concerned, he wouldn't have hesitated to use it against her. Nor would he in the future.

She had to be on her guard. She couldn't let her vulnerabilities where J.B. was concerned fool her into thinking he might really care about her.

Troubled and unsettled, she made her way downstairs. Jonathan might quiz her about the incident earlier in the day when she and J.B. had been trapped, but her father would be oblivious. If the subject came up, she would steer the conversation in a safer direction.

She walked into the dining room, ruefully aware that as usual, the full complement of china and silver and crystal adorned the table. A low arrangement of red roses and holly nestled in a Waterford bowl. Despite the fact that there were only three of them, the Tarletons would dine in style.

Grimacing inwardly, she stopped short when she saw the fourth place setting.

"Who's coming to dinner?" she asked Jonathan, a dreadful premonition already shaking her foundations.

Behind her, a familiar velvet-smooth voice replied.

"It's me," J.B. said. "I hope you don't mind another mouth to feed."

J.B. was accustomed to women's flirtatious maneuvers and their attempts to secure his attention. Rarely had he seen a woman with an expression on her face like Mazie's. She recovered quickly, but for a split second, she was startled, her unguarded look revealing a mixture of dismay and sensual awareness.

He'd be lying if he said the dismay didn't puncture his ego. Nevertheless, he kept his smile.

Mazie circled the room, keeping the dinner table between them. "Of course not. This is my father's house. There's always room for one more."

Gerald and Jonathan sat at the head and foot of the table, leaving J.B. and Mazie to face each other from opposite sides. Just for the hell of it, he moved quickly to hold out Mazie's chair as she took her seat. At the last moment, he unobtrusively brushed the side of her neck with a fleeting touch.

He was almost positive she inhaled a sharp breath, but Gerald was talking in a loud voice, so J.B. couldn't be sure. When the four of them were in place, the housekeeper brought out the first course.

By any culinary standards, it was an amazing meal. The Tarletons' cook was more akin to a chef, and she specialized in Lowcountry dishes that included the best of Charleston's local seafood. Tonight's offering was shrimp and grits with a Caesar salad on the side. J.B. was hungry, so he ate well.

But simmering beneath the surface of the lively conversation was the knowledge that Mazie never once looked him straight in the eye. Nor did she address a single comment directly to him. Her behavior was frustrating.

Things were different between them now…whether Mazie liked it or not.

While J.B. nursed his growing indignation, Gerald Tarleton dominated the evening's debate. Despite his declining health, he continued to go into work every day. He and Jonathan commanded a vast shipping empire that had made the family even more wealthy than it had been in the early days when Gerald took over the reins from *his* father.

At one point, J.B. caught his host's attention. "Mr. Tarleton, my dad wanted me to extend an invitation. He'd love to take you out deep-sea fishing on his new boat."

Gerald shook his head, sipping his wine and for a moment looking oddly fragile. "Tell him thanks, boy. But I don't get out and about much anymore. These old bones give me fits. And call me Gerald. You're not a kid anymore."

"The boat is a honey, Gerald. Almost as comfortable as my own house. The crew would pamper you. Think about it, why don't you? Dad respects you a great deal. I know it would tickle him to have a chance to pick your brain about business."

Gerald's pleased expression told J.B. that he had made inroads into the old man's instinctive refusal.

J.B. turned his attention to Mazie. "What about you, Mazie Jane? I seem to recall that you like to fish. We could make a party of it." He tried to get a rise out of her. Mazie had always hated her full name, because she thought it was too old-fashioned.

She choked on a bite of shrimp. Had to dab her mouth with a napkin before she could answer.

"Sounds fun," she said, clearly lying. "If I can find a free Saturday, I'll let you know."

Her Saturdays would be free when hell froze over. That much J.B. knew.

She was blowing him off, and none too subtly. Her evasion brought out his fighting instincts.

Jonathan's cell phone buzzed. He pulled it from his jacket pocket, gave his three companions an apologetic look and stood. "I have to deal with this. Sorry to interrupt the meal."

Cook spirited his plate away to keep the food warm.

Now it was only J.B., Mazie and an elderly man who was already nodding off, his chin on his chest.

J.B. crooked a finger. "I need to speak to you," he whispered. "In private." He motioned toward the door that led to the covered veranda.

Mazie glanced at her father and then at her plate. "I'm eating."

"This won't take long."

"I don't have anything to say to you."

"But I have things to say to *you*," he said firmly. "Or I can wait until your brother returns, and he can hear it all."

"You're a bully," she said, but she rose to her feet. "Make this quick."

Quietly, they stepped outside onto the porch and closed the door behind them.

Mazie wrapped her arms around her waist. "What?" she asked. "What's so damned important?"

"I want to know why you're looking at me like gum you scraped off the bottom of your shoe."

"I'm not," she said, backing away from him half a step.

"Yes. You are. I'm not an idiot. This morning you and I were—"

She shoved a hand against his chest, halting his words in midsentence. "Stop it. Right there. This morning was a mistake." Then she backed up again, almost as if she were afraid to let herself get too close to him.

He lifted an eyebrow. "You didn't enjoy yourself?"

"That's beside the point. It shouldn't have happened. And it won't again."

He chewed on that for a moment. "What are you afraid of, honey?"

Her eyes flashed. "Typical male response. If a woman doesn't want you, she must be afraid. That's bull crap, J.B."

"No," he said, trying his best to tamp down his anger and frustration. "What's bull crap is you trying to pretend that something extraordinary didn't happen between us today…" He hesitated, unwilling to give her ammunition, but itching to get at the truth. "That kind of connection is rare, Mazie."

She stared at him, eyes wide, posture shouting her unease. "I bet you use that line with a lot of women. You have a reputation, you know."

It was true. He couldn't deny it.

But her wariness went much farther back than that. Yes, he dated plenty of women. Mazie had made her judgments about him a long time ago, though.

"Have dinner with me tomorrow night," he said.

"Why? So you can badger me about my property?"

"Would you rather call it a date?"

He had boxed her into a momentary corner. Even as a child, Mazie never backed down from a dare. Now, he used that knowledge against her.

She lifted a shoulder and let it fall. "Fine," she said. "I'll meet you for a business dinner."

"I'll pick you up instead."

"Something casual."

"I'm taking you to Étoile de Mer."

"Absolutely not."

The French restaurant was intimate and extremely formal. In a century and a city that welcomed tourists in virtually any state of dress, Étoile de Mer maintained the old standards. Men in dinner jackets. Women in long dresses. Dancing beneath an antique Baccarat chandelier. The ambiance was unapologetically romantic and luxurious.

He smiled cajolingly. "It's December, Mazie. Jonathan talks about how much you enjoy the season. The hotel will be decorated to the nines. And Chef Marchon has a special holiday menu. The orchestra will play Christmas songs. Say yes. We'll have fun."

A tiny smile lifted the edges of her lips. "Do you always get your way?"

"Most of the time."

"Why are you doing this?" she asked.

He frowned. "I want to spend time with you. Is that so strange?" It *was* strange. And unprecedented. Both of them knew it. He was supposed to be closing a business deal, not chasing an attraction that could burn them both and end very badly.

He was her brother's best friend. It wasn't as if he could walk away and never see her again.

Her wariness was almost palpable. "I won't give you an answer about selling my property for a couple of weeks. I need time to think it over, to discuss the big picture with Gina. To decide how complicated it would be to move the store. If you're hoping to wine and dine me tomorrow night, so I'll be all mellow and sign on the dotted line, that's not going to happen."

"What if I said this wasn't about business at all?"

The words slipped out before he could snatch them back. To be honest, he hadn't known he was going to say something so revealing.

She put a hand to her throat, nervously playing with the strand of pearls. The necklace was nice, but if he had his way, the pearls would be an entire rope, and he would drape them around her neck while they were in bed.

Mazie made no move to break the silence, so he rephrased the question. "What if I swear that tomorrow night will be entirely personal?"

"You're scaring me."

She said it with humor, but he took her words at face value. "Nothing scary, Mazie. Nothing at all. Just two friends enjoying dinner." He was lying through his teeth. This was about much more than dinner. He was courting danger.

"If this is about what happened in the vault, I have to tell you that I'm not usually so…"

Her wrinkled nose and wry embarrassment touched

him. "You were incredible. I've had a hard-on the entire damn day."

"J.B.!"

Her mortified expression made him chuckle. "I get it, Mazie. You're telling me not to expect anything after dinner. That I get my dessert at the restaurant and not in my bed."

"You make me sound naive and ridiculous."

"You're neither of those things. But I'd be lying if I said you didn't shock me this morning. Hell, Mazie. I guess I've had sex a little more than you have, but you and me today..." He leaned against the porch railing and stared out at the ocean. The sound of the waves usually soothed him. Not tonight.

"What about us?"

There was a world of feminine emotion wrapped up in those three little words. Asking for reassurance.

"We connected," he muttered.

He didn't know how else to explain it. He couldn't even make sense of it himself. Was he headed down a familiar road? Letting sexual attraction drag him into a relationship that was doomed to failure?

"We should go back inside," she said quietly. "Jonathan will wonder where we are."

Something clicked. "Is Jonathan part of the problem? Are you worried about what your brother will think?"

"I don't want to cause discord between the two of you."

"Leave that to me." He sounded more confident than he felt.

Jonathan was likely to punch him, at the very least, if he found out J.B. was dallying with his baby sister. After all, Jonathan was partly to blame for the fact that Mazie had held a grudge against J.B. for so long.

"Daddy's awake," Mazie said. "I can see him waving his arms. Probably bossing the cook. Let's go in."

J.B. took her wrist, holding it lightly, needing to touch her, but not wanting to spook her. "I want to kiss you again."

"You do?"

"Yeah. Pretty badly. Just a kiss, Mazie. That's all."

Slowly, waiting for her to lean in and exhaling on a sigh of relief when she did, he drew her against his chest and wrapped his arms around her. She was tall for a woman. Their heights matched perfectly.

She was soft and warm. He buried his face in her neck, dragging oxygen into his lungs. Reminding himself he wasn't a horny teenager. He could control his emotions and his body.

When his mouth found hers, she murmured his name. Hearing her say it, all low and husky like that, made him nuts. He tangled a hand in her hair and deepened the kiss.

He hadn't imagined it. The fire. The wanting.

Whatever happened with Mazie in that bank vault this morning had nothing to do with his claustrophobia or a stress-induced jolt of adrenaline from being trapped.

It was all Mazie.

Now, she kissed him back. Unmistakably. When he would have pulled away, her hands clung to his shoulders, and she pressed against him. His erection was hard and heavy between them. Nothing he could do about that.

"Mazie," he croaked, trying to back away from the edge of insanity. "We need to go back inside. You said so. You're right."

"Don't listen to me," she said, unbuttoning a button on his shirt and stroking his collarbone.

The little tease was tormenting him on purpose.

He dragged her with him to a less exposed section of the veranda, around the corner of the house. This was not the time for Jonathan to burst through the doorway and find his sister in a compromising position.

"Enough," J.B. begged, wondering when exactly he had

lost the upper hand. He batted her hand away and rebuttoned his shirt. "Say yes to tomorrow night. It's the only answer I'll accept."

She smiled up at him, her eyelids heavy, her lower lip plump and shiny where he had sucked on it. "Yes."

Something inside him settled. "And you'll wear a kick-ass dress so I can make all the other men jealous?"

"I want to dance with you," she said. "If we're going all out for this *date*, I'll expect dancing."

"Duly noted."

"And expensive champagne. Maybe even caviar."

"Yes, ma'am."

"I still don't know why we're doing this," she said, the humor fading from her voice. "It seems awfully dangerous. Southern mamas warn their daughters about men like you."

He rubbed his thumb over her cheek, cupping her face. "You should have had a mother, Mazie. I'm sorry about all you lost."

She pulled away from him as if the sudden switch to a serious topic was more than she could bear.

Though her back was to him now, he saw her shrug. "I was luckier than most kids. My father indulged me."

Sliding his arms around her from behind, he rested his chin on top of her head. "It's easy to do. I have the same tendency myself."

"Which doesn't explain why you're trying to steal my livelihood."

He snorted. "Cut the drama. Besides, we're shelving the business negotiations for now. Isn't that what you wanted?"

It was getting more and more difficult to tell himself that this new détente with Mazie was all about business.

She turned around and looked up at him. "We don't always get what we want, J.B."

Six

Mazie wanted another kiss. But she knew her limits. Already she was playing with fire. Common sense was no match for the beat of her heart and the yearning in her blood.

Could she pursue this attraction and not get hurt? Could she indulge in her passion for J.B. and yet still make him pay for all the pain he had caused her in the past?

She fled the porch, not waiting to see if J.B. followed. Fortunately, her father was enjoying his favorite dessert—warm peach cobbler with ice cream. And Jonathan still hadn't returned.

Her father looked up when she walked into the room. "I wondered where everybody had gone."

"You were dozing," she said, seating herself at the table and picking up the napkin. "J.B. and I were talking business."

Her father raised an eyebrow. "Is he trying to sell you something?"

"No, sir," Mazie said. "He wants to buy the building I'm in."

"Make him work for it."

J.B. sat down as well, smoothing his hair and giving Mazie a steely-eyed glance. "No worries there, sir. Your daughter drives a hard bargain."

Fortunately for Mazie, Jonathan returned at that moment, and she was able to consume her dessert in peace while the men grumbled about sports and politics and whether or not South Carolina was going to have a colder-than-normal winter.

It was the occasional heated glances from J.B. that kept her on edge. Even in the midst of male conversation, he made it clear that his thoughts were on her.

Soon after, J.B. said his goodbyes.

Mazie considered walking him out, but Jonathan beat her to it, so she stayed where she was, telling herself she wasn't disappointed. She had kissed J.B. Vaughan entirely too many times for one day.

When Jonathan came back inside, he shut the front door and began punching in numbers to set the alarm. Mazie stopped him. "Are you in the mood to walk the beach?" she asked in a low voice. "I need to talk to you about a couple of things, and I don't want to do it in the house where Daddy can hear."

Jonathan looked tired and stressed, but he nodded. "Sure. You do know it's December?"

It was a running joke between them. A sort of dare as to which of the two would cry uncle when the temperatures dropped. "I'll bundle up," she said.

As she found her earmuffs and a heavy scarf and slipped on an old thigh-length coat, she couldn't help but wonder if J.B. would have welcomed an invitation to stay for a while. Had Jonathan not been home tonight, she might have been tempted.

On the way down the hall, she stopped by her father's bedroom.

"Jonathan and I are going for a walk on the beach," she said. "We won't be gone too long."

Her father lifted his head from his task and frowned. "It's not safe. I like having you both inside the house, so I know where you are."

She hugged him. "We need the exercise. Jonathan seems awfully stressed. Is everything okay at work?"

"The usual kerfuffles. He's fine."

"Have you heard anything at all from Hartley?"

Her father paled, his gaze haunted. "No. Go for your walk. And make sure you lock up when you get back."

"Yes, Daddy."

Jonathan was waiting for her. He tugged a toboggan over his head. "All set?"

She nodded. "Let's go."

In the brick wall on the back side of the house, a heavy wooden gate with electric voltage across the top provided an exit point. Jonathan disarmed the system and held the door for her to pass. In the soft powdery sand at this level, her feet slipped and slid. They crossed the beach to where the tide was going out, then turned left and started to walk.

Jonathan altered his stride to hers immediately. They found their rhythm and strode briskly. Occasionally, another intrepid beach walker passed by going in the opposite direction, but for the most part they had the beach to themselves.

Sometimes when they walked so late, they carried flashlights. This week, the nearly full moon provided plenty of illumination.

Mazie stared out at the almost invisible horizon. Tonight, the line between sea and sky was barely perceptible. As children, she and Hartley and Jonathan—and often J.B.— had loved watching the huge ships coming in and out of Charleston's historic harbor. They had learned how to spot Tarleton vessels, and how to read the bits of foreign language markings on others.

Often, especially on rainy days when there were no good outdoor activities to entertain a quartet of rambunctious children, they spun stories for each other about mysterious cargoes and whether or not it would be possible to stow away and make a sea voyage on the company's dime.

If they had been particularly well behaved, their father would bring out his expensive, high-powered binoculars and teach them how to focus the lenses. Mazie had stared at the ocean for as long as she could remember.

It was vast and inscrutable. She had seen the sea as placid as a baby's bath or angry and punishing in the midst of a hurricane. Sometimes it seemed as if all the answers to life's weighty questions resided in that enormous expanse of water.

Tonight, though, she sought a more human connection. She loved her brother dearly, but she wondered if he could be objective under the circumstances.

"Jonathan?"

"Hmm?" Her brother was lost in thought, his expression serious.

"Do you trust J.B.?"

Jonathan's head whipped around, his gaze incredulous. "He's my best friend. What kind of question is that? Of course I trust him. Surely you're not worried he's going to stiff you on this business deal. Is that why you're dragging your feet?"

"No, it's not that. I know he'll make me a fair offer. He already has, in fact. The only reason I haven't committed yet is because I wanted him to swing in the wind for a little while. The man is so damned arrogant. I couldn't stand the thought of giving in to him so easily."

Jonathan chuckled. "Well, he *is* arrogant, I'll grant you that. But he comes by it honestly. Everything he touches turns to gold."

"And on a personal level?"

"He and I have never done business together."

"That's not what I meant."

Jonathan stopped and faced her. "You're talking about women." He said it flatly. A statement. Not a question.

"I suppose I am."

"J.B. and I are grown men. We don't share locker room stories. What are you asking me, Mazie?"

She wrapped her arms around herself, feeling a chill now that they had stopped and their blood was cooling. "I'm not sure. I'm wondering what you know about his private life."

"As much as anybody, I guess." He started walking again, leaving Mazie to scamper in his wake to catch up. "He likes variety."

Her heart sank. She had come to the same conclusion. "Yeah…"

"Where's this coming from, sis?"

"He's asked me out on a date."

She threw it out there bluntly. No frills. Wondering what Jonathan would make of it.

For the second time, her brother ground to a halt. This time, his expression was thunderous. "Are you serious? I thought you hated the guy."

"Hate is a strong word. It seems like a bad idea, doesn't it?"

Jonathan made a motion with his hand. "Let's turn around." He walked in silence for a few moments. "Why ask me?"

"Well…" She shrugged. "You and I both agree he flits from one woman to the next. If he and I get something going and then it's over, everything will be awkward. Especially for you."

"Do you *want* to go out with him, Mazie?"

Ah, there was the question. She took a deep breath, inhaling the scents of salt air and somewhere in the distance, meat sizzling on a grill. "I do. Even knowing it's probably self-destructive. I like him. A lot. But J.B. has always been our *friend*. It's weird for me."

"How do you think I feel?"

Her brother's wry comment made her smile. "Well, don't worry. It will probably be a one-time thing. I can't imagine that he and I have what it takes to be a couple." Even talking about it sounded bizarre. There was a very good chance the *date* was an attempt to butter her up.

"Don't sell yourself short. J.B. isn't *only* a successful businessman. He does have a life."

"Unlike you," she said, suddenly eager to change the subject.

"Don't start on me, Mazie. Work has been hell lately. Dad goes in every day and creates messes I have to undo. And then I still have *my* projects to deal with. I don't know how much longer we can keep going like this."

"Is it time for him to step down?"

"I think so, yes. But how do I tell him that?"

"What about Hartley? Couldn't he help you?"

Jonathan's low curse shocked her. It was totally unlike him.

His voice was tense and angry. "There is no Hartley," he said. "He's not coming back. And even if he did, it wouldn't matter. Dad has cut him out of the will."

Sick dismay rolled through her chest. "But why?"

"I can't tell you. Or I don't want to tell you," he said, his voice weary. "He's your brother. I don't want to ruin your illusions. But trust me when I say there are some sins a man commits that are unforgivable."

"But I—"

He cut her off with a sharp slash of his hand. "I won't talk to you about this, Mazie. I love you dearly, but the subject is closed."

Jonathan's vehement tone ended the conversation. Their peaceful walk was ruined.

Tears stung her eyes. Jonathan complained about chaos at the shipping company, but for Mazie, All That Glitters was the stability in her life. At home she had a rapidly declining parent, one brother who was working himself to death and another who had apparently abandoned them all. Even worse—though he didn't say much about it—Jonathan's headaches were increasingly severe. It worried her.

They were almost back to the house. She touched his arm. "I'm sorry. I know you're carrying the business. I wish I could help."

He put an arm around her waist and hugged her. "It will all work out. It always does."

She sighed. "I feel like I should head up to Vermont to see Mama…sometime in the next two weeks."

Jonathan stopped. He rolled his shoulders. "I'm not ready to go inside yet."

They dropped down onto the sand. Mazie linked her arms around her knees. "I'll feel guilty if I don't make the effort."

"She doesn't even know who we are. Hasn't for years."

"I know. But she's my mother. And it's Christmas."

"We were there a month ago."

"Yes." The two of them had flown up to Stowe for a ski trip with friends. Afterward, they had stayed over a day, rented a car and driven to a tiny town near the New Hampshire border to make the sad, difficult visit.

"Have you ever wondered," Mazie said, "why Daddy found a place so damned far away from Charleston?"

Jonathan laughed, but there was no humor in it. "Oh, yeah. To his credit, Ravenwood is tops in the nation for residential care facilities. Believe me, I've checked. So no one can fault him there. He's paying a king's ransom to keep her in safety and comfort."

"But my cynical side tells me he doesn't want to have to think about her. It's easier if she's a thousand miles away."

"That about sums it up."

"When was the last time he went up there?"

"I'm not sure. Two years ago. Three?"

"He could have divorced her."

"I think he probably still loves her, Mazie."

She winced inwardly. Maybe the Tarletons were *every one* cursed…doomed to give their hearts unwisely. After all, wasn't Mazie contemplating doing the same thing? She knew how J.B. had treated her in the past, yet she was still hoping against hope that he had changed.

They sat there in silence, listening to the crashing waves, noting how exponentially many more stars there were the longer they let their eyes adjust to the darkness.

She rested her chin on her knees. "I used to wish we were a family like the Vaughans. Normal. Ordinary. Together."

Jonathan tousled her hair. "I'm not sure I'd call my buddy ordinary, but yeah. I get your point." He leaned back on his hands. "I guess we're all a little screwed up because of what happened. I hated it for you the worst. I remember the day Mom left you cried for hours."

"And you skipped baseball practice so you could come home, sit on my bed and read *Little House on the Prairie* to me."

"She wasn't much of a mom even when she still lived with us. We pretty much raised ourselves."

"I know. It used to scare me when she would sit in front of the window for hours on end and not speak."

"Don't go to Vermont, Mazie. It will make you too sad. Wait until January, and I'll go with you. Or maybe February."

"I'll think about it."

"And J.B.?"

She stood up and dusted the sand from her pants. "I'll think about him, too. Who knows, Jonathan? Maybe you and I are both too messed up to have serious relationships with anyone."

He rolled to his feet and shook himself like a dog. "Speak for yourself. I plan to get laid this weekend on a tropical island with a drink in one hand and sunscreen in the other."

"Really?"

He headed toward the gate, his laughter dancing on the breeze. "You're too gullible, Mazie Jane. I'd work on that before you go out with J.B."

Mazie gulped her coffee, burned her tongue and said an unladylike word. "Can you unlock the door? I don't know what I did with my keys."

Gina scooted past her, punched in the alarm code and wrestled with the cantankerous lock. "I hope we do move. I hate this door."

The two of them entered the shop and dumped their things in the back office. Mazie was usually the bubbly one in the mornings. Gina was slower to wake up. But Mazie had spent a restless night tossing and turning and wondering if she had the guts to call J.B. and cancel.

She didn't know which was worse. Going, or not going. Now she was exhausted *and* conflicted.

Gina sifted through the mail she had picked up from their postal box. "Two bills, an invitation to a reception at the Gullah Cultural Center and seven catalogs. Maybe *we* should consider doing a catalog. The bulk mailings must produce business, or we wouldn't be drowning under the weight of them."

"It's even worse at home. The recycle bin overflows this time of year."

"Look at this one," Gina said. "It's an English company that sells organic scented soaps. Their packaging is really nice. We could add some little things like that to put pops of color in the shop. Even jewelry can get monotonous when it's all gold and silver."

"Bite your tongue," Mazie said, laughing.

As they ran through their morning rituals, Mazie felt the strongest urge to tell Gina everything that had happened in the bank vault, and then last night on the veranda. She needed advice. Support. A dose of impartial sanity.

She was supposed to be planning her revenge, not thinking about how good it felt to kiss J.B. To touch him. To feel his hands on her body.

Gina waved a hand in front of Mazie's face. "Hellooo… you spaced out on me, boss. I need you to focus. We've got not one, but two cruise ships today. And it's Friday, so the Holiday Weekends festival starts. We're going to be run ragged."

"You're right."

Gina cocked her head. "Are you okay, Mazie?"

Seven

Mazie changed the subject and busied herself unwrapping a shipment of earrings.

As the afternoon passed, one thought kept spinning in her brain. She wasn't going to sleep with J.B. Of course she wasn't.

But the whole time she was getting ready after work that afternoon, she couldn't help wondering if he was contemplating taking her home with him after dinner. Given what had transpired in the bank vault, it wasn't an entirely out-in-left-field idea. Clearly he knew that going back to *her* place was out of the question.

She left the shop at three in order to get a mani-pedi before going home. Tonight's encounter required all the confidence she could muster. Whether the evening turned out to be business or pleasure or both, she had to be prepared, mentally and physically.

Fortunately, her wardrobe wasn't a problem. A year ago, for a black-tie charity gala, she had ordered a beautiful holiday dress from an online catalog. At the last minute, she had come down with a twenty-four-hour bug and didn't get to attend the event. The gown had been hanging in her closet ever since.

It wasn't really the kind of thing she could use during another season of the year. The floor-length dress was deep green velvet. The fabric was elegant and classic, the design even more so. A plunging neckline showcased her breasts.

The back of the dress also dipped in a deep vee, leaving her arms and shoulders bare.

She debated longer over her hair than anything else. If it were summer, she would put it up, no question. But the weather was perfect today, and with all that bare skin showing, maybe having her hair down around her shoulders was a good idea.

Fortunately for her nerves, Jonathan hadn't yet returned from the office when it was time for J.B. to arrive. Her father was out of the house also, having dinner with friends. Mazie had said goodbye to him earlier as he left with his driver.

Mazie sent the cook and housekeeper home early, so when J.B. pulled up in front of the house in his luxury SUV, no one was around to witness the moment. She peeked out and watched him lope up the front stairs.

He was a gorgeous man, beautiful enough to make her breath catch in her throat. J.B. would hate being called *beautiful*, but the adjective fit. Though his features weren't perfectly symmetrical, and he didn't have the kind of slick sophistication of a model, there was something intensely masculine about him.

He was a chameleon, really.

In a business setting, she had seen him play the part of the successful entrepreneur, both charming and hard-dealing. But when J.B. and Jonathan headed out to North Carolina to camp in the mountains or took off on a weeklong cruise down the coast in J.B.'s sailboat, his tanned limbs and casual clothing made him look like a rugged outdoorsman.

She took one last quick peek before opening the door.

Tonight, in a classic black tuxedo and crisp white shirt, he was a heartbreaker. Mazie knew that side of him better than most.

J.B. was stunned to find that he was nervous as hell. When Mazie opened the door, his heart slugged hard in his chest. Her glorious chestnut hair spilled across her shoulders, thick and wavy. The green dress she wore showcased her slender figure. His fingers itched to stroke all that soft fabric.

But his sense of self-preservation sounded an alarm.

Instead of touching her, he cleared his throat and smiled. "You look stunning, Mazie. I've got the heat running in the car, in case you don't want to bother with a wrap. It's not really all that cold tonight. You could always throw a coat in the back seat for later."

She had stepped back to allow him to enter. Now he stood in the foyer, wanting to sweep her up in his arms and kiss her senseless. Instead, he jammed his hands in his pockets and practiced self-control.

Mazie's smile was guarded. "Thank you. I'll do that."

The current atmosphere could best be described as wary. The physical awareness between them was on a slow boil, but because he had hurt her once, she didn't trust him. He'd have to work on that.

It took Mazie only a matter of moments to lock the door and set the alarm. When she was done, he put a hand beneath her elbow and steadied her as they descended the stairs. The minimal physical contact was enough to make his blood heat.

He helped her into the front seat before closing the door. Then he ran around to the driver's side. As he had promised, the car was toasty warm.

Mazie buckled her seat belt and folded her hands in her lap, her spine straight. It wasn't the posture of a woman prepared to enjoy an exciting evening. If anything, she seemed to be braced for unpleasant news.

"I don't bite," he said teasingly.

They exited the main gates, and he steered the car toward the Ravenel Bridge.

She shot him a sideways glance. "I'm not sure this was a good idea," she said. "We have nothing in common."

Her tone was prissy enough to annoy him. "It didn't seem that way when you locked us in that bank vault."

"That was an accident."

"So you say." He loved teasing her. "We have history, Mazie."

"I'm surprised you'd want to bring that up."

Bingo. Now he knew for sure what land mines lay in his path. She was pissed, even now, about him turning her down years ago.

"You're still mad about that prom thing?"

"Don't flatter yourself." Her fingers made patterns in the velvet. "I got over my embarrassing crush pretty quickly after that night. You were an arrogant jerk. And unkind on top of that. But I learned from that experience."

"Learned what?"

"Not to trust you."

He flinched inwardly. There were extenuating circumstances, explanations that could clear his name, but he wasn't the only person involved, and he didn't want to cause a rift between her and Jonathan. Even now, J.B.'s behavior was risky. It was the reason he had kept his distance for years.

"I'd like to propose a truce," he said lightly, his fingers clenched on the steering wheel. "What if we start over? A new relationship. A new beginning." He told himself he needed her goodwill so she would sell him her property. Surely he wasn't really considering something so much more unpredictable.

"Why would we do that?"

"It's the season of peace and goodwill. Isn't that enough?" He reached across the small distance separating them and touched her wrist. "This isn't about me stealing your property, Mazie. I want it, yes. But we can do business another day. Tonight, I'm only interested in *you*."

He hadn't meant to be so honest, but her inability to accept him at face value was frustrating.

At the hotel, J.B. handed off his keys with a large tip, large enough to guarantee he'd get the car back with no dings or scratches.

The front door was only steps away. He glanced at his passenger. "Do you want to keep your coat?"

"No. I'm fine."

The seat of the SUV was high. Mazie's legs were long, but her dress was fitted. Without asking permission, he put his hands on her waist and lifted her down to the narrow red carpet that led to the entrance.

Overhead, a canvas awning protected them from nonexistent rain. Huge concrete urns on either side overflowed with holly and magnolia blossoms and burgundy satin ribbons.

Mazie's face lit up, her reserve melting in the festive atmosphere. "This is lovely." She actually squeezed his hand momentarily, leaving him to grin like a kid who'd just gotten a gold star for a perfect spelling test. Unfortunately, the moment was far too short.

He curled an arm around her waist and ushered her inside.

Étoile de Mer was old Charleston at her finest. Five years ago, the series of narrow buildings tucked away on a side street had been an aging inn past its prime with a different name. But new owners had completely renovated the connected eighteenth-century row houses.

The result was a chic, luxurious boutique hotel that catered to travelers with the means to splurge, whether that be millennials or baby boomers. The main floor of the hotel included a bar and lounge along with a five-star restaurant that was booked for six months in advance.

J.B. had called in a few favors, made a handful of promises and wrangled a prime reservation for seven o'clock.

Seeing the expression on Mazie's face was worth every bit of hassle.

The host led them up a shallow flight of stairs to the mezzanine level. Their table was tucked inside a bay window overlooking the street.

Once they had ordered an appetizer and wine, J.B. leaned back in his chair and studied his companion. "Have you eaten here before?"

Mazie shook her head. "No. I do go out with friends often, but we generally pick something more casual. And my social life isn't nonstop. Jonathan and I take turns looking after Dad when we want to be gone overnight."

"He can't be on his own?"

"Oh, he could be," Mazie said. "But Jonathan and I are his emotional crutches. Once Hartley disappeared, I think Daddy gave up and started thinking like an old man."

"Do you know where your brother is?"

Mazie shook her head, her expression bleak. "No. I don't even know what happened. Jonathan won't tell me. Do *you* know?"

J.B. shook his head. "Sorry. No idea. Jonathan and I are tight, but he hasn't said much at all about Hartley."

"Oh." She sighed. "I was hoping you could clue me in. The whole thing is frightening. To be honest, it hurts. He and I were very close. I can't believe he left without saying a word." Mazie traced a pattern in the condensation on her water glass with her fingertip. "I used to be terribly jealous of your family," she said. Her rueful sideways glance told him she wasn't kidding.

"Really? Why?"

"The Vaughans are all so incredibly normal. I never had normal in my life. You're lucky, J.B."

The comment caught him off guard. "I suppose I am,"

he said. The waiter interrupted the conversation, arriving to take their order. Mazie chose shrimp étouffée on a bed of fluffy rice. J.B. asked for the rare filet topped with a crabmeat garnish.

When they were alone again, he picked up the threads of the conversation. "What happens to your father when you or Jonathan decide to get married?"

Mazie wrinkled her nose. "I don't know that either of us has to worry about that. My dear brother doesn't let himself get close to anyone, and I'm…" She trailed off, looking uncomfortable.

"You're what?"

"Scared." She tossed the word at him with an almost visible chip on her shoulder.

"Scared of what?"

"I don't want to love someone so much that it blinds me or traps me. My parents are hardly a shining example of marital success. You know the statistics. You've lived them. No offense."

He winced inwardly. Mazie had faced more than her share of abandonment. She must surely have been conflicted about her father sending her mother away, no matter the circumstances.

"I hear what you're saying, but I'm not sure your argument holds water, though. I had the greatest example of marriage in the world, and still I got duped by a money hungry social climber who ruined my credit and cleaned out my bank accounts in the divorce."

"Did your parents try to stop you?"

"Of course they did. Several friends weighed in, too, Jonathan included. But I was blinded by physical infatuation." Wasn't that what he risked now?

"Not too blind to see what you were getting out of the arrangement."

Mazie's humor soothed old wounds. "I was twenty-two

years old and driven by my hormones. It wasn't my finest hour."

"To be honest, I was away at college most of that year, so I didn't hear more than the occasional flurry of gossip. But I remember being very surprised."

He cocked his head. "Why?"

"Because you were always so sure of what you wanted. At the risk of pumping up your already enormous ego, I couldn't imagine any woman walking away from you after only a few months, even if you *were* difficult to live with. Maybe she had the money thing planned from the start."

"If you're trying to make me feel better, it's not working."

Her grin was impish. "Sorry. I've known you and hated you for too long to tiptoe around your feelings…always assuming you *have* feelings." The smile told him she was making a joke at his expense. She wasn't trying to impress him, that was for sure.

"I have feelings," he said, deadpan. "I'm having a feeling right now." He flirted deliberately, for nothing more than the sheer pleasure of watching her react.

Mazie didn't seem to know what to make of him.

She concentrated on her food, most likely disconcerted by his deliberately intimate teasing. When at last she lifted her head and pinned him with an amber-eyed gaze, he knew in an instant that he had waded into deep water.

"Let me ask you something, J.B.," she said.

He waved a hand. "Anything at all. I'm an open book."

"If we hadn't gotten locked in the bank vault and ended up in an extremely compromising position, would you ever have considered asking me out?"

His fork was halfway to his mouth. The bite of tender beef went untasted. Slowly, he set down the utensil, dabbed his lips with a snowy napkin and frowned. "I feel like this is one of those questions women throw out to trip a guy up."

"It's no trick. I'm merely asking—would we be sitting here right now if you didn't have claustrophobia, and we didn't use sex to take your mind off the fact that we were trapped? You've had a decade to ask me out on a date. Why now?"

Mazie watched J.B.'s face, zeroing in on every nuance of expression. She'd like to think her intuition could spot any dissembling on his part. Then again, the man was a practiced charmer. Girls had been throwing themselves at him since he was in middle school.

It was no wonder he was so confident he could acquire her property. He was accustomed to the dominoes always falling his way. The world cooperated with J.B. Inevitably.

While it was true that his youthful marriage had been a bad misstep, he had survived. He'd been humiliated and chastened and perhaps, at the time, even heartbroken. Still, it seemed unlikely he had suffered any lasting damage.

His silence in the aftermath of her question was ominous. Was he inventing a pretty story? Concocting a tale that would flatter her and woo her?

"J.B.?"

He shook his head. "You ask difficult questions, Mazie Tarleton. Maybe I wanted to be sure I was giving you a thoughtful response. Maybe I needed to comb through my own motives. Maybe I'm not even sure why I invited you to dinner. Or maybe I was afraid the truth would make you angry."

She gaped at him, unprepared for this level of transparency. "So what did you come up with? Don't keep me in suspense."

While she waited, breathless, needing to hear what J.B. had to say, their waiter arrived with the main courses. Though the food looked and smelled amazing, Mazie wanted to banish the poor man to the kitchen. J.B. had been hovering on the verge of complete honesty. She wanted desperately to hear his response.

Instead, she had to be content with a seemingly endless parade of servers and sommeliers and even the manager who wanted to make sure every single thing about the dinner was to their liking.

By the time the two of them were finally alone again, the moment had passed.

Mazie sighed inwardly. An orchestra on the level below them had begun playing a medley of familiar Christmas songs. The restaurant buzzed with laughter and the clinking of crystal.

On any other occasion and with any other companion, Mazie would be basking in a haze of warm contentment.

Instead, she ate her meal automatically. All she could think about was the man sitting across from her. Why was he stalling?

He poured each of them another glass of wine, finished his steak and then stared at her.

"The answer is no," he said. "I wouldn't have. The reason I asked you out has *everything* to do with what happened in the bank vault."

Eight

Mazie froze, sensing danger. J.B.'s eyes were dark…intense. More navy blue tonight than royal. And nothing about him suggested lighthearted teasing.

She swallowed, her throat suddenly as dry as sandpaper. "I see."

He drank recklessly, the muscles in his throat rippling as he swallowed. Without warning, some line had been crossed, some barrier breached.

Gone was the good-natured, sophisticated businessman. The wealthy entrepreneur.

In his place was a primal male with flushed cheekbones, glittering sapphire eyes, and a big body that radiated warmth and raw masculinity.

In his right hand, he held a crystal goblet. His left hand moved restlessly on the white linen tablecloth. Against the pristine fabric, his tanned fingers drummed a rhythm only he could hear.

At last he stared at her moodily, his brows dark, his mood volatile. "Is that all you have to say?"

"I may have given you the wrong impression about me," she whispered, conscious of people coming and going nearby.

"Or maybe you hide the real you from the world."

"I'm not that kind of woman," she said desperately. "It was the adrenaline or something."

"Or something…" He laughed without humor. "You're

a sensual woman, Mazie. Sexy and beautiful and damned appealing in every way. We've been dancing around each other for years, always careful never to get too close. I've seen you move across a crowded room to avoid me. Why?"

"You're imagining things," she said, aghast that he had noticed. But of course he had. The man never missed anything. She'd been protecting herself, plain and simple. And he had known, damn him.

"No." His rebuttal was flat. Certain. "I'm not imagining *anything*. You've kept the width of this city between us, but yesterday when I had my embarrassing meltdown, your compassion was stronger than your need to keep your distance. When we touched, it was gasoline on a fire."

"Please don't say things like that," she begged. "It isn't true."

"You can deny it all you like, but I was there, Mazie. So yes…that's why I asked you out. Even though I knew it was a bad idea. I couldn't wait to touch you again." He stood and tossed his napkin on the table. "Dance with me, sweet girl. Dessert will keep."

His hand closed around her wrist. Gently, inexorably, he drew her to her feet.

Mazie trembled. It was impossible to meet his gaze. Not now. Not when her heart slammed against her ribs and her breasts ached for his touch.

He led her down the carpeted stairs and into the salon where a polished dance floor stretched from wall to wall. Overhead, a phalanx of miniature crystal chandeliers, draped in mistletoe and bows, cast a rainbow of shimmering light over the dancers.

The room wasn't large. J.B. pulled her into his arms and held her tightly. They fell into the music as one, barely missing a note or a step. Some men hated dancing. J.B. moved as if he knew the music by heart.

She felt cosseted in his embrace, but at the same time shiveringly aware of the shark-infested waters that might lie ahead. Already her body responded to his caress. His heart beat a steady rhythm beneath her palm. His fingers were warm on the bare skin of her lower back. They didn't speak.

Words weren't necessary.

It wasn't her imagination that other women sneaked peeks at the man who held her so carefully. His breath was warm at her temple. The scent of his crisply starched shirt teased her nostrils.

Her body warmed and melted into his. They were in a very public venue. Dancing was the only acceptable, legitimate reason for a man and woman to be so close.

One song segued into the next. Mazie knew every word, every chorus. For so many Christmases she had wondered about her future. For so many Christmases, she had told herself she despised J.B.

Now the whole world was changing.

She could have danced all night. Her feet barely noticed the pain in her toes, the strain in her calves. For a woman who spent her days in flats or athletic shoes, tonight's escapade was a dose of reality.

Being glamorous hurt.

At last, J.B. was the one to call a halt. He brushed a strand of hair from her hot cheek. "How about a drink?" The words were commonplace. The look in his eyes, anything but.

She nodded, flushed with a confusing mixture of excitement and dread. Whatever happened tonight was up to her. No matter how many times she told herself she had to stay away from J.B., the truth was far simpler.

He was her kryptonite.

She wanted him.

Hand in hand, they ascended the stairs to their intimate table for two. Dessert menus appeared. She downed two glasses of ice water. Her wineglass was refilled, as if by magic.

When their caramel-laced bread pudding arrived, Mazie shook her head. "I don't think I can. I'm stuffed."

J.B.'s heavy-lidded gaze never left her face. "A taste at least," he coaxed. He scooped up a bite. It was covered in whipped cream.

Mazie opened her mouth automatically when he held out the spoon. Her thighs clenched beneath the table. "Yum," she mumbled, chewing and swallowing.

The man was a devil. She wanted to strip him out of that tux and do naughty things to his body.

His slight smile told her he knew exactly what thoughts were running through her head. Without warning, he leaned forward and kissed the edge of her mouth, his tongue delicately swiping a residue of sweet cream. "You taste delectable."

"Stop," she said, breathing hard. "People are watching."

"It was barely a kiss. Don't worry. No one can see."

She realized he was right. The restaurant lights had been dimmed. A trio of short red candles flickered on their table. With the antique privacy screens and artfully placed foliage, Mazie and J.B. were in a world of their own.

The waiter still stopped by, of course, but not as often now that dinner was almost done.

She sipped her wine, awash in a haze of incredulity. Not only was she enjoying herself, but she was spending time with J.B., and she didn't want to kill him. That was progress, right?

Fortunately for her emotional equilibrium, he didn't try to feed her any more dessert. She ate another couple of bites and left it to him to finish. The man was tall and athletic. He could afford the calories.

While they were dancing, J.B. had left his cell phone on the table, silenced of course. Suddenly, it vibrated. He glanced at it automatically, and before he could say anything, another call came in from the same number.

"It's my sister Leila," he said. "She never calls this time of day. Will you excuse me, Mazie?"

"Of course."

As he stood, the phone buzzed a third time.

Something told her it wasn't good news. As she watched, J.B. hurried down the stairs and out the front door where he could talk in private. Though she was at the window, she couldn't see him on the street.

Less than five minutes later, he returned, his face white beneath his tan. "I'm so sorry," he said. "But I have to go. It's my mother." He swallowed hard. "She's had a massive heart attack. They don't know the damage yet. She may have to have surgery tonight."

Mazie's eyes widened. J.B.'s family was close. The matriarch was beloved. "Go," she said, waving her hand at him. "I'll take care of the bill and grab a taxi. Go. Hurry." She lifted a hand and summoned the waiter.

J.B. hesitated, his usual expression robbed of its suave confidence. "I hate to leave you."

She jumped off the emotional deep end. "I could come with you." Even strong men needed support occasionally.

The waiter handed over the check. J.B. pulled out his credit card. When the man walked away, J.B. looked at her and sighed. "I'd like that. If you're sure you want to."

Were both of them thinking about what they were giving up tonight? "Will it seem odd to your family if I show up with you?"

"You know them all. Nobody will notice."

That was debatable.

The waiter dropped off the bill. J.B. scribbled his name and pocketed his credit card. And they were done.

The valet brought the car in record time. J.B. handed over another generous tip and tucked Mazie into the front seat.

She was hardly dressed for a hospital visit. Neither was he.

J.B. drove the maze of downtown streets with a reckless intensity that was only slightly alarming. At the hospital, he screeched into a parking spot in the emergency room lot and hopped out, pausing to help Mazie.

"I can wait in the car," she said, feeling conspicuous in her fancy dress.

He gripped her wrist. "I want you to come."

Once they were inside, it was only a matter of moments until a nurse directed them to the appropriate cubicle. The heart surgeon had just arrived to talk to the family. They were standing in the hall, though Mazie could see J.B.'s mother through the partially open door. The older woman was hooked up to a multitude of machines.

Most families would probably be scolded for having too many visitors. Since the Vaughans had outfitted an entire pediatric wing in recent years, they were VIPs.

The man's face was grave. "Mrs. Vaughan suffered a very dangerous cardiac event. She is weak and not entirely stable. I don't think we should wait until morning for the surgery."

Mazie recognized J.B.'s father and his two sisters, Leila and Alana. As children, Mazie and Jonathan and Hartley had spent large amounts of time at the Vaughan home. But it had been years since she had been close to them as a friend.

Both of J.B.'s sisters had red-rimmed eyes. His father looked exhausted and stressed. Mr. Vaughan nodded. "We're in your hands, Dr. Pritchard. Tell us what to do."

The doctor made a note on his clipboard. "She's been

asking for her son." He looked at J.B. "Once you've had a chance to spend a few minutes with her, we'll prep her for surgery." He paused, grimacing. "I don't want to alarm you unnecessarily, but I need you to know that the surgery carries significant risk. Without it, she'll suffer another heart attack, possibly fatal. So we don't really have a choice."

Mr. Vaughan spoke up, his eyes sunken and underscored with shadows. "You're saying that her other health conditions make it complicated."

The doctor nodded. "Yes. Her autoimmune disease and the high blood pressure are problematic." He looked at all of them. "We need her to fight and to believe she is going to be okay. So no crying, no drama."

J.B.'s expression was grim, his jaw taut. "Understood."

"If you'll excuse me," the doctor said, "I'll go make sure the OR is being prepped. Once the surgery begins, we'll keep you posted in the surgical waiting lounge." With a brief nod, he disappeared down the hall.

J.B. squared his shoulders. "I'll talk to her," he said.

His father hugged him tightly. "We can't lose her, son. She's the center of this family. She's our rock."

"I know, Dad. I know."

J.B. shot Mazie a look she couldn't read. He hugged his sisters. Then he stepped through the door. "Hey, Mom. What's this I hear about you scaring Dad? That's not nice."

The four people left standing in the hallway strained to hear.

Mrs. Vaughan's expression brightened when she saw her firstborn. "Don't you look handsome. A date tonight?"

"Yes, Mama."

"That's nice."

Tears stung Mazie's eyes when J.B. perched on the edge of the bed and carefully took his mother's hand in both of his. He kissed her fingers. "You gave us a scare, but you're going to be fine."

His mother's wrinkled nose and half frown told Mazie that the woman was well aware of her situation.

"I want you to promise me something, sweetheart." Her voice was hoarse and weak.

J.B. nodded. "Whatever you need, Mom. You name it."

"If anything happens to me, I want you to take care of your dad and your sisters. They will depend on you, J.B."

Leila moaned and burst into tears, though she muffled her sobs and moved away from the door. Alana curled an arm around her father's waist.

Mazie's eyes were damp, as well.

Through the door, she saw J.B. lean down and kiss his mother's cheek. "We're not going to talk like that. I have a surprise for you. I was going to wait until Christmas to tell everybody, but you should know tonight. I've asked Mazie Tarleton to marry me. We're engaged. And the good Lord willing, she and I won't wait too long to get started on those grandchildren you've always wanted."

Mrs. Vaughan's face lit up, and a tear rolled down her cheek. "Really, son? Oh, that's wonderful."

Mazie was stunned for thirty seconds until she realized what J.B. was doing. He was giving his mother a reason to fight, a reason to live. Mazie expected the three Vaughans in the hallway to give her the third degree, but they were too focused on what was happening in the emergency room cubicle.

She sucked in a sharp breath. For a moment, J.B.'s play-acting hit a nerve. If she really hated the man, why did his pretend words reach deep inside her and squeeze her heart?

Mrs. Vaughan peered around her son. "Is she here, J.B.? I haven't seen her in ages."

J.B. looked over his shoulder, his gaze clashing with Mazie's. She nodded slowly, alarmed by how appealing it was to play this unexpected role. Had she honestly blinded herself to the truth so completely? Did she want to be J.B.'s fiancée, even as part of a benevolent lie?

Heaven help her. It felt wrong, but what could she do?

Mr. Vaughan and the two girls stepped aside. Mazie smoothed her skirt. She was still holding her small evening purse. She passed it off to Alana and eased the door open. "I'm here, Mrs. Vaughan."

J.B.'s mother held out her hand. "Come sit where I can look at you. And call me Jane. Oh, honey, you're stunning. That dress makes you look like a model. I know your mother would be so proud."

J.B. stood up so Mazie could take his place. She sat down on the bed gingerly, not wanting to disturb any of the medical equipment. "I haven't seen you in forever, Mrs. Vaughan. Jane, I mean. I'm so sorry you've been ill."

Jane Vaughan beamed, her hand touching the soft velvet of Mazie's skirt. "I couldn't be happier," she said. "Let me see the ring." She reached for Mazie's left hand.

Mazie curled her fingers defensively. "J.B. wanted me to help pick out the ring. So we don't have it yet."

J.B. moved closer. He rested a hand on Mazie's shoulder. His fingers were warm on the bare skin at the curve of her neck. "I won't make her wait long, Mom. This just happened."

"I see."

For a moment it seemed as though J.B.'s mother saw through their subterfuge. But her smile didn't waver.

J.B. hugged Mazie and then leaned down to brush his lips across his mother's brow. "When you're on the mend, we'd like your help with wedding plans."

"Oh, yes," Mazie said. "You know all the venues in Charleston and all the best vendors. I'll need all the backup I can get."

Jane was misty-eyed. She gripped her son's hand…and Mazie's. "I wouldn't miss this wedding for the world."

J.B. chuckled. "Consider it good practice for when Leila and Alana tie the knot."

Mazie stood, keenly aware of the warmth of J.B.'s big frame at her back. "I'll let you rest now."

J.B. nodded. "I love you, Mama. And I'll be here during the surgery. We all will. Don't be afraid."

Jane smiled weakly, obviously tired out by the conversation. "I'm not scared. Your father and I have lived a good life. If it's my time to go, don't let him be sad."

Mazie leaned down and kissed her cheek, realizing how much she had missed having a maternal role model as she reached adulthood. "You can't go," she said firmly. "We all need you."

As she slipped out of the room, the others came in to say their last words of encouragement. The nurse arrived with pre-op sedation.

Mazie leaned against the wall in the hallway and said a prayer for Jane's safety.

When J.B. exited the room, he eyed her warily. Unspoken feelings simmered between them.

She shook her head in bemusement. "You always did think fast on your feet." It wasn't really a compliment.

He scraped his hands through his hair. "I don't mean to make light of marriage, but I wanted her to have a reason to fight."

"Of course you did. But the rest of your family?"

"Let's keep the truth to ourselves for now. Explaining the ruse is unnecessary. They have enough on their plate."

This lie might keep her tied to him indefinitely. She wasn't sure how she felt about that. "I'm going to call a cab," she said quietly.

"I'll drive you home."

"No. You need to be here. I'll be fine." The J.B. she knew had disappeared. In his place, she saw a man who was worried and trying not to show it.

She was getting in too deep. She didn't want to admire him or feel sympathy for him. Her years-long antipathy was the only thing protecting her from doing something stupid.

No one would blame her if she ran far and fast. Getting too close to J.B. threatened her hard-won composure.

For a decade and more she had convinced herself that she didn't even like the man. How could her feelings have changed so radically? Her heart pounded. *Walk away, Mazie. Walk away.* Despite her best intentions, emotionally charged words tumbled from her lips. Words that said her heart was far more involved than she was prepared to admit. "Would you like to me to come back after I change clothes?"

Nine

J.B. looked stunned. Somehow the lie he had spouted was changing everything. This felt intimate. Emotionally charged. She found herself offering help and comfort as if she were a real fiancée.

He nodded slowly, his gaze unguarded for a surprising moment. "Yes, please."

"Do you want me to go by your place and bring you something else to wear?" She knew where he lived. She and Jonathan and Hartley had been to parties there. It was a fabulous home overlooking the Battery.

"You don't mind?" He seemed to be weighing his words as if afraid of spooking her.

"Not at all. I'll call Jonathan and tell him what's going on so Dad won't worry."

He nodded. "I'll text you the alarm code and what to grab for me." When he handed her his keys and their fingers brushed, his touch burned. "Do you feel comfortable driving the SUV?" he asked.

"Not entirely, but I'll take it slow. It's late. There won't be much traffic."

He cupped her chin in his hand. "Thanks, Mazie. I never expected the evening to end this way."

He kissed her softly. At first, it was a kiss of gratitude... of kinship. But in a flash it went somewhere far darker. It seduced her, cajoled her and made her heart beat faster.

His lips were firm and demanding, his smothered groan

telling her that the reluctant connection between them, the one neither of them really wanted or needed, was not easy to eradicate.

This wasn't how they had anticipated the evening would end.

She pulled away. "I should go."

Having J.B. look at her this way was alarming and disconcerting. They had moved from a romantic, flirtatious evening to something far more real.

He nodded, his gaze heavy with emotions she couldn't decipher. "Be careful. And call me if you have any problems."

"I'll be back as soon as I can." She touched his hand. "She'll pull through, J.B. She's a strong woman."

"I hope you're right."

Back at home, Mazie peeled out of the velvet dress with a wistful sigh. After changing into soft jeans and a lemon-yellow cotton sweater, she grabbed a canvas tote and stuffed it with water and snacks. There was no telling how long she would be with J.B. during his vigil.

Entering his home a short while later gave her an odd feeling in the pit of her stomach. Though they had known each other for years, they were not on intimate terms. Or at least they hadn't been until the episode in the bank vault.

She walked through the elegant living room and dining room and climbed the stairs to the upper floor. J.B.'s bedroom commanded the best view in the house, not that she could see anything at this hour.

Though she had already accessed his text for the alarm code, now she checked again, making note of the items he wanted and where to find them. Pants, shirt, socks. A sweater. Casual shoes. A clean pair of boxers. Her cheeks heated. It was a good thing there was no one around to see her reaction.

In his closet she found the leather carry-all he had requested. She stuffed everything into it and took one last look at his text. These few items would hold him until he could come back home. A man didn't need to spend the night wearing a tux, even if it *was* hand-tailored just for him.

She stood in the center of his bedroom for a moment, making sure she hadn't forgotten anything. It was impossible not to look at his massive king-size bed. The wood was dark and heavy, the comforter crimson damask. How many women had J.B. entertained in this luxurious space?

Not her business. Not at all.

Ignoring her hot cheeks, she ran back downstairs, reset the alarm and scooted out the front door. This time, driving the huge SUV was not quite so intimidating.

When she made it back to the hospital, it was the middle of the night. The surgical waiting room was deserted except for the four Vaughans. J.B.'s two sisters were asleep, curled awkwardly on a duo of love seats. Mr. Vaughan was dozing also.

J.B. paced restlessly, looking darkly handsome despite his fatigue.

He greeted her quietly. "That was fast."

"There's no traffic at this hour." She held out the leather satchel. "Here you go. I know you must be ready to get out of that tux."

His sexy grin was a shadow of its usual wattage. "Is that an invitation, Mazie? I'll have to take a rain check."

She pretended his teasing didn't fluster her. "Try to behave. Is there any word yet?"

He yawned. "No. The surgery actually started thirty minutes ago. They said it could take hours."

"Go change," she said. "I'll wait right here."

Though J.B. in a tux was eye candy of the best kind, she

almost preferred the man who returned moments later. A rumpled J.B. in casual clothes was dangerously appealing.

She raised an eyebrow. "Where's your tux?"

"I wadded it up in the bag. Has to go the cleaners anyway."

"Ah. Do you want to sit, or shall we walk the halls?"

"You're probably tired," he said.

"My adrenaline is still pumping. If you want to make a few laps of the building, I'm game."

J.B. poked his head into the lounge long enough leave his bag and to tell his dad where to find him. Then he rejoined Mazie. "Let's go. I can't stand to do nothing but wait."

J.B. was ridiculously glad to see Mazie.

He was a selfish bastard for asking her to stay, but her presence gave him something to hang on to. In front of his sisters and his dad, he had to be strong and unflappable. With Mazie, he could be himself. The distinction should have worried him, but he was too tired to think about the reasons why.

For now, he would ignore his ambivalent reactions to being with her in this charged situation.

They walked the halls in silence. His name and his face were well-known in Charleston, particularly to the hospital staff. His family had been major benefactors for years.

No one bothered Mazie or him. A few nurses here and there said hello. With the lights dimmed and most patients asleep, the building was sleepy and secure.

He ignored the elevators and climbed the stairs, Mazie on his heels.

When they were both breathing hard, he pushed open the door on 4B and crooked a finger at her. "Let's take a look at the babies."

Though the nurse on the other side of the glass frowned, she didn't shoo them away. He could almost watch Mazie's heart melt into a puddle of maternal instinct when she scanned the row of clear plastic bassinets. "They're so tiny," she whispered. "How can they be so small?"

"We were all that little once upon a time."

She bumped his hip with hers. "Not you, surely. I can't even imagine it."

They stood there in silence. A third of the infants slept peacefully. Another third blinked and examined their surroundings with myopic interest. But it was the last third who demanded all the attention. They wailed and scrunched up their faces, making their displeasure known.

He shuddered. "How do new parents do it? You can't Google how to take care of a newborn."

"Sure you can. You can Google anything. Besides, you promised your mother grandchildren. You'd better get over your fear of babies in a hurry."

"Are you volunteering?" His heart squeezed at the thought of having a daughter who looked like Mazie.

"Heck, no." She chewed her bottom lip. "To be honest, I've always been afraid that I might turn out like my mother. I love the idea of kids, but parenting scares me."

"And what about marriage?"

"What about it?"

He sneaked a sideways look at her, noting how intently she studied the helpless infants. "I thought every woman wanted to get married. You didn't object to being my fake fiancée." Under the circumstances, maybe he hadn't given her a chance to protest.

"C'mon, J.B. You can't be serious. This is the twenty-first century. Women have lots of choices."

"That doesn't answer my question." He was inordinately interested in her answer.

She shrugged. "I don't know if I'll *get* married. Watching what my father went through…"

"Did he ever consider divorcing your mother?" Divorce was a painful subject for J.B. His failure still stung deeply.

"No. At least I don't think so. Jonathan thinks he's still in love with her after all these years. But he never goes to see her."

"Because she doesn't recognize him?"

"I guess that's the reason. It must be very painful."

J.B. glanced at his watch. When Mazie let down her guard with him, he actually thought the two of them might finally be able to heal the decade-old rift. But no matter how appealing that prospect was, their timing was off. "We've been gone a long time. I'd better get back to the cardiac floor."

When they reached the surgical lounge, a nurse had just come out of the OR with an update. The surgery was going well. It would be at least another hour and a half, and then recovery.

J.B. grimaced. He took Mazie's arm and drew her away from the others. "Go home," he said. "I shouldn't have asked you to stay." Her skin was smooth and warm beneath his fingertips. He had to resist the urge to stroke her.

"Don't be silly. I'm here. Relax, J.B. I've got nowhere else I need to be." Her smile seemed genuine, though still cautious perhaps.

"This isn't the evening I had planned," he said, his voice husky with fatigue and something else he was too tired to hide.

She cupped his cheek in her hand. "If you're talking about sex, we already took that off the table...remember?"

"Says who?"

His teasing wasn't up to its usual wicked voltage.

"Says me." She paused. "I enjoyed tonight," she said. "Dinner. Dancing. When you're not being a condescending jerk and breaking a girl's heart, you're a pretty nice guy."

* * *

Mazie hadn't meant to be so honest, but it was hard to hold a grudge at 3:00 a.m.

J.B.'s jaw was shadowed with dark stubble. His hair was rumpled. The clothes she had brought him smelled of starch and laundry detergent. The blue button-up shirt and navy cotton pullover strained across his broad, hard chest.

The man looked like he had just crawled out of the covers and thrown on whatever was at hand. And yet he was still the sexiest thing she had ever seen.

She flashed back to his bedroom, for one brief moment imagining herself sprawled on that ruby comforter with J.B. leaning over her.

Her breathing quickened.

To make things worse, she couldn't help remembering the pink and blue swaddled babies. No matter what she'd said to JB, she *wanted* to have a normal family like his. But it just wasn't in the cards for her.

Even her own brother had disappeared.

The Tarletons were a mess.

J.B. took her arm. "Let's sit down. Are you hungry?"

"No," she said. They settled onto a padded bench. Once she was off her feet, the fatigue came crashing over.

He pulled her into his chest, wrapping an arm around her. "Close your eyes. Catnaps are my specialty."

The man wasn't kidding. In seconds he was snoring softly.

Mazie sighed and tried to do the same. But she couldn't relax. Being this close to J.B. lowered her defenses. She didn't *want* to like him. She didn't want to empathize about his worry for his mother. And she surely didn't want to be engaged to him.

Once upon a time, she would have welcomed the chance to be part of J.B.'s life. Those dreams had been crushed early and well. Now, she was almost positive that this sudden affability on his part was a calculated effort to win her trust.

The reality of selling her building to him was not the point. If she decided to go through with it, she would make him pay dearly for the privilege of relocating her.

No, what was really dangerous to her peace of mind was the possibility that J.B. could worm his way into her heart and then walk away when he got what he wanted.

While Mazie struggled internally with the extraordinary feeling of being wrapped in J.B.'s arms, Leila awakened and crossed the room. She tapped Mazie on the knee. "I need coffee," she whispered. "You want to come with me?"

Mazie nodded, welcoming the rescue from her own rapidly eroding good sense. Slipping out from underneath J.B.'s heavy arm, she grabbed her phone and wallet and followed his sister out of the waiting room. The sandwich shop and the main dining room were closed, but near the front entrance, a sleepy barista dozed over her iPad at a coffee counter.

Leila ordered her drink tall and black. Mazie couldn't face that much caffeine in the middle of the night, but she asked for an iced green tea. They found seats in the nearby atrium.

Mazie smiled sympathetically at the other woman. "This must have been really scary for all of you."

"Terrifying." Leila buried her nose in her cup. "My mom is a superhero. Seeing her like this…" She sniffed and wiped her nose.

"Were there any symptoms?"

"Honestly? I don't know. She's the kind of person who would badger the rest of us to get flu shots and go to the dentist, but she might have ignored her own warning signs 'cause she's always so busy."

"Heart surgeons perform miracles these days."

"Yeah." Leila yawned and set her empty cup on a nearby

table. "I'm sorry our family drama ruined your special night."

"Oh, that's okay," Mazie said quickly, wincing inwardly. The ground beneath her feet was quicksand. How did a recently engaged woman react? "The important thing is for your mom to be okay."

Leila grinned, seemingly fortified by her java. "To be honest, I was pretty shocked about this engagement. After the debacle of J.B.'s first marriage, he swore he'd never tie the knot again." Her eyes rounded, and she slapped a hand over her mouth. "Oh, lordy. Please tell me you already knew about that…the marriage, I mean."

"Of course. He's been very upfront with me. You do remember that my brothers and I used to hang out at your house all the time? Not so much as adults, but enough to keep up with J.B. and his escapades. He told me his wife was pretty awful."

"Mom and Dad tried to stop him, but he was madly in love. I was just starting high school, so I thought it was all terribly romantic. It didn't take long for the truth to come out. All she wanted was money. Poor J.B. was collateral damage."

"He seems to have bounced back pretty well," Mazie said, hoping she didn't sound cynical.

"I haven't seen him go out with the same woman more than two or three times. He's rabid about not giving anyone of the opposite sex the wrong idea. He's a workaholic, and he's not interested in anything permanent." She frowned and cocked her head. "How did the two of you hook up? I've watched you avoid each other for years."

"Ah, well…" This was the tough part. She was a terrible liar. "We occasionally crossed paths at a party or a gallery opening. But I suppose we got closer when he started this renovation project down near the Battery. He wants to buy my property. I kept saying no, and he continued to beg."

"Interesting. I've known my brother to do just about anything to seal a deal, but marriage? That's a new one."

Mazie knew Leila was teasing. But her careless comments underscored Mazie's own insecurities. If Mazie had said yes when J.B.'s Realtor called the first time, or even the second, Mazie never would have gone out with J.B., and she never would have been put in the situation of lying to his family.

"Shouldn't we get back upstairs?" she said.

Leila nodded, all animation fading from her face. "Definitely."

As they walked into the surgical lounge, Alana updated her sister with the latest progress report. J.B. and his dad appeared to be asleep.

Mazie kept to herself in one corner of the room until she realized that a *real* fiancée would never be standoffish. Instead, she moved to sit close to J.B., hoping that his sisters would think she didn't want to wake him.

At four fifteen, a weary surgeon came in to talk to them. The siblings formed a united front around their father. The doctor was upbeat. "The surgery went as expected. We did a quadruple bypass, so she'll have a long road ahead of her. Healing takes months, not weeks."

J.B.'s expression was strained. "When can we see her?"

"She'll be in recovery for some time. We'll rouse her slowly. When she's awake, we want everything to be low-key and calm. Nothing stressful at all. I'd recommend all of you go home and get a few hours of sleep. Come back later in the morning. If there's any problem, a nurse will contact you immediately."

Mr. Vaughan didn't like that answer. Mazie could tell. But the poor man looked dead on his feet.

Leila put an arm around her dad. "Alana and I will go back to the house with you, Papa."

J.B. kissed the top of her head. "Thanks, sis." He hugged

his father and Alana. "I'll take Mazie home and then see you guys around lunchtime."

Leila frowned. "But you live the closest of any of us to the hospital."

J.B. didn't miss a beat. "Mazie doesn't," he said.

Mazie could see the speculation in their gazes, but she was too tired to play her part. Did the girls think J.B. would have a fiancée living under his roof already? Fat chance. She'd had it from his own sister's lips that the man didn't like relationships.

In the parking lot, she tried to lobby for common sense. "Let me call a car," she said. "There's no reason at all for you to drive me home."

They had come straight from their date to the hospital. Her car was out at the beach house.

J.B. destroyed her argument by kissing her deep and slow. His tongue stroked hers. "There's a better option," he muttered, as he turned her legs to spaghetti. "For once, just trust me."

Ten

"Trust you?" Mazie eyed him warily.

He grimaced. "I'm so tired my eyeballs ache. Leila was right. It will be dawn soon. I don't really want to spend the next hour driving you to the beach and then heading back to my own place. Come home with me," he said huskily. "My house is five minutes away. We both need sleep."

Mazie hesitated. This family crisis had thrust her into a position of intimacy that was difficult to handle. She was a compassionate person. She could see that J.B. was dealing with stress and fatigue. Still, her sense of self-preservation was strong.

She'd been avoiding this connection forever, and now here it was, rushing her far too quickly into the quicksand of shared desire and impulsive choices.

"I'll be fine in a cab."

He took her wrist and reeled her in, wrapping his arms around her and pulling her close. "Pretty please, Mazie Jane. I don't want to be alone."

She examined his face in the harsh glow of the security lights. If she had seen even a shred of evidence that he was playing her, she would have walked away. But the hell of it was, she thought he was sincere.

"Okay," she said, giving in more or less gracefully. "It will only be for a few hours anyway."

They both climbed into the vehicle without further conversation. J.B. drove with a steady hand on the wheel. His profile was stark. Bold forehead, straight nose, firm chin. Mazie felt as if she was seeing him for the first time. It was clear that his family adored him and that he was someone they leaned on.

At his house, she hovered in the hallway. "I'll crash down here," she said. "Why don't you go on upstairs and get comfortable?"

He frowned. "I have a perfectly lovely guest room right across the hall from my suite."

"I don't want to argue about this J.B. Not right now." If she climbed those stairs, all bets were off. Too cozy. Too everything.

His gaze cooled. "Fine. We'll share the sofa."

She'd had no sleep. Her eyes were gritty, and her body was limp with exhaustion. "If that's what you want."

Most of J.B.'s beautiful home was decorated in true Charleston fashion. No doubt one or both of his sisters had helped, maybe even Jane. But at the back of the house in his personal den, he had opted for masculine comfort. An enormous flat-screen TV. A couple of huge recliners and an oversize sofa that looked as if it was covered in the soft, scarred leather of old aviator jackets.

He kicked off his shoes and grabbed two afghans from the cabinet to the left of the TV. "Make yourself at home. Are you hungry? Thirsty?"

She shook her head, wondering why she had voluntarily stepped into the lion's den. "I'm fine. Go to sleep, J.B. You'll have to be back at the hospital soon." Without waiting to see if he would take her advice, she curled up on one end of the couch and laid her head on the arm. At the last minute, she remembered to send a text to Gina letting her know that Mazie would not be coming in to the store this morning…or at least not until much later. Then she silenced her phone.

Out of the corner of her eye, she saw J.B. sprawl a few feet away from her and prop his feet on the coffee table.

The lure of sleep was strong. How did she end up here? Was this really as innocent as it seemed?

J.B. groaned and rolled his neck. "I'm too damn tired to relax."

Mazie sighed. "Lie down, for heaven's sake. Let me rub your head."

"I can think of other places I'd rather have you rub." His fake leer didn't have enough energy to be insulting.

"On your back, Mr. Vaughan."

As she sat up, J.B. stretched out full-length, his feet propped on the other arm of the sofa. With his head in her lap, he relaxed. Thick lashes, unfairly beautiful for a man, settled on his cheeks.

"Thank you, Mazie," he muttered.

She stroked his forehead, feeling the silkiness of his hair. Keeping her touch light and steady, she watched as the lines of tension in his face and shoulders gradually eased.

Some strong emotion slid through her veins and weakened her resolve. She couldn't fool herself any longer. She was dangerously close to falling for him again. How reckless could she be?

Soon, he was asleep. Only then did she allow herself to lean back and close her eyes.

J.B. dreamed about angels. Perhaps he should have been alarmed. He wasn't prepared for his life to end. But this particular angel whispered to him, words he couldn't quite catch.

He awoke with a start. For several long seconds confusion reigned. Then the familiar surroundings grounded him. Worry for his mother arrived first. And then concern about Mazie.

Good Lord. How long had he been sleeping in her lap?

The poor woman must be a glutton for punishment. He sat up carefully, noting the awkward bend to her neck. A glance at his watch told him it was not quite eight thirty. Still time to rest. And no messages on his phone.

Without overthinking it, he grabbed a pillow and scooped Mazie up long enough to change their positions. She murmured in her sleep but didn't wake. With his back against the couch, he tucked her up against him and sighed. This would do.

The scent of her hair tickled his nose. He had danced around his attraction to her for years, never quite willing to admit it existed. Now here she was. In his house. In his arms.

This relationship was *snakebit* from the beginning. Even if Mazie learned to trust him, what did he need from her? Marriage was out of the question. He'd learned that lesson the hard way.

Women were duplicitous. And he was bad at reading their wants and intentions.

He closed his eyes for the second time, and slept.

When next he awoke, the sun poured into the room through a crack in the draperies. As he crooked his arm to see his watch, Mazie stirred. "J.B.?"

"Right here, darlin'. We both went out cold."

She appeared charmingly befuddled. "Oh."

He stroked her cheek with the pad of his thumb. "Are you always this beautiful in the morning?"

It was a cheesy line. But hell, it was true. Her skin was soft and flushed. Those big golden eyes were underscored with shadows, but still deep enough for a man to lose himself.

Mazie bit her lip. "I must look a mess."

He threaded his fingers through her thick, glorious hair. The waves clung to his hand. His heart beat faster. "I'm going to kiss you."

It was a warning and a plea all wrapped up in one. He felt remarkably off his game. Ever since that incredible episode in the bank vault, he'd been obsessed with the need to touch her again.

He'd been compelled to ask her out. Some would say it was his subconscious that had taken over and proclaimed the false engagement.

He shifted his weight and leaned over her on one elbow. "Mazie," he whispered.

She put a hand behind his head and pulled him closer. "Yes."

The single word shot arousal through his veins like a powerful stimulant. He was trembling, almost out of control. Yet they had barely begun.

Her lips clung to his, not submissive, but challenging. He was hard in an instant. Desperate. Ready to beg. But the incredible woman beneath him was not erecting any barriers at all. She arched into his embrace, melding their bodies from shoulders to hips, completely his except for the fact that they were fully clothed.

The look in her eyes was his undoing, part yearning, part caution. She didn't completely trust him. He'd have to work on that.

"Easy, love." He distracted her with a hungry kiss while he wrestled with her thin sweater. Once he ripped the garment over her head, he was treated to the sight of raspberry-tipped breasts cupped in a lacy confection that was meant to drive a man wild.

He teased her nipples through the semi-transparent cloth. "I've pictured you like this in my head," he groaned. "But I never thought it would happen."

She nipped his bottom lip with sharp teeth. "And why is that? I thought the larger-than-life J.B. Vaughan was irresistible to the female sex."

"You're sassy. And no, I'm not irresistible. You aren't

even sure you like me, Mazie Jane. And you sure as hell don't trust me."

The flicker of her gold-tipped eyelashes told him he had hit a nerve. But her voice when she answered was steady. "I discovered something in that bank vault, J.B. Something that shocked me. Apparently, it's possible to crave someone even if he's a bad boy with a terrible reputation."

His smile widened. "You *crave* me, darlin'? Well, I must be doing *something* right."

"Does your ego ever take a rest?" She caressed his chin, smiling faintly.

He ignored her gibe. "Get undressed before someone like your brother decides to interrupt us."

Mazie wriggled away from him long enough to dispense with her pants and socks. J.B. did the same. He leaned forward to grab his wallet and extract a condom. His hands were shaking.

She curled her arms around him from behind and rested her cheek on his back. "We're probably going to regret this."

"Yeah. Maybe." He pulled her in front of him, standing her on her feet and kissing her cute, tiny belly button. Gooseflesh rose on her pale skin. "You have no idea how much I want you."

"That might be the sleep deprivation talking."

He slid her bikini underwear down her legs and sighed. "Nope. It's you, Mazie Jane." He parted her damp folds with his thumbs and caressed her intimately. Her whimper of pleasure hardened his erection a millimeter more, if that was possible.

In another situation, he would have taken his time with her. He might have paused to savor the smorgasbord of delights. But he'd only been half kidding about Jonathan. Given the situation at the hospital, someone could call at any moment. He dared not turn off his phone.

"We should hurry," she panted, perhaps reading his

mind. "I'm ready for you. More than ready." She played with the shell of his ear, leaning down to whisper naughty suggestions.

J.B. cursed. He shed his boxers with more speed than finesse and sheathed his sex. Mazie was still wearing her bra. It was too late to do anything about it. He had to have her in the next thirty seconds, or he was going to die.

Moving to the edge of the sofa, he gripped her wrist. "Come here, sweet thing. Let me love you." He took her by the waist and helped her straddle his lap, her long, smooth legs spread on either side of his hips.

Mazie took over before he could do more than groan and bury his face in her chest. She sank down onto him, taking him inside her, joining their bodies with the sweet wild slide of passion.

His vision went dark. Everything inside him focused on the sensation of Mazie's tight, hot sex accepting him. Sweat broke out on his brow. "Slower," he begged. He was close to embarrassing both of them.

Mazie combed his hair with both hands, massaging his scalp, toying with his ears. "What if I like it fast and hard?"

He gripped her soft butt so tightly it might leave bruises. "Bad girl." He thrust upward, filling her, claiming her.

Mazie laughed. The soft, husky chuckle drove him mad. Suddenly, he was sorry he had chosen this position. It was too passive. He was in a volatile mood. Lack of sleep blurred the edges of his control.

"Put your legs around my waist." He stood abruptly. Mazie was a tall woman, but he was extremely motivated. He eased past the coffee table and tumbled them both to the carpet, their bodies still joined.

Mazie smiled up at him, her eyelids half closed, her breath coming in short pants. "Who knew you were so strong? I'm impressed Mr. Vaughan."

His chest heaved. "You make me nuts. Why is that, do you think?"

"Mutual antipathy?"

He pumped his hips.

Her eyelids fluttered shut. She arched her back, gasping.

"Look at me, Mazie. I want to see your eyes when you come."

She obeyed. Her amber-gold gaze locked on to his. He felt naked suddenly, raw and exposed. Those eyes saw everything.

Mazie wet her lips with the tip of her tongue. She reached up and traced his features with her thumbs. "I won't break, J.B. Give it all to me."

The sexual challenge dissolved the last of his rapidly winnowing willpower. With a groan of helpless inevitability, he pounded into her, thrusting again and again until his world went black, and his entire body spasmed in hot, desperate pleasure.

Dimly, he heard Mazie's cry of release and felt the flutters of her sex on his shaft as she came.

When it was over, they lay in a tangle of arms and legs and fractured breathing. Mazie was still wearing her bra. J.B. couldn't feel his legs. Her body was soft and warm beneath his. He never wanted to move, though that wasn't a viable choice under the circumstances.

After several long moments of silence, he rolled to his back and cleared his throat. "I don't know what to say. I'd offer to fix you bacon and eggs, but that seems a paltry thank-you for what just happened."

He was dizzy, and his feet were cold.

Mazie patted his cheek. "Don't be silly. It was sex. Great sex, I'll admit. But just sex. I can grab breakfast at home."

When she stood up, found her undies and began to get dressed, he gaped at her. "What are you doing?"

She pointed at the antique clock on the mantel. "It's late,

J.B. Your family will be expecting you at the hospital. And even though I told Gina that I wouldn't be there to open the shop, I still need to get to work." She fastened her jeans and sat down to put on her socks and shoes.

"But you're the boss." What the hell was happening? The sex had been incredible, wild and hot. How could she pretend as if nothing had happened? Was she really as unaffected as she seemed?

"It's the Christmas shopping season. I need to be at my store. But more important, your mother will be asking for you soon. Grab your shower, J.B. I'll call a car service. No worries."

She picked up her purse and jacket. "I'll be in touch to check on your mom later today." She blew him a kiss. "Gotta run."

As he rolled to his knees and stood up, he heard his front door open and shut.

Eleven

Mazie leaned her back against J.B.'s front door for half a second, barely long enough to catch her breath, and then she fled. She jogged three blocks before she called a car service, desperate to make sure J.B. wasn't going to follow her. With her heart pounding and her eyes blinking back tears, she felt like a crazy woman.

Her whole world was upended.

How could puppy love have stayed alive all these years? She *knew* what kind of man J.B. was. Thanks to his sister's candid remarks, Mazie also knew J.B.'s views on relationships and marriage.

Only the worst kind of masochist would allow herself to be sucked back into his realm. Pretending like morning sex was no big deal had required all of her acting abilities. Harder still was erasing the mental image of a naked J.B. sprawled on the plush carpet.

The man had a seriously ripped body.

He was also funny and smart, and kind to his mother and the rest of his family. That didn't erase his willingness to squash other people in his drive to get what he wanted in business.

He had hurt her once before. If she allowed him to get too close, odds were, it would happen again.

Despite her panic and all-out flight from J.B., she arrived home in a slightly calmer frame of mind. She would survive whatever this was. She had to…the past was not worth repeating.

Jonathan was at work, of course. She had texted him from the car to let him know Mrs. Vaughan was stable. He had answered with a single word. *Good.* That kind of clipped response was typical of her brother when he was neck deep in shipping crises.

Her father was dozing in the living room with a paperback novel in his lap. Mazie sat down beside him and touched his arm. "Hi, Daddy."

He opened his eyes. "Hello, baby. What are you doing home this time of day?"

She explained about Mrs. Vaughan's heart attack, glossing over the details about her date with J.B. and why Mazie was at the hospital at all.

Her father nodded. "I'll have Jonathan's assistant send flowers."

"That would be lovely." She paused, shifting gears. "How was *your* dinner last night? Did you have a good time?"

He grew animated as he shared details of his evening.

Mazie spotted an opportunity and took it. "Daddy, have you ever thought about moving to one of those places where your friends live? Here at the house you're awfully isolated and lonely, and besides, you know that Jonathan and I might not always be around."

"I like it here," he said. "It's safe." Then his smile grew wistful. "Are you planning on leaving your old dad, Mazie? I knew it would happen one day."

"No plans," she said lightly, witnessing his frail emotions. This thing with J.B. had made her even more aware of how dysfunctional her family was. She sighed, needing reassurance, wanting answers. "Daddy, please tell me what happened with Hartley. Jonathan won't talk about it."

His face darkened. "And neither will I. It's best you

don't know. Just understand that he's probably never coming back."

She wasn't a child. What secret was so terrible that it had ripped their small family apart?

With an inward sigh, she stood and stretched, feeling the strain of not enough sleep and the fact that several of those hours she did doze were sitting upright on J.B.'s sofa. It was frightening to realize that she already missed him. "I'm going to take a shower, grab a quick lunch and head to work. Do you need anything before I go?"

His eyelids were already drooping. "I'm right as rain. Don't worry about me."

Fortunately for Mazie, All That Glitters was madly busy on this bright, sunny Saturday in December.

She waded into the fray, grateful for something to distract her from the unanswerable questions about her fake engagement and her enigmatic fiancé.

Since Gina was far too busy to dig for details about Mazie's date and the events that followed, Mazie was able to shut out the past twenty-four hours. Mostly.

The day passed quickly. Sales numbers were gratifying. If she took the new building J.B. was offering her, she would have ample room to expand.

The Tarleton shipping business would have had room for her if she had been interested. But she had needed something she could control, a part of her life where she was in charge, where she didn't have to worry about being abandoned.

If she couldn't have J.B.—and did she really want him?—her work was going to be her future.

As they prepared to lock up and head home at five, Mazie cornered Gina. "You want to grab a bite of dinner?"

"Oh, gosh, Mazie. You know I would. But we're having a big extended-family Christmas thing at my aunt's house tonight. Kind of a command performance. You're welcome to come with me."

"No, no. That's fine. Go. Don't be late. I'll wrap things up."

"Are you sure?"

"Positive. You covered for me this morning. Get out of here."

When the store was empty, Mazie turned the deadbolt and flipped the sign in the window to Closed.

She told herself she wasn't jealous of Gina, but it was a lie. Gina came from a huge Italian clan. She had more cousins than she could count. Mazie's parents were both only children.

All Mazie had ever wanted was to belong, to have a big, loving family. First her mother was sent away. Then Hartley left. Now her father's health was precarious. Soon it would be just Jonathan and Mazie. When Jonathan eventually married, Mazie would be on her own.

The prospect was dismal. Was that why she had let herself be drawn back into J.B.'s orbit? Was it the memory of her old crush on him that drove her now, or was there more to this dangerous liaison?

It must be the holidays making her maudlin. As much as she loved the holly and the mistletoe and the beauty of the season, at times all the hoopla amplified her aloneness. She finished the last of the chores that were rote to her by now, and went to the back to get her jacket and purse.

When she returned, her heart stopped. There, standing half-visible in front of the top glass pane of her door, was a huge man. But a familiar one. He was dressed casually in khakis and a forest green sweater.

After her heart started beating again, she opened the lock and let him in. "You scared me to death," she said. It was already dark outside.

"It's dangerous for you to be closing up alone. Anyone could bust in here and hurt you or rob you."

"We have a system," she said calmly, though her fingernails dug into her palms. "Gina and I usually walk out together, but she had a *thing* tonight. I sent her on, so she wouldn't be late. What are you doing here, J.B.?"

He lifted an eyebrow. "Collecting my fiancée?"

"That's not funny." Even so, his teasing smile made her heart wobble. The fact that they had been naked together only a few hours before made her skittish.

"Mom's asking for you," he said.

"Well, crud." She frowned. "I know why you did what you did, but how are we supposed to handle this now?"

"We need to buy a ring. I asked my friend Jean Philippe to give us a private appointment at six."

Mazie heart clenched in alarm. "We're not engaged," she said firmly. "And I'm not picking out a ring."

"You have to."

"I don't have to do anything."

"Be reasonable, Mazie. She's awake and she wants to see you. She's worried that her heart attack messed up our special evening. She's ragging my butt to make sure I put a ring on your finger. Sooner, not later. I couldn't disappoint her."

Mazie was appalled at how much she wanted to play his game. At this rate she would end up abandoned at the altar because she didn't have enough sense to guard her heart. "Tell her I'm picky. Tell her no one in Charleston has a loose stone big enough or perfect enough to suit me. Tell her you and I will be flying to New York after the holidays to hit up Harry Winston and Tiffany's."

"I can't tell her that," he said, visibly grinding his jaw.

"Why not?"

"Because she would insist I book two tickets right now.

The woman is like a bulldog, Mazie. Sick or not sick, she'll grill you until you cave."

"Why don't you borrow a ring from a friend, then. Or pick out something by yourself. It can be anything. Why does it matter?"

J.B. didn't like not getting his own way. His eyes glittered. "I've never had to work so hard to buy a woman jewelry."

Mazie didn't want to think about all those women. "Sorry to inconvenience you," she muttered.

"My mom has spies all over the city. If I don't do this the right way, somebody will spill the truth and she'll be devastated."

"And you'll say it's my fault." She stared at him, shocked.

"Maybe."

Mazie saw a million reasons why this was a terrible idea. "She came through the surgery really well. Why don't you just admit the truth?"

"You mean I should say that I flat-out lied to her on her death bed? Oh, yeah. That's an awesome idea."

"Well, when you put it like that..." Mazie grimaced. That was the trouble with lies. One thing always led to another. "This is ridiculous, J.B. I *know* Jean Philippe. Not as well as you, maybe, but I'm pretty sure he's not going to buy my act as an adoring fiancée."

"I thought about that. We'll just tell him that we've kept our relationship under wraps."

"Why?"

"I don't know. Maybe your brother doesn't approve."

"Oh, crap." She rubbed the center of her forehead where a headache bloomed. "I'm going to have to tell Jonathan and Daddy what we're doing. If word gets back to them that I'm *engaged*, and I haven't told them, they'll be so hurt."

"Can your father keep a secret?"

"Are you asking me if he's senile?"

"Well, he does seem to be slipping."

Mazie shook her head slowly. "He's not as sharp as he was, but he'll understand this. I'll just have to remind him not to talk about it at all. That's the safest bet. Besides, it's only for a week or so…right? Until your mom is recovering well? Then you and I can have a huge fight and end things."

"You don't have to sound so happy about it," J.B. groused.

She moved toward the door and stopped to pat his cheek. "It's going to be the highlight of my Christmas season."

If there was one thing Mazie knew about J.B., it was that he never left any detail to chance. That's why he was such a success in business. That and the fact that he was way smarter than his smiling blue eyes and surfer physique might suggest.

She stood on the sidewalk outside her shop and argued with him. "I'm taking my own car," she said. "It's the only plan that makes sense. That way I can drop by the hospital after we do this jewelry thing, and then head home."

"A couple buying an engagement ring doesn't arrive in multiple vehicles," he said stubbornly. "You have to commit to the role, Mazie."

"We'll improvise. It will be okay." She wasn't going to let him push her around. It was a matter of principle.

"Fine."

J.B. wasn't happy, but she didn't care. She was tired, and this pretending was breaking her heart. Didn't she deserve a man who *really* wanted her?

As far as she could tell, J.B. was simply being himself… taking care of problems. His determination to bend her will to his shouldn't have hurt. She knew who and what he was. But her emotions plummeted.

Jean Philippe's shop made All That Glitters look like a thrift store. He was a fixture in Charleston. He sold wedding rings and engagement rings, fabulous necklaces and even the occasional tiara. The fifty-something jeweler knew all there was to know about gem stones and their provenance.

Clearly, he didn't offer private appointments to anyone and everyone. He was expecting a big sale.

The store was closed, of course, since it was after business hours. A uniformed guard, fully armed, unlocked the front door and let them in. Then he relocked the plate-glass entrance and stationed himself beside the exit.

Jean Philippe was effusive. "Mr. Vaughan, Ms. Tarleton. I am honored that I can serve you in this special way."

Mazie's cheeks heated. "We'll try to be fast. I wasn't sure I wanted a ring, but J.B. insisted."

The older man raised a scandalized eyebrow. "Of *course* you need a ring. Oh, I know how you girls think these days. You're independent. You can buy your own jewelry. You don't need a man. But trust me, young lady, it means far more coming from the love of your life."

When Mazie glanced at J.B., he had an odd look on his face. Maybe he was jittery about the *L* word. "So how do we start?" she asked.

Jean Philippe glanced at J.B. "Would you like to select a handful of rings and let your fiancée pick from those, or do I—"

J.B. shook his head ruefully. "I'll let her have free rein. I trust her."

The other man's carefully manicured eyebrows shot to his hairline. There were pieces in this store that would bankrupt a lot of men. "Well, I…"

"Anything she wants, Jean. Anything."

It was all Mazie could do not to roll her eyes. Her *fiancé* was having entirely too much fun at her expense. It would serve him right if she picked out the biggest, gaudiest bauble in the store.

Unfortunately, she was too squeamish to spend that kind of money for a two-week stint of playacting.

Without much fanfare, she glanced in the nearest case. "That one's nice," she said.

Jean Philippe pulled out the ring she had indicated, a tiny frown marring his forehead. "A decent stone," he said grudgingly. "But rather pedestrian. It's only a single carat."

Mazie jumped, startled, when J.B. slid an arm around her waist. He murmured in her ear. "I'm a wealthy man, darlin'. We need something that befits my bride-to-be. Something that's as beautiful as you are. Don't hold back."

The jeweler nodded eagerly. "Indeed."

Oh, good grief.

She stared at the rows of rings blindly, wishing J.B. didn't smell so good. Also wishing that he would back up so she could breathe.

One at a time, she pointed out rings. One at a time, the two men shot them down. Finally, she began to lose patience.

She took J.B.'s arm. "Perhaps we should come back another day when we have more time. I want to visit your mother."

J.B. ignored her, his attention riveted on a nearby case she hadn't perused.

"That one," he said. "Top row on the right."

Jean Philippe practically danced in his polished cordovans. "Wonderful eye you have, Mr. Vaughan. That is an exquisite yellow diamond from Brazil. The rich color and dazzling clarity are unmatched by anything I've seen in the last ten years. Five and a half carats, cushion cut. The setting is platinum, very simple. Designed to showcase the stone, but if the lady prefers something else, we could always reset."

J.B. narrowed his eyes and picked up the loupe. "Let me take a look."

As he examined the stone, Mazie freaked inwardly. The ring had to be well over six figures. That was a heck of a lot of money for a play prop.

She tugged his sleeve. "That one's too much. Be sensible."

J.B. turned to face her, his half smile intimate, toe-curling. "It's you, Mazie. Rare. Unique. Stunning. The stone picks up the sunshine color in your amber eyes and the gleams of gold in your hair." Before she could stop him, he took her left hand and slid the ring onto her third finger.

For a split second, the world stopped. J.B.'s hands holding hers were warm, his grasp strong. The ring nestled in place as if it had been sized for her and her alone.

She swallowed. "It's beautiful." The stone was actually heavy on her hand. Weighty. Serious.

Everything this engagement was not.

He frowned, perhaps sensing her unease. "We can go with a traditional diamond if you'd prefer. I realize this color is not the usual bridal choice."

Mazie knew J.B. was playing a part. He was pretending to care, pretending to consult her wishes. No matter how much she told herself this fairy-tale moment wasn't real, the little girl inside her who dreamed of fairy tales and Prince Charming was jumping up and down.

Her throat was tight. "I love it," she said huskily.

J.B. turned to the jeweler, pulling his wallet from his jacket pocket and extracting his platinum credit card.

"We'll take it."

Twelve

Mazie found a parking spot at the hospital, turned off the engine and sat for a moment, staring at her newly adorned hand. If alien civilizations actually existed, she could probably pick up communications from other planets on this thing. The ring was huge, stunning.

Even here, in the semidarkness, it seemed to have a life of its own, much like J.B.'s impromptu engagement for his mother's benefit.

Before Mazie and J.B. had left the jewelry store, Mazie had been forced to hover for long embarrassing minutes while the two men conducted the business portion of the transaction. The ring came with a two-page appraisal and a fancy box wrapped in plum satin paper and silver ribbon.

The fact that the box was empty didn't seem to bother anyone. It was part of the pomp and circumstance of purchasing a ridiculously expensive piece of jewelry.

She glanced out the window, suddenly aware—as never before—of the possibility of getting mugged in a parking lot. Because she had insisted on having her own car, she and J.B. had gotten separated on the way to the hospital. He might be close by or on the other side of the building.

As far as she could tell, no was one lurking in the shadows ready to snatch a ring off her finger. Shaking her head at her own vivid imagination, she got out and locked her car.

Before she could take more than a few steps, J.B. appeared, loping across the pavement. Clearly, he had found a parking spot more quickly than she had.

"Did you spend most of the day here?" she asked.

He folded his arms across his chest. "The part of it that I wasn't having sex with you, Mazie. You can't pretend it didn't happen."

"Watch me," she muttered, taking off for the hospital entrance as if she were being pursued.

J.B. kept pace with her mad dash, but he didn't touch her. She told herself she was glad.

In the elevator, they were surrounded by strangers. On the CCU floor, the other three Vaughans kept their vigil. J.B.'s mother was doing very well. The nurses had had her up walking, and all her stats were good. In another twenty-four to forty-eight hours, she would likely be moved to a regular room.

Alana motioned for everyone's attention. "Mama wants to tell us something. But we have to make it quick. They're bending the rules right and left, but we're running out of goodwill, I think."

The five of them entered the cubicle. The two sisters took one side of the bed, J.B. and his father the other. Mazie hung back near the door.

"Okay, Mama," Alana said. "What's up?"

Mrs. Vaughan looked at her son. "You four have been here most of the day." She patted her son's hand. "J.B., I want you to take your sisters and your dad, and go have a nice restaurant dinner somewhere. *Not* the hospital cafeteria. Mazie will sit with me while you're gone."

They all turned and looked at Mazie. She felt her face heat. "I'd be happy to do that."

Leila grimaced. "But Mazie needs dinner."

"I have peanut butter crackers in my purse. I'll be fine." She curled her fingers around the ring. Maybe she could slip it off for the moment.

J.B.'s face had no expression at all. If Mazie had to guess, she'd say he was sifting through his mother's statement for hidden grenades and wondering if it was safe to leave Mazie behind.

Mrs. Vaughan waved a hand. "Go. I'm serious." Her voice was weak, but her color was healthy, and she was clearly in good spirits.

"Okay, Mama." J.B. turned to Mazie and kissed her on the cheek. "Make my mother behave."

"I'll do my best." Having J.B. be so casually affectionate after what had happened between them this morning rattled her composure. What would happen if his careful attentions were rooted in truth? Could she trust him? Would she be glad?

When the room emptied, Jane Vaughan exhaled and smiled at Mazie. "I love that crew, but when they hover, I want to smack them up the side of the head. I'm not accustomed to being out of control. I don't much care for it."

"Yes, ma'am. I understand."

"Pull that chair closer to the bed, Mazie."

"You probably should rest until they bring your dinner tray. I have things to read on my iPad."

J.B.'s mother shook her head. "This may be our only chance to speak in private. I have to carpe diem," she said.

Seize the day? Mazie frowned inwardly. "I'm not sure I understand."

"I want to talk about my son, dear girl. And your relationship to him."

Mazie froze, sensing danger. Here was a woman who had undergone serious surgery. She couldn't be upset or shocked or any other emotion that would impede her recovery. "Okay…"

Jane chuckled. "Don't look so petrified. I know the engagement is fake. You can relax."

Mazie gaped at her. "Why would you say that?"

"Jackson Beauregard is my firstborn. I know him, and I love him. Ever since that stupid woman coaxed him into marriage and humiliated him, J.B. has closed himself off emotionally. I've prayed that he would come to terms with the mistake he made, but J.B. is harder on himself than anyone else. He can't forgive his own youthful blunder. He swore never to let any other woman get that close to him again. And he's kept that vow. He has multiple women in his life, but to him they're as interchangeable as a pair of socks."

"But…"

The older woman grimaced. "He was trying to give me a reason to live. And it was sweet of him, dear boy. But I'm not a fool. Nobody does a one-eighty that fast. If he had been falling in love with you, I would have gotten wind of it." She grinned. "I have *spies* all over the city."

"That's what J.B. told me." Mazie paused, trying to understand. "So you're saying there's no reason to continue with the charade?"

"Oh, no, my dear. Just the opposite. I'm begging you to keep up the pretense in hopes that my sweet boy will see that true love is worth fighting for."

Mazie's head was spinning. In the midst of this extraordinary conversation, a nurse had come in to draw blood and check vitals. Close on her heels was an employee with a dinner tray.

When the medical staff finally wrapped up their assigned tasks and left the room, Mazie uncovered the meal. "Looks like a grilled chicken breast, rice and lemon Jell-O."

"Oh, goody."

Jane's dour sarcasm made Mazie laugh. "You need the calories to get better. Which do you want first?"

"If I eat all that dreadful stuff, you have to agree to my plan."

Mazie cut up the chicken, added sweetener and lemon

to the tea at Jane's request, and raised the head of the bed. "I'm feeling a little bit under the gun, Jane. You have to understand, J.B. and I are…" She trailed off.

How exactly did one define what she and J.B. were to each other? She was letting his masculine charm drag her under his spell all over again, and he was using her as a convenient ploy.

Jane, true to her word, was working her way through the bland food. "Have you slept together?"

"Ah…" A hot flush rose from Mazie throat to her hairline. This woman had endured major, life-threatening surgery, and yet still had the capacity to do an interrogation that would make a seasoned professional proud. "I'm not comfortable discussing that with you."

"Fair enough." Jane finished the rice. "I'm aware you've known each other forever, but how did you come to be on a fancy date last night?"

Mazie chose and discarded explanations rapidly. "J.B. was wining and dining me because he wants to buy my building. It's smack in the middle of his big restoration project. I'm the last holdout."

"How delicious. I hope you haven't made it easy for him."

Were they talking about business or sex?

Mazie uncovered the tiny serving of Jell-O and added a plastic spoon. "I'll have to admit, it made me mad that he thought I would simply give him what he wanted. So I've been cranky and obstructive. But he's offered me another property for my store that is lovely. I've decided to let him stew until after Christmas, and then give him what he needs."

"Well, I'm glad his business dealings are doing well, but I'm more concerned about his emotional well-being. Please let the engagement stand, Mazie. He already trusts you. That's a huge step forward."

"Why would you say that?" She couldn't let herself believe the fantasy that J.B. actually cared for her. There would be too far to fall when the truth was revealed.

"No man enters into a fake engagement unless he is absolutely sure the woman in question will let him off the hook when the charade is over. Clearly, he trusts you not to sue him for breach of promise or something awful like that. And he doesn't have to worry that you're after his money, because you have plenty of your own. You're the perfect woman for him."

But she wasn't.

J.B. didn't want to be married. And no matter how great the sex, no man was going to tie the knot when he wasn't emotionally involved. Mazie wasn't convinced J.B. would allow himself to be that vulnerable.

If she went along with this plan, he might destroy her all over again. Still, she couldn't say no to his mother, not under these circumstances.

"I don't know that I am, Jane. But if it will make you happy, I'll let this arrangement ride for the moment."

Jane beamed. "Thank you dear. Now let me see the ring."

Mazie blushed again. "How did you know?"

"You've been hiding your left hand since you walked into the room. Not only that, I practically ordered my son to take you ring shopping today, and I was fairly certain he wanted to pacify me."

"It's a little over the top," Mazie confessed.

She held out her left hand. Even now, in this sterile, medical setting, the ring blazed with life.

Jane took Mazie's hand in both of hers and studied the diamond from all angles. "Wow," she said.

Mazie wrinkled her nose. "I know. It's too much, isn't it? I don't know what he was thinking."

"I always told my children to go big or go home." Jane closed her eyes, rubbing her chest absently.

"Mrs. Vaughan? Jane?" Mazie looked at her in alarm. "Are you okay?"

"Just tired, my dear. Why don't you read your book now, and I'll nap for a few minutes…"

"Of course." Mazie tidied the mostly empty food tray and covered everything. Then she rolled the little table away from the bed so Jane could relax in comfort.

When she glanced at her watch, she saw that the Vaughans had been gone only fifty minutes. If they followed Jane's directive, they would stay away another hour. Mazie pulled her iPad mini from her purse and queued up the book she was reading. It was a romantic comedy about a dyslexic librarian and a handyman who liked to work after hours. The story was charming and funny, but it failed to hold her interest.

At last, she dropped the device into her purse and studied the woman in the bed. Mothers, in general, were supposed to have keen instincts when it came to the love lives of their children. Jane was more dialed in than most. The fact that she saw through the false engagement ruse meant that she really did understand how J.B.'s mind worked.

What the other woman *didn't* know was that J.B. had already rejected Mazie once. He had broken her heart. He'd left her vulnerable and hurting.

You could argue that something so long ago wasn't real or even very important. But Mazie still carried the scars. For J.B.'s mother, she would let this charade continue a few days or weeks.

Nothing more, though.

She was not going to be foolish enough to believe that the ring and the situation were anything more than a son's desire to cheer up his mom.

J.B. stood in the doorway of his mother's hospital room and studied the two women inside. His mother was napping. Every report they had received so far was promising. Surely that meant she was beyond the worst of the danger.

Beside the bed in an ugly recliner covered in faux leather, Mazie snoozed as well, one hand tucked beneath her cheek. It was no wonder. She had waited at the hospital with him a big chunk of the night, and then this morning at his house, she had been otherwise engaged.

The memory of making love to Mazie disturbed him. He liked keeping things in neat compartments. His feelings for the woman with the whiskey-colored hair and the amber eyes slopped over into several boxes.

Business contact. Longtime family friend. Childhood confidante. Lover.

Most disturbing of all, she was his best friend's sister. It was the last designation that gave him heartburn.

A physical relationship with Jonathan's sister seemed fraught with danger. For years he had kept her in a box labeled *not for* me. Now, to make things worse, J.B. himself had invented a fake engagement to give his mother something on which to focus her goals for recovery. How far would he have to play out that scenario before he put a stop to it?

Not that he thought Mazie would take advantage of the situation. If anything, she was a very reluctant fiancée.

He must have made a sound, because Mazie's eyes flew open.

"Oh, hey," she said. "You're back. Where are the others?"

His mom roused, as well. "Hello, son. Did you all get something good to eat?"

He nodded. "We did, Mom. Dad and the girls have gone home to sleep. I'm taking first shift. I'll be here overnight."

"I don't need a babysitter."

He leaned down and squeezed her hand. "Humor me."

He glanced at Mazie. "If you're ready, I'll walk you down to your car."

"Take your time," his mother said with an arch smile.

Mazie's cheeks heated.

He rolled his eyes. "Behave, Mom."

She was unrepentant. "The moon is out. It's a beautiful night. I'm not going anywhere. And by the way…"

"Yes?"

"You did well on the ring. It's gorgeous."

For some reason, the tops of his ears got hot. "We're glad you like it. I wanted something unique and special… like Mazie."

His fiancée stood and stretched. The stone on her hand flashed and sparked as she moved. "Enough blarney," she said.

She gave his mom a smile. "I enjoyed talking to you, Jane. Maybe I'll see you tomorrow? If you feel like having a visitor?"

J.B.'s mother waved her arms. "Come here. Give me a hug. And yes, I'll be expecting you. I'll send the rest of them out for coffee, so we can gossip."

"As long as you're doing everything the doctor orders, we can gossip to your heart's content. Good night, Mrs. Vaughan. See you tomorrow."

"I'll be back shortly," J.B. said.

He took Mazie's arm and steered her toward the bank of elevators. "Thanks for doing that. It makes her feel good to know that the rest of us are obeying her orders."

"She's not that bad," Mazie protested. "She only wants what's best for all of you."

"Uh-oh," he said, faking alarm. "She's indoctrinated you."

Mazie punched his arm. "Don't be mean. Your mom is a sweetheart."

He tapped the button for the lobby. "I agree one hundred

percent. But don't let her fool you. She'll have you dancing to her tune in no time."

Outside, he walked Mazie across the courtyard and to the far parking lot where she had left her car.

She unlocked the door and tossed her purse on the passenger seat. "You should hurry back inside," she said. "In case she needs something."

He leaned an arm on the roof of the car, boxing her in. "Trying to get rid of me, Ms. Tarleton?"

Mazie looked up at him, her features shadowed. "No."

He stroked a wisp of hair from her cheek, wishing they weren't in a public arena so he could kiss her the way he wanted, needed. "I missed you today."

She murmured something that was neither agreement nor dissent.

He frowned. "You *are* my fiancée, after all."

Her head snapped up, her demeanor indignant. "Fake fiancée," she insisted.

"What are we going to do about this *thing* between us?"

"You're talking about sex."

"Yes. But it's not easy and fun, is it? We're digging ourselves into a pretty big hole."

"I agree. It seems smarter to end things now."

"What if I don't want to? You and I are crazy in bed—crazy good."

"I'd like to point out that we haven't actually tried sex in a bed. We seem to go for more inappropriate locations. Bank vaults. Your living room sofa."

He kissed her temple. "Nothing wrong with a sofa." It struck him suddenly that he didn't want her to leave. He liked having her at arm's length in the midst of his family crisis. She made everything easier.

The implications of that shot alarm and adrenaline coursing through his veins, but he ignored the internal upheaval, intent on having his way.

"I have an idea," he said. "Why don't you move into my place for a few days? My mother likes you, and you could help us keep an eye on her. Plus, my house is close to All That Glitters. Cut your commute time in half."

"That's a fairly elaborate setup just so you and I can have the occasional booty call. What's your end game, J.B.?"

Why did women always want to strangle a man with emotion and romance? This was physical. Nothing more. Mazie had to know that.

"There is no end game," he said gruffly. "With Mom sick and you working and me *trying* to work, this is the only scenario I can come up with for you and I to get a moment alone."

"For sex."

"Yes," he said, grinding his jaw. "For sex."

"How long are you thinking about?"

"I don't know. A week, maybe. Or two."

"That takes us up until Christmas."

"I guess it does." He slid his hands into her hair and cupped her head, tilting it back so he could kiss her. "Spend Christmas with me, Mazie. Today wasn't enough," he said, his body already taut with need. "I want you. Beyond reason. Tell me you feel it, too."

She was soft and warm in his arms, her body a feminine foil for his harder, bigger frame.

"Yes," she said, her voice barely audible. She sounded more resigned than happy. "But I like a lot of things that are bad for me. Rich chocolate mousse. Salted caramel ice cream. Bad boys who insist on getting their own way."

He dragged her closer, closing the car door and leaning Mazie against it until his lower body pressed hers. His erection ached.

"I have to go back inside," he groaned.

Mazie cupped his face in her hands and kissed him slow and deep, her tongue teasing his. "I'll think about your offer, J.B." She flattened her palms on his chest and shoved. "We're not having sex in a parking lot. I have to draw the line somewhere."

He might have whimpered. He nearly begged. But she was right, damn it. Gulping in huge breaths of the chilled night air, he forced himself to back up. "Pack a bag tonight. Please."

"Don't push me. I said I'll think about it." Ducking out of his embrace, she opened the driver's door and got into her little sports car. "See you tomorrow."

Thirteen

Mazie was starving when she finally got home. She'd never actually gotten around to eating the peanut butter crackers in her purse. All of the household staff were long gone by now, but she could cook well enough on her own. Which was pretty surprising for a woman whose mother hadn't been around when she was a teenager. Fortunately, more than one housekeeper had taken pity on a moody preteen and let her putter around the kitchen.

Jonathan found her there. The smell of bacon frying had clearly drawn him away from his home office.

"Late dinner or early breakfast?" he asked, sniffing the air with an appreciative sigh.

She took a carton from the fridge. "I missed supper. You want any scrambled eggs?"

He sat on a stool at the counter. "Actually, that sounds pretty damn good. I had a salad with a client, but I wasn't in the mood for a big meal."

"Still feeling rotten?"

He nodded. "I haven't wanted to tell you this, but I guess it's time. My doctor wants me to go to some hippie-dippie holistic retreat out in the desert to see if we can break the cycle of these headaches. The doctors and counselors who run the program use a combination of meditation and medical assessment and organic or natural medicines."

She tended the eggs carefully. The strips of perfectly crisped bacon were already draining on a paper towel.

"No offense, Jonathan, but that doesn't sound like you at all." His air of brooding exhaustion made her worry about him.

"You're right. In fact, you couldn't be *more* right. But I'm getting desperate."

"Here. I'll have toast ready in a minute. Start on this." She gave him the eggs and bacon. "But why wouldn't you want to tell me that?"

"Because the retreat center is booked months in advance. The only opening they had was the week that includes Christmas."

"Oh." Disappointment curled in her stomach. "Well, it's just one day on the calendar. Daddy and I will be fine."

Jonathan grimaced. "That's the other part. Dad's been invited to go on a cruise with his college buddies. He asked me what I thought, and I told him it would be good for him to get out of the house. But that was before I knew I'd be leaving, too. I feel terrible about this, Mazie. I've dreaded telling you."

She managed a smile. "Don't be ridiculous. I'm a grown woman. Besides, there are tons of places I can celebrate the holiday. Don't worry about me at all. The important thing is for you to get well."

Relief lightened his face. "I'll make it up to you, I swear."

"I'll be fine. Eat your eggs before they get cold."

She added the toast to their plates and joined him. For several minutes, peace reigned in the beautiful kitchen. Mazie often thought about having her own place. A man to cook for, or one who might cook for her. A couple of kids running through the halls, leaving toys scattered about. Maybe a mongrel dog, or two...

"Jonathan?"

"Hmm?" He had cleared his plate and was now slathering butter and honey over a piece of toast.

"J.B.'s mother came through the surgery well. But right

before she went under the knife, J.B. did something kind of dumb. They were all afraid she wasn't going to make it. Even Jane, his mom, wasn't sure."

"And?"

"J.B. told her we were secretly engaged. He said she had to get well so she could play with all the grandchildren we're going to have."

"Stupid bastard." But he said the words with wry affection.

"I know. I couldn't even be mad at him, because he was so worried and scared."

"But now you have to wait a little while before you can break it off so you won't upset her."

"Something like that." She didn't bother explaining that Jane Vaughan had already seen through the ruse. What did it matter?

Jonathan opened the dishwasher, tucking his few items inside. "If you want my advice, I wouldn't bother telling Dad. It will only confuse him. I hate to say it, but I see him slipping a little more with each week that passes."

"And you think that won't be a problem on a cruise?"

Jonathan grinned. "It's not like he can wander off. Seriously, though, I know all of his gang. They'll look out for him."

"As long as none of them is like Daddy."

"The cruise is billed as an all-inclusive event for older adults. Much older. He'll be fine."

"I hope so."

Jonathan glanced at the clock. "Don't move. I have something I want to show you."

When he disappeared, Mazie tidied up the kitchen. The housekeeper could have done it in the morning, but Mazie hated leaving a mess overnight. She had just wiped down the counter when Jonathan returned carrying a small box, much the size of the one that had come with her ring.

This box was red leather, and it wasn't wrapped. Mazie was standing at the sink when Jonathan tucked his arms around her from behind. "I hate like hell to miss Christmas, sis. I want you to have your present early."

He hopped up on the granite-topped island and folded his arms across his chest. "Go ahead. Open it."

Mazie pulled on the hinged lid and caught her breath. Inside was a delicate necklace. A gold chain, featherlight, coiled in the box. It supported a single, gorgeous pearl, as fat as a child's marble.

She lifted the necklace carefully, rubbing a fingertip over the luminescent sphere. "It's beautiful, Jonathan."

"Dad put my name with his on a lot of legal stuff recently. When I was going through the safety deposit box, I found a bunch of Mom's jewelry. Evidently, when he sent her away, she had to leave it all behind. I know how much you miss her, especially during the holidays. I thought you could wear this and feel close to her...until you and I can go to Vermont after the first of the year."

Mazie eyes were damp. "Thank you, Jonathan. I adore it."

He waited as she wrestled with the clasp. "It will all be yours someday anyway."

She frowned. "No. That's not fair. You and Hartley will take a share for your spouses."

"Hartley is out of the picture, and I don't know that marriage is in the cards for me."

"Why do you say that?"

His gaze was stormy, troubled. "I've wondered if these headaches are a precursor of something worse. What if I've inherited Mom's instability? I don't want to doom a wife or a baby to the kind of life you and I experienced. It wouldn't be fair."

She was shocked. Had he been wrestling with this possibility for months? Shaking her head vehemently, she touched his knee. "Oh, Jonathan. I had no idea. I don't think that could be true. You're brilliant. You run a multinational shipping empire. Hundreds of people depend on you, and you handle it all with such grace, including your ability to make sure Daddy still feels needed. You're *not* going crazy. I would tell you if I saw any inkling."

Some of the clouds left his face. "Thanks," he said gruffly.

"Don't worry about the holidays," she said. "I might spend Christmas somewhere else since you and Daddy will both be gone." Was she rationalizing her decision? Trying to put a positive spin on a choice she knew she should never make? "J.B. offered a room at his house." And a whole lot more…

"For a fake fiancé, he sure has a hell of a nerve. Are you sleeping with him?" Jonathan's tone was truculent.

She scowled at him, long accustomed to his protective nature. "I love you, big brother. And I love my gift. But I won't have this discussion with you. Are we clear?" Some things were far too private.

"What will you tell Dad?"

"The truth. That I'm helping out a friend. I'll drop by here and see him every other day or so until he leaves. By the time he gets back from the cruise, all of this will be over."

"So you'll spend Christmas with the Vaughans? That would make me feel better about leaving you."

"Maybe so, or if that doesn't work out, maybe with Gina's crew. She has so many cousins they would never notice one more person. She's always asking me to come to family things. I don't know that Mrs. Vaughan will feel up to having much of a Christmas, anyway."

"Okay. As long as you're not alone."

"Being alone isn't so bad," she said. "It's not the same as being *lonely.* I have you and Dad and all kinds of friends. I'll be fine."

The question remained, would she spend Christmas in J.B.'s bed?

* * *

Her brave statement to Jonathan was tested a few hours later.

With the lights out and the room dark, all she could think about was how much she wanted J.B. here beside her. The strength of that yearning was a wake-up call. How had he wormed his way into her heart so quickly?

It occurred to her that over the years she had whipped up her antipathy toward him for no other reason than to keep from admitting that she still had feelings for him. Not teenage heart palpitations, but full-blown, adult emotions that left her weak and vulnerable and afraid.

J.B. was playing with her. Not cruelly, but for fun. He was intent on having a grown-up sleepover.

A holiday affair.

She would be a fool to let him have that much control over her happiness. To let him lure her into his home and into his bed.

Even knowing every single reason that she had to guard her heart, she couldn't resist the pull of the perfect holiday with J.B.

Admitting the truth was both elating and terrifying.

Come morning, she was going to pack a bag and cast her lot with Charleston's *baddest* bachelor.

When she reached the hospital on Sunday just before noon, she was suddenly unsure about going in. J.B. hadn't called. Or texted. They had left things between them at a rather volatile crossroads last night.

Maybe he was regretting his impulsive invitation.

It wasn't too late to undo that. Her bag was in the trunk. No reason for him to ever know she had come prepared.

Because she had dropped by work briefly before coming to the hospital, she was dressed nicely in a black pencil skirt, emerald green silk blouse and her new necklace. The large pearl nestled just at the top of her cleavage.

She touched the cool stone. Jonathan understood all she had missed as a child…all they both had missed. The pearl couldn't bring her mother back, but it was a tangible link to all the might-have-beens.

Inside the hospital, she headed straight for the information desk and confirmed that Mrs. Vaughan had been moved to a regular room. That was definitely good news. When Mazie made her way upstairs, she found only Alana in residence. Even the bed was empty.

The woman who was only a couple years younger than Mazie smiled. "They took Mom one flight up for cardiac rehab. She'll be back soon."

"And the rest of your family?"

"Dad's an early riser. He got here at six this morning and sent J.B. home to sleep. Pop is downstairs grabbing a snack right now. Leila and I were here by eight. Mom's asking for her favorite coffee. The doctor okayed it, so Leila went to get her some."

"Well, it sounds like you have everything under control. Perhaps I'll swing by later in the day."

Alana hopped up, tossing the paperback book she had been reading into her tote. "Actually, I have a favor to ask."

"I'd be happy to help," Mazie said. "What is it?"

"My sister and I have matinee tickets for *The Nutcracker* at 2:00 p.m. today. Mom remembered and is insisting we go. One of the tickets was for her, so she wants Daddy to take her place. Which is stupid, because the man is *not* a ballet fan, but what can he do? He wants to make her happy."

"I'd be happy to sit with your mother," Mazie said.

"J.B. will be back soon. You wouldn't be here alone."

"I've already said yes," Mazie teased. "No need to over-sell it."

"Perfect," Alana said.

At that moment, an orderly wheeled Mrs. Vaughan back into the room and helped her into bed. Mazie hovered in the hall during the transfer, not wanting to be in the way. Soon, Mr. Vaughan and his other daughter arrived, as well. The controlled chaos lasted for several minutes.

Mazie could hear J.B.'s mother directing everyone's movements. Mazie grinned to herself. No wonder the Vaughans loved and feared Jane. She was a formidable force.

At last the hoopla settled and the room quieted. Mazie could hear Jane asking for her. She stepped to the door. "I'm here."

Jane kissed her husband and daughters as they leaned over her bed. "Go have fun, my loves. Mazie and J.B. will look after me until you get back."

Soon the room emptied, and it was just Mazie and Jane. For the first time since Mazie had arrived, the older woman seemed to deflate.

"I'm toast," she grumbled. "I hate feeling this way."

"You had a major heart attack and serious surgery. It's going to take some time. Why don't you rest until they bring your lunch tray?"

"I'm tired of resting. Tell me about your family. I need distractions. I'm going crazy in this place."

Mazie pulled up a chair. "Okay. What do you remember?"

"Not much," Jane said. "When you children were small, I knew your parents well, but the years passed, you all grew up, and we lost touch."

"You know about my mother, though?"

Jane's expression softened. "I do. The poor woman had demons, I suppose. And you were just a babe."

"Old enough to remember her leaving."

J.B.'s mother patted the bed. "Come sit here." Jane took her hand. "Everyone in Charleston knew what was happening. But the scuttlebutt was never unkind. Your parents were well respected, and to see you children lose your mother…" She shook her head, her gaze sober. "We all grieved for you and your brothers. And your father, too, of course. How is Gerald doing these days?"

"His health is precarious. He's twenty-two years older than my mom, so he's beginning to slow down."

"It must have been hard for him. Sending her away."

Mazie stood up and paced, her arms wrapped around her waist. "Yes. My brothers and I visit her occasionally. Up in Vermont. But she hasn't known us for years. She seems happy, though."

"If you marry my son, I'd be honored to be your mother-in-law."

It sounded like a joke, but when Mazie turned around and stared at her, Jane was clearly dead serious. Mazie hesitated. "You told me you understood that J.B. was inventing this whole engagement charade."

"I do. But sometimes a man does things for reasons he can't even understand until later."

"Mrs. Vaughan… Jane. Please don't set your heart on this." She bit her lip. "It's not real."

"I've seen the way he looks at you."

Mazie swallowed, desperately wanting to believe that Jane was right. "He's physically attracted to me. For the moment. I think it's probably the thrill of the chase. As soon as I sell my property to him, he'll lose interest."

"It's time he settled down."

"J.B. has a great life. I don't think he's missing out on anything."

"And what about you, Mazie?"

Fourteen

J.B. heard just enough of the conversation in his mother's hospital room to realize that poor Mazie was floundering. He bumped the partially open door with his hip and entered. "I brought Chinese for Mazie and me. Sorry, Mom. We can eat in the lounge if it makes you too hungry."

He smothered a grin at the naked relief on Mazie's face. "Thanks, J.B."

A young woman in pink scrubs brought in the noon meal and set it on the bedside table. While J.B. set out the more appetizing of the two feasts, Mazie helped Jane get organized.

As everyone was digging in, Jane smiled genially.

"We should settle on your wedding date immediately," she pronounced, staring at her broiled codfish with distaste. "All the best summer venues will be booked soon."

J.B. took his mother's outrageous efforts in stride. He was used to her tactics.

Poor Mazie, on the other hand, choked on a bite of moo shu pork, her expression impossible to read. Her cheeks turned pink. Was she appalled or intrigued about the mention of wedded bliss?

For his part, the idea didn't bother him as much as it should have.

J.B. shook his head. "Back off, Mom. I love you, but this is between Mazie and me."

Mazie nodded. "Please don't be offended. But we're in

no rush, Jane. J.B. has this big project ahead of him, and besides, we haven't been together all that long."

His mother shook her head, picking at a cup of out-of-the-can fruit cocktail. She shot a sly glance that J.B. intercepted, though he didn't think Mazie saw. "You know how much I hate downtime, son. This wedding could be the perfect thing to occupy me while I'm having to take it easy."

"Nice try, Mom. Guilt and coercion are not going to work on either of us. Mazie and I are adults. You'll have to trust us to decide when the time is right. Now eat your lunch and behave."

The remainder of the afternoon passed without fireworks. His mother napped off and on. In between, he and Mazie entertained her with lighthearted conversation about anything and everything. Mazie was great with his mom. For a woman who had grown up without a female role model, she was remarkably astute when it came to handling a difficult parent.

Caring for her father had shaped her adult life.

By the time the next shift arrived at five, J.B. was more than ready to spirit Mazie away. Watching her all afternoon had been slow torture. He wanted to make love to her again. Badly. And this time in a comfortable bed with soft sheets where he could take his time with her. The prospect dried his mouth and tightened his body.

She was an elegant woman, graceful, fun loving, and above all, kind. Which didn't explain why she had given him such grief about selling her building. The place was a mess. Heating, wiring, water issues in the basement. Everything he had offered Mazie as a trade was far and away better. But she had clung to her hatred of him. He liked to think he had mended fences with her now...that what happened so long ago no longer mattered.

Some people said love was the flip side of hate. Did he

want that from Mazie? Surely not. He'd been vulnerable once, had trusted a woman. The betrayal that followed had cost him his heart, his pride and his fortune.

Mazie wasn't like his ex-wife. He'd stake his life on it.

But did he really want to take a chance?

His mother's heart attack had diverted his attention. But now that she was on the mend, he needed to focus his attention on persuading Mazie to sell.

Perhaps he could combine business with pleasure. He had asked her to spend Christmas with him. Was she going to say yes? The prospect was far more personal than he wanted to admit.

When his father and sisters shooed him on his way—after heaping gratitude on Mazie for spending her Sunday afternoon at the hospital—J.B. followed Mazie outside, breathing in the crisp evening air with a groan of relief.

"God, I hate hospitals," he said. "The smells. The sad faces. I hope Mom doesn't have to stay long."

Mazie rolled her shoulders. "It's a great hospital, J.B. But I know what you mean."

"Are you hungry?"

"Not yet."

"You want to walk the bridge?" The Ravenel Bridge, completed in 2005, had been constructed with both a pedestrian path and a bike lane. It was a popular destination any time of the year, but in December when the weather was kind, it couldn't be beat.

Mazie nodded. "I'd love to. I've been feeling like a slug." She glanced down at her slim skirt and high heels. "I'll have to put on other clothes."

They had made it out of the lobby and were standing on the sidewalk near the main parking lot. J.B. took her arm, his fingertips rubbing lightly over the narrow bones of her wrist. "Did you bring what you needed to stay over?" He felt her pulse jump.

She nodded slowly. When she lifted her gaze to his, he saw deep vulnerability. "I'm not sure why, but I did."

Exultation flooded his veins, though he kept his expression noncommittal. Words he couldn't say hovered on his lips. Words that would change everything. He couldn't do it. He wouldn't. It wasn't really necessary to upset the status quo. Too much at stake. "Good. Let's meet at my house, and we'll both get changed."

Was that disappointment he saw on her face? He felt a lick of shame, but it didn't sway him.

The distance was short, ten minutes at the most. Even so, he held his breath until he saw Mazie's distinctive car pull into his narrow driveway and squeeze in beside his SUV.

He slammed his car door and waited, rifling though his pockets for what he wanted to give her.

Mazie got out as well, with her purse slung over her shoulder and a stylish duffel in her hand.

"I made you a set of keys," he said. "I'll remind you how to use the alarm before we go to bed tonight." He took the heavy bag from her.

She wrapped her arms around her waist. "That's not really necessary, is it? I won't be here long."

"I want you to feel at home."

As he said the words, something about them set off warning bells in his head. When had he *ever* said that exact phrase to a woman? Never that he could recall.

He would have to tread carefully. Mazie might get the wrong idea. Even worse, so might he.

Inside, he led her upstairs, bypassing his bedroom and ushering her into a beautifully decorated guest room. The celadon hues were soothing.

"This is beautiful," Mazie said.

He set her bag on the dresser. "I hope you won't want to spend too much time in here."

Her mouth dropped open in a little O of shock. Hot pink color flooded her face. "J.B., I…"

He held up a hand. "It's your room. Completely private. No strings attached. But I reserve the right to remind you how sweet it is when we both give in to temptation."

She lifted an eyebrow. "Sweet? More like insane."

"So you admit it."

Mazie shrugged, her gaze moody and restless as she dropped her purse on a chair and examined the amenities.

"It would be hard not to," she muttered, running her hand over the bedspread.

Watching her touch the bed was almost tactile. His skin quivered as if she were stroking *him*. He kept his distance, though it strained every ounce of his control.

He loved her.

The admission slapped him like a jolt of cold water on a winter morning. He wanted to snatch her up and kiss her senseless and bury himself inside her until he couldn't breathe with wanting her.

But the consequences of such abandon were very nearly life and death.

He couldn't dive into this thing without remembering the past. Failure. Humiliation. Self-loathing.

Instead, he did the mature, nonreckless thing. "Get dressed," he said gruffly. "We'll walk the bridge, and then I'll take you for fresh shrimp and hush puppies at Lolita's."

This time, Mazie's smile was open and untinged with the wariness that was so much a part of her personality.

"For that kind of positive reinforcement, I'll follow you anywhere."

J.B. needed exercise. Badly.

And though he would have preferred the kind between the sheets, it was probably better this way.

Mazie changed clothes as quickly as he did. Soon they

were on their way toward the bridge. Beneath the magnificent structure with the two triangular sets of silvery spires, an enterprising city had installed parking and a labyrinth of short trails.

While Mazie hopped out and began stretching, J.B. locked the car and tried not to look at the way black spandex cupped her cute butt. Lord help him. He did a few stretches, too, but he was antsy. "Let's go," he said. "We can walk the first quarter mile to warm up."

They were far from the only people enjoying the bridge. Though the sounds of cars whizzing by a few feet away on the other side of the concrete barrier was not exactly relaxing, being able to look down on the city of Charleston made up for it. They started out at a brisk walk.

When Mazie shed her jacket and tied it around her waist, he gave her a nod. "Ready?"

"Yep. I'll drop back when people pass us."

They set off at an easy jog. Tension winnowed away from his body step by step. For weeks he had been totally immersed in the huge project that included Mazie's shop. And then the scare with his mother had left their entire family on edge.

But the emotions that had truly kept him tied in knots day and night were all because of Mazie.

At the top of the arc, he expected her to stop, but she kept on running, her ponytail bouncing in the wind. He kept pace with her, curbing his stride to match hers. At the other end, they did an about-face and headed back. This time, when they hit dead center on the bridge, Mazie paused long enough to stare down into the inky black Cooper River far below.

On sunny, bright days, you could spot dolphins frolicking. Tonight, the deep water was mysterious.

He bumped her hip with his. "We can't stand here too long, or we'll get cold. And I'm starving."

A smile curved her mouth. "Have you ever heard of delayed gratification?"

He took her arm. "Not a fan."

They walked quickly, using the last segment to lower their heart rates. Unfortunately, being near Mazie kept his blood pressure and respiration perpetually in the red zone.

For the moment, he would sublimate with food.

Lolita's was a hole-in-wall place. The kind of eatery the locals patronized and tourists rarely took the time to find. Not on the beach, but near enough the water to have the best seafood in Mount Pleasant.

Even better, the ambiance was definitely casual. He and Mazie didn't look out of place in their running clothes.

The hostess led them to a scarred table beneath a huge stuffed tarpon wearing a Santa hat. She handed them plastic-coated menus. "Wreckfish is the special tonight. Two sides. Thirty-five bucks. It's worth the price. Soup of the day is seafood gumbo. Let me grab you a couple of waters, and I'll be back to take your order."

Mazie yawned. "Sorry," she said as the waitress walked away. "I didn't sleep great last night. Jonathan and I had eggs and bacon late, and I drank half a cup of coffee. I was able to do that in college, but I guess I'm getting old."

J.B. leaned back in his chair and chuckled. "Yeah. You're ancient." He glanced around the restaurant, noting the multiple strands of Christmas lights and the ubiquitous tinsel garlands. "I suppose I should confess something. My housekeeper decorated my place for the holidays. Garlands and lights and such. But I don't have a tree. Seems kind of a waste for just me."

"No worries," she said. "We never have a tree up at our house."

He frowned. "You're kidding. I thought you were the one who loved Christmas. Jonathan jokes about it and how he has to hide his Scroogish tendencies when you're around."

"I do love Christmas," she said. "But we haven't decorated since my mom left. At first, we kids were too little, and by the time we were in high school, the moment had passed. The boys weren't particularly interested, and I was self-conscious about tackling it on my own. Plus, I was afraid it would make my father sad. So we don't deck the halls." She shrugged. "There are enough decorations elsewhere for me to enjoy. It's no big deal."

But it was a big deal. He hated the thought of a little girl yearning for candles and ornaments and wreaths and a tree and having no one to get them for her.

Their meal arrived. Both of them cleaned their plates.

Mazie finished her last plump shrimp and her last crispy hush puppy. "This place is amazing. I'm glad you thought of it."

The blissful appreciation on her face was aimed at the food, but J.B. was equally willing to accommodate any other appetites she might have. His body ached for her. The urgency of his desire was outrageous enough to slow him down for a moment.

Though he would like to take her straight back to the house and strip her naked, he needed to take a deep breath and get some perspective. Besides, she needed some pampering.

After taking care of the check, he ushered her outside. "I have a surprise," he said.

As usual, Mazie's response was laced with suspicion. "I hope it doesn't involve bank vaults."

Was she flirting with him? Or simply giving him a hard time? It baffled him that he still had difficulty understanding her. Usually he could read people like open books. Mazie was a whole damned library with the doors padlocked.

He opened the car door for her and tried to help her up

into the passenger seat, but she waved him away. "I can do it."

"Fine," he muttered. He waited until she was settled and slammed the door. Loping around to the driver's side, he quickly composed and discarded several versions of a plan to make her smile.

It was Christmas. The season of peace and goodwill. He and Mazie were mending fences, but he wanted more. He was tired of living in the shadows of his own failures.

Suddenly, he knew he had to give her the perfect, special holiday.

For a split second, he envisioned a year in the future with the two of them gathered around a fireplace reading books to a toddler. The image shocked him so much, he almost ran a red light. Tonight was about Mazie's broken childhood. He didn't want to examine his other motives too closely.

Mazie shot him a glance. "You okay?"

He swallowed the lump in his throat. "Yeah. Sorry. My mind was on something else."

She patted his thigh. "I understand. You must be so worried about your mom. But she's doing well, J.B. Honestly, she is. When you all were gone today, she told me she's feeling stronger every day."

"Yeah, I know." His mother was definitely on his mind. But her condition was stable. This thing with Mazie was definitely *not* stable.

Up ahead, he finally spotted what he was looking for. He turned into a parking lot and shut off the engine.

Mazie looked through the windshield and then sideways at him. "What are we doing here?"

"What do you think?" He reached across the small space between them and caressed her cheek with the pad of his thumb. "I think you've been a very good girl this year. Santa wants you to have all the trimmings."

Fifteen

Mazie's throat tightened. Tears stung her eyes. How dumb was this? She surely wasn't going to get all emotional because a man was being sweet and kind and indulging her love of the holiday.

J.B. stared at her with a quizzical smile on his face. He had charisma in spades. No wonder he'd dated his way through half the women in Charleston. He was a young George Clooney. Charming. Funny. Hard to pin down.

"Are you sure?" she asked. "Real Christmas trees shed needles everywhere. And they can be hard to set up."

J.B. grinned. "Challenge accepted."

"Okay, then. You asked for it."

She hopped out of the car and inhaled a deep lungful of balsam-scented air. "Take a whiff," she said. "No artificial tree can give you this."

Though it had been dark now for several hours, the proprietor had strung up long swaths of colored lights among his offerings. Christmas carols played in the background from an old-fashioned boom box. Because it was getting closer to the main event, the Christmas-tree lot was crowded with browsers.

Moms and dads and excited children. Young couples. Families with teenagers.

For a split second, Mazie felt like a child again with all the anticipation and wonder and hope of innocence. And she owed it all to the man who had once broken her heart.

But he had changed, she was sure of it. And now his sensual charm was irresistible.

J.B. tagged along behind her with an indulgent smile on his face as she walked through the rows of freshly cut trees. Half a dozen varieties were represented, but the Fraser firs were her favorites.

She bypassed the six-and seven-foot trees and headed for the bigger ones. J.B.'s living room had high ceilings. No need to skimp.

At her request, he held up one tree at a time, twirling them around so Mazie could inspect all sides. Finally, she found the one she wanted. It was perfectly symmetrical, and it was fat and healthy. It topped J.B. by almost two feet.

For the first time, he winced. "You sure about this? It's gonna look bigger when we get it inside."

"It's the perfect tree," she said. "You'll see."

While J.B. paid for the expensive fir, and the man tucked it in a mesh sleeve for the trip home, Mazie gave herself a stern lecture. She would *not* let herself be sucked into a fantasy where J.B. doted on her and actually cared about her. Everything about this weird December aberration was make-believe.

He liked having sex with her. And maybe he was also stringing her along so she would sell him her property, or he was worried about his mother and using Mazie's sympathetic heart to help him get through these difficult days, or both.

That was all this was.

At the moment, he looked like a ruggedly sexy lumberjack. He had hefted the heavy tree on top of the car, and was now securing it with bungees.

She joined him and slid an arm around his waist, feeling his muscles strain as he worked.

"You're my hero," she said, only half joking.

He stepped back and wiped sap from his forehead. "You

owe me for this. Just so you know, I plan to collect later tonight."

His wicked grin curled her toes. "The tree was your idea," she pointed out, leaning into him and inhaling the scent of warm male. "I merely went along with the adventure."

"Smart woman." He kissed her nose and then found her mouth with his. The second kiss started out lazy for five seconds and then hardened.

Mazie arched her neck, kissing him back. "You drive me crazy," she muttered.

"The feeling is mutual." He backed her against the side of the car, his lower body pinning hers to the vehicle. "I haven't needed anyone like this in a very long time. You make me want to be sixteen again."

"No," she groaned, her arms tightening around his neck. "Not that. I want the J.B. who knows all the naughty secrets about women."

He pulled back, his gaze oddly abashed and serious for the moment. "I don't know all *your* secrets, Mazie."

"I don't have anything to hide," she said lightly. The lie was both easy and disturbing.

He sucked in a sharp breath, his chest heaving, as he looked around at all the people keeping them from a private moment. "We still have to buy decorations," he muttered.

"Then let's go."

They hit up a fancy department store nearby, cleaning out a huge percentage of their handblown ornaments and silvery tinsel. Mazie added box after box of multicolored lights to the haul.

When the cashier rang up the total, J.B. never flinched. He handed over his platinum card and scrawled his name on the credit slip, giving the poor woman a smile that made her blush from her throat to her hairline, though she was old enough to be his grandmother.

Mazie rolled her eyes. The man couldn't help himself. His masculinity was electric and compelling.

Back in the car, she yawned. "It's probably too late to decorate tonight."

"I hope that means what I think it means."

She fidgeted in her seat, trying to get comfortable, her breath coming faster. "I could be persuaded."

"Oh, no," he said, staring at the traffic and not at her, so that she saw only his profile. "You're a guest in my home. I'll need a firm, unequivocal invitation."

There was a tongue-in-cheek tone to his voice, but what he said made sense. It would be cowardly on Mazie's part to pretend reluctance when the truth was, she wanted him every bit as badly as he wanted her.

Sliding her hand across the leather bench seat, she placed it on his upper thigh, gripping the taut muscle beneath his pants. "I'd like to have sex with you, J.B. In a bed, in a chair, heck, even in your fancy kitchen." She sighed. "You're a very tempting man. And I'm in a mood to indulge."

He shot her a sideways glance. "You sound like someone prepared to go off a diet. Am I really that bad for you?"

She pretended to mull it over. "Hmm. Let me see. A commitment-phobic bachelor. A relationship that will possibly hurt other people when it ends, including me. That's a yes, J.B. I don't think you're my smartest choice, but I'm not going to run away. You're exactly what I want for Christmas."

They were parked in his narrow driveway now, with two houses looming on either side. The vehicle was dark. What was he thinking? Had she startled him with her plain speaking?

After a long, tense silence, he handed her his keys. "Unlock the front door. I'll carry the tree in."

She did as he requested, and then stood aside while he brought the large Fraser fir into the house. Immediately, the foyer filled with the fragrance of outdoors. Crisp, clean. If they invented a name for this particular scent, Mazie would call it *mountain morning.*

They had bought a tree stand, a fancy one that held a good supply of water but could be tilted carefully to straighten the trunk. Somehow, they had to unwrap the tree, lift it into the container and tighten the bolts.

Suddenly, Mazie realized that she should be the one to call the shots. J.B. was trying to give her a Christmas experience she had missed for many years. He wouldn't stop until the whole damn tree was ablaze with lights and sparkling with expensive ornaments.

After he leaned the tree in a corner and dusted off his hands, she went to him and laid her head on his shoulder. "I'm serious. I don't want to decorate this tree tonight."

She felt his body tense. "You're sure?"

"I'd rather decorate you. Maybe a dab of whipping cream. A little chocolate. What do you say?"

His laugh sounded breathless. "Don't toy with me, woman."

It came to her in that moment that she was in over her head. She had wanted him forever, it seemed. But for years, she had been afraid to admit those feelings or to fight for what she needed and deserved.

In spite of the risks, she was all in now. When it came to a choice, she would always choose J.B. Maybe the aftermath of this little experiment was going to suck, but that was in the future. For now, she wanted him so much it left her breathless.

"No games," she whispered. "But I think I'd like a quick shower first."

He grabbed her hand and dragged her toward the stairs. "We'll do it together and save time."

"I can't remember if I shaved my legs."

"Doesn't matter."

His desperation might have been flattering if she hadn't been so scared of letting him know how she felt. She had to keep this light and physical. No messy emotional connection.

That was hard to do when he was so damned cute.

In his bathroom, he released her only long enough to turn on the water in the shower enclosure and adjust the temperature. When he turned around, Mazie was naked from the waist up.

His cheeks flushed dark red. "I think you're getting ahead of me," he croaked.

"Maybe you should try harder." She stripped his shirt over his head and kissed his nipples. They were flat and copper colored, and he hissed with pleasure when she licked them.

His running pants were thin nylon. They did little to disguise the fact that his sex was rising to the occasion rapidly, thick and eager.

By unspoken consent, they each removed the remainder of their own clothes. She was bashful, but not reluctant. The look in J.B.'s eyes made a woman feel invincible.

When they were both completely nude, he took her hand, lifted it to his lips and kissed her fingers. "After you, my lady."

Her hair was in a knot on top of her head, because they had been running earlier, so she didn't have to worry about putting it up. It would be easy enough not to get it wet. At least that's what she thought until J.B. joined her.

Even though his hedonistic shower was huge, the guy was big. He took up a lot of room.

Mazie backed against the corner, her heart beating far too fast.

"Face the other wall," she said. "I'll wash your back." Anything to keep him from staring at her. When he turned away, she breathed a sigh of relief.

With shaking hands, she picked up the washcloth and soaped it. Then she started at the back of his neck and rubbed hard enough to make his skin pink. Next, his shoulders, his broad back and his narrow waist.

J.B. groaned as if she was torturing him…when all she was doing was playing the role of a bathhouse girl. She kneeled on the slick floor and soaped the backs of his legs… powerful thighs, muscular calves. Even his bare feet were sexy. Now that it was time for him to turn around, she nearly lost her nerve.

She rose to her feet and put both hands on his shoulders. "All done here."

He spun slowly and stared at her. The heat in his blue-eyed gaze made her stomach clench with desire. "You gonna wash the rest of me?" he asked, a tiny smile tipping the corners of his mouth.

"I think you're perfectly capable of handling that," she said primly.

"Then I'll do *your* back. You know…tit for tat."

She tried not to laugh. "I don't believe that word is politically correct anymore."

He lifted an eyebrow. "Tat?"

"You're impossible."

He put his wet hands on her shoulders and turned her away from him. Soon, the feel of his hands on her body made her legs shaky. Especially when one particular part of *him* kept bumping her bottom.

J.B. put a lot of effort into making sure she was clean from head to toe. He seemed particularly taken with her bottom. When he had soaped it up to his liking, he rested his erection in the cleft and slowly massaged her with his sex.

Oh, lordy.

He'd barely gotten started, and she was falling apart.

"J.B.?"

"Hmm?" He kissed the back of her neck, nibbling gently.

"We're using an awful lot of water. Seems irresponsible."

Without warning, his arms came around her from behind. "Let me finish this one part," he muttered. "Then we'll get out."

He abandoned the washcloth. Instead, his big soapy hands caressed her breasts.

Her head fell back against his shoulder. "I don't think my boobs are all that dirty," she panted, trying not to beg him to take her then and there.

"Maybe not." He tweaked her sensitive nipples. "But they're so damned pretty when they're wet and slick."

She was wet and slick somewhere else. Embarrassingly so. But it seemed rude to mention it. Not when J.B. was doing such a bang-up job of bathing her. His hands were gentle and thorough. Much more of this and she would melt…maybe slide right down the drain.

When the water started to run cold, she seized the chance to move their interlude to somewhere less wet and more horizontal. After all, she didn't want to be responsible for either one of them cracking their skull in the shower.

"Bed," she begged. "Let's get in your bed. The water is freezing."

J.B. couldn't argue with that. He turned off the faucet and grabbed towels for both of them. "Your lips are blue," he said. "Poor baby. I'll have to warm them up."

She scrubbed her body with the dry towel and grabbed a robe off the back of the door. "Meet you on the mattress. Bring condoms."

He followed her, pausing only to rummage in a bathroom drawer. "Plural," he teased. "I like how you think."

J.B.'s bed was a testament to fine linens and the ingenuity of an American mattress company. She climbed beneath the covers, tossed her damp towel on the floor and reveled in the unmistakable luxury of thousand-thread-count sheets. It figured that J.B. would have only the best in his bachelor paradise.

Instead of joining her immediately, he stood with his hands on his hips and stared at her.

Mazie clutched the covers to her chin. "I thought you'd be in more of a hurry." The part of him that reared strong and proud against his flat belly seemed not inclined to wait.

One masculine shoulder lifted and fell. "I'm enjoying the prelude," he said, the words low and husky. "You look delicious in my bed."

"Like an apple waiting to be picked?"

"Like a moment I want to paint and record for posterity."

The sappy romantic comment stunned her. Not because he said it jokingly, but because of the utter sincerity in his quiet words.

"I want you here with me," she begged. "Come warm me up." His steady regard made her self-conscious.

He dropped the towel wrapped around his hips. "I can do that."

When he joined her underneath the covers, something inside her sighed with contentment. Which was odd, because she was a long way from satisfied.

She ran her hand down his flank. Questions trembled on her lips. Requests for reassurance. Demands about the future.

What did J.B. want from her? Was any of this more than a lark for him?

Swallowing her uncertainties was much harder than it should have been.

"Thank you for the Christmas tree," she said.

He turned on his side and faced her, resting his head on his hand. This close she could see his thick eyelashes and the sparkles of gold in his blue irises.

"I'm glad we skipped decorating for this instead," he said.

Despite her best efforts, her insecurity slipped out. "What is *this*, J.B.?"

The faint frown on his face told her she had overstepped some invisible boundary. "Do we have to ask that question right now? Can't we enjoy the moment?"

She nodded slowly, swallowing her disappointment. "Of course we can."

Hurt bubbled in her chest, but she ignored it.

J.B. wasn't a forever kind of man. She had known that when she climbed into his bed. She would take this temporary affair and wallow in the magic of Christmas. Reality was something that could wait for the cold, bleak days of January.

"Make love to me," she whispered.

Her words galvanized him. Bending over her, he suckled her breasts and slid a hand between her thighs. When he entered her with his finger, she cried out. Her body was taut with arousal.

A lock of his hair fell over his forehead. His face was flushed. "I want you, Mazie Jane. Insanely, as it happens. Why do you think that is?"

"Maybe you got tired of women who won't stand up to you."

He choked out a laugh, as if her blunt honesty had surprised him. "You're prickly and unpredictable. I've had easier women, that's for sure."

When she reached for his erection, he batted her hand away. "Next time, love. I'm too primed for that." He sheathed himself and moved on top of her, fitting the blunt head of his sex at her entrance. "Lift your arms," he demanded. "Hold on to the headboard."

She obeyed automatically, clenching her fingers tightly around the wavy iron bars. Her eyelids fluttered shut.

J.B. pushed inside her slowly. The feeling was indescribable. She heard a ragged curse, as if he, too, was surprised at the way their bodies fit together. Yin and yang. As old as time. As new and fragile and precious as a morning mist on the beach.

"Open your eyes, sweet girl. Don't hide from me."

She tried. The intimacy was painful. His features were taut, his expression impossible to read.

But she, on the other hand, felt naked. Surely he could see everything she had hidden for so long. Her wrists weren't immobilized. She could have touched him if she wanted.

Still, she didn't move. She held her breath, her body straining against his, her heart soaking up every tender, muttered endearment, every rough thrust, every unbelievably raw emotion.

"J.B.," she cried out, feeling the peak rush toward her.

He buried his face in her hot neck. "Come for me, Mazie."

She wrapped her arms around him, arched her back and obeyed…

Sixteen

Mazie had never enjoyed *sleeping* with a man. Actually *sleeping*. But somehow, curling up with J.B. and letting drowsiness roll over her was the most wonderful feeling in the world.

By the time she awoke the next morning, something had changed. Not in him, maybe, but in her. No matter how foolish or self-destructive, she had to admit the truth.

She had fallen in love with J.B.

There hadn't been far to fall. Deep in a sixteen-year-old girl's heart the memory of her feelings for him had lived on, just as strongly as the memory of her mother's leaving home when she was twelve.

Traumatic events, world-changing events, never really went away. A person just learned to bury them. She had covered her desire for J.B. with animosity, trying to pretend he was nothing to her. It had worked for a long time— years even. But no more.

The covers were warm. J.B.'s big body was warm. He held her cradled in his arms, her head on his shoulder.

What was she going to do? How far could she let herself be pulled into his orbit and still be able to break free?

He stirred and gave her a sleepy smile. "Hey, there, gorgeous."

She cupped his stubbly chin. "Shouldn't you be at work?"

J.B. yawned and glanced at the digital clock on the bedside table. "I've got it covered."

"What does that mean?"

"Isn't All That Glitters closed on Mondays?"

She was surprised he had paid that much attention. "Yes."

He kissed her nose. "I wanted to spend the day with you. My partner is on call for any emergencies. It's almost Christmas. Things are slow."

It bothered her that he hadn't said a word about their long-standing feud or her property or his big project that included her. After his mother's heart attack, he had backed off completely. Two weeks ago, his Realtor had been contacting Mazie every three or four days. Now, nothing.

Was J.B. playing a game with her? Did he think she would cooperate if he wrapped her in romance and soft sheets?

Once before, she had been positive he had feelings for her. When the teenage J.B. had exhibited arousal, she'd been naive enough to believe it was going to lead to something. To a relationship. To a future.

He had disabused her of that notion cruelly.

Was she courting heartbreak a second time? Was J.B. even capable of love? Did he want more than her body and her business?

Was J.B. Vaughan her soul mate or her worst nightmare?

She wanted to take this experience at face value. She wanted to live in the moment. Sadly, she had never been the kind of woman to enjoy sex for the sake of sex. Before this thing with J.B., she had been celibate for two years.

"What did you have in mind?" she asked, snuggling closer.

His eyes were heavy-lidded, his hair tousled. Without his fancy suits and his billionaire persona, he looked far more dangerous.

"I thought after breakfast we could decorate the tree," he said. "Then take a shift at the hospital sitting with Mom."

"I like it."

"But first…" He reached for a foil packet on the night-stand and turned back to press a possessive kiss on her mouth. "I want to play."

After last night's excess, this morning should have been lazy and indulgent. Instead, it was as if the world was ending and this was their last chance to find a mate.

J.B. touched her everywhere, whispering her name, showering her with endearments and compliments. Her first climax hit sharp and hard and left her shaking. Before she could do more than gasp for breath, he was driving her up again…raking her nipples with sharp teeth, pressing kisses to her belly and below. Filling her with his power-ful thrusts.

When she came a second time, he was there with her, a muffled shout buried against her throat. She wrapped her legs around his waist and held him tightly, her eyes damp.

They slept again.

When she woke up the next time, her stomach was growling.

"Feed me," she begged, shaking his shoulder.

J.B. rolled out of bed and padded to the bathroom, giv-ing her a tantalizing view of his male beauty. "You're so demanding."

She could hear his laughter, even after he closed the door.

While J.B. was getting dressed, she took a quick shower, fetched her bag from the guest room, and pulled out fresh clothes. It sounded like the day would be casual, which suited her just fine. Mondays were usually lazy days, her one indulgence in a week that was typically crammed with work and looking after her father.

She followed her nose to the kitchen and found J.B. knee deep in eggs and bacon.

"Shall I make toast?" she asked, pausing to lean her cheek against his arm.

He gave her a quick kiss. "Butter's on the counter right behind me. There's a loaf of bread in the pantry. Coffee's ready if you want some."

The homey scene was entirely bogus. J.B. Vaughan was not a domesticated animal. Mazie didn't even want to calculate the number of women who had wandered into this charming kitchen scene over the years.

She knew this wasn't the same place J.B. lived during his short marriage. That knowledge should have made her feel better. And it did…a tiny bit. Truthfully, she adored his carefully preserved row house.

The copper-bottomed pots hanging over the island might be only for show, but as far as she could tell, J.B.'s kitchen was outfitted like a chef's dream. Mazie liked to cook when she had the time. It wasn't hard to imagine herself right here in the midst of preparing a big dinner for a group of friends.

While J.B. scrambled and fried, she found a cookie sheet and decided to do the toast in the oven. When it was done, she joined him at the table and slid two pieces of perfectly browned sourdough onto each plate.

A jar of homemade plum preserves she had found in the fridge was the finishing touch.

J.B. devoured the meal as if he were starving.

Truth be told, they had expended a great deal of energy since they ate shrimp the night before. And it was already midmorning.

She reached across the table and removed a drop of jam from his chin. "How are you at putting Christmas lights on a tree?" She vowed to keep the day light and easy. No more personal questions that would make both of them uneasy.

He finished the last bite of eggs and sat back in his chair. "Don't know. I guess we'll find out."

J.B. was in trouble.
And he knew it.

Part of him wanted to get Mazie out of his house and out of his bed. It was beginning to feel as if she *belonged* here.

That wasn't possible.

He liked her. A lot. Still, he had done the marriage thing, and he was really bad at it. So he needed to put a stop to this *playing house* gig.

As the morning progressed, he watched her, searching for any sign that she thought this was leading to something bigger. Other than a single, logically female question last night, she hadn't pressed for answers. Maybe because he had shut her down.

He felt bad about that.

By the time they finished the tree, his living room was a mess, but Mazie was glowing. She stood back and put her hands on her hips. "Look at it, J.B. It's glorious." She threw her arms around him in a big bear hug. "I can't wait until it's dark tonight, and we get the full effect."

Her enthusiasm was contagious. He felt a sense of pride that he had been able to give her something so simple and yet so profound. Mazie was a confident, happy, successful woman, but deep inside was that sad little girl who had lost her mother and had spent multiple Christmases on the edges of someone else's celebrations.

Damn Jonathan and Hartley for not noticing. Maybe they were too close to the situation, and maybe they had other interests. It was women who usually created the warmth of holidays, women who knew how to make an occasion memorable.

But J.B. wished her family hadn't dropped the ball where Mazie was concerned.

He tugged her ponytail. "I can't wait until dark either."

She headed for the stairs. "We need to leave for the hospital. You promised we'd be there at one."

He followed her a moment later, only to find that she

had taken her overnight bag and all her things to the guest room to get ready.

Why, damn it? And why wasn't he glad? He felt like he was losing his grip. Nothing made sense.

At the hospital, the news was not quite as upbeat as it had been. His mother was wan and listless. According the doctor, there was infection somewhere in her body. They were pumping her full of antibiotics.

Only Leila was there.

His sister stepped out into the hall to speak to them. "I'm not sure what happened overnight, but she was like this when I got here this morning. Dad is a wreck. I sent him home to sleep. Alana is with him."

J.B. hugged his sister. "You go, too. Mazie and I can be here as long as we need to be."

The afternoon crawled by. His mother alternated between resting and waking, barely speaking at all. Mazie sat beside her and rubbed her hand, the one that wasn't encumbered with the IV.

J.B. paced.

At one point, when their patient was sleeping, he pulled Mazie to a far corner of the room. "I feel like we should be doing something."

She grimaced. "Hospitals are all about waiting. They must think the medicine will work eventually. She's not getting worse."

He pressed the heel of his hand to his forehead. "I hate being helpless."

Mazie wrapped her arms around him. "Whatever happens, she knows how much you love her. That's the important thing."

His blood chilled. Mazie was obliquely referencing what all of them had been thinking. Jane Vaughan might not pull through this. His heart pounded and his knees felt funny. He loved his mom.

For the first time, he truly understood how Mazie must have suffered when her mom was taken away. It would have been like a death.

"I'm sorry," he said, his hands on her shoulders.

"For what?"

"For not realizing how much it has hurt you to have your mother several hundred miles away."

Mazie paled. "She doesn't even know who I am."

"So you feel guilty if you don't go and even sadder when you *do*? That's the worst of it, isn't it? You want to believe that it will be different every time you visit, but it never is."

She nodded slowly. Tears welled into her eyes and spilled onto her cheeks.

He held her close, his heart expanding with an emotion that confused him. Being so close kindled a spark of sexual arousal, but it wasn't only that. He wanted to protect her and make her happy and give her the family she had always wanted. Holy hell. What was he thinking?

Before he could make himself release her, Mazie slipped free of his arms. "Excuse me," she muttered. "I'll be back."

When he turned around, his mother's eyes were open. "You love her, don't you, son?"

He started to deny it, but at the last moment remembered the faux engagement. "Of course I do, Mom." He pulled up a chair beside the bed and studied the machines beeping softly. "How are you feeling?"

She pursed her lips. "Tired. Glad to be alive."

"I don't want you to fret. Can I go get you a hamburger? Medium rare with onions?"

The little joke made his mother smile. "You would do it, wouldn't you?"

"If you asked me. I love you, Mama."

His heart was cracking inside his chest. Breaking wide open. Between his fear for his mother and his need for Mazie, he was turning into someone he didn't recognize.

His mother put her hand on his head, almost like a blessing. "You don't have to worry about me, J.B. I'm going to live to see those grandbabies you promised me."

Guilt choked him. He couldn't tell her the truth. Not now.

Mazie returned at that moment, rescuing him from the need to deal with his mother's loaded statement. His fiancée was pale, but she seemed calm. She had been to the hospital gift shop by the looks of it. In her hand, she carried a vase of pink sweetheart roses.

"Alana told me these were your favorites."

His mother perked up visibly. "Oh, thank you, sweet girl. They're beautiful. Set them right there where I can see them."

J.B. stood. "I'm gonna grab some coffee." He was suffocating. He *wanted* Mazie here. Of course he did. But seeing her interact with his mother signaled an intimacy he was trying his damnedest to avoid.

After that particular Monday, the days fell into a pattern. Christmas was barely over a week away. J.B. and Mazie both went to work every morning, but the evenings were for taking care of family, and later for making love beneath the beautiful, fragrant Christmas tree.

J.B. had discovered Mazie's particular fantasy when it came to holiday sex, so he capitalized on it.

She had no complaints.

It was the happiest she had ever been.

Still, hovering in the back of her mind was the knowledge that she would have to leave eventually. The longer she stayed, the harder it would be to extricate herself from a relationship that was definitely lopsided when it came to the emotional component.

J.B. gave her his passion and his compassion, but his heart wasn't up for grabs.

It hurt. Badly. She couldn't lie to herself. She tried not

to think about it, but deep down was a tiny stupid glimmer of hope that he would come around…that he would feel what she felt.

Because he never said the words, neither did she.

On December 22, she was so glad she had not.

It was an ordinary day, nothing to indicate that her bubble of perfect joy was about to pop.

On that morning, it was raining. J.B. kissed her goodbye as she left for work. She was wearing a black raincoat with a hood, so she thought it would be enough to keep her dry. When she got outside, though, she realized that the light showers had turned into a downpour. Not only that, she had forgotten to pick up her umbrella.

She was running late, but she scooted back inside to grab it.

As she did, she heard J.B. on the phone talking to someone. He must have been in the den, because his voice carried clearly to the foyer.

"I don't think we have anything to worry about. I've got her eating out of my hand. It won't be a problem."

All the blood drained from her heart to the floor. Numbly, she grabbed the umbrella, backed out of the house and fled.

Unfortunately, it wasn't far to her destination. She parked and gripped the steering wheel. Her mind was blank one minute and filled with pain and terror the next. Surely it couldn't be true. Surely J.B. hadn't moved her into his house and slept with her so she would give him a stupid building.

She had noticed him pulling back emotionally over the last few days. Though they had been as close as a man and woman could be from a physical standpoint, it was if J.B. had put up a mental wall between them.

She had assumed, had hoped actually, that it was because his feelings for her were changing. That maybe he was fighting the connection between them.

He had failed at commitment and marriage in the past and was too afraid to try again.

But what if his retreat was more sinister? What if he was getting ready to reject her again now that he had accomplished his goals?

Try as she might, she couldn't think of another interpretation for his words. Especially because he had sounded happy and upbeat.

With his mom on the mend and Mazie no longer a problem, he was going to have a very merry Christmas.

Mazie couldn't bear it. Why did no one she cared about stick around for the long haul?

What was wrong with her?

Seventeen

Somehow, she made it through the day.

Gina looked at her oddly several times, but they were too busy with customers for her to grill Mazie. With only two shopping days left after this one, the store was a madhouse.

Jewelry flew out the door like fake gold doubloons being tossed in a Mardi Gras parade. Fake doubloons. Like everything else in Mazie's life at the moment. Her engagement, her blackhearted lover. Even her smile. Because inside, she was nothing but a child crying in the driveway when everything she loved best was being taken away from her.

At last, the interminable day was over. She had to figure out a way to extricate herself from J.B.'s house. First, though, she had to go by the hospital. Jane was doing much better, but she wasn't entirely out of the woods.

Mazie knew J.B. was working late, so she wouldn't have to see him. Please God, let that be so.

Both Alana and Leila were with their mother. Mr. Vaughan had been home napping during the afternoon but was due back soon.

The three women in the room greeted her warmly. Mazie hung her purse on a chair and cleaned her hands with hand sanitizer.

"How's our patient today?" she asked.

Jane wagged a finger at her two daughters. "If these two will quit worrying, we'll be fine." But J.B.'s mother didn't look healthy. If anything, she seemed frail and pale.

Alana spoke up, looking chagrined. "You're not as well as you think, Mama."

"Oh, pooh. I'm determined to be home for Christmas. You wait and see."

Leila grimaced. Mazie sympathized. Jane wasn't a bad patient, but she was strong willed.

Leila hugged Mazie unexpectedly. "You've been so great to our mother. She told us that you're not actually engaged to my brother. So you've really gone above and beyond. Thank you, Mazie."

Alana hugged her, too. "I was disappointed. I think he needs someone like you in his life, but the guy is stubborn as a rock."

"Don't I know it," Mazie said lightly.

The lump in her throat was more of a boulder. Though the Vaughans didn't realize it, this was Mazie's goodbye visit. She had agreed to J.B.'s charade when she thought something real might grow out of it…when she had trusted him. Now, though, she had to leave him.

Without warning, the door swung open and J.B. strode into the room. He carried with him the crisp masculine scent that was like a drug to her. She put the width of the bed between them and barely acknowledged his presence.

It wasn't so hard. He was chatting with his sisters and sitting on his mother's bed to speak with her.

Suddenly, every alarm in the room began to beep. Jane's eyes fluttered shut and her breathing was raspy. In an instant, three nurses ran into the room and surrounded the bed.

The three siblings clung to each other, ashen faced.

Mazie huddled in the corner, out of the way.

J.B. was wild-eyed as if he couldn't believe what was happening. He looked for Mazie.

"Come where she can hear you," he begged. "Tell her she has to hold on."

Mazie didn't know if he was asking for himself or his mother or both. But she would do whatever he asked, because she loved him desperately.

Before Mazie could move closer, Leila, tears streaming down her cheeks, patted her brother's arm. "Stop, J.B. Quit pretending. It doesn't matter now. Mom knows the engagement isn't real."

His jaw dropped. He stared at Mazie with hot eyes. "You told her?"

Humiliation burned her cheeks. "Well, I…"

His face was stony, his gaze both judge and jury. "We'll talk about this later."

A doctor joined the fray. "I'll need all of you to step into the hall, please." As a team of medical professionals swooped in, J.B. and his sisters and Mazie were kindly but firmly evicted.

J.B. took her arm and steered her a short distance away, far enough for the two of them to speak in private.

His expression was tight with fury. His grasp was firm enough to leave bruises. "Go home," he said. "I have to concentrate on my family now. They are all that matters to me."

The intimation was sharply painful. He blamed Mazie.

This wasn't the time to exonerate herself. And besides. What was the point? It didn't matter what J.B. thought of her. Their relationship—if you could call it that—was over. And this time the pain of his rejection was far more devastating than she could have imagined.

She stumbled her way to the parking lot and got into her car. Driving to J.B.'s house, dealing with the alarm, and unlocking the door took all the courage she had, even knowing that he was not going to interrupt her.

With shaking hands and a stomach curling with nausea, she packed up her clothing and personal items. Most of it was in the master bedroom. A few things in the guest room. There wasn't a lot, really.

Her holiday affair hadn't lasted all that long.

Back downstairs, she went into the den and plugged in the lights on the Christmas tree. The beautiful fir mocked her. The tears came then, hot and painful. She had gambled and lost.

J.B. hadn't cared about her when she was sixteen, and he didn't care about her now.

She was a means to an end.

When she was calm enough to drive, she headed for home. For the last week, Jonathan had been working like a madman, preparing to be gone, so he was keeping late hours. Her father was distracted with chores for his trip and would be leaving in the morning. He was the most animated she had seen him in months.

Mazie had dinner with her father and helped him pack afterward. As she was folding a pair of socks, she blurted out a question she had wanted to ask him for years but had never had the guts.

"Daddy?"

"Hmm?"

"Why do you never go see Mama? Why did you send her so very far away?"

He turned slowly, his face paling. He sat down hard on the side of the bed. "I wondered when one of you kids would finally ask me that." His voice rasped with emotion.

"I don't want to upset you, but I need to know."

He shrugged, playing with a loose thread on one of his sweaters. "When your mother had her complete psychotic break, I took her to the best and most expensive doctors in the country. Your mother was the love of my life. When she came to me, she was young and charming and so full of animation. It was only after we married that I discovered her demons."

"And nothing helped?"

"No. Not really." His jaw worked. "We went through

months and years of diagnosis and treatment. She seemed better for a time, but then her father killed her mother and took his own life. That was too much for her to handle."

Dear God. "But you told us our grandparents died in a car accident."

"I didn't want to frighten you. And as for your mother…" He stared out the window, obviously seeing some painful scene from the past. "I couldn't bear the thought of her taking her own life. When I found the facility in Vermont, it was reputed to be one of the best in the entire world. Your mother thrived there, though she no longer knew me or even that we were married."

"I'm so sorry, Daddy."

He shrugged. "We had eight or nine good years together. They had warned her not to have children, but she was adamant about wanting a family. I've always prayed that none of you would be affected. She continually sabotaged her birth control, and each time she got pregnant, she refused to take the medicines that controlled her mania. By the time you were ten, things had gotten very bad indeed."

"I remember."

"The tipping point was the day I found her playing with knives in the kitchen. She had cut her fingers badly. Swore it was a mistake. But I knew we were nearing the end. Not long after that, she woke up from a dream in the middle of the night and thought I was a burglar trying to strangle her in her sleep."

He stopped and gasped for air, clearly still traumatized after all these years. Shaking his head, he gazed at Mazie bleakly. "I brought doctors here to the house. A dozen of them. They all said the same. The end of her mental competence was coming soon, and if it happened while she was alone with you kids, she might harm you."

"So you sent her away."

"I did. I missed her so badly I thought my heart would break in two. But I had to protect you and your brothers."

Mazie went to him and wrapped her arms around him. "Thank you for telling me."

"I should have done it long before now, but it was so hard to face it…to talk about it."

He was shaking. Mazie felt the lash of guilt for putting him through the retelling, though she was glad to know the truth. "You're a good man. And a good father. I'm so happy you're going with your friends on this trip."

"I'm sorry I won't be here for Christmas."

"No worries," she said blithely. "Gina has asked me to spend the day with her family."

That part was true. He didn't have to know that Mazie had declined the invitation.

She fell into bed that night, but slept only in snatches. Alana and Leila had taken turns answering Mazie's texts. Jane Vaughan had a pulmonary embolism. It was serious… likely a complication from her surgery. But she was being treated with the appropriate medications and would be monitored closely.

Mazie begged both of J.B.'s sisters not to let him know that she was in contact with them.

There was to be no Christmas celebration at the Vaughan homeplace. If Jane stabilized, she might be allowed to leave the hospital for a few hours to celebrate with her family at J.B.'s house, since it was so close to the hospital.

On the twenty-third, Mazie worked all day and then drove her father and brother to the airport. Their flights were only an hour apart, and fortunately in the right order. Jonathan was able to make sure his father got safely on the plane to Fort Lauderdale where he would meet up with his college buddies. Soon after, Jonathan flew out to Arizona.

Hopefully, he would find some relief for the headaches that plagued him.

That night, Mazie walked the floors in the empty house. She felt like a ghost. A phantom. A woman who wasn't actually real.

The pain had receded for the moment, leaving her pleasantly numb.

She slept on the sofa for five hours. Showered. Went in to work.

Christmas Eve was normally her favorite day of the year. This time, she suffered through it, watching the clock, waiting for the moment she could return home and pull the covers over her head.

Her acting skills were top-notch. When Gina asked once again about Christmas Day, Mazie declined with a smile on her face. Gina assumed—and Mazie didn't correct her—that Mazie was spending the holiday with J.B.

There would be plenty of time later for the painful truth.

All That Glitters closed at four on the twenty-fourth. Mazie handed out beautifully wrapped gifts to all her staff, gave a brief emotional speech and sent everyone on their way.

With the inventory secured and the shop locked up and the alarm set, she headed for home. She had to get through the next thirty-six hours. After that, maybe she could find a way forward. Perhaps she would move to Savannah and open another branch of her popular jewelry shop. That would put her far enough away from J.B.'s orbit not to bump into him, but still close to her family.

Maybe Jonathan could hire someone to help out with their father. Mazie couldn't stay in Charleston any longer. She had to change her life.

The long hours of Christmas Eve were a mockery of all her dreams. As a teenager, she had imagined she would be married by now. With a house of her own, children, a husband. Having a career had been important to her, but no more so than building a future with people she loved. Starting traditions. Sharing special moments.

She sat in front of the TV and watched bits and pieces of movie classics. Funny ones. Sad ones. Hopeful ones.

When that pastime lost its allure, she walked the beach in the dark. From the water's edge, she could look into the windows of large rental houses. Families celebrating. Eating. Laughing.

Never had she felt so alone.

Christmas morning dawned sunny and mild as it so often did in Charleston. As soon as she woke up, all the awful memories came rushing back, not the least of which was the look on J.B.'s face when he exiled her from his mother's hospital room. It had shriveled her soul.

She knew now what she had to do to bring closure to this painful episode of her life. Perhaps she had dreamed the solution in her sleep.

First she showered and dressed for the day. Lycra running pants and a long-sleeve tee would suffice. Then she visited the safe in her father's office.

She riffled through a stack of documents, selected the appropriate one and tucked it in a brown envelope. Next she Googled twenty-four-hour delivery services.

Soon, she would never have to see or speak to J.B. Vaughan ever again.

Eighteen

J.B. was in hell. And operating with a split personality. Thankfully, his mother had recovered to the point that her doctor was comfortable releasing her for a few hours on Christmas Day.

The family had strict instructions to rush her back if certain symptoms occurred.

But Jane Vaughan was glowing. Surrounded by her children and her husband, she was ecstatic to be celebrating the holiday in something other than a hospital gown.

Alana and Leila had thrown together a very creditable feast. Roast turkey with all the fixings. Grandmother Vaughan's sweet potatoes. A few other side dishes, and—procured from a local bakery—a stunning red velvet cake.

Since J.B. didn't own any china—only masculine earthenware dishes—the womenfolk had opted to break with tradition and use disposable plates to minimize cleanup. J.B.'s drop-in-thrice-a-week housekeeper had been given the week off between Christmas and New Year's to spend with her family.

The meal was outstanding… J.B. felt deep relief and gratitude to see his mother doing so much better. His father was equally exuberant to have his bride back on her feet. Alana and Leila were in a celebratory mood, as well.

The only nagging thorn in J.B.'s soul was Mazie's absence. He had started to call her a dozen times, but he was still so angry that she had revealed their secret to his mother without asking him. In the midst of all the drama, he had actually been convinced that Mazie's mistake caused his mother's relapse.

Later, he realized the truth. He had overreacted.

He owed Mazie an apology for that. But his righteous anger was justified. The secret about their fake engagement hadn't been hers to reveal.

She had gone behind his back. That was why he was angry—right?

Or was he so devastated, because in the midst of everything that had happened, he had finally realized the complete truth. Not only was he heels over ass deep in love with Mazie, he might be willing to believe he had a second chance at forever.

The three recent nights without her in his bed were interminable. He had come to depend on her soft warmth to help him sleep. He worked too hard and had trouble relaxing. Mazie's presence in his life in the midst of his mother's traumatic illness had helped steady him.

Why had she told his mother the engagement was not real? What did she hope to gain?

Her unexpected and dangerous choice felt like a betrayal.

After the midday meal, his parents dozed in the den. J.B. helped clear the table, but his sister shooed him out of the kitchen.

Leila kissed his cheek. "We love you, J.B., but we can do this faster without you. Relax. Check your email. We've got this."

He wandered toward the front of the house, reluctant to go into the den. There were too many memories there. Seeing the beautiful Christmas tree he and Mazie had decorated hurt. He didn't want to remember. He wanted to throw the damned thing out to the curb, ornaments and all.

When the doorbell rang, his heart leaped in shock and

momentary hope. But of course it wasn't Mazie. Why would it be? He had sent her away most emphatically.

The barely-twenty-something man standing on the doorstep wore the familiar uniform of a well-known delivery service. He handed J.B. a manila envelope. "Sign here, please."

J.B. scribbled his name on the magnetic screen. "Did you draw the short straw today?"

The young kid shook his head and grinned. "Nope. Jewish. I volunteered. Merry Christmas, sir."

J.B. closed the door and opened the envelope. At first he couldn't process what he was seeing. It was a deed. Not just any deed…but a deed to the building that housed Mazie's jewelry store. And she had signed it over to him.

Leila exited the kitchen, drying her hands on a dishcloth covered with reindeer. "What's that?"

He frowned. "I'm not sure. It seems as if Mazie has finally agreed to let me have her property for my renovation project."

"That's good, isn't it?"

"Yes. But I…"

"But what?"

"I don't know why she's giving it to me now after stonewalling for so long. And why the hell did she tell Mom we weren't engaged without asking me first? The shock could have killed Mom."

"And you're still angry."

"Hell, yes," he said.

Alana gave him a pitying look. "You're such a dope. You don't know Mazie at all. Of course she didn't tell Mom anything. Mom guessed the truth from the very first day you lied to her. She knew you wanted to give her something to cling to before heart surgery."

"She did?"

"Yeah. Mazie kept your secret, J.B. And she kept pretending because Mom asked her to. But you yelled at her and humiliated her in front of all of us and a bunch of nurses and doctors. Bad karma, my brother."

His heart sank. The enormity of his blunder crushed him. "I've got to talk to her," he muttered.

"We're about to open presents," Alana said. "And besides, I don't think you should go rushing over there if you don't have your head on straight. You've hurt Mazie. You'd better decide what you want from her, or you'll make things even worse."

J.B. made it an hour and a half before he cracked.

He *had* to go talk to Mazie. It couldn't wait. He needed to apologize and tell her he loved her. Or both.

Fortunately, his mother decided she was ready to go back to her hospital bed. The cardiologist had promised that if this next set of tests was acceptable, he would release her on the twenty-seventh.

When the house was finally empty again, J.B. grabbed his keys. He drove across town and on toward the beach, barely even registering the empty streets. His heart pounded in his chest. Would Mazie be willing to talk to him? He had treated her terribly.

When he got to the Tarleton property, the front gates were locked. Fortunately, J.B. had the security codes. Jonathan had given them to him a few months ago when all the family was out of town at the same time. J.B. had checked on the property for them.

Now, he prayed the codes hadn't been changed.

He breathed a sigh of relief when the gates swung open. All the cars were visible, parked in the partially sheltered bays beneath the house. But there was no sign of life anywhere.

Patience.

He took a deep breath, trying to silence his galloping

heartbeat. He loped up the front steps, entered a second code and eased open the door.

"Mazie? Jonathan?"

As far as J.B. could tell, no one was home. He walked through the main floor of the house. There was no sign of any activity. No meal. No televisions running. No wrapping paper.

He stopped at the bay window and gazed out at the aquamarine ocean.

And then he saw her. Down by the water's edge, a lone figure, unmistakably feminine, strolled along the shore, bending now and again to pick up a shell.

His body moved instinctively. Exiting the back of the house, he peeled off his socks and shoes, rolled up his pants legs and let himself out of the gate, using the same codes he had memorized earlier.

Mazie had stopped now and was looking toward the horizon, her hands on her hips. The sound of the waves masked his approach.

He stopped a few feet away so as not to scare her.

"Mazie," he called hoarsely.

She spun around, flinching visibly when she saw it was him. "Go away, J.B. This is my beach."

"You can't own beaches in South Carolina," he said. "Please, Mazie. Let me talk to you."

"Didn't you get my package? It's over. You have what you want. Leave me alone."

The scales fell from his eyes. The angel choirs sang. His own stupid brain finally clicked into gear. If he hadn't been such a clueless idiot when he was a younger man, he could have had Mazie by his side and in his bed all these years.

Instead, he'd been saddled with a terrible marriage that had almost destroyed him. He had ended up all alone and had convinced himself that he liked it.

"No," he said soberly. "No, I don't have what I want."

He swallowed hard, not quite able to say the words. But he was trying. "I need you, Mazie. I *want* you in my life. I'm sorry I yelled at you and accused you of something you didn't do. I rejected you. Again. Only this time, it was far worse. Alana told me you didn't spill the secret. I should have known better."

She folded her arms around her waist, her posture brittle with *something*. "Apology accepted. And as for the other, I'm no longer interested. Find another woman."

"I can't," he said. "There's only you."

Pain drenched her beautiful eyes. Tears welled in them.

"You don't need to play the game anymore, J.B. I know what you were after. I gave it to you. We're done."

Now he was confused. "Are you talking about the property?"

"Of course," she shouted. "Does any of this sound familiar? *'I don't think we have anything to worry about. I've got her eating out of my hand. It won't be a problem.'*" She paused to catch her breath. "You didn't want me when I was sixteen, and you don't want me now. You've been *using* me, and I was fool enough to go along with it. But I'm done."

All her anger seemed to winnow away. She stared at him, stone-faced.

He swallowed hard. "You misunderstood," he said carefully.

"Liar."

"I wanted to go out with you when you were sixteen, I swear. I had a huge crush on you. But your brother promised to neuter me if I went through with it because he knew my reputation with girls. So I turned you down. And I've regretted it ever since."

She blinked, her expression wary. "That doesn't excuse the fact that you used sex to coerce me into selling my property to you. I *heard* you, J.B. You can't talk your way out of this one."

His knees felt funny. "I love you, Mazie. I think I have in some way or other my whole life. But I got married, and I screwed that up, and after that, I was too embarrassed to talk to you."

"You don't love me," she whispered. "You *don't*. I heard you on the phone."

God, he had hurt her so badly. He'd tried to protect himself from making another mistake, but in the process, Mazie had become collateral damage.

"I was talking about the mayor," he said. "That was my partner on the phone, yes. But we weren't discussing you. I've been sweet-talking the mayor and the city council into letting us build a city park. They have grant money for beautification. We've offered to go in with them, if they agree, and do the project in tandem."

"The mayor?"

He nodded. "The mayor. Not you. In case you haven't noticed, you've been leading *me* around by the nose, and not the opposite. I adore you, Mazie. I'm sorry it took me so long to admit it, but I'll spend the next six months convincing you if you're interested in a June wedding. Or if we're both scared, we can wait a year. Or two. Or four. But nothing will change on my end. I love you, Mazie Jane."

The sun was hot on the top of his head. He felt dizzy and sick and terrified. Nothing in his life had ever been as important as this. And he had bungled the hell out of it.

"Say it again," she whispered.

"I love you?"

She shook her head. "No. The part where you wanted to take me to the dance when I was sixteen."

His heart lightened. "When you grew up, Mazie—overnight it seemed—it socked me in the stomach. For years you had been this cute, spunky little kid trying to keep up with your brothers and me. Then suddenly you were a princess. I got tongue-tied just trying to talk to you."

"But you let Jonathan get in your head."

"To be fair to your brother, I was kind of a jerk in those days. He was probably right to wave me off."

"I adored you back then," she said, the words wistful.

He tasted fear. "And now?"

She didn't say a word for the longest time. He could almost *feel* the struggle inside her. Finally, she held out her hand. "I love you, Jackson Beauregard Vaughan. I didn't want to, but I do. As embarrassing as it is to admit, I think I loved you way back then and somehow never got over it."

He closed his eyes and inhaled sharply, tilting his face toward the sun, feeling the weight of the world dissipate. Then he smiled at her and dragged her into his arms.

"I think I've been waiting on this moment forever." After kissing her long and thoroughly and reveling in her eager response, he pulled away at last. "Why are you alone on Christmas Day, sweet girl?"

She laid her cheek against his shoulder. "I'm not alone, J.B. I have you. Merry Christmas, my love."

"Merry Christmas, Mazie." He scooped her into his arms. "Is that house behind us really empty?"

She grinned at him, her hair tumbling in the breeze. "Completely. Would you like to join me in my bedroom and open your Christmas present?"

He laughed out loud, startling a trio of seagulls. "Oh, yeah. And just so you know, great minds think alike. I got you the very same thing..."

Epilogue

Jonathan sat in his luxurious Arizona hotel room at the retreat center and read through the packet of meditation techniques that were supposed to diminish his headaches. Nothing seemed to be working. Not expensive pharmaceuticals. Not hippie-dippie mumbo jumbo. With each passing week, he became more fearful that something in his mother's messed-up DNA had triggered a cataclysm in his. A mental meltdown that might change everything about his life.

Or destroy it completely.

The intensity of the headaches scared him more than he wanted to admit. He didn't want to end up like his mother, drugged and helpless in a facility somewhere.

A phone call from his sister had soothed some of his other concerns. Mazie and J.B. were together. With a capital *T*. It boggled the mind, but both of them sounded happy.

He wished them all the best, even if it was a little weird for him personally.

More important, it was a relief to know that whatever happened to him, J.B. was going to make sure Mazie was okay.

At least one member of the Tarleton family would find happiness…

* * * * *

NASHVILLE
REBEL

SHERI WhiteFeather

One

Sophie Cardinale couldn't do it anymore.

She couldn't be Tommy Talbot's tour manager, living her life on the road with nothing except the sound of Tommy's music roaring in her ears. She needed to put down roots, to get a desk job, to have a baby. At thirty-four, her biological clock wasn't just ticking; it was on the verge of exploding. She'd been thinking about this for the past year, day in and day out. It *never, ever* left her mind. But she hadn't told Tommy yet. He wasn't just her gorgeous, wild, pain-in-the-ass boss; he was also her closest and dearest childhood friend.

Sophie's father had worked for Kirby Talbot, Tommy's country-music-legend dad. Her dad had been Kirby's guitar tech up until the day he'd passed away, a little over two years ago. Sophie had never known her mom. She'd developed postpartum preeclampsia a month after she'd given birth to Sophie and had died as a result. Mom had been the love of Dad's life. He'd talked about her all the time, reminiscing about how sweet and beautiful she was. Her parents had met on the road, in the mid-1970s, when turquoise jewelry and leather vests reigned supreme. At the time, Mom worked for Kirby Talbot, too, as his wardrobe mistress. They got married, and Sophie had been born a decade later. Kirby had adored both of her folks. They were like family to him.

In fact, after Mom died, Sophie, her dad and her granddad, who'd also helped raise her, lived in one of the guesthouses on the Talbot family compound. That was how she'd gotten to know Tommy so well. According to his mother, they'd bonded as babies when she used to "borrow" Sophie to keep him company in his playpen. But mostly Sophie thought that Tommy's mom just felt sorry for her since she didn't have a mom of her own.

During their adolescence, Sophie and Tommy were inseparable, spending their time jumping out of trees, riding green broke horses and speeding around on his dirt bikes together. In those days, Sophie had been a pixie-haired, doe-eyed tomboy who'd had a crush on Tommy, and did almost anything he dared her to do. But she'd calmed down since then. Tommy? Not so much. He was still a daredevil, especially on stage.

Tommy trained with some of the best stuntmen in the business. His most recent act involved riding a mechanical bull on a rising platform. He even stood up and danced on the bull to the opening riff of "Rebel with a Country Cause," one of his most popular songs. During his dance, the floor below him would erupt into flames.

His stunts weren't always planned or practiced. If he wanted to climb lighting trusses or do backflips into the crowd or douse his guitar with lighter fluid and set it on fire, he merely took it upon himself to do so.

On this latest tour, the one that had just ended, the pyrotechnics guys kept threatening to quit if Tommy didn't follow the rules. But it wasn't Tommy who had to suffer the wrath of the road crew. It was Sophie. Everyone took their complaints to her, expecting her to keep Tommy in line.

In the beginning, working for him had been exciting. She used to get a dangerous thrill out of it. Now, all these years later, she just wanted some peace and quiet.

But mostly she longed to become a mom. She'd already been checking out sperm banks, and soon she would be ready to concentrate on choosing a donor. Sophie had a bad track record with men. She'd given up on finding the right guy, and by now she needed some emotional security in her life. For her, becoming a single mom was the answer, even if it meant quitting her job and finding a new one in order to do it.

So here she was, behind the wheel of her truck, driving to Tommy's ranch, to give him her notice. Sophie lived outside of Nashville, in the same area as Tommy. She had a modest home on a mini ranch, with two horses and two dogs, all of which she boarded at Tommy's place when she traveled with him. His spread was huge, boasting a custom-built mansion and a slew of ranch hands and caretakers. By now, Tommy was as rich and famous as his legendary father. Maybe even more so. Whereas Kirby Talbot had been deemed "the bad boy of country," Tommy had become known as the "the baddest boy of country," surpassing his dad in that regard. Mostly Tommy had earned that reputation because of how reckless he was on stage. But him being such a ladies' man was a factor, too, which had never sat well with Sophie.

As she approached the private road that led to Tommy's estate, she sighed in relief. Thankfully there weren't any fans at the gate, clamoring to see him coming or going on this September afternoon.

She buzzed the intercom and announced her arrival, and his security chief let her through. She'd already texted Tommy and told him to expect her. But she hadn't revealed the nature of their meeting or what it would entail. It wasn't going to be easy—of that she was certain. Tommy wasn't going to want her to quit. He wouldn't be happy about the reason she was quitting, either. Babies had become an anxiety-ridden subject with him. Earlier this year a woman named Kara Smith, with whom he'd had a one-night stand, claimed that he might be the father of her unborn child. He wasn't, as it turned out. Tommy was extremely careful about practicing safe sex. But the possibility that the protection could have failed still scared him and had taken an emotional toll on his bachelor, happy-go-lucky lifestyle.

After Sophie parked in the circular driveway, she exited her vehicle and smoothed the front of her tank top over her flat stomach. Hopefully a few months from now, she would have a cute little baby bump.

She rang the bell, and Dottie, the woman who ran Tommy's house, answered the door. She was the nicest lady, a grandmotherly type, who fussed over Tommy as if he was her own. But she wasn't a pushover, either. When the pigheaded superstar needed a tongue-lashing, Dottie was more than willing to do it, even if her reprimands didn't make a bit of difference.

"Hi, Dot." Sophie entered the colorfully tiled foyer. "Will you let Tommy know I'm here?"

"He's already waiting for you by the pool." When Dottie smiled, her friendly blue eyes crinkled beneath her glasses. Her salt-and-pepper hair was fixed in its usual short-and-simple style.

Sophie had a mass of long, wavy brown locks that never behaved. She was considering cutting it. Not now, but maybe after the baby was born. The baby she hadn't even conceived yet, she reminded herself. She needed to hurry up and plant that seed.

"Do you want me to bring you something cool to drink?" Dottie asked. "Or some lunch, perhaps? Chef already has chicken salad with cranberries and walnuts ready to go."

"Thanks, but I'm fine. I don't need anything, except to talk to Tommy. I'll just go see him now."

She headed for the backyard, with its gigantic, lagoon-style grotto pool. Beneath the center waterfall was a waterproof cave, which had an entertainment room with rock walls, stone floors and a glamorous sitting area, complete with a spectacular sound system, a big-screen TV and a tiki-type bar. Tommy had built that room for his guests. For himself, he'd created a private apartment, accessible from yet another waterfall, for when he wanted to be completely alone and relax beneath his pool. No one except him had ever been inside it. He didn't even take his lovers there.

She saw him lounging in the sun, listening to music on a portable device, the earbuds planted firmly in place. His eyes were closed, and his light brown hair was still damp from a recent swim.

She was lucky that he was wearing trunks. Tommy had no qualms about nudity, and skinny-dipping was one of his favorite pastimes. Tempting as he was, whenever he stripped down in front of her, she tried to avert her gaze from the parts that mattered. She also made darn sure that he'd never seen her naked. Even when they were kids and splashing around in the stream on his daddy's property, she'd never peeled off her swimsuit in front of him—no matter how often he baited her to do it.

Sometimes he still baited her to get naked with him. And not just for swimming. Thing was, Tommy had been trying to hook up with her since high school. Yet even during their teenage years, he had too many other girls around him. After they graduated, Sophie had gone to college, while he focused on his music and gained notoriety. She'd earned a business degree and started working for him. She'd never considered the boss/employee aspect of their relationship a problem. In her own sinful way, she thrived on his playful flirtations. But since she was supposed to be the voice of reason, she made sure that he knew her boundaries. Nonetheless, she also fantasized about having a ridiculously steamy affair with him. Of course, that didn't mean she was going to act on those feelings. Her concern was his inability to settle down.

Tommy used sex like a weapon, a gun he never quit firing. Mostly he partook of groupies. On occasion, he had regular girlfriends, too. But he never made commitments to any of them. Brunettes, blondes, redheads: they were all his playthings.

Not this brunette, she reminded herself. She wasn't going to share his bed, no matter how exciting the experience might be.

Suddenly, he opened his eyes and stared straight at her. Funny how he sensed her presence at the very moment her mind was immersed in sex.

Sophie squinted at him, and he smiled. He had a lopsided grin that made him look like the troublemaker he was. Only his wildness wasn't fueled by anything except his hot-blooded nature. Although he threw some extravagant parties, Tommy never drank alcohol. He didn't do drugs, either. His father was a recovering alcoholic and addict, and Tommy vowed to never be like him, at least not in that regard.

She moved closer. The drink holder in the chair's armrest held his beverage of choice: a bottle of berry-flavored sparkling water. When he was on the road, she made sure that his hotels, dressing rooms, tour buses and private jet were all stocked with it.

He removed the earbuds. "Hey, Sophie-Trophy," he said, using one of the many nicknames he'd given her. Anything that rhymed, he used. Mostly he had to make up words. There weren't a lot that rhymed with Sophie or Soph. Or even Sophia, for that matter.

She sat in the chaise longue next to him and greeted him with a simple "Hello."

Idiot that she was, she stole a glance at his navel and the line of hair that disappeared into the waistband of his trunks. If he'd been naked, she never would have dared to look that low on his body. But for now, she took her fill. Or thrill. Or whatever.

Luckily, she'd worn shorts and sandals today. She didn't feel out of place sitting by the pool. But that didn't make her any less nervous about revealing her agenda.

Before she got the chance to start the conversation and spin it her way, he said, "I hope you came by to talk about extending the tour. I know it's supposed to be over, but I was thinking we could add more dates." He frowned into the sun. "I'm already going bonkers sitting around here and we've only been back for a few days."

She frowned, too. Not at the sun, but at him. "I know

how stir-crazy you get when you're not on the road, but adding more dates is the last thing I've been thinking about."

He grabbed his water and took a swig. After he swallowed a noisy gulp, he asked, "So what's the deal, then? Why did you call this meeting? Am I in trouble? Is the insurance company threatening to raise my rates again?"

"No, it's nothing like that." She steadied her voice. But then she got antsy and just blurted it out. "I'm giving you my notice. I'm quitting so I can get a job with regular hours and less travel and have a baby."

If the pavement had just opened up and swallowed him whole, he wouldn't have looked more surprised. "Damn, really? You're pregnant? By who?"

He sounded offended. Or annoyed. Or frustrated. But he always acted that way when she was dating someone. As reliant as he'd become on her, he got jealous when she gave her attention to someone else. So much so that he tended to butt heads with her lovers. Not that she'd had many men. She'd never been in a relationship that was worth a damn. Her last boyfriend, a record exec, had cheated on her with his twentysomething assistant.

"I'm not pregnant yet," she replied. "But I plan to be."

A muscle tightened in his jaw. "Did you and Cliff get back together? Are you going to marry that jerk?"

She shook her head. "Are you kidding? I'd never get back with him, not after the way he betrayed me. I'm not planning on having my baby with anyone. I'm going to be a single mom."

He had a confused expression. "The last time I checked, it takes two to make a baby."

Sophie rolled her eyes. "I'm going to use a sperm bank."

"You're picking the guy out of a genetic lineup? Come on, Soph. That's crazy." He frowned again. "Besides, when did you get so maternal? I never knew you wanted kids."

"I've been thinking about it for a while now. And at my age, I can't wait forever. The older a woman gets, the more steps she needs to take to ensure a healthy pregnancy."

Tommy sat a bit more upright. "Have you cleared this with your doctor? You're not at risk for what your mom had, are you?"

"There could be hereditary issues, but they can't predict whether it would happen to me. Either way, my doctor assured me that they would closely monitor me for any signs of a problem. My mother didn't report her symptoms when they first appeared. She wasn't aware of how serious it was."

"Yeah, but still. Maybe you should just forget the whole thing."

"I can't." She craved the wonderment of being a mom. It was especially important since she'd never known her mother, and with her dad being gone a few years now, she missed having a family. Her grandpa had passed away a while ago, too. Sophie was all alone. "I'll never feel complete if I don't do this."

He winced. "So you're determined to go through with it?"

"Most definitely." She wasn't giving this up for anything. "I haven't put any feelers out there for another job. I wanted to give you my notice first. But I know enough people in this industry to find something suitable."

"You don't have to stop working for me. I can get you set up in the management office. You can join Barbara's team. I'm sure she would be happy to have you on board. She's always singing your praises, going on about how you're the only person who's truly capable of handling me."

"I certainly try." As for Barbara, she was his business manager, and the poor woman had her work cut out for her, trying to get Tommy to follow her advice. But she stuck by him, was loyal to the core. Of course, Tommy had offered Barbara a lucrative deal to represent him, making him her one and only client.

"Are you interested?" he asked.

"Yes, actually, I am." She would rather stay with his organization than start over somewhere new. But she had certain conditions if she was going to remain with him. "I'll call Barbara and arrange a meeting with her. But I want the same pay and the same benefits I have now, with Monday-through-Friday hours. No overtime, no mandatory weekends and no gigs. I'm not attending any of your shows, not even the local ones."

"Yeah, right," he scoffed. "You say that now, but I know what a workaholic you are."

"I mean it, Tommy. I'm not going to babysit you anymore."

"All right, all right." He held up his hands, Old West style, as if she was preparing to shoot him. "You can have whatever you want." He lowered his hands. "I just don't want you to go off and start working for someone else. It's going to be tough to replace you, as it is. I need you, Soph."

His words sent a jolt of heat through her veins. Damn, she hated it when he had that effect on her.

He raised his water bottle in a mock toast, his hazel eyes locking onto hers. "You're my go-to girl."

She forced herself to hold his gaze. The unwelcome heat was still attacking her body, but glancing away would be admitting defeat. She didn't want him to know he was making her weak.

"You mean 'woman,'" she said.

"What?"

"Go-to woman. I haven't been a girl since you put that rubber snake down the front of my shirt."

He burst into a reminiscent laugh. "You're right— you're all grown up now. Damn sexy, too."

Well, hell. Could he make it any worse? Struggling to form a response, she tried a joke. "Yeah, and I'm going to be one hot mama, too." She made a big, sweeping motion over her abdomen. "Just wait until you see me then."

He kept staring at her. Only now he was looking at her as if she was a specimen under a microscope—a pretty little organism he didn't quite understand.

"I've never touched a pregnant woman's stomach before," he said. "When the kid is kicking, will you let me feel it?"

The heat intensified, deep in her bones. "After your recent baby scare, I'd think you'd be more shy around pregnant women."

He shifted in his chair. "I'm just lucky they were already able to do a paternity test."

"Yes, you got lucky." Kara wasn't due for four more months, but there was no reason to wait for the baby to be born. They'd agreed on a NIPP, a noninvasive prenatal paternity test, where their blood had been collected to do a DNA profile on the fetus. They'd done it just nine weeks into her pregnancy. Tommy's brother, Brandon, had suggested the procedure. He was Tommy's attorney. Overall, everything had been kept quiet. Kara hadn't gone to the press, so Tommy had dodged that bullet, too.

He tugged a hand through his hair. "I'm just glad that poor kid didn't get stuck with me being its dad. Not just from an emotional standpoint, but with the way I travel, too. I'd feel awful if it was waiting around to see me, like Brandon and I used to do with our dad. I don't know how I'd cope with the distress it would cause. Some people take their kids on the road with them, but I couldn't fathom doing that, either."

"Me, neither." Sophie's mom had been prepared to stay home to raise her, but she'd died before she had a chance. "I want to be a traditional parent, tucking my son or daughter into his or her own bed every night."

"Yeah, I'm sure you'll do great. But at some point, your kid might wonder who its father is."

"I've already considered that." She'd spent every waking hour contemplating her options. "But I'm not sure if I want to use an open donor or not."

He sent her a blank look. "Open?"

"It's where the donor is open to contact with the child. But it can only occur after the child turns eighteen, and only if he or she requests to meet him."

"I wonder how much of a difference that would make. I guess it would depend on the type of guy the donor turned out to be. I think having no dad would be better than having a bad one. Or one who is barely around, or drunk or stoned, like my old man was most of the time."

"At least Kirby is trying to make amends and be a better father to all of you."

"He still has a long way to go, especially with Matt."

Sophie nodded. Matt Clark was the half brother in Texas whom Tommy and Brandon had never even met. Kirby had fathered Matt with one of his mistresses while he was still married to Tommy and Brandon's mother, which eventually resulted in their divorce. It was a long and sordid story that was going to be revealed in a biography Kirby had sanctioned about himself. In a strange twist, it was Matt's fiancée writing the book. She'd met and fallen in love with Matt while she was researching it.

Now that Tommy's tour had ended, they were supposed to have a family gathering at the Talbot compound sometime within the next few weeks to get acquainted with Matt. His fiancée was already there, working with Kirby on the book. Both Tommy and Brandon had met her a while back, when they'd agreed to be interviewed for the biography.

No one had asked Sophie to be part of the book. But she hoped that she could attend the upcoming gathering. She was curious about the son Kirby had kept hidden away from the world. At one point, he'd even abandoned Matt.

"So how does it work?" Tommy asked.

She blinked at him. "I'm sorry. What?"

"Choosing a donor."

She quit thinking about his family and focused on his question. "Sperm banks have websites with their donors' information. So all you have to do is search their catalog for donors who fit your criteria. In some cases, they'll provide childhood and adolescent photos of the donors. Some will even let you see adult photos. If the donors who fit your criteria are keeping their profile pictures private and you want your donor to resemble someone specific, you can send the sperm-bank photos showing what you want him to look like. Then they'll go through your donor choices and rank them by how closely they match."

"Really?" His lopsided smile resurfaced. "You should send in some pics of me."

"That's not funny." She swung her legs around and kicked his longue chair, rattling the base of it. She wasn't pleased that he'd put the idea in her head. She wouldn't mind if her child resembled him. He was beautiful to look at, with his straight, easy-to-style hair, greenish-brown eyes and ever-playful lips. There was also a gentle arch to his eyebrows, lending his features a comforting quality—when he wasn't making faces. She'd known him for so long that everything about him was familiar.

He leaned forward, resting his hands on his knees. He had an artist's hands, with long fingers. He played a mean guitar, but her favorite songs of his were ballads he'd mastered on the piano, with hauntingly romantic lyrics. He sang about being painfully in love, even if he didn't know the first thing about it. Sophie had never been in love, either, not where it tormented her soul or ripped her heart apart.

"Maybe I can help you choose a donor," he said.

She all but flinched. His suggestion caught her off guard, making her wonder what sort of nice-guy stunt he was trying to pull. "You want to help me select the father of my baby?"

"Sure. Why not?" He tilted his head nearly all the way to the side, as if he was sizing her up somehow. "Remember when I used to help you with your chemistry homework?"

"Yes, of course." He was good with numbers. Math and science came easily to him. "But this isn't a school project."

"I know." He righted the angle of his head. "But we're like family, you and me. The least I can do is support you on this however I can."

"Thank you." Suddenly she wanted to touch him, to put her hands where they didn't belong, to skim his exquisite jawline, to run her fingers through his still-damp hair. "That means a lot to me." More than it should. It even made her imagine him being the donor, which was about the dumbest thought she could've had. She wiped it out of her mind, but it spiraled back, undermining her common sense.

He asked, "Should we do it tonight?"

She struggled to comprehend what he meant. Her brain wasn't behaving. She was still stuck on the stupid notion of him being the donor, which was complete and utter lunacy.

"Should we do what?" she finally asked.

"Look through the sperm-bank sites. I'll ask Chef to make a batch of his double-chocolate-chip cookies, and I'll bring them with me. I know how chocolate helps center you."

"Yes, let's do it," she said, finally managing to rid her jumbled mind of the idea of having his child. "Let's go through the sites tonight." She needed to find a donor, a stranger.

And she was going to make sure it was someone who looked nothing like Tommy, someone who didn't have the slightest thing in common with him.

Two

Tommy sat next to Sophie at the computer desk in her home office, where they'd been for the past hour. She scrolled the donor search catalogs she'd bookmarked.

He could barely believe this was happening. Not just her wanting a baby, but the fact she was resigning as his tour manager. She was supposed to be a permanent fixture on the road, a constant he could count on. Sure, she would be an asset to his business management team. But that wasn't the same as her managing his tours. Life on the road was the soul of his existence, what he loved most about his job, and Sophie had always been part of it.

He studied her profile and the way her unruly hair framed her face, with one strand falling farther forward than the rest. He'd always been fascinated with her hair. When they were kids, she'd kept it short. She was just the cutest thing back then, following him everywhere he went. He wished that she was still trailing after him, instead of bailing out to have a baby.

So far, her donor search wasn't going well. She rejected one guy after the next. But Tommy didn't mind. He hoped that she might forget the whole idea, anyway.

With a sigh, she reached for one of the cookies he'd brought, dunked it in her milk and took a gooey bite. She kept dunking and eating until it was gone.

A second later, she licked the lingering mess from her lips, making him hungry to kiss her. Of course, that wasn't anything new. He'd been longing to taste that pouty mouth of hers since they were teenagers. If he thought he could haul her off to bed, he would strip her bare this very instant. Some people believed that sex between friends would complicate matters, but Tommy wasn't of that mind-set. Of course he had to consider Sophie's feelings, and he understood that being friends with benefits wasn't her style. She'd made that clear a long time ago.

He leaned closer to get a whiff of her perfume. She always smelled so sweet and good.

She shot him a wary frown. "What are you doing?"

He lied like a schoolboy. "You're blocking my view." Earlier she'd attached a large monitor, mouse and keyboard to her laptop to make their joint effort easier; he could see just fine.

"Sorry." She rolled aside her chair, obviously trying to make room for him. "Is that better?"

He nodded and made a show of looking at the screen, where her latest rejection, a surfer-type dude, offered his best smile. "Why are they all so young?"

"This particular bank only accepts donors in their mid-to-late twenties."

"And you're okay with that?" He didn't like the idea

one bit. "It's as if you're robbing the cradle or something."

She shook her head. "What about you and those fine young groupies who worship at your feet? At least I'm only looking at these guys for—"

"How smart and handsome and virile they are," he interjected. As much as he hated to admit it, he was getting envious of the donors. It almost seemed as if she was searching for a lover. "Maybe you really should send in some pictures of me. You can dredge some up from when I was in my twenties." He paused for effect. "If you're lucky, there might be a match."

She sat back in her chair, giving him a disapproving look. "Gee, could you be any more conceited?"

"Don't act like you don't think I'm hot because I know you do." He grabbed the mouse and changed her search criteria, putting in physical features that matched his. He didn't care if he was annoying her. By now, she should be used to his pesky personality. "Let's see who pops up."

She turned away. "Do whatever you want, but I'm not interested."

"Yeah, right." He didn't believe that for a second. Sooner or later, she would sneak a curious peek.

He delved into his task. There were a variety of donors with his body type, as well as hair, skin and eye coloring. Not all of them had pictures available. He focused on the ones who did.

While he searched, Sophie wolfed down two more cookies. She was still avoiding looking at the screen. It didn't matter, anyway. He couldn't find anyone who fit the bill.

"Never mind," he said. "They're all dorks."

"Really?" She slanted him a sideways glance. "Every last one of them?"

He gestured to the monitor. "Take a gander for yourself."

"All right, I will." She settled back into place. "What about him?" She clicked on a candidate Tommy hadn't given a second thought to—a guy with longish hair and a one-sided grin.

He scrutinized the picture, wondering what the hell she was thinking. "He doesn't look like me."

"His smile does. His hair would, too, if he cut it and styled it like yours." She read the profile. "Oh, and get this? He performs in musical theater."

Tommy rolled his eyes. "Oh, right. That's all you need, for your baby to come out singing show tunes."

She laughed. "Now who's being a dork?"

"I'm serious, Soph. A son or daughter with his genes could turn you into a stage mom. And if you think touring with me is tough, just think of how grueling your kid's Broadway ambitions are going to be. You need to steer clear of Mr. Musical Theater."

She called him out. "You sound jealous."

"Of that guy? My offspring would be way cooler than his."

She gaped at him. "*Your offspring?* I can't believe you just said that."

He hated that his chest had turned tight as he defended the remark. "I was just goofing around, trying to get your goat."

"Well, knock it off." Her voice quavered. Even her hands shook. "You're supposed to be helping me find a donor, but you're only making it harder."

He'd never seen her so worked up. This baby thing

was messing with her emotions. With his, too, dammit. "So take Mr. Musical Theater and be done with it."

"I don't want him." She clicked away from the guy's profile. "I don't want anyone who has your smile. Or anything else that reminds me of you. I already…"

"You already what?" He prodded her to finish what she obviously didn't want to say.

She pushed her hair away from her face. "Nothing. I don't want to talk about it."

He wasn't about to let up. His stubborn streak was stronger than hers. "You better tell me. If you don't, I'm going to stay here day and night, bugging you for an answer."

"Why can't you just drop it?"

"Because I don't like seeing you this way." He wanted the old Sophie back, the woman who didn't freak out about everything.

She fell silent, and he waited for her to respond. Communication had never been a problem for them before.

Finally, she grimaced and said, "Earlier, when I was at your house, I had this crazy notion about you being the donor. It actually crossed my mind."

"Really?" He should have panicked, but somehow he didn't. If anything, he felt weirdly, wonderfully flattered.

She squinted at him. "Don't sit there looking so smug, not after telling me how cool your offspring would be."

"Sorry." He tried to seem less macho, even if he was still feeling his masculine oats. "I shouldn't have pushed it that far, but you were right about me being jealous. I don't like you searching for the perfect guy."

He shrugged, still playing down his machismo. "I'm honored that you thought of me, though."

She got up and strode to the other side of the room. "It was the most insane idea I've ever had." She stopped and sent him a dubious look. "You're not thinking it could be possible between us, are you?"

"I don't know." His mind was whirring, the gears spinning inside his head.

She stood near a bookcase packed with Western novels her dad used to read. Suddenly, she seemed so small and lost—a woman alone, missing her family.

"It'll be okay, Soph," he said.

She glanced up. "What will?"

"You finding the right donor and having the baby you want." Tommy considered the possibility of getting involved. Could he become her donor for real? Since he was on the road more than he was home, he would rarely see her or the child. That would make things easier for all of them, he supposed, with her being the sole parent. But he needed to be sure that the rules wouldn't change on down the line, that she would never ask more of him than he was capable of giving. "Let's say for the sake of argument that you did use me. Would it be a permanent agreement, with no expectations or daddy duties from me?"

"Yes, but you being the donor isn't going to happen. So why are we even talking about it?"

Flooded with feelings he couldn't deny, he went over to her. "Maybe it's supposed to be me. Maybe I'm the guy who's meant to do it."

She looked shocked. "You don't know what you're saying."

"Yes, I do." He knew exactly the direction he was taking, and somewhere deep inside, it felt right.

"You've always been there when I needed you, working day and night, devoting yourself to my career. And as much as I'm going to miss you managing my tours and being on the road with me, it would be nice to know that I participated in making your baby dreams come true."

She looked as if she might cry. "That's really nice, Tommy, but you're making me feel vulnerable right now." She backed away from him. "And I have to keep my wits about me."

Had he already lost his? Offering himself up like that? His heart was beating triple time.

"Do you even know what being a donor entails?" she asked.

He gestured to the monitor, which had gone black. "I know as much as the guys on those websites do."

"But this is different. We're not strangers. In our case, there would be a lot more to consider, particularly with how entwined our lives are. I understand that you aren't interested in playing an active role as the father. I'm good with that, too. I want to be a solo mom. But would we tell the child who you are at some point? Or would you prefer to be completely anonymous, with no one ever knowing it was you?" She set her mouth in a grim line. "I couldn't make those types of decisions for you."

"And I can't make them on the spot." He understood there was a lot at stake, legal and emotional issues that could impact the future. He wasn't taking this lightly. "I need time to mull over the details, and once I've thought them through, we can discuss it further."

"It's just all so much." She seemed scared, uncertain if he could handle it.

He encouraged her to give him a chance. "Why don't

we sleep on it tonight, and in the morning, we can both see how we feel?"

"Okay." She backed herself against the bookcase. "There's no harm in that, I guess."

He didn't move forward or invade her space. He kept a formal distance, even if he ached to press his body against hers. "I am sure of one thing. If I'm your donor, I don't want to use artificial insemination. I want to make that baby the natural way."

When her breath hitched, he knew that he'd just sent a surge of good old-fashioned lust through her blood. At least he had that in his favor.

"I don't know, Tommy. I just don't…"

He tried to help her relax by saying, "You don't have to decide now. I'm not trying to rush you. But I'm not going to pretend that I don't want to be with you, either."

"I'm more than aware that you've always wanted us to be lovers. And you know that I've always been attracted to you, too. But this is a lot to consider."

"Just think it over, and I'll see you tomorrow." Before she made an attempt to fall into step with him, he added, "There's no need to walk me out." He knew the way to her front door.

She nodded and let him go, without another word between them.

Sophie barely slept a wink. She'd spent most of the night wondering what to do. And now, at the crack of dawn, she stood in the kitchen sipping her second cup of coffee with unanswered questions still swirling in her mind. Should she refuse Tommy's offer and choose another donor? Would having a baby by him be too complicated or would it make the process easier? And then there was the sex. Should she give up the fight and sleep with him or keep it professional and insist on insemination?

So much uncertainty, she thought. So much she'd yet to figure out. But maybe all of her worrying and wondering would be for nothing. Maybe Tommy would revoke his offer, and the decision to use another donor would be made for her.

Preparing for that possible outcome, she retrieved her laptop and went into the dining room. Settling in for a brand-new search, she logged on to a different site from the one she and Tommy had used.

After sitting there for what seemed like forever, she glanced at the vintage cowgirl clock on the wall. Two hours had passed, and she hadn't found anyone who seemed right. Now that the donors were in direct competition with Tommy, she couldn't help comparing them to him.

Sophie heaved a sigh and reconsidered the musical-theater guy from the original site, but her attraction to him wasn't strong enough. She needed someone who could hold his own against Tommy, a man who made her heart skip a beat.

Which was stupid, she knew. Before Tommy had offered to be her donor, she wasn't concerned about being sexually attracted to the man she chose. But now that seemed to matter, somehow.

So maybe she should stop looking at donors with current profile pictures and focus on the ones who only had photos from childhood. Maybe that would solve her dilemma.

Unfortunately, it didn't. None of the kid pics looked enough like Tommy when he was young to make her want to choose the grown-up donor.

Dang it, she thought. Tommy had doomed her, ruining her chances of accepting anyone else. But there was still a lot to consider. If she used Tommy as her donor, they needed to discuss every aspect of what the future would entail. They'd already agreed he wouldn't play an active role as the father. But would he want to engage with the child in other ways? Or would he prefer to keep his identity hidden?

Whatever his decision, she was certain that they would always be friends. They'd know each other their entire lives. That was a bonus, particularly in a situation as sensitive as this one. Surely, between the two of them, they could make something like this work.

She could only hope that he hadn't changed his mind. She wanted him to be the donor.

Did that mean she was ready to sleep with him, too? God help her, she honestly didn't know.

Her phone pinged, signaling she had a text. She removed it from her shirt pocket. Tommy was up and wanted to come over now. She quickly replied to his message, as anxious as could be.

She considered changing her clothes, but decided to stay as she was, keeping it real. Her oversize men's shirt had belonged to her grandpa, and she wore it hanging loose over a pair of floral-printed leggings. Her shoes were fuzzy green slippers she'd bought at an offbeat boutique somewhere—she couldn't remember what city or state.

A short while later when the doorbell rang, she nearly skidded across the hardwood floor to answer it.

She flung open the door; the first thing she saw was both of her Pembroke Welsh corgis prancing on the porch. Typically, they came in and out through a doggy door in the den, but they were grinning at her as if they'd just rung the bell. Of course, it was Tommy who'd done it. He'd obviously let them into the front yard by way of a side gate.

The dogs scampered past her, but Tommy stood where he was, strikingly handsome in a simple straw Stetson. He towered over her five-foot frame. She always wished that she was taller, especially around him.

He shifted his booted feet. "How're you doing, Sophie?"

"I'm okay." She didn't want to admit that she was a basket case. "Doing the best I can."

"Me, too." His eyebrows rose slightly. "Are you going to let me in?"

She wasn't blocking the doorway, was she? She stepped back, realizing that she was. Struggling to get a grasp on her emotions, she led him to the living room.

He plopped onto the sofa, the leather upholstery creaking beneath his butt. "I hardly slept."

"Me, neither." She sat next to him, relieved that she wasn't the only one who'd tossed and turned. But she couldn't take any more small talk. "Are you still interested in being my donor?"

"I definitely am." As sunlight spilled in from the windows, his eyes changed color, turning from green to brown to green again. "What about you? Do you want it to be me?"

Sophie nodded. "Yes, I do."

"Good." He removed his hat and tossed it on the coffee table, making his eyes more visible. But at least they'd settled on a color. "There's a lot we have to discuss. Where do you want to start?" he asked.

With kissing you, her whirring mind answered. *With tasting the sexy slant of your lips.* Shaking away the traitorous thought, she said, "Let's start with the type of donor you decided to be."

He had a ready reply. "I want an open situation. No secrets, no lies. I don't want to mimic my dad, having a child no one knows about. I'd prefer that everyone was aware of our arrangement, including the kid when he or she is old enough to understand."

Sophie relaxed a little, feeling as if they were making headway. "I would've respected your wishes if you wanted to remain anonymous. But I agree that it would be better if everyone knew the truth."

"If you want, we can join forces to tell the kid. When the time is right, we can explain that even though I'm not in the traditional father role, I'll always be a family friend. With the way I travel, I won't be around that much. But at least he or she will know who I am and that I care about his or her emotional well-being. Plus, we can share our past, that you and I grew up together. I think the child would appreciate knowing our history." He smiled. "We can make this work. I know we can."

Her heart warmed. "Thank you, Tommy." She wanted to hug him for being so kind and conscientious. But she didn't trust herself to wrap her arms around him, not while the issue of how and when they'd conceive the child hadn't been resolved. She'd spent years keeping her desire for Tommy at bay, and she had to be careful.

He continued with his plan. "We're going to need a legal document to seal our deal. I can ask my brother to handle it. But if you'd prefer to seek your own counsel, I understand."

"I'm fine with Brandon representing both of us, if he's okay with it." He was like a brother, of sorts, to her, too. It was different with Tommy. There was absolutely nothing sisterly about her feelings for him.

Sophie frowned. Then why was she making such a fuss about sharing his bed?

Because he already had tons of women at his disposal, she warned herself, and she'd vowed to never be one of them.

Yes, but for the sake of conceiving her child, wouldn't it behoove her to make love with him?

As her pulse beat mercilessly at her throat, she rubbed the goose bumps peppering her arm. How many times had she fantasized about climbing onto Tommy's lap? Or sliding her hands down the front of his pants? Or making kittenish sounds in his ear? Sometimes she'd even thought about him when she was with other men, and she knew that was a terrible thing to do. Her last boyfriend had cheated on her, but in her low-down, dirty mind, she'd been unfaithful, too.

"Are you okay, Soph?"

She glanced up to find Tommy watching her. "I was just…"

He searched her gaze. "Making a decision about us?"

She nodded, struggling to keep her shameful appetite for him from running amok. "Maybe we should talk about—"

"Are you willing to sleep with me to make this happen? I don't want to pressure you. Maybe we should—"

"I'll sleep with you. But we're not having a random affair."

"I never said this was going to be random, Soph. We'll be doing this to make a baby. Granted, I've always wanted you, but I'm not going to lose sight of our agenda. I'd still like for it to be romantic, though."

She couldn't concentrate on how romantic he wanted it to be. She was trying to hold tight to her emotions. Even with as gentle as he seemed, he was still a playboy, and she was still the woman who was supposed to know better. Deflecting the romance, she said, "There will be certain times that'll be my best chance for conceiving."

"And when will that be?"

"In another week or so." Trying to alleviate the heat dashing through her veins, she presented the clinical side. "Most women ovulate in the middle of their cycle, with about five to six fertile days each month. When we're together, I'll use a test for accuracy."

He furrowed his brow. Clearly, she was talking over his head. "How long do you think it'll take?"

"For me to get pregnant? I don't know. But on the average, most fertile couples conceive within six months."

He tapped a finger against his mouth. "Maybe we should do it more often to be sure. When Mack and Jean were trying to have their kids, that's what they did."

"Mack told you that?" He was Tommy's drummer; she mostly knew him to be a private person.

"No. But at the last party at my house, I overheard Jean talking to some of the other band wives and girlfriends about it."

Sophie hadn't been included in that conversation. Of course, she wasn't one of the band wives or girlfriends, either. "You shouldn't have been eavesdropping on them."

"Are you kidding? I love to hear the stuff chicks yap about." He waggled his eyebrows. "So what do you say? Should we try Mack and Jean's method?"

The notion spun through her like a tornado. "Don't get smart, Tommy. Not now."

His expression became somber. "I know you're crossing a line you never intended to cross by being with me. And you're right—I shouldn't be cracking jokes. But I still think my idea warrants consideration."

"All right. I'll think about it. I might even discuss it with my doctor, to see what he thinks is advisable." She was trying to keep things in perspective, even if her body was hungry for his. "Also, there's one more thing. Before we go any further, you need to see your doctor and get a sperm-count test." She wasn't an expert on semen analysis, but she wanted to be sure there weren't going to be any problems in that regard. She'd already had her AMH level tested, making certain she was fertile. "The men on the donor sites are required to have above-average counts."

"Gee, nothing like putting me under pressure." He nudged her foot, tapping his boot against her slipper. "I'll do whatever you want me to do. Because one way or another, we're going to make a baby. And I promise we're going to have lots of fun trying."

She didn't doubt that. But for now, she needed to catch her breath. She stood and moved completely away from him, letting the gravity of the agreement they'd just made sink in.

After all of these years, they would finally be together.

Three

Eager to see Sophie again and share the results of his doctor's visit, Tommy drove to her house. Only three days had passed since they'd made a decision about the baby business, but if next week was going to be a prime time to conceive, he wanted to be ready.

He drove onto her ranch and parked, then hopped out of his truck and went into the barn. He'd texted her earlier, and she'd told him that was where she would be.

She was hard at work, mucking out a stall, and didn't seem to notice he'd arrived. He stepped back to admire her, with her dirt-smudged jeans and her hair coiled into a messy bun.

"Need some help?" he asked, announcing his presence. He couldn't stand here all day like a teenager with his heart pounding.

She spun around. "Oh, my goodness, you scared me."

"Sorry. I didn't mean to sneak up on you."

"It's okay. I'm about done anyway." She finished the job and patted the mare in the stall.

After she put away the rake, she dusted her hands on her pants. Tommy always thought that she was a fine little cowgirl. When they were kids, she had the gumption to keep up with him, and that was saying a lot. He used to drag her along on his reckless escapades. And now, as adults, they were going to do the most reckless thing of all and make a baby.

She drank water from a canteen and asked, "So what's up? What important news do you have to tell me?"

"I saw my doctor, and my sperm count is great." Then in an old codger's voice, he jokingly added, "Those young whippersnappers on that donor site got nothing on me."

She rewarded him with a laugh. "Glad to hear it."

"So was I." He quit goofing around and glanced at a sensual line of sweat trailing from her neck and down into the opening of her blouse. The top two buttons were undone.

She gestured for them to go outside, as if she needed a change of scenery. He walked out beside her and waited a beat before he asked, "Did you call your doctor about what's advisable? About how often we should…"

"Yes, I called him." She hesitated before she added, "He recommends frequent encounters, especially during my ovulation window."

He moved closer and touched her cheek, marveling at how soft her skin was. "You're allowed to let down your guard and enjoy it, Sophie."

"I know." She met his gaze, and they stared at each other.

He lowered his hand. Suddenly he felt as overwhelmed as she looked. There was another subject he wanted to discuss with her.

They headed for a shade tree. The sun was already bright in the sky. She drank more of her water, and he braced his back against the trunk, feeling the rough bark through his shirt.

Finally he said, "There's something else I spoke to my doctor about."

"What is it?" She sounded concerned. "What's going on? Do you have a health issue?"

"No, it's nothing like that. But I've made a decision. After you have the baby and we know everything is all right, I'm going to get a vasectomy." He tried not to wince. The procedure itself gave him the willies, but the end result was important enough for him to follow through.

Her soulful brown eyes went big and wide. "Why would you do that?"

"Because I'm never going to be a donor again, and I don't want to get caught up in another baby scare like I did with Kara, or accidentally make someone pregnant for real. I figured this way, there will only ever be one child in the world with my genes, and that kid will belong to you."

"I don't know what to say about that, Tommy."

"You don't need to say anything. I just wanted you to know that's what I've got planned. I also want you to know that I'm going to set up a trust for the baby, for when it's older."

She studied him in a way that made him feel emotionally exposed. Then she said, "That isn't necessary."

He shrugged, using humor as his shield. "With a

donor as rich and ornery as me, the kid should get something out of it."

"You're not ornery." She spoke quietly, her voice as whispery as the breeze that had just kicked up.

"Maybe not, but I've got plenty of dough. And I want to make your son's or daughter's life easier."

"Thank you." She fussed with her hair, pressing some of the pins protruding from her messy bun back into place. "That's really nice of you."

He imagined her sprawled out on his bed and tangled up in his sheets, her long dark locks tumbling over a pillow. By now, the tiny trail of sweat between her breasts was making her cleavage glow. He looked away; he had to get control of himself. He knew he had to wait but she was making him hot and breathless.

"I'm going to Brandon's office this afternoon to get his legal input." He'd already briefed his brother over the phone, but they were going to finish their discussion in person. "Do you want to go with me?"

"I can't. I'm meeting with Barbara today."

Right, he thought—to sort out the details of her new job. "Okay, then. We'll talk later, and I'll let you know what Brandon says." He had a pretty good idea of how her meeting was going to go. He'd already instructed Barbara to create a position for Sophie, giving her whatever she wanted. And Barbara, naturally, was delighted to do it.

She glanced toward her house. "I better go. I have to shower."

He merely nodded, and as she bade him goodbye, he envisioned her slick and sudsy and wet. He had to keep these fantasies about her in check until it was time. But on and off he'd been having them for years. In some form or another, Sophie was always on his mind.

* * *

Brandon's office was in the hub of Nashville, with a colorful view of the Country Music Hall of Fame and Museum.

The location served as a reminder of who they were, Tommy thought, and how this city impacted them. Their daddy was featured in one of the museum's galleries. Tommy was, too, with artifacts from his most successful tours. As for Brandon, he was an entertainment lawyer, representing the Talbots and other country heavy hitters. He was also an elected trustee at the museum. But Brandon had always been the high-class type, well-known and well-respected in Nashville society.

Tommy and Brandon had grown up in the same rich, privileged, crazy-ass house, but they were nothing alike. Still, they were as close as two completely opposite siblings could be. And lately, they'd banded together, helping their dad with his now three-year sobriety. They also supported their mom, a former supermodel, in her beauty-business endeavors, making investments and buying stock in her company. Mom had rebranded herself, and was starring in her own infomercials, selling cosmetics and skin-care products.

When Tommy first explained the donor situation over the phone, Brandon had reacted in a perfectly professional way. No personal opinions, no judgments. Even now, he was as cool as a corporate cucumber. He looked the part, too, in an impeccable gray suit, his short black hair slicked straight back, his chiseled jaw clean-shaven. He'd inherited regal qualities from their mother's side. Tommy didn't have any of that.

"I'd be glad to represent both you and Sophie," Brandon was saying. "I can draw up what's called a known-

donor contract, clarifying the details you agreed upon.
But first I'm going to consult with a colleague of mine
who's versed in this area of law. I want to be sure there
aren't any unforeseen events that we should include in
the contract, things you and Sophie might've not considered."

"Whatever you need to do." He trusted his brother to
get it done right. They were two years apart, with Brandon being older and obviously wiser. Besides, Tommy
didn't like to fuss with the business end of things.

The wiser one squinted. "I hate to bring this up, but
has Sophie thought about who she would name as the
child's guardian in case she becomes incapacitated or
dies? Family members are usually preferred, but Sophie
doesn't have any family. And since you'll be signing
away your rights, you wouldn't have any legal claim
on the minor. Not unless you petitioned the courts, and
with you not wanting to have a direct role as the father,
I don't see you as doing that."

Tommy's gut tensed. The kid hadn't even been conceived yet, and now they were discussing the possibility of the child becoming an orphan. When he thought
about how Sophie's mom had died, the tension inside
him worsened. "I have no idea who she would name as
guardian, but I'll bring it to her attention. Then she can
consult with you about it."

Brandon looked him square in the eye. "Maybe she
can appoint someone in our family. Mom would probably be willing to do it."

"Yeah, she probably would." Their mother was hoping for grandkids someday, and the likelihood was
pretty damn close to nil if she had to rely on her sons.
Brandon wasn't any more settled than Tommy in that
regard. "Mom and Dad probably aren't going to like

this donor decision of mine." He'd decided to wait to tell them until he and Sophie worked out the legal details, and now there was the guardian issue she would need to consider, too.

"No, I don't suspect they'll like the idea of you being a donor. Knowing Mom, she'll accept it easier than Dad will. She tends to be more pliable than he is. But it's your life, not theirs."

"Yeah, and considering the lives they've led, they don't have a whole lot of room to talk." Their parents used to have an agreement where their dad had been allowed to sleep with other women. Their mother's only stipulation was that he wouldn't father children with anyone except her, and he'd broken that vow when he'd sired Matt. "Do you think Mom was really okay with Dad screwing around like he did? Or do you think she just accepted it as part of what came with the territory?"

"I don't know. I've never asked her about it. But she'll be telling her side of the story in the biography, so it's all going to become public, anyway. From my understanding, Matt's mom has already been interviewed. Her story will be included, as well."

"Well, I think our mom is a darned fine person for forgiving Dad and choosing to be friends with him again. It's also nice of her to want to meet Matt and embrace him."

Brandon nodded. "It's going to be a heck of a get-together, all of us meeting up like that."

Tommy scrubbed his hand over his face. "Remember when Mom first told us that Dad had another son out there, and how we wondered about him?" They'd been teenagers at the time. Tommy had just turned sixteen and Brandon had been a diligent eighteen-year-old, the senior class president of the private academy he'd attended. Tommy had chosen to go to public school, where Sophie and the rest of his friends were. "I never hated Matt for existing, but I hated Dad for hurting Mom."

"I know how deeply it affected you. But everything about Dad has always been harder on you. You look more like him than I do. You're a performer like he is. You've had to fight your way out from under his shadow, even when we were young."

"It helps that I have a brother who understands." Tommy smiled. "And they say lawyers are heartless sharks."

Brandon flashed a lethal grin. "I have my moments."

No doubt he did. But all Tommy saw was the good in him. "You always supported me, even when I got into trouble."

His brother shrugged. "With the way you and Dad used to fight, I knew you needed someone on your side."

"Those fights aren't over yet. We had a raging argument not too long ago about Kara. He read me the riot act, even after I told him the baby wasn't mine."

"Did you call him on the carpet about Matt? About having a grown son he barely knows?"

Tommy blew out a sigh. "You bet I did. But he just babbled on about how much he's changed and how focused he is on being a dad now. For someone who's trying to atone for his mistakes and be a better parent, he doesn't have a clue how to go about it."

Brandon lifted a glass paperweight off his desk, looked at it and set it back down. "He's been sending me gifts. For all the birthdays and Christmases he missed back in the day." He glanced up. "Have you been getting presents from him, too?"

Tommy nodded. Along with a slew of other things, he'd received the same paperweight, containing a sentimental quote inside. "I know his heart is in the right place, but there's only so much of his interference I can stand. Even when I try not to argue with him, I still lose my temper."

"Do you want me to approach him about you and Sophie so this doesn't turn into a battle?"

As tempting as the offer was, Tommy declined. "I appreciate it, but you don't have to do my dirty work for me."

"Are you sure? I'm good at smoothing things over."

"Thanks, but I'll handle it." Tommy knew that he was doing the right thing by being Sophie's donor, and no one, not even his dad, was going to take that away from him.

Sophie cringed. Tommy and his father were snapping at each other, deep in the throes of a heated argument. Now she wished that she wouldn't have accompanied him to Kirby's house. Mostly she'd only gone with him so she could talk to his mother, Melinda, about being named as the guardian for her child.

But she hadn't gotten a chance to do that, not with the power struggle taking place between the men. Kirby didn't like their plan at all. He'd blown up the moment Tommy had told him.

Melinda seemed okay with the idea, or was at least being supportive, the way a parent should be. She'd tried to ease the tension earlier, but her efforts had been in vain. The whole thing was getting out of control, and Sophie didn't know what to do, either.

The four of them were in the main parlor of the plantation-style mansion, surrounded by the trappings of wealth and opulence. The entire compound had been dubbed Kirbyville by the press. Even the family had begun to call it that. And what a strange bunch they were, Sophie thought. There was nothing conventional about the Talbots, not with a patriarch like Kirby at the helm.

His maid had already brought in a pitcher of iced tea and served everyone, creating a formal atmosphere that had gone awry. Kirby looked like his usual legendary self, with his graying beard and signature black clothes. He paced back and forth, rugged and demanding. Melinda was dressed in white, making an angelic contrast to her ex-husband. At fifty-eight, she was as beautiful as ever, with her golden blond hair and tall, slim figure. She sat across from Sophie on a matching antique settee, heaving ragged sighs.

And Tommy...

He stood near a window, bathed in natural light, his hair mussed from running his hands through it.

"You don't know what the hell you're doing," his dad was saying to him. "It's not right."

"Oh, really?" Tommy countered. "This from the guy who had a secret kid with one of his mistresses?" He glanced at his mom for a second, as if to apologize for being so blunt in front of her. Then he glared at his dad again.

Kirby grabbed his tea and took a swig, as if he was gulping down the bourbon he used to drink. "I never planned on having a baby with Matt's mother."

"And that makes it okay? You lied to all of us, and later you abandoned him, as if he didn't matter. You're the last person who should be giving advice."

"Quite the contrary. I'm exactly the guy who needs to do it. I'm telling you, boy, if you're not going to be the child's father, then you need to remove yourself from the equation."

"Dammit, old man, I'm not a boy." Tommy set his jaw. "So don't treat me like one."

Sophie gazed at Melinda, and they exchanged uncomfortable glances. Nothing was getting solved.

Kirby polished off his tea, put the glass down with a thud and narrowed his gaze at his son. "After the last talk we had, I was hoping you'd start becoming more responsible."

"Responsible?" Tommy scoffed. "This isn't a case of me accidentally making Sophie pregnant, like you did with Matt's mom. We're entering into a legal agreement, with Sophie choosing to be a single mother. The baby will grow up knowing me as the donor and a close family friend, and if there's anything Sophie or her son or daughter needs, I'll provide it. I'm already planning on setting up a trust fund for the kid."

"And you think that's going to help?" his dad replied in a harsh tone. "I established a trust for Matt that didn't make a hill of beans. After he used it to get his ranch going, he paid back every dime, making damned sure I knew that he no longer needed or wanted my money. It's taken years for him to forgive me. So why would you purposely give up the rights to your son or daughter, possibly creating problems like that, too?"

"I'm giving Sophie the baby she wants," Tommy said, seething. "Why is that so hard for you to understand?"

"Because you're too close to the situation, and you're not thinking clearly."

Tommy stormed over to his dad, his dusty Western

boots echoing on the pristine wood floor. He stopped just inches from his father and growled, "You don't know shit about what I'm thinking."

Kirby forged on, his voice getting louder. "I know that you're an adrenaline junkie who's always looking for a fix. And once you come down off this latest high, you're going to be left with a kid who isn't yours."

"It isn't supposed to be mine!" Tommy yelled. "That's the whole frigging point of me being the donor!"

Sophie wanted to tell both of them to shut up. She never used to argue with her dad, not even when she was a teenager. They'd always spoken kindly to each other. She would give anything to have him back. But it was different with Tommy and Kirby; they could fight about the weather. Granted, she understood that Kirby's views were distorted because of the mistakes he'd made with Matt, but his criticism wasn't helping. He needed to know when to quit. But Tommy needed to know when to cool off, too.

"Stop it!" Melinda finally made her way into the fight. She wagged her finger at her ex. "If this is what Tommy and Sophie want, they have every right to do it. They're consenting adults who can make up their own minds, and you need to stay out of it." She left her seat and sat next to Sophie. "I'm happy for you, honey. If you want a baby, then you should have one." She leaned forward to address her son. "And you'll make a darned fine donor."

"For crying out loud." Kirby threw up his hands. "You're all nuts."

For now, everyone ignored him. Tommy shrugged, and then smiled at both Sophie and his mom. How quickly his mood changed once he got his way. But if it hadn't been for his mother, he would still be locking horns with his father. Trust a woman, Sophie thought, to save the day.

She still needed to talk to Melinda about the guardianship issue. Of course, she hoped and prayed that tragedy never struck, leaving her child in someone else's care. But she couldn't pretend that horrible things like that didn't happen, either.

Sophie turned to Melinda and said, "Brandon recommended that I appoint a guardian for the child in case anything ever happens to me. And since I don't have any family left, he suggested you."

"Oh, my." Melinda fluttered her hands in front of her face, her elegantly manicured nails glittering with silver polish. "Do you want it to be me, Sophie?"

"Yes, I do. I think you'd make a wonderful substitute parent." Sophie had friends with children, but they were so attached to their own families, she feared that if she chose one of them her baby would get lost in the shuffle. "My dad used to say how sweet it was of you, bringing me up to Tommy's nursery and sitting both of us on your lap."

"You were so cute together, always grinning at each other. You were just the prettiest baby. Tommy's nanny thought you were a doll, too, with those big brown eyes of yours." Melinda glanced at her son. "He always seemed happier when you were around." She shifted her gaze to Sophie. "I'd be honored to be your child's guardian."

"Thank you." She blinked back tears. She hadn't expected this to be so emotional.

While the men remained quiet, Melinda softly said, "From what I knew of your mother, I really liked her. Kirby spent more time with her and your father than I did, with them being on the road together. In the beginning, I used to travel a lot, too, for modeling jobs, but I cut back after I had my kids. I didn't want to be an absentee mom."

"Me, neither. That's why I'll be working in the management office instead of going back out on tour with Tommy." She glanced at him, and he smiled. He seemed pleased that Sophie and his mom were creating a warm and gentle vibe.

Melinda turned to Kirby and said, "See, this is all going to work out fine."

He quickly replied, "Because Sophie asked you to look after her kid if she's not around to do it? I'm sorry to be so blunt, but that doesn't make everything all right. While she's alive and well, you're nothing to her baby and neither am I. We're not the grandparents, not if our son isn't the father."

Tommy jumped in. "Don't start, Dad."

Sophie spoke up, as well. "You're right, Kirby. You won't be the grandparents, not in a legal sense. But I'd be happy for both of you to get close to the baby. The way Tommy will be close, too."

"As family friends." Kirby plopped down next to his ex-wife, crowding her and Sophie on the settee. "I guess it's better than nothing," he grumbled.

Melinda laughed a little. "I'm going to be the most doting family friend that baby will ever have."

"Me, too." Kirby chuckled. "An old, proud, grandpa-type friend." He shot Tommy a stubborn glance. "And nothing you can say is going to stop me."

"I'm not stopping anyone from doing anything. If Sophie says it's okay for you to spoil her kid, that's her prerogative." He came forward and sat beside her, making the settee even more crowded. He leaned over and whispered, "Thanks for indulging my parents."

"I don't mind," she whispered back. She was certain her family in heaven would approve.

As Tommy touched her hand, a sweet and sexy thrill shimmied through her. Now all she needed to do was conceive this much-anticipated child—with the baddest boy of country as her donor.

Four

Five days later, Sophie knew it was time. She appeared to be ovulating, based on the results of the test she'd just taken.

With her nerves ratcheted up a notch, she reached for her phone to call Tommy. As far as she knew, he was in his studio, toying around with some new songs. He never stayed idle for long. When he wasn't touring, he was writing or recording.

Sophie would be starting her new job next Monday, going into an office every day and working like a normal nine-to-five. Her life was on the verge of change, and if she was lucky, she would get pregnant right away.

Maybe even tonight.

She scrolled through her contacts and tapped Tommy's name. With the phone on speaker, she listened to the line trill.

When they were in elementary school, he used to goad her into making prank calls with him. Back then, hardly anyone had mobile phones. Even caller ID was new. You could get away with all sorts of foolishness on those old landlines.

Tommy's phone went to voice mail, and she blew out a breath. With what they had going on, shouldn't he be more aware of the possibility of hearing from her and pick up?

Sophie didn't leave a message, mostly because she didn't want to say something so personal in a recording.

She sat on her bed, getting more anxious by the second. Her dogs kept running in and out of the room, chasing each other on their short little legs. With their smart and willful personalities, they could be quite bossy. But they were loyal to the core, too. Some people said that corgis weren't suitable for small children, but hers loved her friends' kids. She was certain they would adore her baby, too.

Pressure mounting, she debated calling Tommy again. But he beat her to it.

Her ringtone, an old Hank Williams Sr. tune, chimed with Tommy's name glaring across the screen.

Heart beating in her throat, she answered. A soft and floaty "hi" was all she could seem to manage.

"Hey, Soph. I got a missed call from you, and I—" He stalled, as if her uncomfortable tone had just registered. "Is this it? Is this the day?"

"Yes." She wasn't being much of a conversationalist.

Neither was he, apparently. He went silent. An instant later, he asked, "When and where should we—"

"Tonight," she replied. "At your house." His master suite was a series of custom-built rooms; she'd been there plenty of times before. But this would be the first time she would get to explore his bed, his sheets, his pillows, his body.

That hot, hot body.

"Do you want to go out first?" he asked.

She cleared her mind. "I'm sorry. What?"

"You know, dinner and dancing."

Oh, my God. "Like a date?" She shook her head, even if he couldn't see her. "That isn't what this is about. Besides, you always get bombarded with people asking to do selfies with you. And I'd be too nervous to be in the thick of that."

"I was planning on taking you to a private club, where that wouldn't happen. But we can skip it if you're not up for it." He paused. "I don't want you to be nervous, Soph."

Too late. She already was. "I'm trying to relax."

"I can't wait to be with you tonight. To undress you." He spoke in a hushed tone. "It's all I've been thinking about."

"Me, too." But she couldn't sit here, tangled up in anticipatory knots, edging into phone sex with him. The pulse between her legs was already throbbing. "I have to go, Tommy."

"Go where?"

Anywhere, she thought. "I have errands to run." That was a lie. The only place she needed to run was straight into his arms. "I'll see you later, okay?"

"What time should I expect you?" he asked, before she ended the call. "When is the bewitching hour?"

For a mysterious moment, she imagined creeping over there at midnight, casting dark-of-night spells. The moon was even supposed to be full.

"Sophie?" He was prodding her for an answer.

"How about nine? Or maybe eight would be better?" She couldn't decide.

"Eight," he confirmed. "I don't want to wait any longer than I have to. And you need to come hungry."

Her mind jumped. "What?"

"I'm going to feed you, nice and cozy, in my bedroom."

Was that a double entendre? "Are we talking real food?"

A smile sounded in his voice. "As real as it gets."

With him, one never really knew. "Dinner at your house?" She repeated it to be sure.

"In my bedroom," he reiterated. "I'll ask Chef to whip up something special."

So now he was arranging a different kind of date? She should have known he would have a backup plan. "You don't have to fuss over me."

"I'm doing it anyway. So just go with it, Soph."

Clearly, she didn't have a choice. He was taking control and sweeping her along, determined to start their baby-making affair with a romantic bang.

As evening rolled around, Sophie labored over deciding what to wear. She knew that her clothes shouldn't matter, not when she would only be removing them later. Still, she wanted to look pretty. Her underwear seemed especially important, so she rummaged through her drawer for her best lingerie—soft cottons with bits of ladylike lace. She didn't do the supersexy stuff.

After scenting her skin with a silky lotion and layering it with her airy perfume, she donned a cherry-red blouse and a short, chiffon-trimmed skirt, pairing the ensemble with Western boots.

She plaited her hair into a long, loose side braid, with unbound tendrils falling around it. For makeup, she went for a sheer bronzer, a light coat of mascara, a hint of blush and lipstick that complemented her blouse.

Sophie gazed at herself in the mirror. Was it too much? Should she undo her hair and change into something less frilly? In spite of Tommy's interest in wining and dining her, this wasn't a real date, and she wasn't supposed to be getting romantically invested in it.

She looked at her reflection again. Her outfit was nice, bright and pretty. So she needed to stop worrying about it. With the effort she'd taken to get ready, she should just stay as she was.

Earlier, Tommy had sent a text telling her to use the private entrance to his house, the one that led directly to his suite, from an outdoor stairway near the pool.

Sophie packed an overnight bag, but that didn't mean she was staying the night. She might skip out after the sex and return to her own safe little haven. It depended on her mood and if she needed to escape.

She drove to Tommy's place, taking the same route she always took. But it felt different. Bumpier, she thought. Not the road, but her emotions.

When she arrived at the main gate, security buzzed her in.

She made her way to the back of the mansion and took the designated staircase, stopping on the landing to glance out at the pool and the brightly lit waterfalls. From her vantage point, the entire grounds looked spectacular, with their flourishing greenery, vibrant southern gardens and long and winding riding trails.

Instead of knocking, she tried the knob on the door that would take her into Tommy's suite and found it unlocked. She was familiar with the layout and knew how expansive it was. She entered a marble-floored sitting room with silvery gray sofas and shiny black tables. The hallway beyond it offered a media room, a library and a music room, each designed for Tommy's personal use. Somewhere in the middle was a glass elevator. Then, finally, at the end of the hallway, she would encounter his bedroom—complete with a fancy dining alcove, a luxurious bathroom built for two, separate dressing rooms for him and his lovers, and a breathtaking balcony.

She didn't mind that he hadn't come out to greet her. It made her feel independent to go to him. Then again, for all she knew, he was watching her on a security camera in his room and getting a thrill out of it. She'd heard rumors that he had voyeuristic tendencies, but she'd never been brave enough to ask him if they were true.

Sophie actually had fantasies about being watched, but she'd never told him that. She'd never admitted it to anyone. She was way too shy to act out her fantasies, unlike Tommy, who probably did all sorts of wild stuff.

She ventured down the hall, feeling like a virgin on a warped wedding night. But thank goodness that wasn't the case. He wasn't her first lover, and they were nowhere near being married. She was only having this mini affair with him so she could get pregnant. She almost laughed to herself. As if that scenario was so much saner.

Almost there, she thought, as she stopped in front of the big, beautifully carved double doors to his room.

She rotated the brass handle on the right one and crossed the threshold. There was no turning back now. She was in for the count, or the date, or whatever the heck this was.

Sophie gasped. The room was dimly lit with burning candles, in different shapes and sizes and colors, scattered everywhere. She made her way to the dining area. The table was elegantly set, and a portable foodwarming cart stood nearby, the entrées covered with metal lids. Another cart presented a small but fully stocked salad bar. The third unit offered a decadent assortment of desserts. There was a beverage-and-coffee bar, too, with a refrigerator and stainless-steel sink built into a wall.

She looked around for Tommy, but didn't see him. She didn't see his chef or a maid or anyone else, either.

Maybe Tommy was on the balcony. Or maybe he was taking a last-minute shower and getting dressed. She took a moment to check out the main course, lifting the lids on the entrées. It was three of her favorite Italian dishes: chicken marsala, gnocchi with red sauce and baked artichokes stuffed with Parmesan-seasoned bread crumbs.

"Evening, Sophie." Tommy's voice sounded behind her.

She closed the lid on the artichokes and spun around. Suddenly she realized that he'd been there the entire time, sitting in a darkened corner of the room. She could see him now, gently illuminated in a pale gold light he'd just turned on.

"You're cheating," she said. "Catching me off guard like that."

"I just wanted to enjoy the feeling of watching you." He stood and left his wingback chair.

He definitely seemed like a voyeur. But instead of viewing her on a security camera, he'd waited until she entered his room, observing her in person. Sophie got desperately aroused. But the feeling was wrapped in a dangerous sensation, too, with how easily it triggered her fantasies.

He looked incredibly handsome, dressed in a classic white shirt, a Western bolo tie and black trousers.

But as sharply attired as he was, he hadn't gotten ready all the way. His feet were bare. Call her crazy, but that struck her as sexy. It was just so... *Tommy.*

"Everything looks wonderful," she said. Him, his room, the food.

"So do you." He came closer. "So beautiful." He leaned in and whispered, "I can't wait to make love with you."

She nearly teetered in her boots. "You're supposed to feed me first."

He nuzzled her cheek. "Are you hungry?"

"You told me to come hungry." His whiskers scratched her cheeks. But she better get used to it. He always shaved with one of those trendy trimmers, creating perfectly even stubble. She knew a lot about his personal habits. Too much, she thought.

He turned his face more fully toward hers. Was he going to kiss her? Or was he being playful, letting her soak up the heat between them? She was already tingling.

"What are you doing?" she asked.

"I want to kiss you," he replied.

"Then do it," she said, a millisecond before his lips crushed hers.

Sophie moaned beneath his onslaught. Quick and wet and wild, he pillaged her mouth. He tugged her tight against him, and she kissed him back, her tongue sparring with his.

This had been years in the making. The buildup, the desperate desire had always been there, below the surface. And for now, it was only a kiss.

While her mind spun, Tommy toyed with her braid, pulling it gently, then roughly, then lightly again, keeping his mouth fused to hers the entire time.

So good, she thought, so hot and dizzying.

But it didn't last. He broke the connection and let her go. She blinked at him, struggling to breathe.

"Now we can eat," he said.

Sophie blinked again. He only smiled and turned away.

"Do you want wine?" He headed over to the wet bar. "I brought up a bottle of merlot for you."

"Yes, please." She could definitely use a drink.

He uncorked the bottle and poured the rich, red liquid. He handed her the glass, and she took a much-needed sip.

"Have a seat, and I'll serve you."

"Thank you."

He fixed her salad and brought it to her. He tossed his, too, and filled their water glasses from a chilled pitcher, garnished with lemons.

"Did you know that there are hundreds of fertility gods and goddesses from cultures all over the world?" he asked. "I got curious and looked some of them up."

She couldn't help being intrigued. She settled her napkin on her lap. "Do you have a favorite? Someone we should call upon tonight?"

"Venus would probably be pleased to hear from us. She's the most widely known. Aphrodite, too. They're similar in nature, but are from different origins. Roman versus Greek. Also, from my understanding, Aphrodite is more of a sexuality goddess than one of fertility." He scooted in his chair. "I like her for sure."

"Yes, I'll just bet you do." She dug into her salad, fascinated.

"Overall, I think Liber is my favorite. He presides over male fertility. There was even a cult that worshipped phalluses in his honor. His female counterpart

is Libera. They're Roman deities who represent libera-
tion and being wild and free." He gestured to her merlot. "They're gods of wine, too."

"Then I'll enjoy this in their honor." She toasted him
with her glass. "You should write a song about them."

His voice turned low, rough and carnal. "I think I'd
rather write one about having this affair with you."

Sophie didn't reply, but somewhere deep down, she
wanted to be the subject of one of his rebellious songs.

They finished their salads in silence. He served the
main courses, and she studied him from beneath her
lashes. He was watching her, too.

Once it was time for dessert, she said, "Maybe we
should share the pastries. In bed," she added softly. She
needed to get closer to him, to do away with the table
between them.

He took an audible breath. "Whatever you want,
Soph." He got up and approached the pastry cart.

She left her chair and walked over to him. "Let's try
a few bites of each." She wanted to tempt her palate in
as many ways as possible.

He arranged a mini fruit tart, a chocolate éclair and
a slice of marshmallow pie on a glass plate. He studied
his masterpiece, before squeezing in a caramel-pecan
cannoli. "Now, that's a sugar overload."

"It's perfect." She followed him to his massive four-
poster bed. All of the furniture in his room was big and
heavy and ornately carved.

He placed their desserts, two gold forks and two linen
napkins on a nightstand. "I think we should unmake
the bed for later." He lowered the quilt and fluffed two
pillows that already looked gloriously soft. "We should
get more comfortable, too." He unfastened his bolo tie

and took it off. He untucked his shirt and opened the buttons, leaving the tails hanging loose.

Sophie joined in, pulling off her socks and boots.

"That's it?" he challenged her. "That's all you're getting rid of?"

"We're not playing strip poker. But if you insist on treating it that way, then how about this?" As brazen as could be, she reached under her skirt. Then, without letting him see anything, she peeled off her panties. She flung them a distance away. "Game over."

He gaped at her, and she smiled. It felt good to tease him. But she still wanted her sweets. Perched on the edge of the bed, she took a creamy bite of the pie. She was going to taste the éclair and the tart next, saving the cannoli for last. But for now, the pie was delish. She fluffed up another forkful. "Want some?"

"No." He plopped down beside her. "You've got about two seconds to finish that before I pounce."

She held the untouched bite between them. "We're supposed to be sharing dessert."

"It's too late for that." His voice vibrated with anticipation. "You can't sit there, so nice and polite, after whipping off your panties like that, and not expect me to go mad."

Sophie should have known better than to bait him. With a man like Tommy, she was bound to lose. But she was enjoying the game, too.

"Hurry up and eat it," he said.

With a burst of excitement, she shoved the marshmallow filling into her mouth, swallowing it quickly. She'd never been so aroused.

He grabbed the fork away from her and speared the éclair with it, causing the custard to seep out. Then when the fork toppled over, it jarred the plate and sent the cannoli rolling onto the floor.

Ignoring the mess he'd made, he nudged her down, slid his hand under her skirt and kissed her deep, causing her pulse to skyrocket.

He used his fingers, making her wet, teasing her with his foreplay. He didn't stop, not until he flipped up her skirt in one fell swoop.

"Do you want more, Soph?"

"Yes." *Please, yes.* Her modesty was all but gone. She was fully exposed to his view.

He went after her blouse. "Let's finish getting you naked first." Her bra came next. Then her skirt. He blew air over her stomach as he pulled it off. "Now I can ravage you for real." He lifted her legs onto his shoulders and pulled her against his mouth.

She tunneled her hands through his hair, the intensity of his touch rippling through her. He used his tongue like a warm, slick weapon: he licked; he swirled; he stabbed; he kissed.

Sweet heaven, he was good at this.

A waxy scent from the candles filled the room. She inhaled the aroma, flames dancing to and fro.

He glanced up at her, making the connection stronger. She kept her eyes open, wanting to see him, too. Steeped in sensation, she leaned forward, putting her fingers near his mouth. She wanted to touch the source of all that wicked pleasure.

So much warmth, so much wetness.

Sophie couldn't have stopped the orgasm if she tried. She came in a series of long, gasping shudders.

Tommy waited until the last wave subsided before he sat up.

"Do you know how long I've wanted to do that to you?" He spoke softly, sexily.

She was too hazy to respond. Her mind had gone numb. She could barely move, barely think.

He undid the button on his trousers, and her brain kicked back into gear. She took a thrill-seeking peek at the bulge pressing against his zipper.

"This is going to be a first for me," he said.

She adjusted her line of sight, zeroing in on his handsome, sharply defined face. "A first what?" she asked, her voice coming out raspy.

"I've never been with anyone without protection." He removed his shirt and tossed it onto the floor. "But tonight I'll be skin-to-skin with you."

A newly awakened pulse fluttered between her legs. "I've never done it that way, either." She'd always insisted that her lovers use condoms. Not just for birth control, but to stay safe in other ways, too. "Do you think we'll notice a difference?"

"I don't know. But we're about to find out." He ditched his pants, peeling off his crisp white briefs with them.

He was big and hard, beautifully endowed and already beading at the tip. She reached down to stroke him. When she spread the moisture in gentle little circles, she felt him shiver.

He touched her, as well, roaming his hands along her curves. He climbed on top of her, fondling her breasts and licking her nipples. She opened her legs, making more room for him, and he lifted his head.

They looked into each other's eyes. By now, he was poised at the juncture of her thighs.

"My Sophie," he said.

Her heart pounded. "I'm not supposed to belong to you."

"It's just for tonight. And every other day or night that we're together." He skimmed his mouth over hers, whispering against her lips. "Then it'll be over."

She wrapped her arms around him, and he entered her. But he didn't move. He just stayed there, letting both of them savor the moment.

"It does feel different," she said. There was an unsheathed closeness she couldn't deny—warmth of the most intimate degree.

"Oh, yeah." He pushed deeper. "Oh, hell, yeah." He angled his hips for their mutual pleasure. "I'm going to try to make this last, but it still might happen fast."

She met his gaze. He already had a feral gleam in his eye, his hair falling rebelliously over his forehead.

"But you're going to come lots of times tonight," he continued, nipping her earlobe.

"Promise?" She was more than ready, eager and willing.

"Definitely." He rocked her body with his, setting a passionate rhythm.

Holding him to his promise, Sophie dug her nails deeper, eager to take every mind-spinning, heart-hammering, love-making thrust he gave her.

Five

The reality of being with Sophie went beyond Tommy's expectations. He couldn't get enough. He wanted more and more of her, of this feeling. Every nerve ending in his body had come alive, sparking beneath his skin. She matched him stroke for stroke, lifting her hips and taking him deeper.

In his mind's eye she was part feline, a beautiful hellcat, using his back as a scratching post. Even her hair—that pretty braid and the messy strands falling around it—drove him crazy.

She moaned, and he rolled over the bed, taking her with him and tangling the sheets. He changed positions, so she was on top. He wanted her to ride him as wildly as he'd been riding her. It was her turn to buck and spin.

She didn't miss a beat. She straddled his lap, moving up and down, giving him a cowboy's thrill. He watched her, captivated by the fullness of her breasts, the flatness of her stomach and roundness of her hips. Tommy gripped her waist, and she bit her lip in naughty concentration. Then he reared up, putting his face next to hers. They kissed on contact. The exchange was sloppy, but deeply carnal, too. He slipped his hand between their bodies and rubbed her where it counted.

The kiss ended with a jolt of electricity, and she latched on to his shoulders. Was she anchoring herself for the orgasm that was building inside her?

"I can't… This is…" She struggled to speak.

She couldn't what? Stay grounded while she came? He rubbed her a little softer, a little sweeter, giving her a moment to breathe. She slowed down the pace, riding him in a more languid way. Like silk over skin, he thought.

Sophie came softly, her lashes fluttering, her body shimmying. Tommy skimmed her cheek, so damn glad she was his friend. He couldn't imagine a world where she wasn't in it.

When the final wave subsided, she put her head on his shoulder. He eased her down, switching positions again. She looked up at him, and he reentered her.

A new dance. A new awakening.

No matter how fast or slow or easy or frantic their rhythm was, it worked. She wrapped her legs around his waist, and he pumped into her. They were compatible as lovers, even though this could never last beyond their attempts to conceive.

They kissed and caressed and made hungry sounds. By now, he knew every lovely inch of her, mapping her for pleasure. He made her come another time, pleased with how responsive she was. But finally, Tommy needed a release, too.

So damn badly.

On the heels of Sophie's most recent orgasm, his muscles went taut, as his mind was consumed with lust. He inhaled the scent of sex, her heat mingling with his. He caught a misty veil of her lingering perfume, too.

So light, so pretty.

As his vision fogged, he gazed at Sophie, trying to keep her in his sights. She seemed to be watching him, too, in the same blurred way he watched her.

Tommy came, feeling strong and invigorated, knowing his seed was spilling deep and warm inside her.

After he was spent, he kissed her, then fell into her arms. She stroked a hand down his back, soothing the scratches she'd put there.

A few beats later, he rolled off her. But he remained close, right beside her, where he intended to stay for the rest of the night.

He trailed a hand along the flare of her hip and asked, "Do you want to finish dessert now?"

"Thanks, but I'm good." She stretched, as agile as the hellcat she'd become in his mind. "I should probably leave soon, anyway."

He frowned at her. "What are you talking about?"

She sat up and held the sheet against her. "I left my bag in the car, in case I decided not to spend the night."

"And now you decided to go home? Come on, Soph. Don't leave."

"But I don't want to get too cozy, to make too much of this."

He tried to persuade her to stay once again. "There's nothing wrong with a little coziness. Afterglow is supposed to be this way, isn't it?"

"Yes. But this isn't a real relationship, and we already did what I came here to do."

"That doesn't mean you have to dash off in the dark."

"I guess it wouldn't hurt to stay." Her expression softened. "I'm just a little nervous, cuddling with you like this. It's all so new."

"There's nothing to fret about. We both know the rules, and a little cuddling isn't going to change anything."

"Then I'll have to go to the car and get my things."

Because he didn't trust her to skip out on him, he said, "I'll get it in a while. And don't worry if there's anything you forgot to pack. I've got plenty of toiletries you can use. I'm well stocked with guest supplies."

"Right. The big bad musician and all of his overnight guests." She shook her head. "I shudder to think of how many women have slept in this very same bed with you."

"You knew who and what I was when you agreed to be with me."

She made a face. "Boy, did I ever. But I only agreed because of the baby."

"Yeah, and I'm still the best guy for the job." He tried to ease the tension by tugging on her braid.

She poked a finger into his ribs. "There you go, being conceited."

"About me being the right guy for the job? That's just a fact. And you know what else? I should make you eat the rest of the pie you teased me with. You and your seduction trick with the panties." He feigned offense. "It was shameful."

"Really? Well, I should make you eat the éclair you took a stab at with your fork. Look at that poor thing."

He glanced over at the nightstand. The éclair was a bit of a disaster. The pie looked sort of pathetic, too. The cannoli was definitely a lost cause, smooshed up on the floor. "The tart hasn't been touched. Maybe I'll eat that instead."

"You can't wolf it down without giving me some."

"I thought you didn't want any more dessert."

"That was before you convinced me to stay the night." She practically pushed him out of bed. "Go get it and bring it over here."

"One romp in the hay, and I almost forgot how bossy you can be." Amused, he leaned over to kiss her.

She returned the favor, and they tasted each other with their tongues. A minute later, he grabbed the tart, along with both forks. They sat cross-legged on the bed, bare-ass naked, sharing the treat.

Tommy smiled and stole a strawberry from Sophie's side of the tart. She nudged him away, and he laughed, immersed in the long-awaited exhilaration of this moment.

Sophie was glad that she hadn't gone home. It was still strange, though, to be snuggled in Tommy's bed. But at least she didn't feel the urge to escape. Odd as it was, she was enjoying their postsex rapport.

"Do you think we made it happen?" he asked, gesturing to her stomach with his chin.

"Your guess is as good as mine. But it can take some time."

"A guy can hope." He lifted one shoulder in a brawny shrug. "Will you feel anything right away if it does happen?"

"I have no idea." She smiled and ate more of the tart. "This is yummy."

"I wonder what food cravings you'll get. My mom said she used to crave Mississippi mud pie when she was pregnant with me. But I think she made that up because I was always covered in mud when I was a kid."

She remembered being covered in it with him, especially after a good hard rain. "Actually, mud pie is a great craving. I could do worse."

"Wouldn't it be funny if you craved me?"

She glanced up from her fork. "What?"

"I was just saying that it'd be funny if you craved me instead of some sort of food. But I'll be off-limits by then, so you better have me out of your system before you're waddling around with my donor bun in the oven."

"Your donor bun?" She laughed. Sometimes he had the goofiest way with words.

He laughed, too. "You know what I meant."

Yes, she did, indeed. And she agreed about getting him out of her system. When this was over, she needed to be done with him. No more sex. No more cozy afterglows.

They finished the tart, and he set aside the tin. After that, he propped a pillow and leaned against it.

Struck by his nonchalant pose, she said, "Just so you're aware, pregnancy doesn't make women crave men. So you better get that thought out of your head."

He shrugged. "You might be the exception."

Lord, she hoped not. She didn't want to crave him after she was pregnant. It was bad enough wanting him now. In the silence that followed, her mind spiraled in a new direction, one she hadn't expected to take. And just like that, she asked, "What's Kara like?"

Tommy merely stared at her. "What?"

Sophie couldn't blame him for his reaction. She had sprung the question on him; she wasn't even sure why she'd asked it. "I was just wondering what kind of person she is. With all this pregnancy talk, it made me think of her, I guess."

He sighed. "Truthfully, I hardly know anything about her, except she's a bartender at the Miami hotel where we hooked up. It was such a quick thing, we didn't spend a lot of time chatting each other up. But I can tell you this much—I don't think she wanted her baby to be mine. I called her after the DNA results came in, just to see how she was doing, and she sounded relieved that I'd been eliminated as the possible father."

She contemplated Kara's plight. "Maybe she cares about the man who turned out to be the real father. That could be the reason she didn't go to the press."

"I don't know. Maybe. I didn't ask her about him. I didn't think it was my place. But calling her still seemed like the right thing to do." He ran a hand through his hair. "Should I get your bag now?"

The quick change of topic threw her, but she understood how it was a sensitive subject for him. "Sure. My keys are in my purse." She stood up to get them while he climbed into a pair of sweat shorts he removed from a drawer.

"You can blow out the candles while I'm gone," he said.

"Okay." They certainly couldn't leave them burning all night. "They were a nice touch, Tommy."

He smiled and came over to kiss her. She melted from the sensation, from the taste of his lips, then warned herself to stop being so girlie. But darn it, being close to him felt good. For now, she told herself it didn't matter. As soon as she conceived, their intimacy would end.

He left the room, and she extinguished the candles. Keeping busy, she picked up their clothes from the floor and placed them on a chair. Without thinking, she put on his shirt and rolled up the sleeves. She buttoned it, too, keeping the fabric next to her bare skin. She was being girlie again. But she didn't want to remove it.

When Tommy returned, Sophie was clearing the

table and stacking the dishes in a rack on the bottom of the salad cart.

He set her bag near the bed and dropped her keys back into her purse. "Look at you," he said, roaming his gaze over her.

Yes, look at her, traipsing around in his shirt. "I was just borrowing this for a second." She fingered the hem. "But I can put my robe on now. It's in my bag."

He approached her. "You can stay like that. It looks better on you than it does on me. And you don't have to fuss with the dishes. I was going to do that."

"It's all right. When I'm finished, you can wheel the carts into the hallway and call the kitchen to have someone pick them up." She knew that was Tommy's habit when he dined in his suite. It was similar to being in a five-star hotel.

After everything was done and the room was clear, Sophie said, "I'm going to remove my makeup and get ready for bed."

"I have to do that, too. Not the makeup part. But I need to brush my teeth and whatnot."

They went into the bathroom together. Since it had been designed for Tommy and his lovers, there was lots of elegant space for separate routines.

He finished before she did, but he didn't return to the bedroom. He sat on the edge of the freestanding tub and observed her every move, making her self-conscious. But she liked it, too. The forbidden feeling of him watching her.

She went ahead and said, "I heard rumors that you were a voyeur or something."

"Not the way you're suggesting. I'm not a Peeping Tom or anything." He smiled his crooked smile. "Get it? *Tom? Tommy?*"

Of course she got it. She reached for her moisturizer and asked, "Then what do the rumors mean, exactly?"

He moved his gaze up and down her body. "I just think it's sexy when my lovers…you know…"

Touch themselves and let him watch? Sophie clutched the bottle in her hand, holding it tighter than necessary. What he'd just implied was her deepest, darkest fantasy. The manner in which she often imagined being watched.

Should she tell him? Should she admit it? No, she thought. She would rather keep it a secret, especially since she wasn't brave enough to actually do it.

She looked in the mirror and saw that her skin was flushed. Of all things, she was blushing. Her nipples were hard beneath her shirt, too. Or Tommy's shirt, as it were. But thankfully, it was baggy enough to conceal what was happening. She didn't want him to know how this was making her feel.

She hurried up and finished her routine. She didn't even take her hair out of its braid. It was easier to just get the heck out of the bathroom.

Once they were back in his bedroom, he asked, "Did you make a wish when you blew out the candles?"

She rummaged through her bag and found the short, simple nightgown she'd brought. "Isn't that only for birthday cakes?"

"I don't know, but why are you putting on clothes? Don't you sleep naked?" He was already peeling off his sweat shorts.

"Typically, no." And this wasn't the time to start.

"Then why don't you just sleep in my shirt instead? You can unbutton it to make it more comfy."

So that she would be seminaked?

He walked over to her. "I'll do it for you."

She stood like a statue while he made the adjustment. Heaven help her, but she could scarcely breathe. Her fantasy was rattling around in her head all over again. But she needed to stop thinking about it.

"That's better." He dusted his fingers over her protruding nipples. They were showing through the fabric now. "Are you cold?"

"A little," she lied. She was still aroused by him.

"I can warm you up." He led her to bed, and they got under the covers. He spooned with her, pressing the front of his body to the back of hers. "How's this?"

"It's nice." *So very nice.* She was tempted to turn around and initiate another round of sex, but she closed her eyes instead. There was something incredibly sweet about being held by him.

Sweet and complicated, she thought. For such a rough and reckless man, Tommy had a dreamy side. He reached across her to turn out the light and then settled back into place, where they slept for the rest of the night.

Sophie awakened in a breathless flutter. Tommy had one hand wrapped around her breasts and the other resting low on her stomach. She barely had time to open her eyes, to focus on the light creeping into the room, let alone assess the situation.

Was he awake and aware of what he was doing? Or was he asleep? In case it was the latter, she kept still, trying not to disturb him. But either way, she liked the position she was in. Her pajama top, the shirt she wore of his, was riding up in the back, and his morning erection was pressed against her bottom.

She had no idea what time it was, but it seemed early. It hadn't taken much for him to talk her into sleeping there. She'd given in easily. But that had always been the nature of their relationship. Tommy could convince her to do just about anything.

As the hand on her stomach moved, sliding toward the V between her legs, Sophie took a stirring breath. He must be awake. Surely he didn't play around like that in his sleep. Then again, with Tommy anything was possible.

When he started peppering her neck with suckling little vampire kisses, her pulse jumped. He knew exactly what he was doing.

"Oh, my," she said, her voice coming out crackled. "That feels good."

"Uh-huh." His response sounded rough, too. By now, he was spreading her with his fingers, getting ready to stake his masculine claim.

Sophie knew that she shouldn't be reacting to him with such desperate passion. He had more than enough women who flocked around him. But she was here for the sake of her baby. It was different for her.

Different or not, he was making her eager for more. Of course, Tommy had lots of practice. She even remembered the first time he'd gotten laid and how jealous she was. Not that he'd had sex, but that he'd done it with the prettiest and most popular girl at their school.

She closed her eyes, struggling with the memory. She could have been with him back then, too. She'd just been smart enough to refuse his advances.

He took his hand away, and she opened her eyes. Had he sensed what she'd been thinking? God help her, but she didn't want him to stop.

"Tommy?" she asked in a concerned tone.

"It's okay, Soph." He whispered against her ear. "I

just want you to get on your hands and knees so we can do this right."

Without hesitation, she removed the shirt so it didn't get in their way and climbed on all fours. He got behind her and steadied her hips as he rubbed against her. She arched her body, anxious to feel him inside. But first, he undid her braid, removing what was left of the plaiting and letting her hair cascade over her shoulders and down her back. Then, on something akin to a growl, he pushed all the way inside.

Sophie keened out a moan. She'd been taken this way before, but it hadn't been as primal as this. With each and every thrust, he tugged on her unbound hair.

She pushed back against him, meeting his determined strokes. He was at the right angle to stimulate her G-spot. But sex god that he was, he probably already knew that.

Soon he was doing all kinds of wild things—reaching around to fondle her breasts, biting her neck, scraping his teeth along her collarbone.

Sophie was on the verge of losing her mind.

She came hard and fast, jutting and jerking against him. Primed and ready, Tommy exploded, too, groaning and growling and spilling into her.

In the moments that followed, she collapsed headfirst onto the bed. He scooped her into his arms, and they both rolled over, face-to-face once again.

Sophie relaxed in the bath, or she tried to. The tub was certainly big enough to accommodate two people, so that wasn't the problem. It was Tommy. They were seated across from each other, and he kept staring at her.

She splashed some water at him. "Knock it off."

"Knock what off?" He tossed the soap in her direction, and it landed directly in front of her.

"Looking at me in that hot-and-bothered way of yours." She tried to grab the floating item, but he leaned forward and retrieved it.

He sat back and said, "I have no idea what you mean."

"Yes, you do." He couldn't play the innocent. She knew him far too well. "We just had sex, and you're still thinking dirty thoughts."

"So I'm a guy with an active mind." He placed the French milled soap back in its dish and braced his arms on either side of the tub. The way he reclined made him look regal, like the Nashville prince that he was.

Gorgeous and oh-so idolized.

She sighed. "Maybe we should talk about something else."

"All right." He ran a damp hand through his hair. "We can discuss our schedules and plan for what's ahead. I think you should move in with me while we're trying to conceive."

She blinked at him. "You want me to stay with you?"

"Not forever. I'm just trying to make the baby-making process easier. It might help for it to happen spontaneously instead of us having to arrange it every time."

He probably had a point. But for now she couldn't think clearly.

He continued, "You can bring the dogs and horses, the way you always do when we're on tour. This is already like a second home to them." He drew up his knees. "Think about it, Soph. We're going to be together as much as we can, and it doesn't make sense for us to bed-hop when we could be in the same house."

And his mansion was the logical choice, of course,

with how big and private and secure it was. "I don't know. It just seems so…" She didn't know what word she was searching for. All she knew was that she'd never imagined living with him, not even temporarily. But there was a part of her that liked the idea. It seemed oddly thrilling, somehow, to always be ready for each other. And if it helped make the baby…

"Did you tell Dottie about us?" she asked, wondering what to expect if she stayed here.

He shook his head. "I didn't tell Chef Bryan, either. They didn't know who I was entertaining last night. But since we're not keeping our arrangement a secret, I was planning on mentioning it to them today. Come on—move in with me. And as soon as you're pregnant, you can go back home."

"What if it takes six months to conceive?"

"What difference does that make? We've practically lived together before. Growing up together as kids, and then all those years on the road."

"None of that is the same as our current situation." Of going to bed together each night. Of waking up beside each other every morning. "You've never even had a girlfriend who's lived with you."

"I know. But that's the beauty of it. We're not a couple. We're just making a baby. And we're used to each other, Soph. I mean, really, how bad can it be?"

As bored as he got when he wasn't on tour? It could get bad, she thought. But maybe she was worrying for nothing. He was right about how much time they'd spent together in the past. That definitely counted for something. "All right, we'll try it. But only for the first month, as a trial period, just to see how it goes."

He smiled. "That works for me."

"I just hope we don't get on each other's nerves." Or

that she didn't start enjoying it more than he did. With his restless nature, there was no way to be sure.

"I think it'll be fine." He swirled his hand in the bath. "The water is cooling off. Should we have Chef send up some breakfast, then go back to bed?"

She laughed a little. "You're insatiable."

"I can't help it if I'm hungry." He swooped across the tub to kiss her, sloshing the cooling water.

When his mouth sought hers, she latched on to his shoulders, pulling him closer.

She was hungry, too.

Six

Sophie had been living with Tommy for nearly a week. So far, they'd made love every day. At some point they would take a break and rejuvenate, but for now he wanted to make the most of their time together.

He glanced over at her. They were both getting dressed, putting on casual clothes. Today they were going to Kirbyville to meet Matt. Tommy had invited Sophie to join him for the family gathering, a picnic by the stream his dad had arranged.

He was feeling overwhelmed. Not just about meeting Matt, but about how things were playing out with Sophie. Was she enjoying his company? Was their arrangement working for her?

"Am I getting on your nerves?" he asked.

"What?" She sent him a baffled stare.

"You said before that you hoped we weren't going to get on each other's nerves, so I'm just checking to see where your head is at now."

"I only said that because of how restless you get when you're not on the road. By next week, you're probably going to be bored out of your gourd."

"Are you kidding? Sex with you is never going to bore me."

She batted her lashes. "My own personal sperm donor."

He laughed. "Darned right." He strode over to her, reached out and put his hand on her stomach. "I wonder if it happened yet."

"It's too early to tell." She looked into his eyes. "And to answer your question, you're not getting on my nerves. I like playing house with you."

"Is that what we're doing?" He splayed his fingers, where her baby would grow. "Well, whatever it is, I'm glad you're coming to the picnic with me."

"So am I. I want to meet Matt and his fiancée. Her name is Libby, isn't it?"

He nodded. "She seems nice enough. She has a six-year-old son. He's supposed to be there, too."

"I didn't know she had a child."

"I guess I forgot to mention the boy to you." Tommy was still trying to grasp the details himself. "Dad told me that Libby is widowed. That she lost her husband about three years ago."

"Oh, how sad. What's her son's name?"

"Chance. And get this—his middle name is Mitchell."

"Chance Mitchell?" Sophie's eyes went wide. "Like the fictitious outlaw from your dad's song?"

"Yep. Libby and her late husband were fans of my father's. She's probably going to be the only one at the picnic who hasn't been hurt by my old man."

She sat on the edge of the bed to put her boots on. "Kirby has never hurt me."

Uncertain about her remark, Tommy asked, "You aren't hurt that he doesn't approve of our donor arrangement?"

"I'm disappointed that he thinks we're making a mistake. But I'm not hurt."

He grabbed his boots and sat next to her. "I totally forgot to tell you that Dad called this morning. He wanted to know if he could include us in the biography."

"Us? As in you being my donor?"

He nodded. "He made a valid point about the time line. The book is scheduled to be released next summer, and if everything goes as planned, you'll be pregnant or maybe even ready to give birth, and we would've made a public statement by then."

"Do you think that's what we should do?"

"Contact the media ourselves? Definitely. I'd rather take things into our own hands than let the press put a spin on it. I can have my publicist handle it when we think the time is right. But for now, I'll have everyone who is aware of the situation sign a nondisclosure so it doesn't get leaked before we're ready to share the information." Tommy knew how easily people could turn on you and sell your story for personal gain. He knew how brutal the gossip sites could be, too. "If we agree to have it included in the book, Kirby said that we can tell our side of it. But he wants to be able to state his opinion, too."

"And tell the world that he wishes that the child was going to be his official grandbaby? I suppose we can't fault him for that." She sighed. "Has he already confided in Libby about it?"

"Yes, but it won't go into the book unless we say it's okay. But I don't think it'll matter, either way. The biggest part of the biography will be the unveiling of Dad's secret son, not the baby you'll be having."

"Well, thank goodness for that." She tossed him a smile.

"Yeah. You know Dad. He wouldn't dare let us upstage him in his own book." As cute as her smile was, he couldn't help but frown. "So are you ready for this little family gathering?"

She reached for his hand and squeezed it. "I think the real question is if you're ready."

He avoided the issue. Instead, he said, "Dad already took precautions to keep the picnic private and away from the press, so no one needs to worry about that. He doesn't think anyone would suspect who Matt really is, anyway. As far as Dad's household staff knows, he's just Libby's fiancé who comes to visit her when she's there."

"That's not what I meant about you being ready for it. I was talking about you meeting Matt."

He finally admitted how he felt. "Honestly? I'm nervous about making a favorable impression on him. I'm not like Brandon. He always gets people to warm up to him. I don't know how to do that, not without pouring on the celebrity charm, and Matt isn't going to give a crap about that."

"Just be yourself, Tommy."

"But that is who I am." A superstar's rebellious kid who'd blasted his way to the top, too. "You've seen me in action all these years. You know that I'm not good at being a regular guy. If I'm not performing or being the life of the party, I don't know how to act around people."

She kept holding his hand. "If it's any consolation, Matt is probably as nervous as you are."

"No doubt he is." But Tommy was still worried that he was going to be Matt's least favorite brother.

* * *

By midafternoon, the picnic tables were laden with leftover food and the family had divided into separate groups. Sophie and Tommy's mom were engaged in girl talk with Libby, and Brandon, Matt and their dad were goofing around with six-year-old Chance and playing tag in the grass. Tommy was the odd man out, just as he'd suspected he would be. He'd barely exchanged more than a few words with Matt. He didn't know how to interact with Chance, either. He'd never been particularly good with kids. So instead of joining the men, he walked beside the stream, letting the breeze skim past his face.

What the hell was wrong with him that he couldn't just behave like a normal guy? Even his dad was pulling it off. Not that Kirby was in any way average. He used to do weird things, like wear his sunglasses in the house. Not all the time, but often enough for Tommy to recognize the signs of his old man's hangovers. Dad used to find all sorts of ways to shut out the family. But today, Kirby looked like Grandpa of the Year, with how easily he was playing with Libby's son.

When Matt took a break from tag to grab himself a cold drink, Tommy decided to approach him. Matt was only going to be in Nashville for a few days, and he would be spending most of that time with Kirby. If Tommy wanted to make a halfway-decent first impression on his brother, he needed to do it today.

He headed over to Matt, and as they stood beside the cooler, Tommy asked, "Will you grab me a bottle of sparkling berry water?"

"Sure." The Texan reached into the ice chest and handed him one.

"Thanks." Tommy twisted the cap, and they gazed

awkwardly at each other. Matt was tall, like Tommy, with a long, lean frame, but other than that, they didn't resemble each other. The other man had short black hair, dark skin from his mother's Cherokee side and stunning amber-colored eyes. He owned a recreational ranch in the Texas Hill Country that was a major success, but he still carried himself like a down-home guy.

"So how's it going?" Tommy asked. It was all he could think to say.

"Fine. How's it going with you?"

"I'm all right." But this conversation was stilted. They both took a swig from their drinks.

After a beat of silence Matt said, "Everyone says you're like him."

Tommy hated the comparison to his father. "I'm not. Or maybe I just hope I'm not. He can be such an SOB at times, with that arrogant manner of his."

Matt smiled for a split second. "Yeah, I know." The smile didn't return, not even a flicker. "He treated me awful when I was a kid."

"He wasn't a good father to me or Brandon, either. I used to fight with him, where we'd get right in each other's faces. We still do that, even now."

Matt glanced over his shoulder. "Brandon seems to get along with him okay."

Tommy followed his line of sight. Kirby and Brandon were swinging Chance by his hands and feet and making the kid laugh. "Brandon makes more of an effort than I do. He's the peacekeeper."

Matt turned back around. "And what are you?"

"The daredevil, I guess. That's what I'm known for, even within the family. Brandon and I used to refer to you as our lone-wolf brother. We always wondered what you were like."

"To be honest, I always wanted brothers or sisters, but not strangers who only shared half of my blood." Matt shifted his stance. "It was hard for me to think of you as anything other than Kirby's legitimate sons. But now I know that you were just as miserable as I was being his kid."

Tommy barked out a humorless laugh. "I'm still miserable about it." He quietly added, "If I was you, I never would've forgiven him."

"I had to work at it, believe me." Matt blew out a breath. "Mostly I did it for Libby and Chance. I knew that I couldn't be a strong and loving husband to Libby or a kind and caring father to Chance if I was harboring hatred toward my own dad. I had to make things right. It was important to Libby, too. She's gotten to know a side of Kirby that no one else has, with how deeply he's confiding in her for the book. She knows he's screwed up, but she sees how much he cares and how sorry he is."

"Sometimes I see it, too. And other times, he just seems like a pompous ass, poking his nose into my life."

Matt nodded. "When I first reunited with him and told him that Libby and I were getting married, he took credit for our relationship. He actually patted himself on the back about it. He brags about Chance being named after his song, too. But he is wonderful with the boy. Chance thinks he's cool."

"I can tell." Tommy noticed how the kid hung all over Kirby. "He's not taking credit for anything I'm doing right now. He's pissed at me for what I've got going with Sophie. I know that he told Libby. Did he tell you about it, too?"

"The sperm-donor arrangement?" Matt furrowed his brow. "Yeah, he mentioned it. But I think you have a right to do whatever you want to do."

"Being a donor suits me." He glanced back at Kirby, who was still playing happily with Matt's new stepson. "I don't want to end up like Kirby, having children I don't know how to raise. It's better if Sophie parents the child on her own."

"I always wanted kids. I was even married once before to a woman who had two little twin girls. But it didn't work out. She divorced me within six months. She wasn't who I was meant to be with."

"I'm not meant to be with anyone. Sophie and I are just friends." Friends and temporary lovers, he thought. And for now, he was content to have her as his housemate, too. He shook his head. "I can't believe I'm having a personal discussion like this with you."

Matt made a tight face. "As much as I hate to say this, I used to think of you as an idiot. I never liked your public persona."

Tommy laughed in spite of himself. "Sometimes I don't like it, either."

Matt laughed, too. "I'll keep that in mind." His expression sobered. "It's going to be tough when the book is released and everyone finds out that I'm Kirby's son. Dad said that we can do some press conferences ahead of time and announce it beforehand, but it's still going to disrupt my life. As much as I hated being his secret kid, I got accustomed to it."

"I guess we're all accustomed to the roles he has us playing in his life."

"I used to ban his music at the barn dances at my ranch. I never let the band cover his tunes. Your music was off-limits, too. But I'm letting that rule go now."

Curious, Tommy asked, "What reason did you give for banning our songs?"

"I never said, but I think people drew their own conclusions, assuming that the Talbots' music reminded me of something bad from my past. They just didn't know how bad it really was. I didn't even tell my ex that I was Kirby's kid or that you were my brother. Only Libby knows."

"I'm sorry that you felt that way." Tommy didn't want his music to be a source of anyone's pain. "But I'd love to see your ranch someday."

"That'd be great. You're welcome anytime. But if you visit sooner rather than later, we'll have to stick to a cover story about how we know each other. We can't admit that we're brothers until after my identity is revealed."

"We can just say that we became acquainted through Libby since she's my dad's biographer and you're her fiancé. We can tell everyone that we're newfound friends." Tommy paused to add a silly joke. "Unless I'm too much of an idiot for that."

Matt flashed a teasing smile. "You're not so bad."

"Ha. You say that now. You only just met me." But at least they were off to a good start, taking steps toward the future, where they could actually become real-life friends.

After the picnic ended, Tommy and Sophie returned to his house. She followed him into his music room, where he tuned one of his prized guitars, and she scanned a music trade magazine from the 1950s. Tommy had a huge collection of them. But he could tell from the way she was absently paging through it, she wouldn't stay quiet for long. Tommy was in a reflective mood and was being silent. He got like that sometimes, especially after emotional encounters, and today had been chock-full of emotion.

As expected, she set aside the publication and said, "I had a nice time. It seemed like you did, too, after you got over that hump with Matt."

Without looking up at her, he adjusted the Stratocaster on his lap. It was a prototype of the signature model that had been designed for him, with plans to market them next year. "It turned out better than I expected. But I made a conscious effort to talk to him."

"Yes, I noticed that you sought him out."

He finally lifted his gaze. "You were keeping tabs on me?"

"Not the entire time, but I wanted to be sure you were doing okay. I've gotten used to having you on my radar."

It wouldn't be like that once he started touring again. He wouldn't be anywhere near her radar. He didn't want to keep dwelling on that, though, not with as much as he was going to miss traveling with her. But at least he was helping her to have a baby. Whenever he was on the road, he could envision her with her child, being happy as a single mom. "What did you think of Libby?" he asked, taking his mind in another direction.

"I adored her. I mean, really, what's not to like? She's upbeat and smart, with a glittery sense of style, white-blond hair, big blue eyes and two perfect little dimples. I can see why Matt fell head over heels. Then again, he's quite the catch, too."

Tommy felt a pang of jealousy. "So he impressed you, did he?"

"Oh, my word, yes. Not only is he tall, dark and broodingly handsome, he's thoroughly devoted to Libby and her son." Sophie leaned back in her overstuffed chair. "He's everything they need."

Tommy got up and placed the guitar back in its case.

When he returned to his seat, he said, "I guess you're going to look for a guy like that someday?"

"Are you serious? I'd never find anyone who wants me that badly. Besides, I just need to focus on being the best single mom I can be."

"A lot of men would want you, but I'm glad you've got your priorities straight." He couldn't stand the idea of a stranger coming along and sweeping Sophie off her feet.

"Libby wasn't looking for anyone, either. But still, her situation was different from mine. She didn't set out to be a single parent." She sent him a coy smile. "And for now, I'm just happy I have you as my baby-making lover."

"Oh, right." He scoffed, even if her remark warmed him in all the right places. "Now you're kissing up to me? After you swooned over my brother?"

She rolled her eyes. "I wasn't swooning. I just think it's nice that Matt and Libby found each other. Mostly what she talked about was how amazing Matt is with Chance. Isn't he just the cutest thing? A ball of energy, but so bright and clever, too."

"He seemed like a sharp kid. But children have always been a mystery to me."

"He reminded me of you when you were that age— not as mischievous, but there was just something about him."

"What I remember most about being six is us being in first grade together. I was afraid that we might not be in the same class, but we were." For all the good it had done. He'd yapped so much to her, their teacher had separated them, putting him on the opposite sides of the room. "You never got in trouble, but I was always getting a time-out."

She laughed. "I wasn't the one disrupting the class, Tommy. You were."

He shrugged, trying to brush it off. "I can still be disruptive, I guess."

"You guess?" She wagged a finger at him. "You make everyone crazy with worry. Every time you step out on stage, it's another broken bone waiting to happen."

"I've never gotten that busted up." Just a few typical injuries, he thought, and certainly nothing that had stopped him from performing.

"It still makes me crazy."

"Then we're even because you make me crazy, too." If he'd gotten her out of his system years ago, he probably wouldn't be so damn attached to her now. "Sexy crazy," he clarified.

She stared at him for a second. "I knew what you meant."

Before things got awkward, he said, "I guess it's safe to assume that Matt and Libby are going to have more kids. That Chance will have brothers or sisters."

"Oh, most definitely. Libby told me that they're going to get married first, though, and the wedding isn't scheduled until next year. They want time to plan it right." Sophie paused for a second, then prattled on. "Libby is originally from California, so she and Chance relocated to Texas to be with Matt. But since she's been spending so much time here with Kirby on the book, Matt has been looking after Chance when she's gone. He's really close to her son."

"So I gathered." This was the second time Sophie had mentioned Matt's tight-knit relationship with the boy.

She tucked her feet under her, getting cozier in her

chair. "When Matt and Libby get married, Chance will be your nephew. Kirby already treats him like a grandson."

"I noticed that, too. But I'm not surprised, not with how my old man is champing at the bit to be a grandpa." He squinted at her, thinking how pretty she looked, with her now-wrinkled picnic attire and long hair in a ponytail. "It's funny how people can be crappy parents, and then end up being wonderful grandparents."

"Some folks mellow with age. And in your dad's case, I'm sure it has a lot to do with his sobriety."

Tommy nodded. He'd hated having a drunk and stoned father more than he'd ever hated anything. "I just hope he never starts drinking or using again."

"He seems really committed to staying clean and sober."

"For now, he definitely does." But lots of alcoholics and addicts fell off the wagon. "I think that's why my mom is able to be friends with him again."

"It was great that she was at the gathering today. She really liked Matt and Libby. And she thought Chance was a doll, too." A moment later, she asked, "Did you know that Matt competed in junior rodeos when he was a kid?"

"No. We didn't talk about anything like that."

"You ride and rope, too."

"But I never competed." He wouldn't have been able to follow the rules. "I'm not a structured-sports guy. Never was, never will be."

"I know, but Matt is teaching Chance to ride and rope, and I was thinking that maybe someday you could teach my son or daughter to be a cowboy or a cowgirl, too."

The gravity of this conversation was making him nervous. What if her child didn't give two figs about him? It wasn't as if he was going to be the dad. "You can do that, Soph. You ride and rope as well as I do."

"Yes, but what I learned, I learned from you. So that's why I thought you could teach my child, too. That seems like something a family friend could do, and since that's going to be your role in his or her life…"

"Sure, okay. But only if that's what the kid wants." Tommy was already concerned about overstepping his bounds. There weren't any hard-and-fast rules for family friends, not like there were for dads.

She glanced around the room, settling her gaze on the piano, before returning her attention to him. "Maybe you can teach the baby to play music, too."

He battled a quick, shaky breath. He hoped her son or daughter didn't blame him for not knowing how to be a parent. "The way I tried to get you to master 'Chopsticks'?"

She primly folded her hands on her lap. "At least I tried."

He chuckled in spite of how he was feeling. "Who are you trying to fool? You were the most impatient student I ever had."

"I was the *only* student you ever had," she countered.

That was true. He didn't share his skills with just anyone. "Let's hope that kid of yours inherits musical aptitude from me."

"I hope it inherits a lot of things from you."

"You do?"

"Of course," she softly replied. A heartbeat later, she winced. "But if it's a boy, it better not be a womanizer. That's a quality I don't want my son to have."

Instead of taking offense, Tommy combed his lusty gaze over her. "I should seduce you for even saying that."

She turned flirtatious, too, making naughty eyes back at him. "Here, in your music room, amid the instruments I don't know how to play?"

"Hell, yes." He stood and dragged her out of her chair, backing her toward the piano. "We're going to make our own wild brand of music."

She laughed, and they kissed, hard and rough. After they yanked off each other's clothes, he pressed her bare butt against the piano keys and said, "If you're not pregnant already, you sure as fire will be."

Just as soon as they were done.

Seven

Sophie wanted to cry. On this quiet October morning while she was getting ready for work, her period came.

Determined to stray strong, she pulled herself together and took the elevator to the first floor of the mansion, where a buffet-style breakfast was being served. Tommy had already gone downstairs ahead of her. In fact, he'd gotten up early to ride a new mare he'd bought, so she hadn't seen him since he'd rolled out of bed. He'd taken her dogs with him, letting them run around in the yard today.

As she reached the dining hall, she spotted Dottie coming toward her. The older woman smiled and said, "Tommy is back from his ride and is having his breakfast in the garden room. He'd like you to join him there."

"I will. Thanks." When the urge to cry returned, she bit back the tears. She had no business getting upset after only a month of trying. But still, she felt cheated. She wanted so badly to be pregnant.

"Are you okay?" Dottie asked. "You seem sort of sad."

"I'm fine. I just have something on my mind." She couldn't reveal what was wrong, not without telling Tommy first. "I'm going to grab my food now."

"All right, hon. Chef made a lovely spread today with the sweet-potato-and-spinach strata you like so well. He enjoys having you here, and so do I. Just let us know if there's anything else we can do for you."

"Thank you. That's sweet. You've both been so accommodating." She wanted to put her head on Dot's shoulder, but that would provoke the tears she refused to cry. "I'll talk to you later. Okay?"

"Sure." Dottie walked away, returning to her household duties.

Sophie fixed herself a plate, taking an extra helping of the dish Chef Bryan had prepared specially for her. She also went for crab cakes and avocado sauce. She added fresh fruit and whole wheat toast, along with a frosty glass of milk. She'd already had coffee in Tommy's suite.

She put everything on a tray and carried it to the garden room, located just off the dining hall.

Tommy sat at a mosaic-tiled table, surrounded by a spectacular array of plants and flowers, with several fountains bubbling nearby. He looked exceptionally rugged wearing his Western riding gear in this glamorous setting.

He glanced up and noticed her. "Hey, there."

"Hi." She put her tray on the table and took the chair across from him. When she unfolded her napkin on her lap, she skimmed her stomach and frowned. Instead of dragging out her news, she hurriedly said, "I just got my period." To keep those stupid tears at bay, she sipped her milk.

"Damn. Really? I was so sure that we were going to…" He moved around a half-eaten crab cake on his plate. "It'll happen next time."

"What if it takes longer than we anticipated? What if it goes on for years or never happens at all?" Nature was difficult to predict, and now a fearful burst of gloom and doom was setting in.

"Come on, Soph," he admonished. "Don't talk like that."

"But what if that's our fate?" Or more accurately, *her fate*. He wasn't the one who wanted a baby. "You're not going to keep doing this with me forever."

"I'll do it as long as it takes. I already told you that."

"Yes, but years? Come on, Tommy. It's unrealistic for you to think you could stand it for that long."

"Stand what? Having you as my lover? Or console you when you get your period?"

Both, she thought. But she said, "Maybe I should just go back to my own house."

He scowled. "You're giving up already?"

"No, but it might be less emotional if I wasn't living with you."

He stared across the table at her, the fountains gurgling in the background. "Don't you like being here?"

Truthfully? She loved the pampered warmth he provided, and that was beginning to seem like a problem, too. What if she started getting crazy ideas about living here for real? She wasn't supposed to be a permanent fixture in his home. "I just don't want to overstay my welcome." Or get more attached to him than she already was.

"You're not overstaying anything. I want you here,

Sophie. I want to see this through, the way we originally planned."

She debated what to do. Maybe once her period ended, she would be able to think clearly. Besides, how much more attached to Tommy could she get? They'd been ingrained in each other's lives since they were born. "All right," she conceded. "We'll keep things as they are for now. But I can sleep in one of your guest rooms until we start working on the baby again. We don't have to keep sharing your bed."

He shook his head. "Don't be ridiculous. You're sleeping beside me, just like you've been doing." He resumed eating. "So now that we got that over with, I have something to ask you. There's a fund-raiser I'm supposed to attend later this month. You know how I hate those stuffy high-society balls, but Brandon gave me the tickets. It's an art auction, and I promised him that I would buy something. He can't attend because he has another event that night. Anyway, I thought it might be more interesting if you joined me." He paused. "So, will you be my date?"

"Do you think that's wise? Us dating like that? People might misunderstand and think that we're a bona fide couple."

"What people? Everyone close to us knows we entered into a donor agreement and that you're living here for now. The assumption is that we're sleeping together, anyway. That's part of why I had everyone sign nondisclosures. Even the management team you work with signed them."

That was true. He'd taken the necessary steps to stop people from talking about them. "What about the press? If there are any photographers there, our pictures might show up on gossip sites."

"Don't worry. That's not going to happen."

Did that mean this was a carefully screened event? It certainly seemed so. She relaxed a bit. "Okay, I'll go with you." Maybe it would be good for her to have an evening on the town, to get dolled up and get out of the mansion, to quit stressing about their relationship seeming real. They would be back to the baby-making business by then, too, and that was her priority.

"Great." He tossed her a boyish grin. "Since the media won't get wind of it, we can dance really close and kiss and make sexy spectacles out of ourselves."

She shook her head. Even if they weren't in danger of ending up on gossip sites, she wasn't going to get wild at a charity ball. "We're going to behave, Tommy. No PDAs."

He didn't reply. He drank his orange juice and gazed at her over the rim of the glass, as if he was daring her to do it when the time came.

Sophie felt like Cinderella getting ready for her famous ball. Tommy had brought a beauty expert to the house to do her hair and makeup. He'd purchased a designer gown for her. He'd also made certain that loaner jewels were available. She'd gotten dressed up for award shows and industry parties and whatnot in the past, but not where Tommy had hired a stylist for her or orchestrated what she would be wearing. No matter how much she tried to squelch the Cinderella feeling, it wasn't something she could seem to shake. Of course, it wasn't as if Tommy was her fairy godmother. She even laughed at the thought.

Her appearance wasn't anything to snicker at. This was the most elegant she'd ever looked. She stood alone in the private dressing room designed for Tommy's lovers, gazing into a full-length mirror. Her hair was swept into an intricate updo, and her champagne-colored, mermaid-style gown was embellished with hundreds of shimmering glass beads. She'd chosen a red garnet bracelet and diamond drop earrings as her accessories. Her heels were red, with shiny gold soles.

Suddenly, she caught a tall, dark reflection behind her. *Tommy.* He'd just entered the dressing room. He stayed quiet, admiring her from where he stood. Attired in a classic black tuxedo, he held a delicate red-rose corsage.

Her handsome date bearing a gift.

She turned to face him, and they gazed silently at each other. He moved forward to put the flower on her wrist.

"Thank you," she said. "It's beautiful."

"You're the one who's beautiful." He lingered over her. "I have something else for you."

He led her out of the dressing room and over to the bed. On top of it was a champagne-colored mask that matched her gown.

She stepped forward without touching the mask. It had long, red fluffy plumes incorporated into the design. "We're going to a masquerade ball? Why didn't you tell me before now?"

"I wanted to surprise you."

"Now it makes sense why you said us being seen together won't matter. If we're wearing masks, no one will know who we are."

"Yes, but don't get too excited. It's still going to be the same stuffy function." He picked up the mask and handed it to her. She held it against her face, and he tied it into place.

"How does it look?" she asked.

He circled around to face her. "Gorgeous. Sexy." He opened an armoire equipped with a mirror. "See for yourself."

She turned and saw a mysterious stranger, hot as fire, gazing back at her—gold beads, red feathers and crimson lipstick. "Where's *your* mask?"

"In here." He removed it from a drawer in the armoire. "It's a stylized version of the Phantom of the Opera."

He put it on. The black mask consisted of bold carvings and flat, smooth pieces of metal, curving around the edges. One side completely covered his face, leaving only his mouth exposed. On the other side, where a small portion of his face was visible, he still wasn't recognizable. He'd been transformed into a mysterious stranger, too, with prominent changes to his forehead, the shape of his eyes and bridge of his nose.

She placed her hand against the section of his jaw that she was able to touch. "I'm going to want you when we come back." She wanted him now, but she wasn't going to start tearing off his tuxedo.

He smiled, much too wickedly. "You're turned on?"

Her skin tingled. "Aren't you?"

His smile turned even more sinful. "You have no idea."

Before they decided to ditch the ball and tumbled into bed, she said, "We better go. You promised Brandon you'd buy some art."

"He's probably counting on me to bid on something no one else will want." He shrugged. "Either that or he's trying to teach me to have some class."

She gave a sputtering laugh. "Can that be taught?"

He laughed it off, too. "Probably not. But let's find out, anyway." He got serious and offered her his arm. "I've already got the limo waiting."

* * *

The ball was being held at an elaborate Gothic revival mansion, with architecture that mimicked the icing on top of a wedding cake. Sophie was in awe and thought it was the perfect setting for a masquerade-themed art auction. The proceeds from the fund-raiser were being donated to a wildlife foundation, which factored into the building's motif, as well. Not only was the mansion's decor punctuated with animal prints and faux furs, but the pieces being sold also depicted rare and exotic animals.

Sophie and Tommy wandered the grand halls, trying to hunt down the artwork. All of the pieces were hidden within the house, and there was a treasure map of where to find them. Sophie thought it was a clever tactic, enticing people to uncover whatever they wanted to buy. A security guard was stationed at every treasure site, and to place a bid, guests were required to use a specially designed app they'd downloaded onto their phones.

Other activities included sipping Southern cocktails on the veranda, eating delectable appetizers in the dining room and waltzing to elegant music in the ballroom. There were people everywhere, doing whatever struck their fancies.

Tommy checked the map and pointed in the direction of a narrow staircase that led to the attic. "There's supposed to be a jeweled tiger up there."

Curious, she asked, "What is it, exactly? A painting, a sculpture, a piece of jewelry?"

"I don't know. That's the only description. But the opening bid is pretty high."

She followed him up the staircase, the wood creaking from years of wear.

They entered the attic, which was a steeple-shaped room, cluttered with furniture. They weren't the only people poking around up there. Another masked couple was searching for the tiger, too. But it didn't matter who found it first. Even if they all wanted it, only the highest bidder would win.

The attic was staged to seem as authentic as possible, even if there wasn't a speck of dust in it. The floors were spotless. But you couldn't expect people at a sophisticated ball to crawl around and get dirty.

While Tommy went through some old boxes, Sophie rummaged through a trunk filled with ladies' clothing from the era of the house. If the tiger was a brooch, maybe it would be pinned to one of these dresses.

"I already looked in there," the other woman said to her. "We've been searching everywhere."

Sophie glanced up. Her competitor was a young, slim blonde in a green sequined gown and butterfly-shaped mask.

Sophie politely said, "It's supposed to be in this room."

The blonde knelt beside her. "Maybe he has it on him." She nodded toward the security guard. "Should I frisk him and check?"

Sophie glanced his way. The man was tall and broad, as strong and thick as a live oak. "That's probably not a good idea. He doesn't seem as if he would be receptive to that."

When the guard shot them a stern look, both women clammed up. A second later, they put their masked heads together and giggled like a couple of school-aged kids.

The blonde waited a beat before she stood and smoothed her dress. "There's a hand-carved giraffe my boyfriend is interested in. I think we'll go see if we can find that. Maybe we'll run into you later."

"Sure thing. I'm Sophie, by the way."

A pretty smile appeared on the woman's face. "Jenny." She smiled again. "Good luck with the tiger." She collected her man, and they left the attic.

Soon more people arrived, crowding the small room. By now, Tommy had stopped searching and was gazing out the lone window at the garden below.

Sophie quit sorting through the trunk and went over to him. He turned and leaned into her, then whispered in her ear, "I know where it is."

"Where?" she whispered back.

"Come with me, and I'll show you."

"But—"

He shook his head, silencing her, making her heart pound. Were they going to leave the attic and return when no one else but the surly guard was there?

Tommy escorted her down the narrow stairs. Once they reached the second floor, they took the main stair-well to the lower level. From there, he whisked her into the backyard.

Was this a ploy to get her alone, to kiss her, to touch her, to leave her breathless for more?

He said, "We need to keep going."

He was taking her to the garden, but she didn't see another living soul around. "I don't think we should be out here."

"It's okay." He threaded his fingers through hers. "There's a lighted path."

They were soft, warm, romantic lights, she thought. "Are you going to seduce me?"

He squeezed her hand. "You bet I am. But not before I show you the tiger."

He led her through a maze of greenery. At least there were flagstones below their feet and they weren't traipsing through the soil. She inhaled a gust of the night air. She wasn't sure if she believed him about the tiger.

Then she saw it: a huge statue in the middle of the garden, surrounded by cottonwoods. Its eyes were amber stones, along with the stripes on its body. A row of floodlights encompassed it, shining up at its muscular frame.

"Oh, my word. Look how big and beautiful it is." She inched closer. "How did you know it was here?"

"When I was looking out the window I caught flashes of gold through the trees, and I realized that the tiger wasn't in the attic, but was visible from it."

"So the map had a trick clue," she concluded, stating the obvious. "There's no one out here to protect it, no security." She reached out to touch one of its legs. "But I guess someone couldn't just cart it away. It would take a crane to lift it. I wonder if anyone else uncovered it yet or if we're the first."

"I don't know. But it's magnificent." He removed his phone from his pocket. "I'm going to place a bid."

"And if you win the bid, then what will you do with it?" She couldn't fathom buying a piece like that, but she didn't have Tommy's money. Or his impulses.

"I'll put it in my garden. I think it'll look as spectacular there as it does here."

He was right—it would. He had plenty of space to accommodate a treasure like this.

When he put his phone away and moved closer to her, she asked, "Is this the part where you seduce me?"

"Not out here, Sophie. We're going back inside, where I can seduce you into kissing me on the dance floor."

Her pulse jumped in her throat. "I told you before that I wasn't going to do that."

"I know. But somewhere deep down, you know you want to."

Heaven forbid, but that was true. She imagined a wicked kiss on the dance floor. "You're right," she said. "I do want to. But I'm glad our identities are hidden." Of course that only added to the mystique, the feeling of the forbidden. "I told Jenny my name, but we're still strangers to her."

He stood in front of the statue, and with the way the floodlights were illuminating him, he looked down-right sexy, especially in his mask. "I have no idea who Jenny is."

"The blonde in the attic."

"The other tiger hunter? If you see her again, don't tell her we found it. I want to keep this bad boy to myself."

Sophie wanted to keep her bad boy to herself, too. But suddenly, the thought of their affair ending and him resuming relationships with other women made her uncomfortably possessive. To combat the feeling, she reminded herself that her only concern should be the baby, not hanging on to Tommy. "I'd like to grab a bite before we dance."

"Sure. Let's get something spicy."

She glanced at his mouth. "Appetizers to enhance the taste of our kiss?"

He smiled. "That sounds good to me."

To her, too, she thought. But she didn't reply.

They proceeded to the dining room, and he made up their plates. They ate in silence, indulging in honey chipotle wings, cheesy jalapeño poppers and hot-and-smoky meatballs, then topping it all off with fresh mint ice cream from the dessert bar.

"Are you ready to dance?" he asked, when they finished their last sweet-and-creamy spoonfuls.

"In a second." She set aside her empty bowl, battling a case of nerves. Aside from proper little pecks, she'd never kissed anyone in public.

He fingered the edges of his bow tie. "I can wait as long as you need me to."

She suspected that he was turned on by her hesitation. "How is it that you always seem to get your way?"

He lowered his hand. "You don't have to do this, Sophie."

But she wanted to. Nervous or not, she was too aroused to backpedal. She linked her arm through his, encouraging him to escort her to the ballroom. "I can handle it."

"Yes, ma'am. Whatever you say."

Off they went. Once they arrived on the dance floor, he immediately swept her into a glorious waltz. He moved naturally, easily. But he knew the steps, too. She knew he didn't like these types of events, but apparently he'd learned to waltz just fine.

"I've always wanted to slow-dance with you," he said. "Except in my fantasies, we would be at a honky-tonk bar with a bit more hip action." He softened his voice. "Then again, this is pretty damned nice, too."

Yes, she thought, so incredibly nice. The chandelier above their heads cast a magical glow, giving her the Cinderella vibe again. She leaned in to kiss him. At this point, she just needed to fill her senses.

The taste of him burst on her tongue, causing a tangle of excitement to unfurl in her belly. This could have been their very first kiss, it was so thrilling.

She pressed closer, and as he held her, they kissed some more. Spices and lust, she thought. Cool mint and fiery heat. Sophie moaned, her frilly mask bumping against his.

This was no fairy tale, she thought. This was heat and hunger. She rubbed herself against him, needing more of it.

Finally, she pulled back, putting a proper distance between them. In that reckless instant, she wished that they were at a honky-tonk bar. She'd practically been mauling her date at a charity ball.

She sucked in her breath and peered at the other masked dancers. As far as she could tell, no one was gawking at them. Or gossiping about who they might be or why they were being so ill-behaved. Hadn't anyone noticed that something inappropriate had just happened?

Of course they did, she thought. She just couldn't read the expressions on their masked faces or hear their voices. Besides, at this point, Sophie's mind was fogged. Her skin was still tingling, too. She could barely contain her reactions to Tommy.

"You survived it," he said.

"Yes, I suppose I did." But would this high-society crowd think she was a fool if they uncovered the truth? Would they scorn her for how she was handling this situation? Sooner or later, the public would know. She and Tommy had agreed that once she was good and pregnant, his publicist would announce their news.

His lips curved. "Should we kiss again?"

She glanced at his mouth, and the heat in her belly grew tighter, stronger. But she fought the craving. "I think we should wait until we get home."

"I want to swim naked with you. In my pool, under the waterfalls."

Her mind spun. "Sounds tempting. Do you think we really should?"

He nodded. "It's a great evening for it. The weather is mild, but even if the temperature drops later, it won't matter. I always keep the water warm at this time of year. We can use the pool house to get undressed." He softly added, "Or if you want to let go of all of your inhibitions, we can strip outside and leave our clothes wherever they fall."

Could she do something like that? She didn't know. But for now, she and Tommy were still dancing, swaying in each other's arms.

Until the masquerade was over.

Eight

Tommy was a lucky son of a gun. First he'd gotten Sophie to kiss him at the ball, and now he'd baited her to strip down by the pool. He probably shouldn't be so damn thrilled about corrupting her, though. With the moon shining brightly, she looked like a deer in the headlights, standing there in her pretty little panties and bra.

"What if the bracelet or earrings get lost or damaged?" She grouped them together on a patio table. "They must be terribly expensive, and they're only on loan to you."

"They'll be fine." He was in his underwear, too, and anxious to peel it off and dive into the water. "No one is going to come out here and mess with anything." He'd already notified his staff that the area was off-limits tonight.

She sighed. "I shouldn't be leaving a dress like this

draped over a chair. You must have spent a fortune on it, and here we are, treating it like a gunnysack. It's such a beautiful gown, so delicately made. And our masks." She arranged them just so, beside the jewelry.

Tommy wasn't concerned about what happened to their clothes. He didn't even care if the diamonds or garnets she'd worn got lost or damaged. He had enough dough to pay for them, if need be. "I just bought a tiger the size of a tree." He'd won the bid and was having the statue delivered in a few days. "What things cost isn't an issue."

"I know, but…"

"Stop fussing about it." He glanced at the pile of jewelry on the table. "I should have bought it for you, anyway."

She sent him a you're-a-madman look. Then she said, "It's bad enough that I let you pay for the dress. I'm not going to let you turn me into your mistress and start giving me jewelry, too."

"Don't be so dramatic. I've given you expensive gifts before."

"Not jewelry."

"Women make too much of that. Are you ready?" He yanked off his underwear and dived into the pool. He waded in the water, watching her, curious to gauge her reaction before he swam away.

Still wearing her lingerie, she stepped closer to the edge of the pool. "The second waterfall is where your private apartment is. The cave no one except you is allowed to enter."

"I'm going to disengage the alarm, so you can come inside with me." He couldn't explain why he wanted her to share that space with him. He'd built it as his own personal haven, the ultimate man cave. For the most part, Tommy maintained it himself. He didn't have to swim to get there, not unless he wanted to. An elevator on the other side of the pool descended to a water-free entrance, but he rarely used that door.

"What's going on with you?" Sophie asked. "First you're talking about buying me jewelry and now this?"

He smoothed back his wet hair. "I'm probably just feeling macho. I like trying to make you pregnant." He couldn't fathom why else he was behaving this way. "Maybe it'll be lucky for us." Without saying anything else, he submerged himself in the water and swam to his destination.

He dived under the waterfall and reached the cave. Once he was on solid ground, he punched out the numbers on the alarm and went inside.

The first room was merely a place to dry off, with heat lamps and towels. He waited for Sophie there. He was certain that she would find her way.

She appeared a few minutes later, soaking wet in her bra and panties. Little cheat, he thought. But dang, she looked good. Her makeup wasn't even smeared, at least not to the degree of having raccoon eyes. The stylist who'd done her face had probably used the waterproof stuff. Her upswept hairdo was drenched, but given how naturally pretty she was, it only enhanced her appeal.

"Here you go." He wrapped her in a towel and gave her one for her hair, too, which she was already hanging down.

"Thank you." She removed her underwear and dried off. She moved closer to the heat lamps, her damp locks tumbling down her back. "I'm curious to see this private place of yours."

"Sorry, but you're not getting the grand tour. I'm taking you straight to the bedroom."

"Lead the way, then."

Needing no further invitation, he scooped her up and carried her exactly where he wanted to go, passing the living room, kitchen and dining room to get there. The walls throughout the apartment were landscaped with limestone formations. The imperfections pleased him. The furniture, in contrast, was smooth and simple.

"This is quite the cave," she said.

"Yes, it is." No windows, no outside interference, nothing but deliberate solitude.

He'd never wanted to bring anyone here, especially a lover. Sophie was obviously different, somehow. But she'd always been part of his life, so maybe it wasn't so much of a stretch.

He placed her on the bed and followed her down. He didn't hesitate to kiss her. He went full bore, pushing his tongue past her lips. She made sounds of arousal, then arched her back and lifted her hips. He used his hands, playing her like an instrument.

When they stopped kissing, he said, "I really am going to write a song about you."

She gazed curiously at him. "A sexy one?"

"The sexiest." He climbed on top of her. "But I might come up with a ballad, too."

Her breath hitched. "So you're going to write two songs about me?"

"I might do an entire album." At the moment, he wanted to share his feelings for her, send them out into the universe.

"Just don't write any of your phony love songs about me."

He nudged her thighs apart. "Phony?"

She traced rings around his nipples, coiling closer to

their flat brown surface, making him feel as if he had jumper cables attached to his body.

"You know what I mean," she said.

Yeah, he knew. Tommy had a poetic side that didn't fit the rest of his personality. She snaked her arms around him, and he entered her, wet and deep.

Together, they made lust-drenched love, holding each other close. The fire between them burned bright. And so did his fascination with her.

She looked mystical, like a mermaid he'd captured at sea. He twined his fingers through her long, ropy hair, grateful that she'd chosen him to sire her child. The more they worked on the baby, the closer he was to making her dreams come true. He'd already gotten his dream of fame and fortune, making music that touched people's souls. He wanted to touch hers, as deeply as he could.

She sighed, and he reached between her legs, rubbing her softly, then with more intensity. She bit her bottom lip and scratched her nails down his back.

When she came, she gasped and shuddered, her breaths warm and silky against his neck. Tommy came, too, his pulse roaring in his ears.

Afterward, they lay side by side, staring up at the rugged limestone ceiling, a languid silence between them. As always, he hoped that he'd made her pregnant. That he'd done his job. But right now, he wasn't going to worry about being the donor and not the dad, and whether the kid would resent him for it. He knew better than to stress about Sophie's baby. She would be parent enough for both of them.

He turned to her and said, "We're still going to skinny-dip later. We didn't actually get to do that."

She shifted onto her side, facing him, as well. "You did."

"Not with you, I didn't. We swam here separately, and you showed up in your bra and panties. I want to see you under the water, bare as the day you were born." He revealed what he'd been thinking about her earlier. "You already remind me of a mermaid."

"So if we swim naked together, I can seem like one for real?" She wiggled her toes. "Problem is, I don't have a tail."

"That's something I'm willing to overlook."

"You have a lot of fantasies, Tommy."

"When it involves you, I do. I've never obsessed over anyone the way I have over you. Just think of all those years I flirted with you, letting you know how badly I wanted you, while other women were throwing themselves at me."

"That's easy to define."

He frowned. "It is?"

She nodded. "I presented a challenge, and you thrived on the chase."

And he was still chasing her, he realized. "Aside from you, I've always been careful not to go after the ones who might reject me." He didn't put himself in positions of getting hurt. Or having his pride damaged or whatever. "That's hardly anything to brag about."

She flashed a cat-that-ate-the-canary smile. Or maybe she was the canary, devouring the big ol' tomcat.

"You're amused that I'm being humble?" he asked.

"Can you blame me? You're normally so conceited."

"I just pretend to be." He wasn't going to lie, not after the way she'd trapped him with that satisfied smile of hers. "I act more confident than I am."

She squinted, a bit skeptical now, it seemed. "So you don't really think you're handsome and charming?"

"Well, I wouldn't go that far." He shrugged, making a silly joke. "But in all seriousness, I know I'm a terrible catch and that my inability to commit makes me less desirable."

"I wouldn't be sleeping with you if it wasn't for the baby," she reminded him.

"That just proves how deep our friendship really is." He ran his hands down her body, caressing her, letting her know that he needed her again.

"You're definitely the best friend I've ever had, even if you drive me crazy."

He leaned over her. "Am I driving you nuts now?"

"Absolutely." With a sweet and dreamy sigh, she returned his touch, showing him how much she needed him, too.

After they made love for the second time, Sophie cuddled in Tommy's arms, feeling warm and toasty. Romantic, she thought, like one of the ballads she'd told him not to write about her.

She pressed closer to him. "I shouldn't have said what I did."

He trailed a finger along her spine. "About what?"

"Your ballads being phony. Your slow songs have always been my favorites."

"I'm not offended by what you said. Everyone knows that love isn't my thing. But it's easy for me to write about because I've seen how it affects other people, when they're happy or sad, when it makes them euphoric, when it breaks them. Remember how devastated Conrad was when his wife left him?"

"How could I forget?" His guitar player had nearly lost his mind over his divorce. "But he wasn't faithful to her." She frowned. "I hated being witness to that."

Sophie got tired of seeing the infidelities that occurred on the road.

"I try to stay out of the band's personal affairs. But it bothers me when they cheat on their wives and girl-friends, too. It reminds me of how my dad treated my mom, I guess, and that stupid arrangement they had. I never understood how that benefited my mother."

"It didn't, obviously. Especially when Kirby didn't even follow the rules they'd agreed on."

He blew out a breath. "I'm glad Mack has never stepped out on Jean. She's everything to him, her and the kids."

She thought about his drummer and how madly in love he and his wife were. "They definitely have something special." She kept her head on Tommy's shoulder. "Do you think that you shy away from com-mitment because of the effect your parents' marriage had on you?"

"I don't know. Maybe, probably." He expelled an-other audible breath. "This is as committed as I've ever been, and it's not even supposed to last."

"*This?* You mean us? Our affair?"

When he nodded, she said, "You're right. It's not supposed to last." But for now, she wanted to make the most of it. She just hoped that she didn't long for him when it was over. That she didn't stay awake at night, pregnant and alone, wondering what he was doing or whom he was with. To keep her mind from straying too far in that direction, she bit playfully at his arm. The last thing she needed was to pine after him, the way she did when they were younger.

He laughed a little. "Why'd you do that?"

"It's your punishment."

"For what?"

"Being so good in bed." And for making her think painful thoughts.

He rolled over on top of her. "Then I should bite you back because you're just as good." He peered into her face. "We should go skinny-dipping now."

"Sure. Why not?" Maybe it would benefit her to jump into the water, to feel it rush over her. "Are we coming back here afterward or going back to your house?"

"Whichever you prefer."

"We'll go back to the house." She didn't want to leave their clothes and masks outside all night. Or the jewels he'd claimed that he should buy her.

"Then let's go." He got up and reached for her hand.

When they left, he reset the alarm, and they stood at the edge of the water, diving in at the same time.

She felt like a mermaid, sleek and smooth and free. Tommy seemed like a merman, too, gliding effortlessly beside her.

They came to the surface, and he swam over to a corner seat at one side of the pool. She followed him, and they shared the space, as close as two beings could be. Naked and wet, they kissed. Taking it a bit further, she crawled onto his lap and made him hard, simply for the fun of it.

After that, they played in the water, splashing and flirting. Once they quieted down, she floated on her back with her hair fanned out around her. Tommy watched her with longing in his eyes.

A short while later they climbed out of the water. He produced a stack of towels and two thick robes from the pool house, and they dried off and bundled up.

"Did skinny-dipping with me live up to your fantasy?" she asked, as they prepared to gather their belongings and return to the mansion.

"Oh, yeah." He grinned boyishly, happily. "It definitely did."

She thought about her bad-girl fantasy and her desire to be watched. She'd convinced herself that she was too shy to do it. But there was a part of her that desperately wanted to. If she told Tommy how she felt, would he be shocked? No doubt it would arouse the hell out of him. But she kept quiet. She just wasn't ready to go there.

Nonetheless, she was still feeling sleek and sexy. She grabbed a hold of him, and they kissed with heat and vigor. They even slipped their hands into each other's robes, feeling for whatever flesh they could find.

Would they ever stop wanting each other?

Of course they would, the practical side of Sophie's mixed-up mind answered. Just as soon as she was pregnant and their skyrocketing affair came crashing back to earth.

A week after the masquerade ball, Sophie returned from the office and changed into comfortable clothes. She loved being home by five thirty and kicking back for the rest of the night. Overall, she appreciated her new job and enjoyed assisting Tommy's manager. Sophie already knew how to run a tour, and now Barbara was teaching her more about advertising, marketing and the financial end of the business. She'd had a particularly interesting day today. While they were going over current contracts and negotiations, Barbara informed her about a highly lucrative reality-show deal that Tommy was refusing to consider.

Funny, but he'd never even mentioned it to Sophie. Clearly, he didn't tell her everything that pertained to his career...or his personal life, for that matter. She was still learning new things about him. Especially sexual things, she thought. She certainly knew his bedroom preferences now.

As for herself, her voyeuristic fantasy was getting stronger. Should she do it? The idea of being really, really bad thrilled her. But she was still grappling with the self-consciousness of it.

Clearing her mind, she made her way to the kitchen and opened the fridge. Chef knew that she liked to nibble between meals and always had something ready for her. If he wasn't there to give the food directly to her, he wrote her name on the containers.

Just as Sophie turned around, Dottie entered the kitchen, with her twinkling blue eyes and short graying hair.

She smiled and said, "I see you found what Chef left for you."

"I did, indeed." He'd been spoiling Sophie since the day she moved in, and she adored him for it. Chef Bryan was a quiet man, in his late fifties, with a shiny bald head and a heart of gold. "Where is he, anyway?"

"He left early today. He has a date."

"Really?" Instantly intrigued, Sophie wondered more about it. She'd always been interested in other people's love lives. When she was a teenager, she used to document her friends' experiences in her diary and then read them her entries to see if they approved. She never wrote down who Tommy went out with, though. She hadn't wanted to put his conquests on paper or discuss them with him. "I didn't know Chef was seeing someone."

"It's his first time meeting her. They connected on an online dating site. For older folks." Dottie made a goofy face. "Tommy is going to send someone out for pizza tonight. That's what he decided to have since Chef isn't here."

That sounded good to Sophie. "Where is Tommy?" She hadn't seen him since she'd come home.

"In his studio. But he should be taking a break soon. He has your dogs with him. They were with me earlier, but he nabbed them. Hokey and Pokey are such characters."

"Yes. They're a couple of rascals." They dashed around the mansion as if they owned the place, and Tommy indulged them as if they did.

Dottie leaned closer. "So, what type of snack did Chef prepare for you?"

"I don't know. I haven't peeked inside yet." Sophie lifted the lid and poked around. "Cheese, crackers, artichoke dip, roasted chickpeas, turkey-and-cucumber roll-ups. Good, healthy things. Oh, and look, he included ants on a log. I told him they were my favorite when I was little. That my dad used to fix them for me, and now Chef made them for me, too."

"That's so nice. He catered my niece's birthday party and made the most adorable appetizers. Not just ants on a log, but butterflies, caterpillars and snails, too. He used celery sticks and peanut butter with crackers and fruit and pretzels to create them. He also made apple bites that looked like happy-faced monsters and desserts the kids could decorate themselves."

Sophie imagined him catering her child's parties, too. "How old is your niece?"

"Five. She's my grandniece, actually. My sister's spunky little granddaughter." Dottie removed her phone from her pocket and flashed a photo of a freckle-faced girl with a gap-toothed grin. "Her name is Kelly."

"She's darling." Sophie smiled. "As cute as can be."

"I think so, too, but I'm biased. I got her a trampoline for her birthday. It's what she wanted. Thank goodness it has a safety net around it." Dottie sighed and stepped back, rolling her neck and arching her back. "I'm about ready to quit for the day and put my feet up."

Sophie nodded. Dottie lived on the premises and had been managing Tommy's household since her husband died. She'd never had any children, and hence had no grandchildren of her own, either. She needed to be commended for taking such good care of Tommy, even if she didn't always approve of his lifestyle.

"You do a wonderful job around here," Sophie said.

"Thank you, honey. That means a lot coming from you. Now go and enjoy your snacks."

"I think I'll eat in the garden and visit the tiger Tommy bought."

Dottie laughed. "At least it's only a statue. Be sure to text him in case he wants to see you on his break. Otherwise he'll be searching high and wide for you."

"I will." Sophie grabbed a bottle of water and exited the kitchen through a back door. She took the grassy path to the garden. The weather was starting to cool off a bit, but not enough to need a jacket. At least not right now. In an hour or so, it could get breezy.

She parked herself on the bench in front of the tiger and texted Tommy. He didn't reply, so she munched on her goodies. While she was on her second turkey-and-cucumber roll-up, her phone signaled a text. Tommy was on his way to see her.

When he appeared, he looked downright dreamy, rugged to the core, in crisp denims and battered cowboy boots.

"Sophie-Kophie," he said and sat next to her. "How are you?"

"I'm good. So where are my dogs? Dottie said they were with you."

"They're asleep in my studio. They were watching animal videos on the internet earlier."

She raised her eyebrows, picturing it in her mind. "They chose what to watch all by themselves?"

He shrugged. "I might have had a hand in it."

"No doubt." She offered him the snack box. "Are you hungry?"

"I'll take a few of those." He picked through the roasted chickpeas. He eyeballed the ants on a log and grinned. "What are you, in kindergarten again?"

She defended herself. "I can't help it if Chef babies me."

"Everyone loves having you here. They're never going to want you to leave."

With the way things were going, she was afraid that she was never going to want to leave, either. But she was still trying to get pregnant, so there was no need to rush. When the time came, she would quit obsessing about being Tommy's live-in lover and return to her own home. She mulled over the way she'd phrased it. *Live-in lover.* It sounded so real. But it wasn't. Not with how temporary it was.

He took another handful of the legumes. "How was work today?"

"Funny you should ask." She paused to regroup her thoughts. "Barbara told me about *Music Mentors* and how badly they want you to do the show. I don't understand why you're not considering it."

"Because I'd have to commit to two years of being a mentor and hold off on touring on my own. Then I'd have to tour with my protégés as my opening acts, with the show controlling the whole thing."

"Yes, but they book some exceptional tours. Besides, I think you'd enjoy scouring clubs for up-and-coming artists to mentor. You'd have a lot of clout in that regard. You'd get to pick your protégés yourself. And your segments would be filmed right here in Nashville."

"I agree that it would be nice to help new acts make it in this business. But doing television would still be too much of a commitment for me. I need more freedom than that."

"Then I guess there's no point in discussing it. But the amount of money they're offering you is staggering. More than anyone else who's ever been on the show." Tommy had the perfect personality for reality TV and the producers obviously knew it.

He shrugged. "I should get back to my studio."

"Okay. Then I'll see you later for pizza."

"So you know about that, huh? Chef taking the rest of the day off for a date? Speaking of which, I haven't kissed you since this morning." He homed in on her, putting his face wonderfully close to hers.

Her heart pounded with excitement. After he kissed her, she decided that she was going to unleash her fantasy. This very evening. With him. No holds barred. She was going to make it happen.

At this point, there was no reason to put it off. She had a right to explore her sexuality, to become her own woman.

She said, "I'm going to give you a thrill tonight."

He touched her cheek. "You always thrill me, Soph."

"I'm capable of thrilling you even more." Dizzying as this feeling was, she liked the power it gave her. "But you'll have to wait to see what I mean. And you'll have to say 'please.'"

He furrowed his brow. "Even if I don't know what I'm saying it for?"

"Yes." Him not knowing made it more exciting for

her. She needed this. She really, truly did. "When we were younger, you used to make me say 'pretty please with five pounds of sugar on top' when I wanted something from you. But you didn't always give in."

"I'm giving in now." He lowered the tone of his voice. "How about 'pretty please with all of the sugar in the world on top'?"

She couldn't help but smile. "Then what choice do I have?" She was going to fulfill her own fantasy, giving him a night to remember, too.

Nine

At bedtime, Tommy waited for Sophie to get undressed, but she stayed in her jeans and blouse. She'd told him to keep what he had on, too. So he stood there, fully clothed and thoroughly confused.

Ignoring him for now, she moved two chairs from his dining alcove to the center of the bedroom. She placed them across from each other, but not too close, leaving a purposeful span between them. Earlier she'd promised that she was going to give him a thrill, and he was intrigued by the mystery of it all.

"That's your chair." She pointed to the one on the right. "And that's mine." She gestured to the second seat.

He noticed that hers was in shadow. "What should I do now?"

"Just sit and behave."

If he weren't so fascinated by whatever she was

planning, he might've laughed. She was being adorably bossy. He parked his butt in the chair. "Can I at least take off my boots?"

"No."

"Why not?"

"Because they're sexy, and I like how you look in them."

He thought they were old and dusty, but who was he to argue?

She roamed her gaze over him, assessing him in ways he couldn't begin to understand. Then she said, "Open your legs some more."

He was already slouched in a wide-legged spread. But he wasn't foolish enough to protest. He followed her order. Nonetheless, he asked, "Is there a reason I have to sit this way?"

"Other than me enjoying seeing you that way? No, there isn't."

Tommy shivered all the way to his battered boots. "Can I unzip my jeans to alleviate the pressure?" By now, he was getting hard.

She shook her head. "I'll unzip them for you later."

"You're making me suffer, Soph." But he liked it, and was eager for whatever came next.

She took her seat. "This is nice, isn't it?"

"If *nice* is another word for *hot*, then, yeah, this is the nicest thing anyone has ever done to me." He could barely breathe. He'd never had a woman torture him this way.

"Just so you know, this is my fantasy, Tommy. Something I always imagined, something forbidden I always wanted to do. But it's also something you told me that you like your lovers to do."

His brain kicked into gear. Suddenly he knew; he understood. "I'm going to watch you."

"Yes." She removed her bra without even taking off her blouse. She simply maneuvered her arms, pulling it out from beneath the hem.

He was impressed by her slick move. She was definitely giving him a thrill, making good on her promise.

She dropped her bra onto the floor. Her nipples were poking against her blouse. He'd heard that women's areolas sometimes got darker with pregnancy. He wondered if that would happen to her.

"I'm not taking my jeans off," she said. "I'm just going to…" She opened the zipper and tugged them down, just enough to expose her panties.

Tommy let out the breath he'd been holding. Her panties consisted of multicolored lace and a cute little bow. She slipped her hand past the waistband, and he feared he would lose his mind.

She moved her hand, sliding it lower. He watched her, bewitched by her modesty, by how sweet and sensual she was. Everything about her turned him on: the way she nibbled on her bottom lip, the dreamy expression in her eyes, the cascade of her unbound hair.

She rubbed gently, touching herself ever so lightly.

"Is that how you always do it?" he asked. "Softly like that?"

"Yes," she responded breathlessly.

"Have you ever thought about me when you were doing it?"

"Yes," she said again. "More times than I can count."

"You look beautiful." So damn gorgeous, he thought.

"Maybe I can…" She pulled her jeans farther down. She tugged her panties lower, too.

Now Tommy could see the top of her mound. She was getting braver, letting some of her modesty go. He couldn't take his eyes off her.

"Come for me, Sophie," he whispered. "Come while I'm watching you."

She peeked at him through drowsy eyelids. She looked stoned, high on seducing him. He was hooked, that was for sure.

She opened her legs, caught her breath and rocked in her seat. She kept touching herself; it was perfection in every way. So hot. So erotic.

Tommy studied every move she made.

When she came, her orgasm was a thing of beauty, of sugar and spice and everything nice. Now that word made complete sense.

Nice, nice, nice.

Fixated on the sweet sounds she made, he absorbed her emotions, taking them deep inside.

She sighed and removed her hand from her panties.

He waited until her eyes were less glazed before he said, "That was incredible. Thank you for letting me be part of it."

Her smile was rife with sensuality. "I needed to make that happen, to free my inhibitions. But now it's your turn to feel good."

"I'm already feeling good." He was still mesmerized by her.

"Then it's your turn to feel even better." She stood and righted her clothes. "This is part of my fantasy, too." She got on her knees in front of him, and their gazes locked.

Desperate to touch her, he caressed her face. Silent, she undid his jeans and freed him, his desire more than evident.

When she lowered her head and took him in her mouth, everything went blank, except the mindless pleasure she gave him.

* * *

Tommy and Sophie spent the next two weeks working on the baby, doing what they were meant to do. And now he waited nervously outside the bathroom door. Sophie's cycle was four days late, and she was taking a pregnancy test. According to the instructions, this test could be taken as early as one day after a missed period. Bearing that in mind, he figured that four days was plenty of time for an accurate reading.

As soon as the door clicked open and she emerged, he anxiously asked, "What did it say?"

"It says that we did it, Tommy! I'm going to have a baby!" She squealed and leaped into his arms.

He spun her around, like they were kids on a carousel. He couldn't remember being this excited, not even when he'd gotten his first number one hit. Lord almighty, but nothing compared to creating a life. An embryo in her womb, he thought. A teeny, tiny speck that would develop into a human being. Amazing how something so minuscule could be so monumental.

They stopped spinning and broke into laughter. Sophie was going to be a mommy. She was going to have the child she wanted so badly.

A second later, they went warmly, sweetly quiet. He lifted her T-shirt and splayed a hand across her stomach.

Her eyes glistened with tears. "Thank you for doing this for me."

"You're welcome." He poked her belly button, proud and awed that he'd become a successful donor. He couldn't imagine what being an actual dad would be like.

But then he stopped himself; that wasn't part of the plan. Tommy being the father wasn't in the baby's best interest. Still, he couldn't help but wonder if he would be as terrible at it as he first thought. Not that it mattered. This was Sophie's baby. He'd signed a contract that absolutely, positively said so. Besides, he was just feeling all good and manly about making her pregnant. And that had nothing to do with being a parent.

"So what happens now?" he asked.

She stepped back, out of his arms. "I'll call my doctor and make an appointment to see him."

That was the logical answer, but he was thinking on a more personal level. "Is it okay to tell my family? Or Dottie or Chef Bryan? And what about Barbara? You work with her every day."

"We can tell the people we're closest to, but I don't want the public to know. It's too early for that. I want to be at least twelve weeks along before we make a formal announcement. The first trimester is the most precarious, and I don't want to jinx it."

He didn't like the sound of that. "Maybe you shouldn't go back home right away. It'd probably be better if you stayed here."

"I'll be fine, Tommy."

"I know. But it just seems safer." He would worry if she was by herself. "Plus, I'd like to see how you're progressing each day. I'd be glad to go to your doctor appointments with you, if you don't mind the company."

"Really?" She sounded surprised by his offer, but appreciative, too. "Thank you. I'd like that."

He made another offer, a riskier one, this time. "You can keep sleeping in my room."

She blinked at him. "But our affair was supposed to end when I got pregnant."

"I realize that's what we agreed on. But it doesn't have to be over this soon, not if we're both still enjoying it." He wasn't ready to let her go just yet, and he hoped she wasn't ready to be rid of him, either. He just wanted a little more time together.·

She met his gaze. "I do enjoy it."

"I do, too." So damn much, he thought. "So should we keep at it?"

Her breath rushed out. Was she going to agree? Or would she decide to stick to their original plan and go back home by herself? He waited, hoping her decision would go in his favor.

Finally she said, "I'll stay." They gazed silently at each other, and she hurriedly added, "But once I'm farther along, after this first trimester is over, I'll go home and that will be the end of it. Does that work for you?"

"Yes, of course." He wasn't expecting anything more. "I'm going to try to get back on the road later, anyway. I'm still hoping to add some dates to this latest tour."

"You better hurry up and hire a road manager to replace me." She paused. "Or have you found someone already?"

"No, not yet. But I will." He teased her. "You just keep sidelining me."

She smiled. "Me and my zest for motherhood?"

"Yep." He drew her into his arms again, holding her close and resting his hand on her stomach, where her baby was destined to grow.

The next morning, Sophie sat across from Tommy on the balcony, picking at her breakfast. She'd barely slept a wink the night before. Was she doing the right thing by remaining at his house? By sleeping with him? A less attached woman would have returned to her own home, her own life, her own everything.

Moving the eggs around on her plate, she glanced

up at him. What if she didn't want to leave later? What if she started craving a real relationship with Tommy, something committed, something long and lasting and deep? She would be in major trouble if that happened.

"Do you think you're going to be sick?" he asked.

She stilled her fork. "I'm sorry. What?"

"Do you think you're going to get morning sickness and all of that?"

"I don't know. Most women do, I guess. But there should be ways to alleviate it. I'll talk to my doctor about it, just in case." She studied him in the overcast light. The clouds blocked the sun, creating a hazy ambience.

He refreshed his coffee from the carafe on the table. She was drinking herbal tea. She knew that caffeine wasn't good for pregnant women.

"When are you going to call your doctor?" he asked.

"Today, as soon as his office opens. I'm hoping they can get me in within the next few days. But maybe it would be better if you didn't go with me to any of my appointments."

Tommy frowned. "Why not?"

Because having him there might make her feel even closer to him, and she was already struggling with those feelings. "I think it'll create some problems." In all sorts of ways, she thought. "You're too famous to walk into my doctor's office without anyone recognizing you. And since it's an OB-GYN, it might make people wonder what you're doing there. Another patient might snap a picture of you and Tweet about it. And then the media will start speculating, and our plan to keep this under wraps could fall to pieces."

His frown deepened. "So we'll arrange to go through a private entrance like I do with my doctor."

"I don't want anyone making special allowances for me. Besides, it could still turn into a three-ring circus if someone on the nursing staff is a fan of yours." She knew how giddy people got in his presence, especially the young, crush-crazed types.

"You didn't have a problem with this last night."

"I was caught up in the moment. But now I'm thinking a bit more clearly." Or she was trying to, anyway.

"I understand that having to deal with my celebrity can get overwhelming. But it doesn't have to be the three-ring circus you talked about." He leaned forward in his chair. "I can get you your own private physician, and he or she can come to the house. You can have your appointments right here."

"Oh, my goodness, Tommy. That's way too much. I want to see my own doctor in his own office. And I want to do it by myself."

He expelled a hard sigh. "All right. But when we announce that I'm your baby's donor, you're still going to have to cope with the media side of this."

"I know. But I'll be geared up for it by then. Plus, I won't be living here anymore. I'll be at my house, and you'll be working toward getting back on the road." They would be separate entities. Or at least that was the plan.

He sent her a concerned look. "You're not having second thoughts about staying here now, are you?"

Yes, she most definitely was. But she didn't want to bring her fears to his attention. Nothing would be worse than falling in love with him. She knew what a disaster that would be. Yet even as panicked as she was, she wasn't ready to give him up completely.

"Are you?" he persisted.

"Am I what?" she replied, confused.

"Having second thoughts about staying here for the next twelve weeks?"

"No," she lied. But with any luck, she would be prepared to part ways with him by then.

"I'm really glad you're going to stay." A devilish smile spread across his face. "You're as beautiful as ever, Soph. Sexy, too. Pregnancy suits you."

She clucked her tongue, playing down his desire. "You say that now, but you're not going to think I'm sexy when my hormones kick into gear."

"Nothing is going to change how hot you are to me. Now, get over here, little mama, and climb onto my lap." He patted his thighs for effect, flirting shamelessly with her.

Was it wrong that she liked him calling her "little mama"? Or that she wanted him as badly as he appeared to want her? She gave up the fight and flirted with him, too. "I'm not going to bump and grind with you over breakfast. But if you sit perfectly still, I might come over there and give you a long, luscious kiss."

He flexed his hands. "I won't move, I promise."

She left her seat and scooted onto his lap, looping her arms around his neck. He groaned, and she kissed him soft and deep. When she broke her lips away from his, he nuzzled her cheek.

"So is there anything new going on with you?" she asked. "Besides making your best friend pregnant?"

"Ha ha. Funny lady. Actually, I've been thinking about going to Texas to see Matt. And I'd love for you to join me. If your doctor says it's all right for you to travel, do you want to go? Maybe even this weekend?"

"Oh, wow. Really? That soon?" She'd spent a portion of her life being on the road with Tommy, and now he was suggesting a quick getaway. But maybe a little vacation would be a nice change of pace. "I'll check with my doctor. But I'm sure it won't be a problem. Pregnant women travel all the time."

"I'll need to call Matt to arrange it, but he told me before that I could visit anytime. It'll certainly be a lot more fun having you there, sharing the experience with me. Since Libby has been going back and forth and is returning to Texas this weekend, we could offer her a seat on my plane with the three of us making the trip together."

"I like that idea. It would be good for you to get to know your brother better." And Sophie could get to know Libby better, too. With everything that had been going on, they hadn't seen each other since the picnic at Kirby's.

"Then it's a date." He rocked her gently, keeping her on his lap. "Since it's a recreational ranch, there will be plenty of things for us to do. The weather is nice at this time of year, too." He paused and added, "Of course, for now we can't reveal that I'm Matt's brother. But Matt and I already have a cover story, where we'll just say that we're friends."

She understood that they were protecting Matt's identity until the book came out. Just as Sophie was protecting the secret of her pregnancy until she was further along.

But the biggest thing she needed to protect was her heart, and keep it far, far away from Tommy.

Sophie was used to flying on Tommy's private jet. It was the same plane he used when he toured. At the moment, he was kicking back in one of the bedrooms, and Sophie and Libby sat side by side in the main compartment.

"This is so luxurious," Libby said, with her big blue eyes all aglow. "Up until now, I've been taking commercial flights. Kirby pays for me to travel first class, though, so I can't complain."

"How's the book coming?" Sophie asked, curious about the process.

"I'm working on the rough draft, so it's moving along. I still have a few more interviews to conduct, but I can fill those areas in later." Libby tucked a strand of her wavy blond hair behind her ear. "I still need to talk to you and Tommy about the details of your donor agreement and how much of it you're comfortable sharing in the book."

"We can discuss all of that this weekend. It won't really matter because by the time the book comes out the news will be public knowledge anyway." At that point, Sophie would have gotten used to people knowing who her baby's donor was.

"Yes, but it's important for me to tell it in the way you and Tommy want it to be told. For example, do you want me to disclose the fact that you're together?"

Sophie's heart bumped inside her chest. "We won't be together by then." Libby obviously knew that Sophie and Tommy were lovers. Kirby probably told her, maybe even in reference to the book since that seemed to be a concern of Libby's. "Me moving in with Tommy was just a temporary arrangement while I became pregnant. I'll be staying just a bit longer now, but it's still going to end."

The blonde flashed a dimpled smile. "Are you sure about that? If it was a regular donor situation, you wouldn't have been together to begin with, and now that you're pregnant, you're still together. That seems more like a relationship than a business arrangement to me."

"It isn't." Sophie defended the absurdity of remaining Tommy's bedmate. "I'm only staying with him through my first trimester. Then I'll be going home."

"And you'll stop…sharing a bed?"

"Yes, definitely." She tried to sound less worried than she was. She didn't want to admit that she had fears about falling in love with him.

Libby shifted in her seat. She sat near the window, with clouds floating by. "I hope I'm not meddling, but I think you'd make a great couple."

Sophie shook her head, trying to keep calm. This wasn't a conversation she'd expected to have. "It just seems that way because Tommy and I are such close friends."

"Yes, but that's what gives you the background for developing a relationship. And it's obvious how strong your chemistry is."

Determined to lessen the significance of their attraction, she waved her hand, brushing it off. "That'll go away."

"Really? How? Just by willing it away? Matt and I tried to have a no-strings affair and now look at us."

Engaged and raising a family together? None of that applied to Sophie. "It's different for me and Tommy. We only got together so I could have my baby. I never would have been with him otherwise. He's just too much of a player."

"I'm aware of Tommy's history. But he doesn't seem that way now that he's with you."

"That's just an illusion." A magic trick, she thought. "He'll go back to his old ways when the newness of what we're doing wears off."

"I guess you know his patterns better than anyone."

"Yes, I do." She knew how flighty he could be, how

easily distracted, and she couldn't imagine him being any other way. "Besides, I'm not interested in having him as my partner." She knew better than to want the impossible.

"Okay. But if things get complicated, and you ever need someone to talk to, I'm a good listener."

"Thank you. That's sweet. But I'm fine with how things are." Or so she kept telling herself.

Either way, she didn't think that Libby believed her. Matt's fiancée seemed to know that Sophie was struggling with her feelings. She just hoped that Tommy didn't figure it out, too.

Ten

The Flying Creek Ranch was a magnificent place. Sophie loved the layout of the land and the vast beauty of the Texas Hill Country. Some of the regular activities included horseback riding, hayrides, hiking, swimming, fishing, skeet shooting, campfires, barn dances, horseshoes and Ping-Pong.

Matt insisted that they stay at his house instead of in one of the guest cabins or at the main lodge. The single-story, custom-built home he shared with Libby and Chance was beautifully crafted, big and woodsy with stone floors.

Sophie had already gotten a glimpse of the three of them together at Kirby's, but seeing them here in their own environment was even more compelling. But that wasn't the half of it. Tommy's interaction with Chance was really doing a number on her.

She stood in the doorway of the den and watched

them from across the expansive room. Tommy was playing a video game with Chance and getting along brilliantly with the boy. Typically Tommy didn't click with children; it wasn't his forte. But soon after they'd arrived, six-year-old Chance started following Tommy around like a wolf cub, drawing him into the kid zone.

Dang it, Sophie thought. She was already worried about falling in love with Tommy, and this wasn't helping. Still, it made her heart glad to know that he was honing his kid skills.

Nonetheless, Chance was kicking his ass in the game. Funny, too, because it was a rodeo game and Tommy could ride mechanical bulls like nobody's business. The virtual ones? Apparently, not so much. But he was still enjoying himself. He laughed every time he screwed up, with Chance ribbing him along the way.

Libby came up beside Sophie and whispered, "They're cute together."

"Yes, they are." She spoke quietly, too. "So cute, so sweet." But she was trying not to get sucked too deeply into it, at least not where it would knock her into a lovesick abyss. "This is the first time Tommy has bonded with a child."

"Then I'm glad it could be with Chance."

"So am I." She moved away from the door, making sure their conversation remained private. Libby followed her down the hall and Sophie said, "You'd never know it by the way Tommy is playing that game, but he's an incredible cowboy. We already talked about him teaching my child to ride and rope. When we were kids, he helped me be a better cowgirl."

"Your relationship with him is really special—to be such close friends for so many years. You did right by choosing him as your donor."

"Thank you. It's important for me to hear you say that." Especially since Sophie was in a state of emotional distress. "I'm not doing as well as I let on earlier." At this point it didn't make sense to pretend, not when Libby already appeared to sense the truth. "But I'm sure you figured me out."

"I can tell how Tommy affects you." She put her hand on Sophie's arm. "He has a powerful presence."

"I'm afraid of falling in love with him." She couldn't bear to need more from him than he was capable of giving. She would never recover from the problems it would cause.

"I understand how daunting your concerns must be. But maybe in time loving him will seem like a good thing."

"I hope so." Because for now just the thought alone made her ache.

On Saturday night, a barn dance was under way. But at the moment, Tommy sat next to Matt at a rustic wooden table, away from the crowd. They'd already eaten a country-fried meal, and now Libby, Sophie and Chance were line dancing, leaving the men by themselves.

Tommy's celebrity had caused a stir, but he didn't mind. Earlier, he'd taken tons of selfies with other guests and signed cocktail napkins and whatever else they gave him to scribble on.

He'd made nice with the cover band, too. He'd sat in on a couple of old country tunes with them. He'd also offered to Tweet a link to a YouTube video that featured their original material. Overall, they were a damn fine group of musicians, talented in their own right.

Tommy checked out the line dancers. Chance was

doing what he could to keep up, but he missed most of the steps, turning the wrong way nearly every time.

Amused, Tommy said to Matt, "You need to teach that pint-size cowboy to dance."

His half brother chuckled. "I'm working on it. But dancing doesn't come easy to him. He's a hell of a roper, though."

"That's what I've heard. He's a great kid. Being around him is making me more excited about the baby Sophie is going to have. It's still really early, but it's kind of cool to touch her stomach and know there's a little peanut in there."

Matt picked up his beer. "So you're going to call it Peanut Talbot?"

Tommy laughed. A second later, he realized that he had no idea what Sophie was going to call her child. They hadn't discussed what her choices might be. But to make things clear, he said, "It'll be more like Peanut Cardinale. It'll have Sophie's surname." That much he did know.

"Oh, of course. Sorry. I have my mom's last name, too."

Tommy nodded. "Are she and her husband going to stop by the dance tonight?" Matt's mom lived on the ranch with a man she'd recently married.

"They should be here soon. She's interested in meeting you."

"I guess it's only fair since you met my mom." It was strange, too, to think about the way their mothers had catered to their father back in the day, giving Kirby whatever he wanted. "What's on your birth certificate? Who's named as the father?"

"It says 'unknown.' Whenever anyone asked about him, I'd just say that he was a drifter and that my mom never even knew his real name. But that's what I was instructed to say." Matt set down his half-empty beer. "When Kirby first started coming around, I didn't know he was my dad. Eventually I sensed it, though. And then my mom told me the truth."

"At least it didn't take you by surprise. That must have made it a little easier."

"Yeah, I suppose it did. Is your name going to be on the birth certificate for Sophie's kid?"

"No. But we're still going to tell him or her who I am."

"It sounds like you have it all worked out."

"We certainly tried to." Tommy glanced at Sophie, thinking how natural she looked in this setting. A moment later, something inside him went tight—he felt a sudden fear about how easily she could shut him out of her child's life. Of course, that was a stupid thing to think about. Why would Sophie do that to him? He wasn't going to contest their agreement or try to be the dad. Yet Sophie seemed different now that she was pregnant. More cautious, he thought. He even got the sinking feeling that their friendship could be on the line. And if Sophie stopped being friends with him, then he wouldn't get to see the child, either. He would be left out in the cold.

"There's my mom," Matt said suddenly, interrupting Tommy's mental ramblings.

He turned and saw an attractive fiftysomething brunette heading toward them. As for her husband, he was tall and lanky, fair-skinned, with thinning gray hair and a kind face. He already knew that their names were Julie and Lester.

Soon Sophie, Libby and Chance joined them at the table, and they spent the rest of the evening together.

Chance dashed over to the buffet and brought back a huge slice of apple pie. When Sophie caught sight of it, she went and got some, too, and with the way she moaned over its cinnamon flavor, Tommy wondered if she was having her first pregnancy food craving.

She offered him a bite but he refused, not wanting to take it away from her and the little peanut he'd planted in her womb.

After the dance, Tommy lay next to Sophie in the guest room they were sharing, staring up at the ceiling. The bed was warm, the covers smooth against his skin. Outside the window, the night sky was sprinkled with stars.

He leaned onto his elbow, shifting to look at her. "How long will it be before you know if it's a boy or a girl?"

She turned in his direction. "Between four and five months, I think. I didn't really talk to my doctor about that. I don't even have to go back to see him for another six weeks. That's when my prenatal visits will start."

Tommy wouldn't know anything about that, considering that she'd banned him from going with her. "When are you going to start thinking up names? Are you going to wait until you know if it's a boy or a girl? Or are you going to start playing with ideas now?"

"I don't know. I haven't gotten that far."

He wouldn't mind if she involved him in the process, but with the way things were going, that seemed doubtful. "It wouldn't hurt to start making a list."

"I suppose I could do that." She adjusted the covers, loosening them around her body. "Chance's name certainly suits him, with the whole outlaw thing from your dad's song."

"Chance does seem like a little wilding. Your kid will probably be that way, too, with my blood running through its veins."

She placed her hand on her stomach. "I'll bet it'll kick up a storm in my belly."

He wanted to cover her hand with his, but he kept his paws to himself. "I've taken to calling it Peanut."

"Really?" She glanced up and smiled. "Oh, that's so cute."

"It's probably a common nickname, but it's what jumped into my mind. After the way you devoured that apple pie tonight, maybe I should be calling it Seedling."

She laughed. "I did chow down. But gosh, it was good. I'm still partial to Peanut, though." She paused. "Here's something I could consider—if it's a boy, I could use my dad's name for its middle name, and if it's a girl, I could use my mom's."

"Sure. Why not?" He appreciated her bouncing her ideas off of him. "That would be a nice way to honor your parents."

Her voice turned low, soft and sad. "I wish they were here."

"I know. I'm sorry." Tommy had been a pallbearer at her father's funeral. But her mom had always been a bit of a mystery to him. Since she'd died so soon after Sophie was born, he didn't really know much about her. "Do you think it'll be okay for you to just have one kid?"

"What do you mean?"

"Being an only child seems like it would be lonely."

"It was a little lonely for me. But I had you to hang out with, so that helped." She angled her head. "Are you offering to be the donor of my second child, if I ever decided to have another one? Because I thought you were getting a vasectomy after this one is born."

"Truthfully, I don't know what I'm saying or doing or offering. I'm kind of mixed up tonight. I got a little worried while we were at the dance."

"About what?"

"How easily you could shut me out of the kid's life." He tried to make sense of the insecurity churning inside him. "But I think some of this might be coming from how it hurts that you don't want me going to the doctor with you."

"I already explained why—"

"I know. But it just makes me realize how much control you have over this situation. It even feels like a blow to our friendship, and since us being friends is my only connection to the child, it makes me being the donor more difficult, too."

"I don't mean to make you feel that way." She hesitated, closing her eyes, keeping them tightly shut. A second later, she opened them and said, "I'm just trying to cope with everything, too."

Of course she was, he thought. This was a whole new experience for her, as well. "Don't worry about it, Soph. I shouldn't have even brought it up. We came here to have a nice getaway, and I'm ruining it." He reached for her. "Just forget I said anything."

She nuzzled against him. "You're still my friend, Tommy." She trailed a hand down his body, her touch sensuously familiar. "You're still my lover, too."

That was all the invitation he needed. He rolled on top of her, kissing her, tasting the heat of her lips. She sighed, and he lifted the hem of her nightgown. It was a delicate garment, as white as a wedding gown and just as lacy.

Before he thought too deeply about that, he raised the material even higher. She was bare underneath, and he was already naked.

She parted her thighs, and he slid between them, getting an immediate sense of belonging. But being inside her always affected him in that way.

He thrust slowly, his body rocking hers. She whispered something incoherent in his ear. Which was understandable, especially on a scattered night such as this. He'd already created an uncomfortable situation, that was for sure.

Silent, he focused on making her feel good, sweeping her into a sea of sensation, where nothing else was supposed to matter.

Except the comfort of sex.

On their last evening at the ranch, Sophie and Tommy went on a hayride in a straw-filled horse-drawn wagon. They were part of a caravan, en route to a campfire and marshmallow roast. They rode with Matt and Libby and Chance, and the boy chattered the entire way.

Sophie enjoyed listening to him. He was being their tour guide, telling them about the scenery and the colorful glass bottles hanging from the trees. Most of the bottles were blue because Matt was a Cherokee from the "Blue Clan." It was obvious that Chance was repeating things Matt had told him, but he did it with such love and admiration, it made Sophie smile.

Libby interjected and said, "The first time I took this ride with Matt, we were alone, just the two of us, and gazing up at the stars. But since neither of us knows much about the constellations, we made up names for them."

Sophie could tell that Libby was reminiscing about

an early memory with Matt, a night of romance. Or maybe it had been during a time when they'd been longing for love and fighting their feelings for each other.

Sophie was certainly battling her feelings for Tommy. Nothing had changed in that regard. She stole a jittery glance at him while he was looking the other way. Last night he'd shared his concerns with her, and tonight they were behaving as if that conversation had never happened. But deep inside, she wondered if she should tell him what was troubling her.

"What did you name the stars?" Chance asked his mother, pulling Sophie back into the night's festivities and giving her something else to think about.

"We called some of them tic-tac-toe because they were in the shapes of *X*s and *O*s," Libby replied.

Matt piped up and said, "I thought we called them hugs and kisses." He reached for his fiancée's hand and gave it a light squeeze.

She flashed her dimples at him. "Maybe it was a bit of both." She turned her attention back to her son. "Do you want to name some of them now?"

"Heck, yeah." He wiggled in the straw. "Tommy and Sophie can help me. Come on, guys. Let's give 'em better names than my mom and Matt did. Tic-tac-toe is okay. But hugs and kisses… That's kind of stupid."

Tommy laughed. "You won't think it's stupid when you're older. But let's give it a go and see what we can do." He gazed up at the sky. "I've never seen this many stars until I came here, and I've been all over the world."

Chance scooted closer to him. "Where's your most favorite place you've ever been?"

"Honestly, I don't know. I've enjoyed them all. But there is one place I'd like to go that I've never been."

"Where's that?" the boy excitedly asked.

Tommy smiled. "Neverland. Or Never Land or whatever you want to call it."

Chance's eyes went big and round. "Where Peter Pan and Captain Hook and all of them are?"

Tommy nodded. "Sophie looked like Peter Pan when she was little. She had pixie hair like his. And she was tough and scrappy and boyish." He winked at her. "Sometimes I even used to call her Pan, and she'd get mad and throw sticks at me, saying that I was more like him because of how boastful I was." He softened his voice. "We've both grown up since then, but Neverland still reminds me of her."

While Sophie's heart skipped a foolishly dreamy beat, Chance roamed his curious gaze over her. Was he trying to picture her the way she'd just been described?

The child turned back to Tommy and said, "We should name the stars after the people in Peter Pan."

"Sure." Tommy leaned against the back of the wagon, his knees bent in front of him. "That'll be fun. But from here, they all pretty much look like Tinker Bell."

The six-year-old appeared to contemplate that and come to a conclusion. "Then that's who all of them can be, except the ones we give other names to." He gazed up at the night sky, an earnest expression on his little face. "That bunch over there can be Captain Hook and his crew. And that one by itself can be the alligator who ate off Hook's hand."

Tommy chuckled. "Well, that sounds gnarly."

Sophie meant to laugh, too. But she remained quiet, immersed in watching Tommy and Chance. She glanced over at Matt and Libby. They were watching the scene unfold, too.

Tommy pointed upward. "Should that group at the very top be Peter Pan and the Lost Boys?"

Chance followed his line of sight. A second later, he looked at Sophie. "If that's okay with her, then it's okay with me."

She smiled, touched that he was taking her Pan persona so seriously. "It's totally fine with me. I think Peter and his friends would like that spot."

The boy returned her smile and finished his task by naming a star after Wendy. But hers wasn't quite as bright. According to his youthful wisdom, Wendy was just a normal girl who was going to grow old. Someday her star would burn out.

To keep from going sad, Sophie thought about how many Tinker Bell stars were twinkling down on them and wondered if she should make a wish. Or maybe she should just get her head out of the sky and work on staying grounded.

The wagon bumped along, with Sophie trying not to frown.

Once they arrived at the campsite, Matt and Tommy helped the ranch attendants build the fires, and Sophie and Libby unpacked the supplies.

Later, as they sat at their campfire eating s'mores, Chance made a sticky mess, gobbling up the treats and wiping his hands on his pants. He ignored the packages of wet wipes that had been provided. He even dropped one into the dirt.

After Libby picked up the packet and dusted it off, Matt told a nice story. He revealed that he and Libby had gotten engaged on National S'mores Day and would be getting married on that same day next summer.

Sophie commented on how "sweet" their wedding was going to be, and everyone else laughed. But she wasn't laughing herself. As she admired the other couple with their marshmallow-and-chocolate-smeared child tucked between them, she fretted about her feelings for Tommy.

He leaned over and whispered, "You okay?"

"I'm fine." Hating that she'd gotten caught with a less-than-happy expression, she plastered a smile on her lips. But maybe once they got home, she would give up the fight and tell him what was wrong, and admit how deeply afraid she was of loving him.

Eleven

The Texas weekend ended, and on Monday morning Sophie was at work, debating what to do about Tommy. Should she talk to him tonight after dinner? Should she tell him about her struggle?

Yes, she thought, she should. If she didn't, her feelings were going to eat her alive. She wished she could leave the office early and just get it over with. She could feign morning sickness, she supposed. So far, she wasn't having any of those symptoms. But she hated to lie to Barbara and pretend to be ill when she was feeling fine. Or as fine as an anxiety-ridden pregnant woman could be.

Hours later while Sophie was immersed in paperwork, her cell phone rang. She saw Tommy's name on the screen and answered it.

"Soph?" he said right away. "I need to talk to you."

She noticed that he sounded upset. "Is everything all right?"

"No, it's not. Something happened, but I don't want to get into it over the phone."

She panicked. "Is someone hurt?"

"It's nothing like that. It's just…" He hesitated, blowing a raspy breath into the receiver. "I need for you to come home so we can discuss it in person."

"Should I do that right now?" The urgency in his tone worried her, and she was already having issues of her own. This certainly wasn't helping her anxiety. Whatever was wrong in Tommy's world sounded serious.

"Yes, but don't tell Barbara you're leaving because I'm freaking out. This is personal, and I don't want anyone to know besides you. Brandon knows, but he's my lawyer, so I had to tell him."

Sophie couldn't begin to guess what was going on, especially since Tommy had involved Brandon. "Maybe I can tell Barbara that I'm not feeling well. That I have morning sickness or something." It was the excuse she'd considered earlier.

"Sure, that will work. In fact, you can tell her that I called to check up on you, and you told me that you were sick. So I insisted that you come home and rest."

Sophie wished that she actually was returning to the mansion to relax. Tommy's unease was making her tense. "I'll be there as soon as I can."

"Okay. Thanks." He paused. "And I'm sorry, Soph. I'm so sorry."

Her heart punched against her ribs. Was he apologizing for making her rush home? Or was it the news itself that required an apology?

They ended the call, and she smoothed her dress, trying to compose herself. She left her office and headed down the hall, to Barbara's. The door was partially open. She poked in her head, but she knocked, too.

Barbara glanced up from her computer and waved Sophie inside. At forty-six, she was a hardworking Southern gal who wore her dyed red hair expertly coiffed. She had a truck-driver husband and three teenage sons who drove her batty. Tommy sometimes overwhelmed her, too. But he had that effect on the people who worked for him; Sophie was no exception.

Between her fear of falling in love with him and whatever problems he was currently facing, she was getting more nervous by the minute.

She approached the other woman's desk and said, "I'm not feeling well." She went into her morning-sickness spiel, also repeating what Tommy told her to say.

"Oh, sugar, don't worry about needing to go home. I was as sick and surly as an old hound dog with my kids. Sipping cola syrup used to help. Keeping crackers and pretzels beside my bed and at my desk was a lifesaver, too. I heard that some women sniff lemons to alleviate their symptoms. It's supposed to be an aromatherapy thing." The redhead sighed. "But if it gets really bad, you can get a prescription for an antiemetic drug."

Sophie had already discussed morning-sickness remedies with her doctor, but she appreciated Barbara's input. "I'll check back with you tomorrow. I just need to get off my feet today." By now, her story wasn't so much of a lie. She was getting weary. But whether it was the baby or a reaction to the stress, she couldn't say.

Barbara wished her well, and Sophie left the office and climbed into her truck. She rolled down the windows, taking refuge in the cool November air.

By the time she got to the mansion, she'd already listened to a slew of songs on her playlist. None of them were Tommy's. As nervous as she was, she couldn't handle his music today.

She entered the property through the main gate and drove around back. She didn't want to risk seeing Dottie or Chef Bryan or anyone else. Instead, she took the poolside steps that led directly to Tommy's suite.

He was in his bedroom, trapped in a state of dishevelment. He'd made a mess out of his hair—he'd obviously tugged his hands through it—and he'd rubbed his forehead raw, the friction making his skin turn red. He was rubbing it now, even pressing his fingers against his eyes.

"You look awful, Tommy."

"I'm so scared, Soph." He came toward her. "And I'm worried about how this is going to impact you."

"Just tell me what it is." She needed for him to come clean. "Just say it."

"I just found out that Kara's baby could be mine, after all."

She felt the color drain from her face. "What?"

"The lab that did the paternity test called today and said there might've been a mix-up in the results and that I might actually be the father instead of the other man."

"Oh, my God." Sophie sat on the edge of the bed. She could barely think straight. "How is it even possible to mix up a test like that?"

"They think the labels on the vials of blood might've gotten switched. They just discovered that a disgruntled employee was deliberately tampering with stuff, and it's possible that our samples were compromised by this person. We won't know until we retake the test."

"Then that's what you'll have to do." She rocked forward, clutching her stomach. No way was she going to allow herself to love Tommy. Or tell him that she'd been struggling with it. She was already in deeper than she should be. "Did you talk to Kara?"

He nodded. "I called her, and she's freaking out, too. She's afraid that if the baby is mine, she'll lose the other man."

"She's in love with him?" Sophie had wondered about that all along.

Tommy nodded again. "She told me that his name is Dan, and she met him a few days after she was with me. She was on the rebound from her ex, and that's why she hooked up with me. But she said it was different with Dan. That she developed a true closeness with him, an immediate bond."

"It's too bad that she didn't meet Dan before she had that one-night stand with you."

"That's what she said. She hadn't meant to be with two guys in the same week, but she liked Dan so much, she slept with him, too. She used protection with both of us. But obviously it failed with at least one of us." Tommy squeezed his eyes shut for a second. "She and Dan started a relationship, but she didn't tell him about me, not until she found out she was pregnant."

Sophie contemplated Kara's plight. At that point, she could have pretended the baby was Dan's and left Tommy out of it. Of course, Sophie wouldn't have done that, either. Not with something as important as the paternity of a child.

Tommy cleared his throat. "This nearly destroyed them the first time, waiting to see whose kid it was. And now they're going through it again. But it's worse this time, all these months later. Dan is having a breakdown over it. They both are."

Sophie kept her arms around her stomach, holding on to her baby. "I can only imagine the toll it's taking on their relationship."

"Kara told me that it's a boy. She had an ultrasound

a little while ago. Dan was excited about having a son, and now it might not even be his." Tommy rubbed his forehead, making the red spot redder. "I'm scared out of my mind, but I can't just walk away if the kid is mine. I'd have to try to be his father, to be involved in his life, somehow." He sat beside her. "And then there's your baby. I think I should be a father to him or her, too."

She flinched. At first he didn't want any children and now he was willing to claim both of them? "I understand that you're trying to do the right thing by taking responsibility for Kara's son, but that doesn't have anything to do with me."

"You're my closest friend, Soph. I should be the father to your baby, as much as I should be to hers."

"No, you shouldn't." She didn't want him to parent her child, not out of guilt or duty or obligation. If he loved her, then maybe it would be different. But he wasn't talking love. He was talking friendship. "You're the donor. That's what we agreed on. That's the contract we both signed."

"I'd try to be a good dad. I promise I would."

He sounded beautifully sincere. But that only made her feel worse. "That's not how this is supposed to work." She couldn't let him change the rules, not at the expense of how painful it was for her. "We need to keep things as they are." *No,* she thought, *not as they are.* Things needed to return to normal. "Actually, I should go home. I can't keep staying here. I can't keep doing this." She already wanted to curl into a ball and cry.

He frowned. "Do you regret us being lovers?"

She regretted the holes that he'd poked into her heart, but she didn't have the courage to say that. "It's not going to help either of us to lament what we should or shouldn't have done. We just need to move past it."

"I'm going to miss you not living here." He touched her arm briefly, cautiously. "I'll miss you so much."

She was tortured over leaving, too. But it couldn't be helped. "Our affair was always supposed to end."

"I know, but this seems like an awful way to let go."

It was beyond awful, she thought, especially with her fears of loving him. "I'm going to start packing now."

"I have to see my doctor. I promised Kara that would have my blood drawn right away, so they can send it to the lab that finalizes the results. But I can help you move your stuff over later."

"I'd prefer that someone from your staff did it. But thank you for the offer." She studied his forlorn expression, wishing that she could make him feel better. But she couldn't even do that for herself. "Did you tell Kara about us? That I'm pregnant and you're the donor?"

He shook his head. "I would never do that without your consent. Telling her wouldn't have changed anything, anyway. She would still be dealing with her own problems."

Sophie felt bad for Kara and how she might lose the man she loved if the results didn't go in his favor. But on the other hand, should it really matter? "Do you think Dan loves Kara as much as she loves him?"

Tommy shrugged. "I don't know. I guess so."

"Well, if he does, then he should accept her and the child. Even if the baby doesn't turn out to be his, he can still stay with Kara and help her raise it. And you can still be its father, too."

"I wish you'd reconsider my role in Peanut's life."

His nickname for the baby made her hurt even more. "Your role is the same as it's always been." She stood and moved away from the bed. "I'm sorry, but I really need to go home."

He came to his feet, too. "When will I get to see you again?"

"You can call me or come by when you get the test results." She owed him that much.

"It normally takes about a week, but they're supposed to put a rush on it. Brandon said we could sue the lab for the duress this has caused, but I don't want to create more havoc."

"Try to relax until you hear something." She didn't know what else to say to him.

"You need to take care of yourself, too."

"I'll be okay." She headed for the closet to get her suitcases.

When she glanced back at Tommy, she noticed that he was watching her, with a painful goodbye in his eyes.

The following day, Sophie got morning sickness for real. At first it was just a bout of queasiness. So she nibbled on crackers. But that didn't work. So she sniffed a lemon, which didn't help, either. As the nausea progressed, she ran to the toilet, vomiting to the point of exhaustion.

Later, after her stomach settled, she brewed a cup of chamomile tea and called Barbara, letting her know that she wasn't coming into the office today. Between being ill this morning and yesterday's news, she was just too worn-out.

To keep from going hungry, she made some dry toast and ate it slowly. So far, so good. She wasn't having afternoon sickness, too.

She went into the living room and sat on the couch. God help her, but she missed Tommy. She even wondered if she should agree to let him be the father to her child.

No, she thought. Her life was already too entwined

with his. She couldn't handle a deeper connection to him, not if it meant battling her heart for control. Besides, how long would it be before Tommy started hanging out with groupies again? Before he went back to his old lifestyle? She didn't want to be witness to that.

So maybe she should quit working for him and move out of Nashville. She could relocate to Los Angeles. There were plenty of music-related jobs there.

Tommy could come to LA and visit now and then, she told herself. He could still be a friend.

A faraway friend. A man in the distance.

But wasn't that better than staying here and fighting her feelings for him? He would still be the donor. Her son or daughter would still be told who he was. He just wouldn't be living nearby. Then again, with the way he traveled, he wouldn't be around Nashville much, anyway.

She glanced over at her dogs, where they were curled up near the fireplace. Hokey and Pokey seemed depressed now that they were home. They missed Tommy as much as she did, especially with the way he spoiled them. Unfortunately, she didn't know how to cheer them up. She could barely cope with her own turmoil.

The doorbell rang, chiming noisily. The dogs barked and ran to the door, eager to discover who it was. Sophie assumed it was a ranch hand from Tommy's stables bringing her horses back.

But she was wrong. It was Tommy himself. Except that the horses weren't with him. There was no trailer attached to his truck.

"May I come in?" he asked, as he knelt to pet the pooches. They danced happily at his feet.

"Why don't I come out there?" She didn't want to be cooped up in the house with him. Now that he was here, she decided that she needed as much fresh air as she could get.

They sat side by side on the porch steps, and she hurriedly asked, "Did you get word from the lab already? I didn't know it would be this soon."

"There's no news yet."

"Are they going to call you when the results are in?"

"No. They'll be sending them, like they did last time. That's the standard procedure." He angled his body a bit more toward hers. "But that isn't the reason I stopped by."

Her pulse skittered. "Then what is it?"

"I called Kara today and asked for Dan's number. I wanted to talk to him about what you said."

Sophie started. "About his feelings for Kara?"

"Not in so many words, but yeah. I just told him that no matter whose baby it is, he can still be part of its life if he wants to be with Kara. I also told him that I hope things work out for them."

"How did he react to what you said?" she asked, trying to keep her voice from betraying her. She hadn't expected him to take her views about the other couple so deeply.

"He seemed to appreciate it. But I don't know if it helped. He really wants the kid to be his." He leaned forward. "And do you know what I want?" He answered his own question. "For you to agree to let me be the father of your baby."

"I just think it's better if you remain the donor," she said. "I'm probably going to be moving. I was thinking of going to LA."

"What?" He looked as if he'd just stopped breathing.

"I need a change, to start over with the baby."

"I knew something was wrong in Texas. Dammit, I knew I was going to lose you. That our friendship might be ending." His voice went shaky. "I never meant for what I did with Kara to affect you, and I'm so sorry for the stress it caused. But why did you start pulling away from me when we were in Texas? What's going on, Soph? It can't just be this added problem with Kara. Not when I noticed it before."

She couldn't say it. She just couldn't admit that she was afraid of loving him. Or how badly she wished that he would love her, too, in a fully committed way. Tommy had been loyal to her during their affair, but that didn't mean he'd morphed into a one-woman kind of man. "We'll still be friends and you can still visit me. Besides, you'll be back on the road before you know it, living the life you love."

"I can't believe that you want to leave this area. Nashville is where you were raised. This is your home, the place where you've always belonged."

"I can belong somewhere else." She had to find a way to do that. Desperate to escape the confusion she saw on his face, she said, "I hope you don't mind, but I want to go inside and rest. I got sick this morning, and I'm beat."

He searched her gaze. "Can I do anything to help?"

He could love her, she thought. "No, there's nothing. But you can still contact me when you get the paternity results."

He helped her to her feet. "I don't want you to move away."

"I can't talk about this right now." She took her hand away from his. "I need to lie down."

And try to keep herself from crying.

Tommy paced Brandon's office, immersed in panic and fear. Two days had passed since he'd seen Sophie, and all he'd done was obsess about losing her. He couldn't stand the thought of her going to LA and raising the baby there.

As for the other baby, he still didn't know if it was his. The results were supposed to arrive by special delivery in tomorrow's mail. But at the moment, that seemed like light-years away. Everything did.

"You need to chill out," Brandon said.

Tommy scowled at him. Chill out? Was he kidding? "I talked to Matt yesterday and told him what was going on."

"About Sophie wanting to move or about Kara's baby?"

"About both. I thought he would be a good authority on women and children and all of that. But he sounded a little cautious when I mentioned Sophie."

"Cautious how?"

"I don't know, exactly. There was just something in his voice. But then I figured he was probably just uncomfortable about being dragged into it. The only advice he gave me was to be patient with Sophie." But how could Tommy be patient if she left the area? He wouldn't even be seeing her. "I'm not saying that this new problem with Kara isn't an issue, but something was already going on with Sophie before that happened. And you know what makes it worse? That Dad was right. He kept saying that my baby arrangement with Sophie was going to create problems."

"You didn't tell Dad about what's going on now, did you?"

"Hell, no. It was hard enough to tell you and Matt. I don't want Dad rubbing my problems in my face."

Brandon left his chair and came around to the other side of the desk. "I should have advised you the way

Dad did. I should have told you to think twice before signing the donor contract. But honestly, I never expected you to change your mind and want to be a father. I never figured Sophie for wanting to skip town, either. With how tight your friendship has always been, it seemed like a solid arrangement to me. But either way, I'm proud of you, brother."

Tommy blinked at him. "You are? Why?"

"For trying to do right by both babies. And for being respectful of Dan and Kara's relationship."

"I just wish Sophie wasn't shutting me out. She started pulling away once she got pregnant, and she seemed even more preoccupied while we were in Texas. I mentioned it to her while we were there, but it didn't make a difference. I understand that things went awry after we got back, and this situation with Kara is probably pushing her over the edge now." He couldn't deny his part in that. "I feel awful that something from my past is creating stress and anxiety for her. Just so damn awful." Sophie was the last person in the world he ever wanted to hurt. "But I still think there's more going on with her. Something she isn't telling me. She says we'll still be friends, but it doesn't feel that way to me."

Brandon leaned against his desk. "Maybe something happened in Texas that you're not aware of, and that's why Matt sounded so cautious. He might actually know what it is."

Tommy's pulse jumped. "I need to talk to him again."

His brother went into lawyer mode. "We can call him, right now, both of us together. Better yet, let's get him on Skype. I think he'll be more likely to tell us what's going on if we can see him face-to-face."

"And you can grill him?" Tommy was willing to do anything at this point.

They arranged a video chat for an hour later. When Matt appeared on the computer screen, he looked dusty, as if he'd been out riding or working the ranch.

Brandon jumped right in and ambushed him, and soon Matt was squirming under fire. He even pulled his hat lower, shielding his eyes as if that might help.

"It's not my place to talk about it," Matt said.

"Talk about what?" the attorney pressed.

"About what Sophie told Libby. Hell, Libby probably shouldn't have even repeated it to me."

"I understand that you're trying to protect Sophie's privacy and not get into trouble with your own woman over it." Brandon shoved Tommy toward the monitor. "But look at this guy. If you don't tell him what's going on, he's going to lose his mind."

Matt lifted the brim of his hat and stared at Tommy. After a beat of silence he said, "You need to ask Sophie what's going on. She should be the one to tell you."

Tommy replied, "I've been asking her what's wrong, and all she does is pull further away from me. Please, just tell me what she told Libby."

Matt made a pained expression. "Okay, but if this comes back to bite me in the ass, I'm holding you responsible."

"Fine. I'll take the heat." He would take anything anyone threw his way.

His Texas half brother blew out a ragged breath. "All right. Here it is. She's afraid of her feelings."

"Her feelings about what?" Tommy was as confused as ever.

"About you."

Tommy still wasn't getting it. "About me being the donor or the dad or what?"

Matt shook his head. Clearly, he thought Tommy was

being dense. Did Brandon think so, too? Sure enough, he was shaking his head, as well.

"What am I missing?" Tommy asked.

Finally Matt said, "She's afraid of falling in love with you." He gently added, "Is that plain enough? Does that explain it?"

Yes? No? God help him. Tommy dropped onto a chair. He shouldn't have pursued this. He shouldn't have asked Matt to tell him. Because now that he knew, he was afraid, too.

So damn scared of what it all meant.

Twelve

Tommy went home, changed into his swim trunks and dived into the pool. The winter air was cool, and the water was warm.

He couldn't stop thinking about love and what it meant. He had no idea what being in love felt like. But he knew that it could be good or bad, blissful or painful. He'd seen it happen to enough people, where they either flourished from it or curled up and died. He'd been an observer, watching from the sidelines, and now he was drowning in Sophie's fear of it, triggering fears of his own.

He swam over to the second waterfall, submerged himself beneath it and headed for his underground lair.

Once he entered the apartment, he pushed his hair out of his eyes and grabbed a towel. Images of Sophie were playing in his mind from the night of the masquerade, when he'd brought her here. Now on this moonlit evening he was alone, sulking like the phantom that inspired the mask he'd worn.

Everything reminded him of Sophie: his house, his music, his family, his childhood. She'd been a part of nearly every aspect of his life. If she left town, he didn't know what he was going to do without her.

He went to the fridge and grabbed a sparkling water, uncapped the bottle and took a bubbly swig.

Sophie was obviously hurting over him. He was hurting over her, too. He ached inside, his emotions twisting him in two.

He kept saying that he was going to write an album about his affair with her. But the songs would only be mournful ballads. Because, really, who was he trying to kid by saying that he didn't know what being in love felt like?

Sophie had always been the number one person in his life, and he could barely function without her.

He'd been with scores of other women over the years, but he'd never gotten attached to any of them. With Sophie, the two of them had been joined at the hip. At the heart. At the soul.

What they shared was more than physical, and the equation added up to love. Tommy loved her, pure and simple.

No, he thought. There was nothing pure or simple about it. If he went to her this very instant, offering to make a commitment, to marry her and raise their child together, he would also be asking her to accept the results of the paternity test, regardless of the outcome.

If Kara's baby belonged to Tommy, there was no denying that the press would chastise him for having two kids with two different women. And if Sophie chose to stay with him, she would get dragged through the mud, too. The internet trolls would criticize her at every turn. It wouldn't be easy on the kids, either. He knew from experience what having a famous father was like. Yet in spite of that, Tommy had sought fame and fortune, too.

He frowned at the water bottle in his hand. He understood why Sophie was fighting her feelings for him. Regardless of how deep their attraction was, he'd never had the qualities she'd yearned for in a man. She'd refused to date him in the past because he didn't know how to settle down. Because he was too restless, too wild, with too many women around.

Only things were different now. He loved Sophie, and he didn't want anyone except her. She was it for him, the person he wanted to spend the rest of his life with.

But with how precarious everything else was, how was it going to work between them? Not just with the Kara situation, but with his job, too. How would Sophie cope with him going back out on the road? Would she expect him to alter his career and stay home with her?

Tommy had a lot to think about, so many jumbled things tormenting his mind and making a mess out of his heart.

On Thursday afternoon, Sophie got a text from Tommy asking if she would come to his house. He'd received the paternity-test results, but he didn't want to open the envelope unless she was with him. She assumed he was too nervous to do it alone, so she agreed to meet him in his garden. For her, it was a neutral location. She couldn't bear to return to his suite. Being in the vicinity of his bedroom would only make her ache more than she already did. She missed cuddling in his arms at night. She missed him during the day, too. She just plain missed him.

What choice did she have, except to leave Nashville? She needed to find a way to survive without being consumed by him, without his mansion being nearby, without everything that reminded her of him.

She'd taken the week off from work, but she hadn't given her notice yet. She hadn't put her house on the market yet, either. But as soon as this meeting with Tommy was over, she would be doing both of those things.

Sophie cut across the lawn and took the garden path. She passed the tiger statue and headed to the koi pond, where Tommy was supposed to be waiting for her.

She spotted him soon enough—tall and long and lean in his slim-fitting jeans and black vintage Western shirt. Sometimes he favored those old styles. This one had red-rose embroidery and white piping. She was familiar with the design. She'd given it to him on his last birthday, but she hadn't expected him to be wearing it today.

He turned in Sophie's direction, and her heart skipped anxious beats. He was holding the unopened envelope, the yet-unknown paternity results, in his hand.

"Hi, Soph," he said, once they were close enough to speak.

She sucked in her breath and repeated his greeting. "Hi."

They sat beside each other on an ornate iron bench. When he folded the envelope and tucked it into his shirt pocket, she got confused.

She said, "I thought you were going to open that once I got here."

"I don't want to know the results just yet. First I want

to talk to you about something." His leg was jittering, bouncing up and down.

She considered putting her hand on his knee to help calm him, but she didn't. She was too antsy herself. "If I was in your position, I would want to know right away."

"I'm prepared for either outcome. But what I'm not prepared for is losing you."

Her pulse went haywire, was now even jumpier than his leg. "What do you mean?"

"I've been thinking a lot about the pain I've been in since you moved out. And now you're talking about leaving Nashville. With everything going on, I keep coming back to that. I've never felt pain like this before."

"I know that it probably seems cowardly for me to run away. But I can't just hang around here and be your friend. It hurts too much, Tommy."

"But that's what I'm saying. I can't live without you, and I finally understand what that means. I love you, and I want us to have a life together, you and me and our baby. But I'm worried about how it'll affect you if the other child is mine, about how the press will treat the situation and the emotional impact it will have on you. There are other things to consider, too, like me going back out on the road. I came up with a partial solution to that, but it still might not be right for you."

Sophie was still reeling from his initial admission, let alone having the ability to focus on the rest of it. "You love me? Since when?"

"Since the beginning, but I didn't know it, not until I was losing you. I just took it for granted that you'd always be there for me, and I was wrong to expect that from you. You deserve better than someone like me."

"So what are you saying? That you want us to be together, but you don't think it'll work?"

"I just don't want to make life harder for you. I want to be the man who makes you happy, not the guy who creates agony and stress."

"It matters that you love me." It mattered more than she could say. She *never, ever* thought she would hear those words from him.

"Is there a chance you feel the same way, too?"

She nodded, barely able to contain her emotion. "Yes. My God, yes! But I'm still scared of the things you said. Are you sure that you want to be with me, Tommy? It's not just about the situation with Kara and with our baby?"

"I'm positive about how I feel. But that doesn't change the hardship that us being together might cause you."

The look in his eyes was so deep and sincere, she wanted to cry. "No one said love was supposed to be easy."

"I know, but I'm just about the worst catch there is. Who in their right mind would want me as a husband?"

Her heart leaped to her throat. "Is marriage on the table?"

"It is, if you want it to be. But you'd have to be sure, more certain than you've ever been about anything in your life."

In spite of the anxiety still swirling around them, she actually laughed. "That's the most troubling proposal I've ever heard."

He laughed, too. "I know. I'm sorry. But I've been up all night stressing about this." His expression turned serious. "I want to fight for you—I want to convince you that I'm the man of your dreams. But how can I be your dream man if I've never been the type of guy you wanted?"

"I always wanted you. I just didn't want to share you with a zillion other women."

"There's never going to be anyone ever again. It's just you, Soph. It'll always be just you from now on." He looked longingly at her. "Commitment used to scare me, but it feels right with you. Do you believe me? Do you trust me?"

"Yes." He wouldn't have asked her to marry him if he didn't mean it. Tommy knew better than to toy with commitment, especially with how disloyal his father had been to his mother. "I trust you."

"But what about Kara's baby?" He took the envelope out of his pocket. "If this child is mine, it's going to affect you, too. The media will tear me apart for having two kids with two different women, and people will slam you for being with me."

She refused to back down. "I'll just have to learn to handle what they dish out."

"It'll be tough on the kids, too."

She put her hand on her tummy. "I wouldn't allow either baby to be hurt. Kara's son would be mine as much as he would be yours. And I would hope that Dan would be protective of both babies, too, regardless of who fathered them."

He gazed at her as if she was the most amazing person on earth. "You really mean all of that, don't you?"

"Yes, I do." She didn't want to run away from him anymore. She wanted to stay and fight for the love between them. She took the envelope from him, but she didn't open it. She tucked it into her pocket, giving them time to finish their conversation. "Now first tell me about the partial solution you've come up with to you going back out on the road."

He smiled softly, a bit shakily, and was still giving her an awed look. "I was thinking that I could take the reality-show deal so I could stay here with you and our baby for the next few years. Then when it's time for the *Music Mentors* tour, I was hoping that you and Peanut could travel with me. I know you never wanted to haul a kid around on the road, but touring is part of my job. And if we did it as a family, maybe it would be a nice adventure."

"That sounds like a beautiful compromise." She recognized the sacrifices they would both be making. But Sophie wanted nothing more than for her and Tommy and their child to be a family. She reached into her pocket and removed the envelope. "Should I open this? Or do you want to do it?"

"You can do it."

She tore open the seal and removed the results. She glanced at the paper and revealed what it said. "You're not the father, Tommy."

He only stared at her for a second. "I'm not?" He took the paper from her and read it himself.

Then he reached for her, and they held each other, warm and tight.

His mouth sought hers, and they kissed, the two of them wrapped in love and commitment. And friendship, she thought.

Tommy was still her oldest and dearest friend, only now he was going to be her husband, too.

Tommy took Sophie's hand and led her to the mansion. Where she belonged, he thought, where they could be together.

They ascended the private staircase that led to his suite. He was so anxious for the future to unfold that he wanted to start planning their wedding right away. But first they needed to get properly engaged.

Once they were inside his room, he said, "I have something to give you." He went to his nightstand and opened the drawer. He removed the ring he'd bought her from its case and turned to face her. He hadn't brought it outside with him because he'd been afraid to presume that she would marry him. So he'd kept it here, shrouded in hope.

Her eyes went wide, and he went down on bended knee. "I love you, Sophia Marie Cardinale, and I'm going to do everything in my power to be the best husband and father I can be." He released the breath he'd been holding. Making it official, he asked, "Will you marry me?"

Her eyes glistened with tears. "Yes, I absolutely will."

He slid the five-carat solitaire onto her finger and came to his feet. "When I told my jeweler that I wanted a diamond that shined as bright as a star, he said that the ancient Romans considered diamonds to be pieces of stars that had fallen to earth. So that's what this is. A piece of one of the stars we named in Texas."

"It's incredible." She gazed at the ring. "I can't wait to marry you. My father really liked you, Tommy. I think my mother would have, too. Dad always told me what a romantic she was."

"I wish I could have met her. That she could have lived to be part of your life, and mine, too. She's going to be looking down on you on our wedding day. Both of your parents will be there."

"Is it okay with you if I ask your dad to walk me down the aisle? I'd like for him to fill in for my father."

"He'll be thrilled, I'm sure. My mom will be jumping for joy that we're getting married, too."

"We'll have to figure out a way for her to be part of the ceremony, as well. We can't leave her out of it."

"Should we do it here at the mansion? As soon as we can? I don't want to wait or have a long engagement."

"Me, neither. How about a March wedding? That's only four months away and should be just in time for my first ultrasound."

"That works for me. It'll be a whirlwind, but we can pull it off." Tommy had the money and the resources to make it happen in a quick and grand way. "Brandon can be my best man, and Matt can be one of my ushers."

She smiled. "I'll include Libby as one of my bridesmaids. And Chance can be our ring bearer. I'm not sure about the flower girl. Maybe one of Mack and Jean's daughters."

He put his hand on her tummy. "I'm starting to get the feeling that Peanut will be a girl."

"Really? Why?"

"I don't know. Daddy intuition, I guess." He paused. "I want this to be a family-style wedding. I can enlist a nanny service to help with everyone's kids. At some point, we're going to need our own nanny, too, especially when we're on the road. It wouldn't hurt to have an extra set of hands."

She slipped her arms around his waist. "That sounds good to me. I'm just excited to become your wife."

"The next four months are going to be crazy, with the CMAs, Christmas, New Year's and our wedding."

"I almost forgot about the CMAs."

"They changed the time slot, scheduling them a little later this year. I'm not nominated this time, but they asked me to be a presenter."

"Oh, poor boy." She teased him. "You've won Record of the Year and Entertainer of the Year for the past two years. It's time to give someone else a chance."

"Yeah, well, when I produce an album with songs about you and our baby, I'll be winning all sorts of future awards for it. Yesterday I worried about how downhearted my new songs were going to be. But today, I know that they're going to be my best ever."

She laughed. "There you go, boasting as usual. Call me crazy, but I love that side of you."

He grinned. "I just pretend to be conceited, remember? But I'm glad you love my ego as much as the rest of me." He swept her off her feet and carried her to bed. He loved everything about her, this perfect woman who'd agreed to be his wife.

Tommy's hands on Sophie's body felt magnificent. So warm, she thought. So passionate. He removed her clothes, touching her in places that made her sigh and arch and purr.

Whatever made her think that she could live without him? She was still aching from the need to be close to him, and he was right there. Tommy. *Her* Tommy. He belonged to her now, just as she belonged to him.

He went down on her, lifting her hips and raising her bottom in the air. She gripped his shoulders as he did deliciously wicked things with his tongue. Soft and silky heat, she thought, and wild, wild wetness.

The diamond on her finger shimmered in the light. He'd captured a piece of a star and given it to her. He was a star, too, she thought. A superstar who entertained millions of people with his music, and she was his biggest admirer.

He gazed up at her, his hazel eyes changing colors. Sophie was trying to hold on, to make this moment last, but she was already spiraling toward an orgasm.

He smiled like a mischievous schoolboy and pushed her over the edge, making her come.

Shaking and shuddering, she closed her eyes and tugged on his hair, the short, stylishly messy strands slipping through her fingers.

While the room seemed to spin, she felt him shift his weight. She opened her eyes and saw that he'd climbed on top of her, his face temptingly close to hers.

She reached for him, and they rolled over the bed, kissing and caressing and making hungry sounds. She pulled open the snaps on his shirt and bared his chest. She shoved her hands down his jeans, too, giving him an even bigger hard-on than he already had.

"Damn," he said. "What you do to me."

"Likewise." Her skin was tingling from her orgasm, her body still damp from where he used his tongue. "I want you inside me now."

"Yes, ma'am." He exaggerated his country charm and dragged his jeans past his hips.

He didn't take them all the way off, but she didn't mind. It seemed hotter this way, the desperation between them turning her on. He thrust into her, and she dug her nails into the part of his ass that was exposed.

He moved inside her, the friction from his pants abrading her bare legs. She curled her toes and keened out a moan. He kept going, deeper and deeper, every thrust more thrilling than the last. Flesh melded with flesh, twirling and spinning into a chasm of lust.

And love, Sophie thought. So much love.

The sex was ragged, but the commitment between them was gentle. They took a moment to savor it.

"Together," she whispered.

"Always," he whispered back, thrusting warm and deep.

She kissed him, and they tumbled over the bed again, locked in intensity. They messed up the covers, knocking pillows onto the floor. His body tensed, his abs rippled.

She thrashed beneath him, and he tossed back his head and spilled into her. She came, too, his climax jump-starting hers.

In the afterglow, he held her. She didn't know how much time passed, but the room was still brightly lit and immersed in daylight. Eventually, their breathing slowed and the sheen of sweat on their bodies evaporated. When they separated, they retrieved the fallen pillows and rested their heads on them.

"If I had already proposed to you, I would ask you to marry me all over again," he finally said.

"And I would say yes again." She would marry him a million times.

He shifted onto his elbow. "I can't believe we almost lost each other."

"I'm so glad we didn't." She turned to look at him. "Are we still going to tell our donor story in your dad's biography?"

"Sure. Why not? Only now it'll be a story about friends who made a baby and fell in love." He skimmed a hand down her stomach. "Are you going to let me attend your doctor visits now that we're a couple?"

"Yes, of course, and I'm not going to care who sees us or Tweets about it. If I'm going to be your wife, then I'm going to have to get friendlier with your fans.

I might have to start Tweeting more myself. I can even change my Twitter handle to Mrs. Tommy Talbot."

"You'll be famous, too." He kept touching her tummy, his fingertips light and gentle. "Speaking of which, you'll have to get used to having your own body-guard. And walking red carpets." He circled her navel. "Will you go to the CMAs with me?"

"I'd be honored." She smiled. "It'll be our first date without wearing masks."

He smiled, as well. "Can I announce our engagement to the press at the after-parties?"

"You most certainly can." She didn't want to keep anything hidden anymore, not after what they'd just been through. "You can tell them you're going to be a daddy, too."

"Really?" He searched her gaze. "You don't want to wait until the first trimester is over?"

"I don't want to wait for anything." She wanted the world to know that she and Tommy were going to be parents. "I'm not worried about jinxing it anymore, not with as happy as I am."

"Who knew we could be this kind of happy?" He made a perplexed expression. "I wonder if Brandon will ever find anyone."

She raised her eyebrows. "You're concerned about your brother's bachelorhood?" First he was trying to help Kara and Dan stay together, and now he was think-ing about Brandon. Sophie couldn't help but be amused. Tommy the matchmaker. "I wouldn't mess with your brother's love life if I were you. I don't think he would appreciate that."

"I'm not going to say anything to him about it. But now that I have you, and Matt has Libby, he's going to be the odd man out."

"If he's meant to find someone, he will."

"Yeah. You're right. If there's a woman out there for him, he'll drive her as crazy as I drove you."

Sophie moistened her lips. "You Talbot men are a dangerous breed." She glanced down. He'd pulled up his jeans, but he hadn't zipped them all the way. She ran her hand along the denim. "I'm going to want you again."

He climbed on top of her. "That can be arranged."

They kissed, and he rubbed against her, showing her that he wanted her again, too. Hot and dreamy, she thought.

For the rest of their lives.

Epilogue

The wedding was beautiful, exactly as Tommy and Sophie had planned it. She loved every moment of it. For now, they were at the reception, mingling with their guests inside the mansion.

They'd exchanged vows in the garden, beneath a billowy tent, with the jeweled tiger standing guard. She wore a long silk white dress, similar to the gown her mom had worn when she'd wedded Sophie's dad. She definitely felt her parents' presence, like angels from above.

Tommy's family was in full swing. Kirby had walked Sophie down the aisle with pride, and Melinda had lit a glittery gold candle with a romantic scent.

Chance had been a fabulous ring bearer. They'd decided that Hokey and Pokey could walk with him, and he'd gotten a kick out of the dogs being his loyal companions.

Matt and Libby had done their parts, too. And Brandon. He'd looked exceptional in his tux, standing beside the groom.

Sophie's groom. She glanced across the room at him. At the moment, he was engaged in conversation with a group of their guests.

She placed her hand on her growing belly. Tommy was right about their child. They were having a girl. They hadn't come up with a name for her yet, so they were still calling her Peanut. Sometimes Tommy called her Miss Peanut.

"How's my new sister-in-law?" a voice asked from behind her.

She spun around to meet Brandon's gaze. He'd brought a date to the wedding, one of the socialites he sometimes bedded. But it wasn't serious. It never was with Brandon. His date was off sipping champagne somewhere.

"I'm wonderful," Sophie said. "How are you?"

"I'm doing just fine." He leaned in close, his black hair shining beneath the chandelier above their heads. "This is a smashing event. But Tommy always did know how to throw a party."

"He does have his talents. But so do you." She reached for his hand. "The Talbots wouldn't be the same without you."

"Right." He squeezed her hand. "I'm the one always trying to keep the rest of them out of trouble. But I don't have to worry about Tommy anymore. He's your responsibility now. Then again, I guess he always was. The two of you, like peas in a pod. I should have figured out that you'd get married one day. But I was too busy seeing Tommy for the rebel that he was."

She nodded. "We all were."

"You're the best addition this family could ever have. I'm so glad you and my brother are together now."

"Thank you." She thought about Tommy's hope that Brandon found the love of his life someday. But she wasn't going to say anything about it. She'd already warned Tommy to stay out of Brandon's affairs.

Speaking of her husband, he was making his way over to her. Sophie glanced past Brandon and smiled at her man.

"I think this is my cue to leave." Brandon released her hand. "The groom is enticing his bride."

"He does have that effect on me." As Brandon left, he passed Tommy and patted him on the shoulder.

Eager to be near her husband, Sophie walked straight into his arms. Nothing felt more natural, more glorious, more right.

"This has been the best day of my life so far," she said. She knew they were going to have lots of amazing days.

"Me, too." He kissed her, soft and slow. Then he said, "I wrote a special song for you."

He'd been working on the album inspired by her and the baby, but she assumed this was something she'd yet to hear. "You're going to serenade me?"

He roamed his hands along the fabric-covered buttons marching down the back of her gown. "Yes. But it's a sexy song, so it'll have to wait until we're in bed."

"Mmm." She bumped against him. "A honeymoon song."

"Yep." He circled her waist. "For my naked wife."

"I'm not naked yet." But tonight she would be stripping off her dress for him. The country star she'd just married, the friend and lover who would always have her heart.

* * * * *

COMING SOON!

We really hope you enjoyed reading this book. If you're looking for more romance, be sure to head to the shops when new books are available on

Thursday 13th December

To see which titles are coming soon, please visit **millsandboon.co.uk**

MILLS & BOON

LET'S TALK
Romance

For exclusive extracts, competitions
and special offers, find us online: